Praise for
The Blue-Ribbon Jalapeño Society Jubilee

"Brown brings her cowboy-romance writing talents to bear on this hilarious tale of women in a gossipy small town… A high-spirited, romantic page-turner."

—*Kirkus*

"Humor and down-home charm make this a first-place prize winner. All the character quirks and small-town appeal are used to fullest advantage."

—*RT Book Reviews*, 4 stars

"A book so charming it makes you want to crawl inside and live there for a while."

—*The Royal Reviews*

"Reminded me a bit of *Fried Green Tomatoes at the Whistle Stop Café*… Heartwarming and fun."

—*Long and Short Reviews*

"In this laugh-out-loud read, bestselling [ ] s up among four female friends, proving that, no matter w [ ] atters most."

—*Booklist*

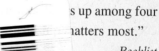

"I couldn't put it down... You just can't s [ ] dillac until you absolutely have to."

—*Minding Spot*

"Absolutely vibrant and fun-loving."

—*Shelly's Journal*

"This is a book I'll keep for whenever I want a good helping of southern sass, spitfire, and heart. To the very end, it had me entertained."

—*The Romance Reviews*

Also by Carolyn Brown

Lucky in Love

One Lucky Cowboy

Getting Lucky

I Love This Bar

Hell, Yeah

My Give a Damn's Busted

Honky Tonk Christmas

Love Drunk Cowboy

Red's Hot Cowboy

Darn Good Cowboy Christmas

One Hot Cowboy Wedding

Mistletoe Cowboy

Just a Cowboy and His Baby

Billion Dollar Cowboy

Cowboy Seeks Bride

The Cowboy's Christmas Baby

The Cowboy's Mail-Order Bride

Women's Fiction

The Blue-Ribbon Jalapeño Society Jubilee

THE RED-HOT CHILI COOK-OFF

CAROLYN BROWN

sourcebooks
landmark

Published by Sourcebooks Landmark, an imprint of Sourcebooks, Inc.
P. O. Box 4410, Naperville, Illinois 60567-4410
(630) 961-3900
Fax: (630) 961-2168
www.sourcebooks.com

Library of Congress Cataloging-in-Publication data is on file with the publisher.

Printed and bound in the United States of America.
VP 10 9 8 7 6 5 4 3 2 1

To Margaret A. Brown
For all the encouragement and love

Dear Readers,

Welcome back to Cadillac, Texas!

It's Cadillac at its best…jalapeño peppers, undying friendship, and blistering hot rumors.

I'd like to extend a huge thank-you to Sourcebooks for allowing me to write two more books about the goings-on in Cadillac. *The Blue-Ribbon Jalapeño Society Jubilee* came out in 2013 and *The Yellow Rose Barbecue Ball* will finish the trilogy. And there are no words important enough to express my thanks to my fabulous editor, Deb Werksman, for her awesome help and expertise. Also thanks to my agent, Erin Niumata, who pushed me to try my hand at writing women's fiction. Again, I have to thank my husband for putting up with me while I write *one more chapter*. Being the spouse of an author is not an easy job.

I'd also like to thank each of you readers who continues to support me, tell your friends about my books, and share them with other folks and post reviews. Y'all are truly awesome!

So settle in, enjoy the fun, and stir up some chili. Be careful with the cayenne pepper, now.

Until next time,
Carolyn Brown

Chapter 1

SOME MEN ARE JUST born stupid. Some don't get infected until later in life, but they'll all get a case of it sometime. It's in their DNA and can't be helped.

Carlene could testify with her right hand raised to God and the left on the Good Book that her husband, Lenny, had been born with the disease and it had worsened with the years. Proof was held between her thumb and forefinger like a dead rat in the form of a pair of bikini underwear. They damn sure didn't belong to her. Hell's bells, she couldn't get one leg in those tiny little things. And they did not belong to Lenny, either. Even if he had become an overnight cross-dresser, his ass wouldn't fit into that skimpy pair of under-britches, not even if he greased himself down with bacon drippings.

They were bright red with a sparkling sequin heart sewn on the triangular front. They'd come with a matching corset with garter straps and fishnet hose. Carlene recognized them, because she'd designed the outfit herself at her lingerie shop, Bless My Bloomers. They belonged to a petite, size-four brunette with big brown eyes who had giggled and pranced when she saw herself in the mirror wearing the getup.

Carlene jumped when her cell phone rang. The ring tone said it was Lenny, but she was still speechless, staring at the scrap of satin in her hand.

She dropped to her knees on the carpet and bent forward into a tight ball, her blond hair falling over her face. She felt as if someone had kicked her firmly in the gut and she couldn't breathe. In a few seconds she managed a sitting position, wrapped her arms around her midsection, and sucked in air, but it burned her lungs. The noise that came forth from her chest sounded like a wounded animal caught in a trap. Tears would have washed some of the pain away but they wouldn't flow from her burning green eyes. Finally, she got control of the dry heaves and managed to pull herself up out of the heap of despair. Dear God, what was she going to do?

The brunette who'd bought the red-satin outfit had told her that she and her sugar daddy were going to Vegas, and she wanted something that would make him so hot he'd be ready to buy her an engagement ring. What was her name? Bailey? Brenda? No, something French, because Carlene remembered asking her about it. Bridget…that was it! Bridget had been to Vegas with Lenny. On how many other trips had he taken a bimbo with him and how many of them had been ten or fifteen years younger—and a size four, for God's sake?

In seconds, the phone rang again. She picked it up and said, "Hello." Her voice sounded like it was coming from the bottom of a well or, maybe, a sewer pipe.

"Carlene, I left my briefcase in my office. I slept on the sofa to keep from waking you, since I got in so late last night. Bring it to me before you go to work, and hurry. There's a contract in it that I need and the people will be here to sign in ten minutes. I'll hold them off with coffee until you get here."

No good-bye.

No thank you, darlin'.

Not even a please.

Did he talk to Bridget like that?

Anger joined shock and pain as she dropped the panties back in the briefcase and then removed the little card she'd made for him to find that morning. She'd written that she was sorry she had fallen asleep before he got home and that she'd make it up to him that night with champagne and wild sex. She stood up, straightening to her full statuesque height of just a couple of inches under the six-foot mark. Damn that sorry bastard to hell. How could he do this to her?

Ripping the note into confetti-sized pieces and throwing them in the air did nothing to appease her anger. Dozens of questions ran in circles through her mind. Had Lenny brought his twenty-something-year-old bimbo to her house for a romp on her bed while she was at work? Did that sorry sucker have sex with his mistress at noon and then with his wife that same night? Just how long had the affair been going on, anyway?

Among them all came one solid answer. She was not living in the same house with a lying, cheating, two-timing son of a bitch. She was leaving his ass and nothing or no one could convince her to stay another night under the same roof with him.

Five Red-Hot Chili Cook-Off trophies looked down from the mantle at her. She picked them up one by one and hurled them across the room. Not one of the damn plastic things broke, which made her even angrier, but she didn't go to the garage and get a hammer to work them over. Instead, she turned into a feverish packing fiend. In less than half an hour her van looked like an overflowing Salvation Army donation hut. Clothing and shoes were stuffed into the back like sardines. Plastic grocery bags filled with items from her dresser drawers were stacked in the backseat, and the briefcase sat right beside her on the front seat.

She gave it looks meant to fry holes through the leather, but it just sat there as cool as Lenny. Damn his black soul to hell for all eternity. She hoped that he was given a place sitting naked on a barbed wire fence and every time he fell off the devil shot him with a cattle prod.

From their house in Cadillac, Texas, to Lenny's car dealership in

Sherman was exactly seven miles and she made it in a little less than five minutes. If it hadn't been for good brakes on her van, she would have plowed right through the plate-glass windows and rammed into that pretty brand-spanking-new red Corvette in the showroom. Some days started off bad and got worse as they went along.

Tears begged to be turned loose but she blinked them back. Be damned if he'd see her cry or reduced to a heap on the floor, either. It might happen, but he wouldn't bask in the glory of seeing it.

Her hands shook and her jaw ached from clenching her teeth. She took a deep breath and pushed open the door of her van, remembering to grab his briefcase before she slammed the door shut. Her bravado left when she looked through the window and caught sight of him through the glass windows in his office right off the showroom floor. Her stomach churned and nausea set in again. Could a person love and hate someone at the same time?

Her legs felt like they were filled with steel when she pushed open the glass door and headed toward Lenny's office. He looked up from behind his desk and with a flick of his wrist motioned for her to come on in.

She was still staring at him trying to figure out whether to beat him to death with the briefcase or just set it in the middle of the floor and get the hell out of there before she started weeping, when she saw a movement in her peripheral vision.

"Well, hello!" Bridget appeared from behind the Corvette parked just inside the doors. "It's good to see you again."

Either the woman did not know Carlene was Lenny's wife or she was a fool who'd caught an acute case of stupid from Lenny Joe Lovelle. Either way, she was crazy as hell and didn't value her hair or eyeballs. Anyone with two sane brain cells in their heads could see that Carlene Lovelle was a time bomb with a lit fuse.

Bridget's eyes twinkled and she lowered her voice to say, "The red outfit drove my sweet sugar daddy right up the walls. Honey, we had the honeymoon suite and we didn't hit the blackjack tables one time all weekend. He didn't even leave to go to his business meetings. We spent the whole two days in that big round bed or else in the heart-shaped hot tub. It was our five-month anniversary and he said that he got luckier in that room than he ever did at the gambling tables. I'll be back in to buy something else for the sixth month. We're going to Florida to celebrate my twenty-second birthday as well as our anniversary. I'm thinking naughty nurse so get the bling out and I betcha I get my ring on that trip. Oh, and guess what else? We are both members of the mile-high club now."

Carlene plopped the briefcase down on the hood of the Corvette and wished that she'd bought one of those shiny metal ones for Lenny's birthday instead of one made of soft kid leather. Hell, if she had a metal one, she really could beat him to death with it, but that fancy leather thing wouldn't even leave bruises.

Bridget's eyes widened out to the size of saucers when she saw the LJL initials on the top of the familiar case and had trouble staying in their sockets when Carlene popped it open. Right there on the top of a big manila envelope were the red panties.

Using a pen with the car dealership logo, Carlene picked up the underpants and threw them at the woman. Then she dumped documents, pens, sticky notes, and everything else in the briefcase onto the tile floor and stomped holes in the papers with her spike heels.

Bridget caught the scrap of red satin and all the color drained from her face. "What are you doing with my panties? And why do you have Lenny's briefcase? Who in the hell are…oh, my, sweet Jesus!" She slapped a hand over her mouth. The panties hung on her pinky finger, and it looked like she was trying to swallow the evidence.

Carlene picked up the empty briefcase and lobbed it like a rocket toward the window between her and Lenny. It lost momentum and didn't even crack the glass but it made him drop like bird shit behind his desk.

"I…I…" Bridget stammered.

Well, praise the Lord, her vocabulary now had two vowels. Maybe by the end of the day, she could add a consonant or two and be able to speak in whole sentences again.

Lenny must've jumped up as fast as he dropped because suddenly he was beside her. "My God, Carlene, what in the hell…oh!" He stopped dead.

His eyes darted from Bridget to Carlene. "I can explain. Bridget, honey, tell Uncle Sam to close the deal with Mr. and Mrs. Reynolds. He'll have to reprint the contracts. And would you please clean up this mess before anyone sees it? Carlene, we'll go discuss this over some coffee in the lounge."

Then he proved just how damned stupid he was by reaching out and touching her shoulder as if he could charm her into forgiveness. Well, Lenny Joe Lovelle wasn't charming jack shit out of her that morning, and it would be a cold day in hell before she ever forgave him. Even Alma Grace, with all her religion and praying, would agree that the Good Book did not condone adultery or fornication—even though it didn't mention skimpy under-britches.

She doubled up her fist and landed a good right hook in his left eye. He went down on his knees and yelled, "Why in the hell did you do that?"

"Because you touched me, you son of a bitch. If you ever lay a hand on me again, I will snatch you baldheaded and then start on your bimbo over there," she yelled.

Shit! Had she really raised her voice right out in public like that? Carlene Carmichael Lovelle was a lady who did not air her dirty laundry, but dammit, he'd broken her heart, twisted it up into a pretzel, and now he was acting like it was nothing. She glared at him, hands on hips and back as straight as steel.

Bridget instinctively covered her hair with her hands, the panties now looking like dangly earrings as they floated down from finger-tips to shoulders.

He stood up and narrowed his eyes. "Come on, Carlene, we have to talk."

"You can talk to my lawyer."

He laid a hand on her shoulder and smiled. "Darlin'…"

She slapped him with her open hand hard enough to put a blaze of red on his cheek, but he didn't drop to the floor. "Dammit, Carlene. You are making a scene."

"A scene. You want a scene? I'll give you a damned scene that a sugar daddy can appreciate." She placed the toe of her high-heeled shoe on the bumper of the Corvette and marched up across the hood, leaving dents that looked like hail had peppered down on the pretty red car. When she was standing on the top of it, she looked right at Bridget.

"Bridget, *honey*, you had better never show your face at Bless My Bloomers ever again."

"Get off that car. You've already done thousands of dollars worth of damage. Sam is going to sue the hell out of you for this," Lenny shouted.

Sam, a robust man with a rim of gray hair, a belly that hung out over his belt, and five-thousand-dollar eel cowboy boots, rushed out into the showroom. "My God, Carlene, have you lost your mind?"

"She's gone crazy, Uncle Sam," Lenny said.

"You want to see freakin' crazy? I will show you crazy." She stepped down to the hood and did a stomp dance. By the time she finished, the showroom was full. She took a deep bow and hopped down from the hood. "When I'm done, you'll be damn lucky to have potatoes with your beans once a week, much less plan little weekend trips to honeymoon suites where you wallow around in a round bed with office girls rather than going to meetings. Dock his pay for the damage, Sam. You'd be wise to fire his ass, but since he's your nephew, that won't happen, will it?"

"Come on, Carlene, it was just a fling. It only happened one time and I'll never do it again," Lenny whispered.

"Fling! Just a fling?" Bridget's voice was as loud as a fire siren. "You promised me that you were leaving her. You promised me an engagement ring with a two-carat diamond as soon as you left your fat wife. You promised me we would have our own apartment by the time the chili cook-off happens and I could be your cheerleader for the event and you'd hang our picture above all those trophies in your office."

"Well, he's not leaving his fat wife. I'm leaving his cheating ass and he's all yours. Better keep him on a short leash. He charming, but he's a two-timin' son of a bitch." Carlene's high heels sounded like fire crackers as she stormed out of the dealership.

She drove until she reached the outskirts of town, pulled over, and laid her head on the steering wheel. That lyin' cheating bag of shit didn't deserve her tears but they flowed down her cheeks anyway as she sat there with the engine running and the air conditioner turning her warm, salty tears as cold as her heart felt.

❧

Monday morning was Josie Vargas's favorite time of the week. She'd cooked all weekend, put up with whining grandkids and great-grandkids, sons in her living room arguing about football on the blaring television set, and daughters-in-law sipping iced tea at her kitchen table while they gossiped about people she didn't even know. The most beautiful sight in the world was the taillights as they all went home Sunday night after supper. Maybe by Friday she'd be glad to see them again, but right then she rolled her eyes toward the ceiling and gave thanks that she'd only birthed two sons.

"Okay," she muttered at the ceiling. "They say they are bringing the kids to see me so I don't get lonely since Louis died. Me, I think they are coming home to be waited on and to eat my cooking. Tell me I'm wrong. No? You can't lie?"

She warmed two leftover waffles from the day before in the microwave and drizzled a mixture of hot butter and maple syrup over them. That and coffee would keep her until she arrived at Bless My Bloomers where she sewed fancy lingerie for all sizes of women. Crazy women who wanted pearls and ribbons and fancy crap all over their under-britches. Josie couldn't imagine wearing the things that she made. Plain old white cotton panties were good enough for her butt and Louis had never complained one time when he took them off.

He would turn over in his grave if he knew she'd gone back to work. She'd retired at sixty-five and she and Louis had twelve good years together before he died. But she got lonely after he was gone, and when Carlene came to ask her if she wanted a job at Bless My Bloomers, she'd jumped at the chance.

She was ten minutes early and parked her twenty-year-old car around back, leaving the curb space and driveway for customers. She was a short woman with a touch of gray in her hair and brown eyes set in a bed of wrinkles. She was eyeballing her eightieth birthday in another year and she loved those three girls she worked with as much as her own granddaughters. Before she got out of the car, she took out the little compact that Louis had given her for their first anniversary and reapplied her trademark bright-red lipstick.

No one else had arrived yet so she let herself in the back door with her key and headed straight to her little room. It had been the library when the house was a residence but nowadays it was her sewing room. The living room was the store. The parlor had been divided into four fitting rooms. The dining room was the stockroom and the walls were lined with basic bras, corsets, and panties in all sizes, shapes, and colors. There were three bedrooms upstairs, and sometimes the owners, Carlene, Alma Grace, and Patrice, kept extra stock up there if the dining room overflowed.

She'd been working on a fancy corset for a bride when she left

Friday evening. She pulled up her rolling chair, picked up the pearls, and started sewing them one-by-one onto the lace panels between the boning. She'd always liked intricate work. Even as a child she was the one who loved embroidery and needlepoint.

"I don't remember Carlene ever being out sick before. I hope she ain't sick today. Alma Grace will have a prayin' fit if she has to fit all those choir women from her church without any help."

∽✑∾

Alma Grace stopped by her mama's house on the way to work every morning so they could have a mother/daughter devotional. They read the daily pages from the study Bible, said a prayer, and then had breakfast.

Few people in Cadillac even remembered the Fannin sisters' real names. Sugar's birth certificate said Carolina Sharmaine, but she'd always been called Sugar. The same with Gigi; her real name was Virginia Carlene. And Tansy had started out life the day she was born as Georgia Anastasia. They'd each had a daughter within a year of each other twenty-seven years before. Alma Grace belonged to Sugar, Patrice to Tansy, and Carlene to Gigi.

"Are you planning a surprise for the Easter program this year?" Her mother pushed a strand of ash-blond hair back behind her delicate ears. Diamond studs glittered in the morning sunlight. Both of her sisters told her that the television show *Good Christian Bitches* had really been modeled after Miz Sugar Magee. Those women damn sure hadn't given up a bit of their bling or their style to be religious and neither had Sugar or Alma Grace.

Alma Grace's curly blond hair, the color of fresh straw, was held back that morning with a silver clasp. Cute little cross earrings covered with sapphires matched the necklace around her neck and her blue eyes.

"Now Mama, you know I never give away all my secrets about the Easter program. That's why we have such a crowd. Everyone knows it'll be spectacular and even bigger than the year before. But I will tell you this much. The teacher from the drama department at the school is working on a gizmo to make me fly as I sing the final song and there will be sparkles on my wings. It's going to be breathtaking. They'll still be talking about it at the chili cook-off. Maybe even at the festival this fall."

Sugar's eyes misted. "It will be the best thing that's ever happened in our church, and when your sweet voice starts to sing the final song, it will be like the heavens open up and the angels are singing."

Alma Grace dropped a kiss on her mother's forehead. "Thank you, Mama. I've got to go to work."

Sugar sighed. "Lord, I wish you wouldn't have…"

Alma Grace laid a hand on her mother's arm. "I prayed about it, remember? And God told me it was just underwear. Carlene, Patrice, and I are making a good living at Bless My Bloomers. And just think of all the happy men in the world who are staying home with their wives because of our jobs."

Sugar nodded seriously. "That's the only thing that I take comfort in, darlin'. Now let us have a little prayer before you go. We'll pray the blood of Jesus will keep you pure as you work on all those hooker clothes."

"Mama!"

Sugar tilted her chin up. "Well, God didn't tell *me* that those things were fit for decent God-fearin' women so I intend to pray about it every day."

"I've got to go or I'll be late. Dinner at Miss Clawdy's at noon?" Alma Grace asked.

"Not today. Gigi and Tansy and I are going up to Sherman to look at a new car for Gigi. She's still driving one that's four years old. It's a disgrace, I tell you. She's got a son-in-law in the business and she drives a car that old. Why, honey, it's almost a sin. I guess I should be happy that she's driving a car instead of a truck, but honestly, four years old!"

"Well, y'all have a good time and bring the new car back by the shop for us to see. That Lenny is so good to his family. Maybe someday I'll find a husband like him. Carlene is one lucky woman."

Sugar waved from the front door. "Yes, she is."

Alma Grace parked the car beside Josie's and went in through the back door. "Hey, no coffee? Where's Carlene?" she yelled.

"Ain't here yet. Hope she ain't sick. Y'all have got all those church women coming for a fitting today."

Alma Grace rolled her eyes toward the ceiling. She'd forgotten about that appointment. Thank goodness her mother was tied up with Aunt Gigi's new car business or she'd have had to cancel lunch with her. Sugar Fannin Magee pouted when she got all dolled up and didn't get to go out and it was not a pretty sight.

"Think I should call her?" Alma Grace asked.

"Hell, no! She'll call us if she's sick. Maybe she's finally pregnant and got the mornin' sickness."

"A baby." Alma Grace almost swooned.

"I didn't say that she was. I said that she might be, and if she is, she'll tell us when she damn well gets ready. Why don't you make coffee?"

"Because Carlene says that my coffee isn't fit to drink. I'll get the lights turned on and the doors opened. I'm sure she'll be along in a little while. Patrice is late all the time but I've never beat Carlene to work since we opened the shop last year."

❧

The alarm rattled around in Patrice's head like steel marbles banging against the edges of a tin soup can. She groaned and shoved a pillow over her eyes with one hand and used the other hand to slap the hell out of the clock, sending it scooting across the floor. That the plug came loose from the wall was the only thing that saved the damn clock from being stomped to death that morning.

Damn Monday mornings after a weekend of hell-raisin' sex and booze. Wine, beer, Jack Daniels, and half a gallon of rocky road ice cream after the fight with her boyfriend did not make for a good start to a new week. Hangover, bloat, and tears were poor bed partners, especially on a Monday morning.

She kicked the covers off, took a warm shower, drank a cup of tomato juice laced with curry, ate half a can of chilled pineapple, and popped two aspirin. It was her special recipe to cure a hangover.

Her job at Bless My Bloomers was keeping books, inventory, and anything to do with a computer. Lord, she hated to face columns of numbers and deal with the wholesale sellers all morning with her head pounding like she was standing next to a jackhammer.

No one at the shop could help her, either. Alma Grace, bless her heart, could sell a blinged-out corset to a saint, but she could not add up a double column of figures even with a calculator. Carlene, God love her soul, could design something so sexy that the devil would hock his horns to buy it, but she was all thumbs when it came to keeping track of what went out and what came into the shop. If things got hectic in the sales room, Patrice could talk to customers, show them the merchandise, and even make a sale, but she didn't enjoy it.

The bathroom mirror brought about a loud groan. Her aqua-colored eyes looked like two piss holes in the snow and her platinum blond hair, straight from a bottle down at the Yellow Rose Beauty Shop, was only slightly better looking than a witch's stringy strands in a kid's movie. Hell, next week, she might cut it all off and wear it in a spike hairdo. It would damn sure be easier to fix than getting out the curling iron every damn morning.

"Grandma Fannin would have your hide if you did that," she whispered to her reflection.

When she'd done enough to cover up most of the hangover, she pulled a pair of skinny jeans from her closet, along with a tight-fitting shirt that hugged her double Ds and black, shiny, high-heeled shoes that she could kick off under her desk.

Evidently Lenny had brought Carlene to work that morning, since her car wasn't parked out behind the shop. Patrice laid her head back against the headrest for a minute and shut her eyes against the blinding sun, vowing that she'd find her sunglasses before she stepped out into the sun again. She needed coffee, good black strong coffee, and lots of it. Thank goodness Carlene always started a pot first thing in the morning.

Her head throbbed so bad, she'd almost be willing for Alma Grace to lay hands upon her and pray that God would heal her, but then she'd have to listen to her asking God to forgive her for drinking. She just needed something to relieve the headache. She hadn't killed her boyfriend, so she didn't need forgiveness, and even Jesus drank wine, so Alma Grace could keep her preaching to herself.

Shading her eyes with her hand against the bright sunlight, she made her way to the porch. Coffee! She needed coffee and lots of it. Bless Carlene's heart; she always had it brewing first thing in the morning. But that morning the wonderful aroma of fresh coffee did not greet her when she opened the door.

"Dammit!" she swore.

"Carlene?" Alma Grace yelled from the front of the house.

"It's Patrice, not Carlene. Where is our cousin? She's never late," Patrice said.

Josie poked her head out of the sewing room. "From the looks of your eyes, I'd say you have a supersized hangover."

Patrice held up a palm. "Guilty. Don't tell Alma Grace or she'll start praying."

"Come on in the kitchen. I'll fix you up," Josie said.

"I already did my magic."

"Did it work?" Josie pointed at the kitchen table.

Patrice shook her head and it hurt like hell.

"No." She sat down, put her head down on her arms, and poked her fingers in her ears when Josie started the blender.

"What is it?" she asked when Josie set a green drink that looked like ground-up bullfrogs in front of her.

"Don't ask and don't come up for air. Drink it all down without stopping," Josie said.

Patrice did and then slammed the glass on the table with enough force to rattle the salt shakers. "Holy damn shit! That's hotter than hell's blazes."

"Yep and it'll burn that hangover right out of you in five minutes. Now let's go to work. Carlene's not here. I hope she's not sick. Y'all have the church choir coming today for fittings."

"Dammit all to hell!" Patrice groaned. "I'm not in the mood for praisin' God and blessing souls or fitting bras to those holier-than-thou gossiping women."

"Me neither but they've got boobs that have to be roped down, so suck it up. Must have been a helluva a weekend that you had." Josie smiled.

"I don't even want to talk about it until my head stops pounding. God, I hope Carlene isn't sick. I don't want to wait on customers today."

Alma Grace poked her head in the kitchen door. "I hope she's not sick, too, but it would be wonderful to have a baby in the family. My mama and your mama and Aunt Gigi are going to Lenny's this afternoon to look at a car. It'd be a shame if Carlene isn't here when they drive it by to show us."

✑

Carlene breezed in the back door of the shop with an armload of clothing, her head held high, her makeup repaired, and a vow that no one else would ever see her cry again. That damned Lenny Lovelle would never, ever know how much he'd broken her spirit and her heart with his cheating.

"I'd appreciate it if y'all would lend a hand and help me bring in all that stuff in my van before customers start coming into the shop."

Patrice peeked outside and frowned. "Good God, girl. You did more than clean out your closets while Lenny was gone this weekend. Did you buy out a store? Are we going into more than lingerie or what? And the look in your eyes is damn scary. What's going on? You look like you could commit homicide on a saint."

"I'm divorcing that two-timing sleazy sumbitch Lenny Joe Lovelle. I should never have married him in the first place. Aunt Tansy read my palm and told me that you can't change a skirt chasin' bastard, but would I listen? Hell, no! Now are y'all going to help or not? And if you start praying, Alma Grace, I'm going to slap the shit out of you," Carlene said. She sounded mean, but truth was she was just like those hollow chocolate Easter bunnies. If anyone pushed her, she'd crumble into a million pieces.

"Dear Lord," Alma Grace whispered.

Carlene shot her an evil look. "I forewarned you."

"I wasn't praying, although I should be. You want that unloaded up in one of the bedrooms or where? I can't believe you are talking about a divorce." She whispered the last word like it was something dirty.

"Just put everything on that old sofa up there in the first bedroom on the left. I'll decide which room I'm going to live in and hang them all up later."

"Dios mio, tell us what has happened," Josie said.

"Help me get the van unloaded first to give me some more time." Carlene pushed the screen door open and it slammed behind her as she led the way outside to the company van.

"Shit!" Patrice followed her.

"Fool must've gotten caught," Josie said.

"Until death parts us. I heard her say the words," Alma Grace whispered.

"Yeah, well, way I see it is that don't necessarily mean death of the body, girl," Josie said. "I'll be right here when y'all get that stuff all carried upstairs. I'm not making trips up and down those steps with these knees."

It took several trips up and down the stairs to get everything brought inside. When they'd finished, the bedroom looked like a tornado had struck a clothing store. The sofa was completely obliterated and Walmart bags bulging and overflowing with panties, bras, and nightgowns were lined up against the wall.

"Why in the hell didn't you pack in suitcases? I know you've got at least three sets," Patrice asked.

"I was so damn mad I didn't even think about suitcases. He promised her that he'd be living with her by the time the chili cook-off happens and that's only a few weeks from now. And that he'd hang their pictures above those damned trophies. He doesn't have a picture of me in his den, in his office at work, or even in his wallet." Her voice quivered but neither of her cousins heard it or Alma Grace would have started praying again and Patrice would have got out a sawed-off shotgun.

Alma Grace touched Carlene on the arm and said, "Okay, darlin', tell us what happened and we'll take it to the Lord in prayer."

"Coffee first and the Lord can't fix this so I'll be damned if I take it to Him. The person that I'm taking it to is Carson Culpepper and I hope that he's as good as everyone says he is when it comes to divorce court."

"Poor old Lenny." Patrice giggled then grabbed her aching head. Laughter and hangovers did not go together.

Carlene whipped around and glared at her. "He deserves it."

"Hell, yes, he deserves it and Carson will make him wish he'd never even looked cross-eyed at another woman. Who was it and how did you find out?" Patrice asked.

"Remember that cute little brunette who came in here and bought that red corset and matching bikinis? Bridget is her name and we laughed about her going to Vegas with her sugar daddy. Well, she works at the dealership and Lenny is the sugar daddy."

"Then go get him, darlin'. I'm right behind you. You want us to shoot his sorry ass? Ain't a one of us that can't handle a firearm, and we're strong enough to dig a six-foot hole," Patrice said.

"Now girls, there's two sides to every story." Alma Grace folded her hands in front of her, shut her eyes, and prayed. "Dear Lord, please help Carlene forgive and forget. Help Lenny to mend his ways *if* he has transgressed and help them to work this problem out because they have both made vows to you. Amen."

Carlene glared at her cousin. Not one time in the past hour had she thought Patrice and Alma Grace wouldn't both stand behind her in any decision she made. True, they were all different. Patrice with her wild ways and cussing. Alma Grace with her religion. Carlene with her business sense. But they were knitted together with blood that ran as deep as sisters. So why would Alma Grace want her to forgive a two-timin', cheatin' sumbitch like Lenny? She reached up and caught a tear as it escaped from the dam behind her eyelids.

"Why in the hell would you pray like that? You should be praying for God to strike him dead," Patrice said.

"There's two sides." Alma Grace squared her shoulders defensively.

"You got that right," Patrice said. "There's the truth and then there's the lyin', cheatin' bastard's story. Which family are you in anyway?"

"I'll put Carlene on the prayer list and we'll all pray that God will guide you to make the right decision and forgive poor old Lenny for being so weak," Alma Grace said. "Now let's go have some coffee."

"There is no coffee because Carlene is the only one who knows how to make it, and if I was her, I'd poison yours," Patrice said.

Carlene was still amazed that Alma Grace hadn't supported her. Tears stung her eyes and her heart felt heavier than it had all morning. "Coffee might clear our heads," Carlene said as she started down the stairs.

They trooped into the big old kitchen: Carlene with curves that stretched a size sixteen; Alma Grace, the petite cousin; Patrice, the tallest one of the three at five feet eleven inches and slim as a runway model. Carlene put on a pot of coffee and then slumped in a chair. She started at the beginning. Surely when Alma Grace heard the whole story, she'd be more sympathetic.

"The sorry bastard. Let's poison him," Patrice said when she finished.

"You promised to love him through good times and bad. You need to give him a chance to make this all right," Alma Grace said.

Josie stood up from her chair, rounded the table, and hugged Carlene. "Honey, I'm not much younger than your Grandma Fannin would be and I got a feeling that she would tell you the same thing I'm about to tell you. Cut your losses right now and move on with your life. He's not worth it. Life's too short and hell ain't half full for you to put up with that kind of shit."

Alma Grace threw a hand over her eyes. "Dear God."

"You pray for me and I'll hurt you, girl. I swear I will," Carlene said.

"I wasn't praying. I promise that I wasn't. I just remembered that our mothers are going to Lenny's this morning to buy a new car," she said.

The sound that came out of Carlene's throat was somewhere between a giggle and a sob. It quickly turned into nervous laughter, followed by a guffaw that echoed off the kitchen walls, and then tears flooded her cheeks again.

She could tell by the looks on her cousins' faces that they thought she was laughing until she cried.

Patrice threw a kitchen towel across the table toward Carlene. "Dab, don't wipe or you'll ruin your mascara. What do you bet that he runs the other way when the Fannin sisters come through the door? He won't remember that Aunt Gigi has been talking about a new car for weeks. Enough of this shit. We've got a business to run."

Carlene pushed the end of the towel up under her eye. "And I've got to call the furniture store and tell them to deliver a bedroom suite before dark or I'll be sleeping on the floor."

"You can stay with me," Alma Grace offered.

"Hell, no! I'm staying right here. All I have to do is walk down the stairs into the store every morning. It's a perfect setup until the divorce is settled. I hope he loses that damn chili cook-off trophy this year. It would serve him right after promising that bimbo that he would hang her picture above the trophies. I threw them across the room but they didn't break."

"You will make the coffee every morning, right?" Patrice asked.

Carlene shot a look across the table.

Patrice fended it off by putting both her palms up. "Don't be killin' me with your mean looks, woman. I didn't cheat on you and I'm supporting your decision to leave that scumbag. I can't believe he's so stupid he didn't even check his briefcase."

"I can't believe you are so stupid that you married him. Everyone knew he was a skirt chaser," Josie fussed.

"Well, I can't believe you aren't going to live up to the vows you said before all three of our mamas and God. And the fact that the trophies didn't break is a sign that your marriage isn't broken, just cracked, and that it can be mended," Alma Grace sniffed.

"I thought he meant it when he said his womanizing days were over, Josie. I hear the front door. Let's go to work," Carlene said, walking out of the kitchen.

"And he broke more vows than Carlene did, Alma Grace, so stop your sanctimonious shit," Patrice said.

"It's going to be the ruin of us. The church didn't like it when I threw in with y'all to put in a lingerie shop but a divorced woman in the mix? I don't know what's going to happen to me," Alma Grace whispered.

"We've done got past the fifties, cousin. Divorce happens. Get over it and you better not ever let me hear you praying for that bastard again or I'll snatch you baldheaded," Patrice said.

Carlene returned with a white carryout box and opened it before she set it in the middle of the table. "That was Beulah from across the street. She ran over to Miss Clawdy's and brought us a dozen pecan tarts. Said that she'd heard the bad news and would be praying that me and Lenny could work things out. Don't you *even* roll your eyes at the ceiling Alma Grace! She said that she hoped that the tarts would help us get through the morning."

"Bad news travels fast," Josie said.

"Fat chance of working it out," Patrice said. "Lenny Joe has treated you horrible, Carlene. It's over."

Alma Grace reached for a tart. "You had these at your wedding. All arranged on a silver platter on the groom's table. You want one? Remember all the good times, Carlene. God wants you to forgive Lenny."

"I'd rather lick the white tops off of chicken shit." Carlene marched out of the room before she had another emotional outbreak just thinking about her wedding day.

Chapter 2

THE FANNIN SISTERS, GIGI, Tansy, and Sugar, arrived in force at Bless My Bloomers at ten minutes until twelve. Gigi was the oldest at fifty-eight and she didn't mind carrying the responsibility of being the firstborn. But her exact year of birth was only known to a choice few and she'd promised to cut their tongues out if they ever told a soul, living or dead. Her champagne-blond hair was swept up into a high Texas style twist, and her pecan-colored eyes were not glittering with happiness that morning.

Taking the trash out without her high heels was right up there next to coveting her neighbor's ass in the list of sinful abominations and that day she wore black three-inch spikes with gold touches on the toes. They looked good with her skinny jeans, a western-cut shirt with pearl snaps, loop earrings with diamond Texas Longhorns dangling from the ends, a gold wide-cuff bracelet with a big Longhorn in diamonds on her right arm, and a watch that matched it on the other wrist.

Tansy was the middle sister and the shortest of the three. Her thick medium-beige hair, according to the box that Stella used down at the Yellow Rose, rested in bouncy natural curls on her shoulders. She fancied herself a bit of a psychic and said that God had given her brown eyes so she could see into the future. She looked like she could pull a crystal ball from her oversized purse or maybe a deck of tarot cards from her flowing tiered skirt with bright blue peacocks scattered over an orange background. The matching orange T-shirt, a lime green stretchy belt with a multi-colored stone buckle, and hot-pink high heels did not tone down her outfit one bit.

Sugar had pulled her hair back with a bright red scarf and let the ends hang over her shoulder. Her slim skirt was red, her button-up blouse pure white with red buttons, and her high heels were black. She wore a quadruple strand of pearls that had belonged to her mother and a pearl and diamond tennis bracelet.

"Dear Lord," Patrice muttered when they paraded into the store.

"You can't pray either, especially after coming here with a hang-over this morning," Carlene hissed.

"Mary Carlene Carmichael Lovelle, why didn't you call me first thing when you found out?" Gigi did not beat around the bush.

Carlene had never even heard all four of her names strung together.

"Have you talked to Lenny?" she asked.

Alma Grace poked her head out into the foyer where the women had stopped. "Did you go buy a car this morning?"

Tansy poked a finger toward Carlene. "Hell, no, we didn't talk to Lenny or buy a car from that bastard. If you will remember, young lady, I told you I had a premonition about that boy before you married him. Everyone in Grayson County knew that he was a womanizer just like his daddy. So you can't say you weren't warned."

"Yes, ma'am, you did." Carlene nodded. "I should have listened."

"None of this is her fault." Patrice joined the ladies.

Sugar frowned at Patrice. "We ought to have a time of prayer before we even hear Carlene's side of the story. Why did you create such a public scene? I heard you ruined a perfectly good Corvette by dancin' on it like a low-class heathen and you screamed at him and that horrible woman in public. I know you were angry but Lenny might be sorry and straighten up. You need to pray to God for guid-ance in how to save your marriage."

"Yes, ma'am, I surely did create a scene and even God can't save this marriage," Carlene said.

Tansy popped her hands on her hips. "Sugar, we are not going to pray so get that out of your head. Prayer is not penicillin and it won't cure everything from philanderin' husbands to ingrown toenails. And who gives a rat's ass if the town is talkin'. I'm proud of you, Carlene. Lenny had it comin' if he's been cheatin'. I wouldn't put up with it and neither would you, Sugar, so don't go all holier than thou on us."

The bell above the entrance door rang and more than a dozen women pushed their way into the store. Church ladies, gossip, and her mother all in five minutes! Carlene hadn't even had time to process everything that had happened that morning and hell had just arrived in the form of a dozen church women.

The first one through the doors said, "We're here for our fittings. We brought our brown-bag special lunches with us because we only have an hour before we have to be at the church to practice for the Easter program. You know it's less than three weeks and we have to be strapped down securely during the part when we all jump for joy. Last year I was wearin' a button-up shirt and two buttons popped off and darlin', the bra I was wearing did not do its job. Had to turn my back and work fast, I tell you. It was downright embarrassing. Alma Grace, I'll go first."

"Y'all can wait in the kitchen," Carlene whispered to her mother and aunts. She'd managed to hold it together and not cry like a baby on her mother's shoulder but it had taken a lot out of her.

"Hell, no! We ain't waitin' in no kitchen," Tansy said. "We'll go over to Clawdy's and have some lunch. But we will be back and you hold your head up, girl. I mean it. Don't you let those women talk you into changin' your mind. I swear, I'll kick your ass myself if you forgive that sumbitch. I knew something like this would happen. My poor bird, Dakshani, wouldn't even eat his special treat this morning so I knew trouble was on the way."

"Jesus couldn't change my mind," Carlene said.

Sugar shook her finger at Carlene. "Don't you be using the savior's name like that."

"It's the truth, Aunt Sugar."

Her mother, Gigi, hugged her tightly and whispered, "I'll gladly put out a contract on his sorry ass. You be thinkin' about it."

Sugar kissed her on the cheek and whispered, "I'll lift you up to Jesus in my prayers and he will help you to forgive Lenny."

Forgive Lenny? No way in hell. It was a black-and-white issue with no fuzzy gray edges. He cheated. No trust, no marriage.

❧

Tansy, Gigi, and Sugar lined up in order of birth and paraded across the street and down to the next corner. The Fannin girls had come to Cadillac and whether they thought Carlene was right or not, they'd stand by her. But of all three, Gigi was the one with smoke coming out of her ears. Her jaws ached from clamping them shut and she wanted to strangle someone just to get a little practice in for when she faced off with Lenny. If he'd abused her baby girl in addition to cheating on her, there would be more than a Corvette at the dealership with holes in it.

Trixie was working the register at Clawdy's that day. She and her best friends, Marty and Cathy Andrews, owned and operated Miss Clawdy's Café, which was located across the street and down the block from Bless My Bloomers.

"Afternoon, ladies. Is it Sugar's time to treat y'all?" Trixie asked.

"Hell, no!" Tansy said. "It's my turn. That's why I brought them to a buffet. Gigi has a mad spell on and when she's mad she eats a lot."

"I heard there was trouble in the Lovelle paradise," Trixie said softly.

"You'd sure understand how my Carlene feels today since you've been through the same thing. You had a lyin' sack of shit for a husband, too," Gigi said.

Trixie circled around the counter and hugged Gigi. "Yes, ma'am, I sure do know how she feels. It'll take a while but she'll move on and he'll be sorry that he lost a good woman like Carlene."

"You ever think about working it out with Andy back before he remarried?" Gigi asked.

"Hell, no! Trust is the foundation for a marriage. Once that's gone, the marriage is gone. It'll take y'all a while to adjust but time helps." Trixie went back to the cash register, ran Tansy's credit card through the machine, and laid the receipt on the counter for her to sign.

Tansy picked up the pen and hurriedly put her name on the paper. "Carlene is pretty mad. I can see it in her eyes. I don't think even Sugar and all her prayers could talk her into giving him another chance."

"I'm not going to talk her out of anything. She's twenty-seven years old and I'll support her decision even if it means giving her an alibi after she's killed him," Gigi declared.

"There has never been a divorce in the Fannin family." Sugar sighed.

"Miz Sugar, some things even God don't forgive," Trixie smiled. "Y'all enjoy the buffet. Cathy made blackberry cobbler today so leave room for dessert. Got to get back to work."

Gigi picked up a tray at the end of the buffet and set a plate, two bowls, silver wrapped in a napkin, and a sweet tea glass on it. She loaded the plate with sweet potato casserole, jalapeño cornbread, fried potatoes, and fried okra, and then filled one bowl with beans and the other with greens.

"I knew you'd go for food therapy," Tansy said.

"Always." Gigi found a table for four, arranged her food, and set the tray on a nearby table. "Food always helps me see things clearly. It's the same as reading palms or cards is for you and praying is for Sugar."

"Speakin' of which." Sugar bowed her head and whispered, "Dear Lord, thank you for this food and help us get through this catastrophe that has befallen our family. We lift it all up to you and leave it in your hands. Amen."

"A-damn-men," Tansy said. "Now do just that."

"What?" Sugar asked.

"Leave it in your sweet Jesus' hands and don't bitch at him when he strikes that damn Lenny Joe Lovelle with boils and pestilence. Screwin' around with another woman…why, it's a damn disgrace, that's what it is. He's the one who's brought all this catastrophe shit upon our family so ask God to give him a case of impotence that even Viagra can't fix." Tansy picked up a piece of cornbread and crumbled it into her bowl of beans.

"I wonder how Carlene found out, anyway," Gigi mumbled.

Trixie brought a pitcher of sweet tea and filled each of their glasses. "You didn't get the whole story? Well, I heard that she found a pair of red bikini underwear in his sock drawer and since she'd made them over at Bless My Bloomers, she even knew who they belonged to and"—she lowered her voice—"they were a size four. But I also heard that she didn't know the woman worked with Lenny until she got there this morning and the woman didn't know that Carlene was Lenny's wife. And they had a face-off right there in the showroom. Gossip says that Bridget, that's the other woman's name, tried to eat the red thongs."

"Holy shit!" Tansy said.

Gigi frowned and her eyebrows shot up a notch. "I'd have shot both of them on the spot. Carlene could do it, too. She's a fine shot. I taught her myself. I would never put up with philanderin' and Hank Carmichael knows it."

Tansy jabbed a fork into a chicken-fried steak. "I'll call both of you so you can get your black suits out of the cleaners if Alex Cordell pulls a damn stunt like that. Our poor Carlene."

"Nothing is an unforgivable sin except blaspheming the Lord's name," Sugar said.

Gigi went back to the buffet for a second bowl of beans.

❧

Carlene could determine a woman's bra size just by looking at her, but she brought out three tape measures, strung one around her neck and tossed one to each of her cousins. It made the customers feel like they were getting their money's worth if they got the full treatment with measurements and lots of choices.

She'd come up with the idea of Bless My Bloomers when she couldn't find fancy lingerie to fit her size-sixteen figure and had started making it herself. The original plan was that it would cater to plus-size women, that it would be sexy, stylish, and affordable. But it had quickly become a store for all sizes and it was sexy, sometimes downright slutty, and they took credit cards, cash, and checks to make it affordable.

She wrapped the tape around her customer's breasts and wrote the number down on a sticky note. "You need a 38D."

"Is that the size the woman had on that you slapped the devil out of this mornin'?" The woman's eyes bored into Carlene's. "I heard that you flat out put her on the ground and Lenny had to break up the fight. And then you jumped up on a Corvette and stomped holes in it and that you pulled a pistol out of your bra and waved it around. Also that Sam is so mad at Lenny that he's making him pay for the Corvette. Is that hussy really pregnant with Lenny's baby?"

"Didn't lay a hand on her. She did the talkin' mostly and I just listened and I don't own a pistol. I do have a rifle but Daddy keeps it at his house," Carlene said. "I'll be back in a minute. I'll bring four different styles in for you to try on."

The lady snorted. "I'd have liked to have been there to see whatever went on even more than having a good fittin' brassiere. But you know you vowed to love him for better or worse. It don't say that you can't make him miserable when you take him back. Lord knows, I'd get a new car out of the deal and maybe a new diamond ring, too. Sam might even give you a new car if you'd go back to Lenny. And once you settle your differences with him, we'll all have a night of prayer for that young lady to see the error of her ways. There's lots of good homes she can put that baby into for adoption. Did she know he was married?"

"Yes, ma'am, she did," Carlene said.

Dammit! Carlene didn't want to talk about Lenny. She didn't want advice. Just hearing his name made her angry yet wrung out her heart like an old rag mop. How in the hell had the news already gotten all over Grayson County? Her Mama was right when she said that gossip spread faster than the plague and did as much damage. She inhaled deeply, held her breath, and then let it out very slowly, and wished that the day would end.

Her phone rang while she was picking 38D bras from the rack in the stockroom and she answered it without even looking at the ID.

"You over your mad spell? How about dinner at our favorite little Italian place in McKinney tonight? I'll pick you up at five in a limo. We can discuss this over champagne on the way." Lenny lowered his voice seductively.

"Are you insane? You cheated on me. Is Bridget pregnant?" Carlene screamed into the phone.

"I only slipped this one time, Carlene, and no, she's not pregnant," Lenny said.

"And now you are lying. Your precious Bridget told me that you've been seeing her for five months."

Silence.

"Well?" she said.

"When you cool down, call me. We can work through this. You've been so busy with your business that you haven't had any time for me," he said. "I even made time for you when the Chili Kings and I were working on the cook-off every year. But since you got that damned old store, you've been ignoring me."

"This is not my fault!" She wished that cell phones had a button that made the sound of someone slamming a receiver down violently. But they didn't so she beat it against the door frame and hoped that it burst his eardrum.

⟅⟆

Patrice always used a tape measure when she had to leave her lair of figures and computers to help out in the sales department.

Kim measured out to be a 34C. Patrice was envious. She'd love to be that size so that she could buy her bras anywhere but oh, no, she got a healthy dose of the Cordell genes and they shared DNA with Guernsey milk cows.

Carlene took a common C-cup bra and Patrice had always been jealous of her, too. And she'd been jealous of Carlene when she'd landed Lenny Lovelle. He'd chased everything that wore a skirt from the time he was old enough to know the difference in little girls and boys. Everyone in Cadillac had figured he'd have a trophy wife if and when he ever settled down. So it had come as a big surprise when he proposed to Carlene Carmichael, a slightly overweight woman who worked at a bank in Sherman.

She met Carlene coming out of the stockroom with a dozen bras lined up on her arm. "What or who were you screaming at in there? Did Lenny call?"

Carlene nodded. "He's acting all cool as a cucumber. He wants me to go with him to dinner. Limo, wine, and the whole works while we talk about the problem. And it's my fault because I've been working too hard. According to him he even made time for me during this beloved old chili cook-off," Carlene whispered.

"Screw him and feed him fish heads." Patrice rattled off one of their favorite sayings.

"I don't want to screw him and I'd rather feed him poison."

They walked away from each other and Patrice picked out a

dozen bras to take back to the dressing room. She looked down at her own endowment and sighed. It was a good thing that she wasn't in the church choir. If she had to jump around doing choreography while singing "Shout for Joy" she'd sure enough have a problem with her shirt popping buttons and her boobs falling out for the whole congregation to see.

When Patrice hung the bras around the dressing room, Kim picked out her favorite two and Patrice waited outside. It wasn't long until Kim jerked the curtain back. There she stood in jeans and high heels and a black lacy bra.

Damn, that brought back memories.

Patrice had been the last one of the three cousins to turn twenty-one and the other two girls had taken her out for a party in Dallas. That was six years ago and her first and only one-night stand. That damn Lenny Joe Lovelle was sexy as hell, smooth talking, and he'd come on to her after the other girls had already gone up to their hotel room. She'd stayed for just one more drink and suddenly there he was on the bar stool next to her with that big smile on his sexy face.

Thirty minutes later she was weaving in front of an oversized mirror in the hotel room in nothing but jeans, a black lacy bra, and high-heeled shoes. The next morning she had chalked it up to too much whiskey and he never called her like he said he would when he left her hotel room. Who would ever have thought he'd wind up married to Carlene a year later or that he was stupid enough to leave a pair of underpants in his briefcase? Or that Carlene had been the one who sewed the fancy beads on that pair of bikinis?

Shit fire! Did she tell Carlene or take the secret to the grave with her?

"So do you think they'll get back together?" Kim asked as she pushed back her dark hair and looked at herself in the three-way mirror.

"Who?" Patrice frowned.

"You know. Carlene and Lenny. I heard that his mistress might be pregnant and is definitely pushing for an engagement ring. If they don't get back together and if she's not expecting a baby, I'd sure like to have another chance at him. He's a real sex machine in the bedroom." She turned this way and that way, looking at the bra. "I like this one just fine. I don't need to try on any more. I will come back when I don't have the rest of the choir hovering around. I want something sexy and pretty to have on hand just in case. I would like to have that cute little corset that y'all got in the window."

"How do you know that Lenny is a sex machine?" Patrice asked.

"Honey, he hasn't always been married and I'm just one of dozens and dozens of notches on his bedpost. Experience makes perfect and Lenny Joe is near perfect in the bedroom." One of Kim's hazel eyes slid shut in a slow wink. "Would you put that corset back for me? I checked and it's exactly my size. And I'd also like a pair of boy-cut panties to match it and maybe some hot-pink hose."

"Shhh," Patrice said. "Don't you even want to know how much all that will cost?"

"It'll be worth every penny, I'm sure." Kim winked again.

Patrice slowly shook her head. That woman would be singing "I've Just Seen Jesus" in the church before the whole town.

Alma Grace's first customer was the director of the church choir. She was even higher up on the righteous ladder than Alma Grace, who had been in charge of the Easter program for the past four years. Even though Alma Grace was the president of the Easter committee, Floy Gastineau was the big boss of anything that had to do with the choir. She was the drill sergeant and the girls, no matter age or size, were her recruits. And they'd better not be late to practice unless they were sick nigh unto death. Missing it altogether better mean they were in the hospital on a ventilator and hanging onto life by a thread. Jesus might forgive. Floy didn't.

Floy started talking the minute Alma Grace showed her into the dressing room. She was a wiry little woman who always wore long-sleeved dresses buttoned all the way up to her skinny neck, her hair in a knot on the back of her head, and a frown on her face. "I wear a 36B and I want an unadorned black bra. The shirts we're wearing are black. I don't agree with that part, Alma Grace, and you know it. But you are right about us looking uniform if we all wear black. Reds, yellows, and pinks wouldn't all match like black. But it is Easter and we should be wearing spring colors."

"Yes, ma'am." Alma Grace nodded.

"And before you go, what is this I'm hearing about Lenny and Carlene?"

Alma Grace sighed. "They are having a bit of a rough time but I'm praying for them to see the error of their ways and put their marriage before their anger."

"Once a womanizer, always a womanizer, but she knew what she was getting when she married him. So she needs to remember her vows and forgive him. I thought she was woman enough to keep him from straying but I guess I was wrong," Floy declared.

"Maybe we could have a special night of anointing prayer for her," Alma Grace suggested.

"She'd have to be willing for it," Floy said. "Can't lay hands on a woman that ain't willing for help. I don't know what we'll do about her being on the Easter egg committee."

"I'll go get your bras." Alma Grace slipped out of the room.

There was no way that Carlene would be willing to show up for a night of prayer. Too bad. They could have a potluck and she'd talk her mama's cook into making her famous pecan sandy cookies for the refreshment table.

She met Patrice coming out of the stockroom.

Patrice stopped in the hallway and raised a perfectly arched eyebrow. "I wish we would have done this Friday. Is Floy talkin' about Carlene?"

Alma Grace nodded. "Oh, yeah, but I told her that I was praying about it and God would surely give them the good sense to get back together. And I am praying, Patrice, whether you like it or not."

"I'm already sick to death of hearing about it and you'd better not pray in my presence, girl. Not if you value your life. Blood is supposed to be thicker than water, you know." Patrice headed into the stockroom.

Alma Grace took three bras from the rack and carried them back to the dressing room. Floy chose the plainest one and shooed Alma Grace outside. "I don't need an audience to put on my undergarments. If you want to be the head of the Easter committee, Alma Grace, you'd best fix this mess."

❧

Carlene sunk down into an overstuffed vintage chair beside the dressing room and threw a hand over her eyes when the choir ladies had gathered up their new bras and the remains of their brown-bag lunches and took off toward the church with Alma Grace in tow. She was glad that her cousin was the head honcho when it came to the Easter program. Maybe she'd go get a dose of the Holy Spirit with her singing and come back with a smile on her face. She'd been walking around all morning like she'd just been diagnosed with some dread disease and only had two hours to live.

A marriage had died that morning but there wouldn't be a funeral. The more she thought about it, the more Carlene didn't want a damn thing that Lenny had. She wanted her business and half of the equity in the house, since she'd made half the payments the past five years. The rest he could keep because she'd never know if one of his women had touched it. Well, all of it except for her Granny Fannin's crystal candleholders. For those she'd fight him to the death.

Patrice fell into the chair beside her and covered her eyes with both hands.

"Did you have a rough weekend, too?" Carlene asked.

"Had a wonderful weekend at the beginning. Spent it with Yancy in my house, drinking and having sex, watching a movie and having sex while we watched it, eating supper naked, and then we broke up and I ate a quart of rocky road ice cream. Must be the weekend for breaking up. I'm sorry, honey." She got up quickly and crossed the room, dropped down in front of Carlene, wrapped her arms around her, and hugged her tightly. "I'm a sorry excuse for a cousin. I was so damn mad at Lenny that I forgot to console you."

Carlene leaned on Patrice's shoulder. "Rocky road with whipped cream and nuts?"

"Ain't no other way to eat it. Now I'm bloated all out to hell, hungover, and I've got a wicked headache even after Josie's hotter'n hell cure," Patrice said.

Carlene managed a weak smile. "Don't tell her or she'll make you drink another one."

Josie slid into the third chair. "I'm taking my lunch break. I wasn't about to poke my head out the door until all those church women left. I bet all they wanted to talk about was Lenny. Am I right? Beulah called my cell phone twice but I didn't answer it."

Carlene nodded. "Looks like I opened a fifty-five-gallon can of gossip. Sometimes it's hard to think of you, Beulah, Agnes, and even Violet all being the same generation, Josie."

"Well, we are, honey. They're all a couple of years older than me but we come out of the same era. We ain't had nothing juicy in town lately. Folks is needin' something to talk about and you just delivered it up to them on a platter. Only thing you can do now is what you know is right and ignore the gossip," Josie said.

Carlene tried to steer the conversation away from her problems. "Thank you, Josie. Did you get that corset done?"

Josie nodded. "Seems a shame to me to do all that work when it's going to spend most of its time on the floor or the back of a chair."

"Oh, but that new bride will be pretty for her husband for a little while, won't she?" Carlene barely got the words out before she buried her face in her hands and her shoulders began to shake.

Josie threw an arm around her. "Let it all out and get it over with. He ain't worth a single tear but you've got to get past this stage and to the one where you don't give a damn. A divorce is like a death in the family and there's steps you got to go through. You don't get to skip one, neither. It is what it is, darlin'."

"How long does the cryin' one take?" Carlene asked between racking sobs.

Josie patted her on the shoulder and let her sob. "Never know just how long any of them will take but one day it'll all be in the past and you won't even give a damn no more."

The bell above the door said that customers had arrived. They should shut the shop for the day, hang a black wreath on the door, and turn out all the lights. But Fannin women didn't run and hide from problems; they faced them square on. That's what her mama always said and Lenny wasn't taking a bit of her power.

Gigi led the way into the shop and instantly went to Carlene's side. She dropped down on her knees in front of her daughter and wrapped her arms around her. "Do you want me to take care of him, honey?"

"I don't want him dead. I want him to suffer," Carlene wailed.

"I could just shoot him in the knees," Gigi said.

Josie headed toward the kitchen. "I'll bring coffee for everyone."

Tansy patted her on the shoulder. "What can we do to help, darlin'?"

The hiccups had set in with the sniffles. "I don't even have a bed to sleep in tonight."

Patrice handed her a box of tissues. "You can stay with me."

"Don't you worry about a thing." Tansy pulled a cell phone from her oversized purse. "Alex, go out in the yard and bring in our strongest gardeners. Take them up to that bedroom at the end of the hallway, the pink one on the left beside the linen closet. Have them load up every bit of that furniture, including the drapes and rugs, on their pickup trucks and bring it all down here to Bless My Bloomers. Lenny Joe, the sorry bastard, has done cheated on Carlene and she's moving into one of the bedrooms upstairs."

Gigi hugged her daughter one more time before she stood up. "Where are your personal things?"

"Upstairs and it ain't pretty," Patrice said.

"It will be when we are done. Y'all go right on about your business here. We're going to set things in order. Tonight you'll have a bedroom and everything will be organized. Have you called a lawyer yet?"

"Sweet Jesus," Sugar gasped. "This all just happened this morning. When the dust settles, they might reconcile. Don't call a lawyer until we've had time to think about it and pray that God will put his hands on both of you."

Carlene shook her head. "I'm not calling a lawyer right now, Aunt Sugar. And you can pray the wings off the angels but I'm not going to reconcile with Lenny."

"Well, you might go ahead and put Carson on retainer. You sure don't want Lenny to get to him first," Gigi said. "Come on Tansy and Sugar. We'll get her room ready before the movers get here with the furniture. Thank God they bought a house to put the business in. At least she's got a decent bedroom to move into and, Sugar, not another word from you the rest of this day."

Chapter 3

CARLENE WAS SO GRATEFUL when five o'clock arrived that she could have danced another jig on the top of that damned Corvette or gone back to the house and blown holes in every one of those damn chili cook-off trophies. So Bridget had been promised a picture above the mantel. Maybe if she thought of a picture of her and Lenny all hugged up together, the tears would dry up and she'd move on to the next step, which had to be fightin' damn rage.

She was tired of even hearing Lenny's name, thinking about him, and worrying about what happened next. She opened the door into a room that looked like it had been sprayed down in bubblegum pink. Her mother and Aunt Sugar had driven out to the Carmichael place and brought in towels and bathroom rugs after the bedroom had been set up, and they were all pink, too.

She threw herself back on the bed and glared at the pink roses trailing on the wallpaper. If she went to sleep, would they attack her and turn her into the first plus-sized Barbie doll?

Her phone started playing "Hell on Heels," and she reached for it without blinking.

"Did you forget your keys again?" she asked her cousin.

Patrice laughed. "No, I got my keys and I didn't forget anything at the shop. I just want to make sure you aren't suffocating in all that pink. You can still come live with me. I've got an extra bedroom with a red satin bedspread, white walls, and a zebra-striped throw rug. Plus there's a full bottle of Jack Daniels in the cabinet."

"I'm a Jim Beam girl, and thanks but no thanks. The pink didn't kill me when I was a kid. I don't expect it will now. However, if you find me curled up in a ball tomorrow morning just tell the undertaker that the rose vines strangled me plumb to death."

"Well, if it starts getting to you in the night, just come on over. My guest room at least looks like an adult lives in it. Has Lenny called any more?"

"No and I hope he doesn't. I need to get past the crying jags before I talk to him."

"Well, hurry up and get mad as hell. That's the way I want to see you from now on," Patrice said.

She'd barely hung up when the phone started playing "Jesus, Take the Wheel."

"Yes, Alma Grace," Carlene answered.

"I ran by the grocery store and put a half gallon of chocolate marshmallow ice cream in the freezer just in case you want it later and there's a special prize on the kitchen table for you. I wish you'd come on out here to the ranch. There's plenty of room in my house for you or you could stay at the big house. Mama would love to have you."

Carlene was tempted. Aunt Sugar's cook would fuss over her and make sure that she had all her favorite foods. But she'd have to endure the morning devotionals and all the praying that would mention Lenny's name in every single sentence. It wasn't worth it, no sir!

"Thanks but I need time alone to think," Carlene said.

"The doors are always open," Alma Grace said.

"I know. Good night," Carlene said.

The third ring was her mother. "I'd offer you a room here but you need to be alone to sort things out. I've got a Confederacy meeting tomorrow night but Wednesday you will come home for dinner with me and your dad. I hope he's cooled down enough by then to talk sensibly. Right now he's threatening to do unspeakable things to Lenny."

"Yes, ma'am," Carlene said.

Maybe she'd be cooled down enough to talk sensibly but not by the upcoming Wednesday—maybe one of those on the calendar in six months.

Her head ached. Her body felt like it had been put through a wringer washer backward. Every time she shut her eyes, she saw those red bikinis on Bridget when she came out of the dressing room. She alternated between tears and cussing, yelling at the walls and dead silence. If only that blasted chili cook-off was open to women contestants, she'd enter it and win the damn thing just to get back at him.

It was not a good time for Lenny to call and she was sick of talking on the phone, of hearing prayers, and of listening to advice, so she didn't answer the phone. Not the first time, the second, or the third, but when the phone rang the fifth time, she figured if she didn't pick it up, he'd drive across town to the shop and she damn sure didn't want to see him.

"What do you want?" she yelled into the phone.

"You," he whispered.

"Well, good luck with that," Carlene said.

"Come on, honey. I promise it won't happen again. I've learned my lesson," he said.

"No thank you." Carlene's words were clipped and came out from between clenched teeth.

"I'm through playing games. Come home right now. You don't get to wait a week to decide. It's either now or never," he growled.

"Guess it's never." She hung up the phone and headed to the kitchen. Chocolate marshmallow was one of her favorite ice cream flavors.

A surprise waited on the kitchen table. She picked up the paperback book, hoping it was a historical romance that would take her to another time and another world but it was something entitled *Making Your Marriage Work*. The note from Alma Grace on the top said, *Carlene, reading this book is a must for all who seek to enjoy lasting peace, joy, and honor in their homes. One little baby step at a time will put your marriage back together and reading the words on these pages will be the first one. Love and blessings, Alma Grace.*

Lenny had taken the honor right out of their marriage. Maybe she should send it to him. And she wasn't interested in baby steps, giant steps, or any other kind of steps. She forgot all about the ice cream, opened the back door, and heaved the damn thing toward the dumpster. It landed in the open container dead center and Carlene nodded without smiling. Who said her career in high school basketball wouldn't come in handy someday?

She slept poorly that night, waking every time a car went down the street or a tree limb brushed against her window. When dawn came, she finally gave up, took a shower, dressed for the day, and went down to the kitchen. Breakfast was a bologna and cheese sandwich, a glass of milk, and two of the pecan tarts that she swore she wouldn't touch the day before. She made coffee, drank four cups, and made another pot while she waited on everyone to arrive.

Josie was first in the back door. She went straight for the coffee pot and asked, "How are you this mornin'?"

"Better than yesterday morning, not as good as I'll be tomorrow morning. He called me to try to make amends."

Josie clucked like a hen gathering her chicks. "That boy ain't got a lick of sense. If Alma Grace and Patrice get too busy, I'll go out in the shop and help. You know that gossip travels faster than the wind and you don't need to answer forty thousand questions. I stopped by the convenience store and brought you two maple donuts. I know how you like them." She patted Carlene on the shoulder and sat down at the table.

"Thanks, Josie. Gossip does travel faster than a tornado, doesn't it?" Carlene said.

Patrice shut the door behind her and poured a mug of coffee. "There are already five cars parked out front and women waiting on the porch. You and Josie might as well put those needles down and get ready to help. Josie, if you'll run the cash register, we'll take care of fittings and sales. "

"Well, crap!" Josie exclaimed.

Alma Grace yelled that she'd come through the front and the shop was open. She went right to work helping customers who had already been packed on the porch when she had arrived. Every fitting room was soon full and women waited on the front porch swing for their turn at the racks and the gossip.

At noon it finally cleared out and Carlene threw herself into an overstuffed chair in the corner of the beading room. "Jesus, Mary, and Joseph. We weren't that busy at Christmas."

Patrice slumped into another chair. "I hope it's not like this all week. It's good for the cash register but hell on my disposition."

Lenny strutted into the room, bigger than life in his khaki slacks, pale blue shirt, and striped tie. His dark hair was feathered back perfectly thanks to a standing appointment over at the Yellow Rose Beauty Shop every Saturday at five thirty. He was so sexy that it wasn't any wonder he had women lining up to go to bed with him. The first thing Carlene noticed was that he was not wearing his wide gold wedding band.

"Mornin', ladies. Y'all think I might have a word with my wife?"

Patrice sat up on the edge of the chair. "Whatever you got to say to her, I'm going to hear."

"I'm not going anywhere," Josie said.

"I want you to know I'm praying for y'all to put this behind you and for you to repent. I've got customers so I'm leaving," Alma Grace said from the doorway right behind him.

He laid a hand on Carlene's shoulder and said, "April Fools', darlin'! How'd you like that joke? I really pulled a good one on you, didn't I?"

For a split second she believed him and then she remembered the look on Bridget's face when he'd said it was just a fling. That was no joke. There wasn't an actor in Hollywood that could pull off shock that genuine.

She shrugged off his hand. "I'm not buying your brand of bullshit this morning, Lenny Joe. I'm not an idiot."

"I told you when we married that I was hanging up my player jeans. I'm sorry that I took the April Fools' joke too far but you got to admit it was funny." His words were smooth; his tone, icy.

Patrice stood up, crossed the room, and leaned on the doorjamb. "That's not what I heard this morning. Couple of customers told me tales that would fry your little brain. They said that they were surprised that Carlene hadn't caught you before. And honey, they were not a bit bashful. They named places, times, and positions."

Carlene narrowed her eyes at Lenny. "How many were there?"

"Before we got married, a lot," he said.

"And after?"

"Go on and take your shoes off." Josie pointed at his shoes. "But even then you probably ain't got enough fingers and toes to count them all, do you? Carlene is not stupid, Lenny, and that was not a joke."

He glared at Josie. "I don't have to listen to this. Those women are spreading untrue rumors. This has all been blown way out of proportion."

Carlene caught Patrice's eye. "Would you bring the Rolodex in here—the one where we keep the hard copy of the customers' names and numbers so we can email them when we have a big sale?"

Lenny crossed his arms over his chest and waited. Carlene fished her phone out of her purse and when Patrice set the round file on her desk, she flipped through it until she found Bridget's personal number. She poked the numbers in and stared Lenny right in the eyes as she waited.

"Hello," Bridget said cautiously.

"This is Carlene Lovelle. Was this all a big joke?"

Lenny grabbed at the phone, missed, and clamped a hand around her wrist. "My God, Carlene, who are you calling?"

Carlene slapped his hand away. "You touch me again and I'll break your arm."

"Is he there? He promised me last night that he'd never call or see you again. That you were getting a divorce and, hell, no, it's not a joke. Did he say it was?"

"And did he make a single meeting at the dealership conference in Vegas?" Carlene asked.

"No, he did not. That was our five-month anniversary trip. We take one every month to celebrate the first time…well, you know. He promised to marry me as soon as the divorce is final. He said he was glad that you found out because he was tired of living with your fat ass…oops, that wasn't nice, was it?"

Carlene snapped the phone shut and glared at him. "You've got until I count to five to get out of here. One, two…"

He spun around before she said "three" and slammed the front door so hard that several beads rolled off the table.

"What now?" Josie asked.

"Now we send Patrice over to Clawdy's to get us some lunch and Alma Grace has a meeting at the church for the Easter program." Carlene's tone was matter-of-fact. Too bad her aching heart didn't feel the same way.

Alma Grace appeared in the doorway as soon as Lenny left. "Did you make up? Did my book work? I'm so happy for you."

"Hell no, they didn't make up," Patrice shouted. "And what book are you talking about?"

"A book on making a marriage work that I bought for Carlene," Alma Grace answered.

"I threw the damn thing in the dumpster. I'm not interested in saving my marriage, Alma Grace, so don't bring another shitty book in here." Carlene pinched her nose with her two fingers but it didn't help the raging headache.

"You did what? That book cost good money and it's got priceless information in it." Alma Grace took off for the kitchen with Patrice right behind her.

"No, no, no!" Alma Grace's screams brought Carlene to a standing position. She jogged toward the back door just in time to see her prissy cousin sticking her head into the dumpster and bringing out that blasted book all covered with coffee grounds and potato peelings. "Look what you did! This could have helped you fix the marriage you broke."

"Are you crazy, woman? Accept it! Lenny broke the marriage. She didn't," Patrice yelled right back at her.

"But she could've fixed it even if it was a tiny baby step at a time." Alma Grace carried the book back into the house like it was a hurt kitten.

Patrice snatched it out of her hands and threw it in the dishwasher in one fluid motion. "If it survives a good washin', then I'll make her read the damned thing. Hell, I'll read it out loud to her word-for-word."

"You're ruining a brand-new book," Alma Grace whined.

"Yes, I am. I'd set it on fire if we had a gas cook stove. No books. No praying. No shit."

Carlene could never remember a time when there had been so much contention between the three of them. Lord, it might be easier to go back to Lenny than to have to listen to those two argue every day. She wished she could run away and hide but Carmichaels did not run from their problems. Time was supposed to heal but this anger between Patrice and Alma Grace seemed to get worse with every hour.

∽⚬∼

Committee meetings always meant finger foods, so Alma Grace arrived at the church fellowship hall with a platter of jalapeño poppers and a dozen peanut butter cupcakes. God bless her mama's cook. Alma Grace could sweet talk a nun into a black lace corset and fishnet hose but she couldn't make toast without it resulting in sirens and fire trucks.

She set her offering on the table and picked up a purple paper plate. A hard morning of running back and forth from fitting room to stockroom to cash register had flat out worked up her appetite. She started with two chicken salad sandwiches and added a handful of chips on the side.

"You need some sideboards there?" Floy asked from the head of a table where only one seat was left. It was pretty quiet for a committee meeting, which left no doubt that they'd all been talking about the divorce.

"I think I can manage it." She smiled.

"Okay, while we eat, we'll talk business," Floy said. "I heard that Lenny put Carson on retainer this morning so I suppose this divorce is going to happen."

She bit into the sandwich. "I'm not surprised. I hear he even told his new girlfriend that he'd hang a picture of them together above the mantel."

"Why would he do that?" Floy asked.

"Well, you know he's won the chili cook-off every year since he and Carlene married. I guess he plans to win it this year and put his and Bridget's picture holding the trophy up on the wall. But we are praying that he comes to his senses and repents," Alma Grace said.

"We had an executive meeting before you got here and we've voted to change the bylaws for the Easter committee," Floy said bluntly.

The sandwich stuck firmly somewhere between Alma Grace's throat and stomach. It took three big gulps of sweet tea to send it on down. "What does that mean?"

"It means that the person in charge of the Easter program has to be above reproach. It was bad enough when you threw your lot in with your cousins and went into business in a panty shop, but now there's going to be a divorce and talk will be bad. They'll say that Carlene is doing all kinds of things in that room above the store."

"It's pink," Alma Grace stammered.

"What's that got to do with anything?"

"It looks like a little girl's Barbie room. There's no way it could ever be misconstrued as hooker paradise," Alma Grace said.

Floy set her jaw and shook her head. "Even your language has been affected by working in that place. We just can't abide it, Alma Grace. So we put an amendment into the bylaws. It's to save you and your sweet mama embarrassment. From now on the president of the Easter committee can only serve two terms, each one lasting one year. You've already served far longer than that, so as of today someone else is taking over your spot and Kim will help her out. No hard feelings, now. It does say in the Good Book that those who the Lord loves will be chastised. Women need to learn their place and stay in it. If she'd been doing her part in the marriage, Lenny would not have strayed."

Steaming hot tears welled up in Alma Grace's eyes but she didn't let a single one escape. "What about me? I'm the angel who sings the final song and this year we were working on bringing me down from the rafters like I was flying."

Floy's smile was as stiff as that tight little gray bun at the back of her head. "Kim is going to do that. Bless your heart, you can sing in the choir. We'd never take that away from you. Not with your sweet soprano voice."

Alma Grace pushed the plate away from her. If she had to smell that dill pickle another minute, she would throw up. She was ruined and she hadn't done a blasted thing. The fault lay on Carlene's shoulders for leaving Lenny before the Easter program. If she'd stuck around and tried to work it out, none of this would be going on.

Her voice cracked but she didn't let the tears loose. "I suppose you're putting me on the back row, right?"

Everyone in the committee knew that a place on the back row was a slap in the face. There was no way that anyone could even see Alma Grace or hear her either. She'd just been demoted from heaven to hell.

Floy's skinny shoulders popped up a couple of inches in a shrug. "It's the only chair open right now. If someone gets sick, we might make a place for you toward the front."

Alma Grace pushed her chair back. "I'll make it easy for y'all. Just give my chair to someone else and I'll sing with the congregation this year. Have a nice lunch."

She picked up her cupcakes and poppers on the way out, put them in her car, and was about to get inside when she remembered the wings and halo had been bought from her personal checkbook, not the church's money. She marched straight back to the choir robe room to get them. She looked in the closet but they were gone. She checked everywhere but she couldn't find them. Those rotten women had taken her position and stolen her wings, too.

〰️

Patrice looked up when Alma Grace stormed in the back door. She slammed the cupcakes and pepper poppers on the kitchen table and slumped in a chair. Josie opened the cupcake holder and rubbed her hands together.

She grabbed a cupcake and peeled the paper off the sides. "I love peanut butter cupcakes. I can gain five pounds just smelling them. And poppers, too. What happened? Did they call off the church thing?"

"No, they fired me. If I can't be the Easter angel, they aren't going to eat the food I took to the meeting," Alma Grace said.

Carlene dropped her spoon and it rattled across the floor. "They did what?"

"Fired me! To make it less of an embarrassment, they changed the bylaws and now the Easter program committee head can only have that office two years running. Since I've had it a lot longer, I'm out. Just like that and they stole my wings and my halo. Kim gets to wear them."

"Why?" Carlene asked.

Patrice swallowed the first bite. "Floy probably already had Alma Grace on probation for going in with us to buy a sexy panty store. That was a big enough blot on their sweet little sanctimonious self-righteous asses. They sure couldn't deal with a divorced cousin. Dear God, that would singe their wings for sure. Am I right, Alma Grace?"

"You've got to be kidding me," Carlene gasped. "Wait until Aunt Sugar hears this. I'll be taking my name off the Easter egg committee."

Patrice giggled. "Aunt Sugar might even cuss or change churches but you will not take your name off that committee. We've got to have an inside woman or they'll line all of us up before the firing squad."

Alma Grace pointed a long slim finger at Carlene. "This is your fault. I love you because we're kin folks. I respect you because we are business partners. But right now I don't like you. Why'd you have to leave him before the Easter program? Couldn't you have stuck around until it was over? Maybe by then you would have ironed things out. You did promise to stay with him through bad times and good times and it's only been two days and look what a mess you've made. And Patrice is right, if you leave the committee, it'll look like they've won, so you have to stay." Tears streamed down her face, making wet circles as they landed on her cute little white shirt.

"If you have got to blame someone, then blame Lenny, not Carlene," Josie said.

"I do blame him but he could repent and make things right. And I hope Kim is too fat for my wings and I'm mad at you for ruining that book because it might have helped Carlene go back to him but now he's been to see Carson so he's not going to repent," Alma Grace whined.

"He's been to see Carson!" Patrice raised her voice. "Carlene just left yesterday, for God's sake. What are you going to do now, Carlene? He's already retained Carson."

"Guess she pissed him off pretty good when she called Bridget, but he deserves it." Josie got up and busied herself washing up the dirty cups and saucers.

"There goes the house and everything in it." Patrice sighed.

"I don't want anything except Granny Fannin's candlesticks. Mama gave them to me for our first anniversary and I want those back. The rest of it he can have, long as he doesn't try to touch Bless My Bloomers. I'll fight with him until my dying breath before he touches a dime of our profits," Carlene said.

"Surely he wouldn't be that stupid," Patrice said.

"I don't know. Hell hath no fury like a woman scorned or a man who's been caught with his under-britches down around his knees," Josie said.

"Amen," Carlene muttered.

Alma Grace hit the table with her fist. "Or an angel who got her wings stolen. I hope Kim gets laryngitis and can't sing a note. When they come to ask me to step in, I'm going to tell them to…"

"Spit it out. Might as well say it as think it." Josie grinned.

Alma Grace bit her lower lip. "I will tell them to go to hell. That's not a cuss word, it is a destination. And I'm not praying for them or their program. I hope it's a big flop. And I'm still mad at you, Carlene."

Chapter 4

ALMA GRACE SLID INTO the back pew of the Christian Nondenominational Church. No one called it that, but in keeping up with the current trend toward using initials for everything, it was simply the CNC church. She kept her head down and felt condemned for not going to the church where she'd gone her whole life. But the Bible said that under no circumstances was it okay to commit murder even if it was justifiable. If she had to sit in the same room that night with those so-called sanctimonious witches who'd stolen her halo and wings, she'd be sorely tempted to blow the bottom right out of the sixth commandment.

When she was a little girl, the building where the CNC church was located had been a grocery store and her mama brought her along to do the weekly grocery shopping. When the grocery store went out of business, it was converted into a convenience store/gas station and she remembered filling up the gas tank on her little hot-pink Mustang and buying candy bars and Cokes in the store.

Now it was a church and there she was sitting on the back pew. She'd been in the church a few months earlier for a wedding but it had been all decorated that day and had looked real pretty. Now it was bare and kind of sad looking, but peace wrapped around her like a nice warm fleecy blanket on a cold winter night.

Surely God did not want her to attend services there? Her spiritual gift was her voice and there was no choir loft. Not even a few folding chairs back behind that hideously old pulpit that had been painted crimson red. Pews lined either side with a center aisle between them but not even one tapestry or stained glass window graced the bare walls.

The clock behind the pulpit dinged seven times and Darla Jean took her place behind the podium. "Happy Wednesday, everyone. Let's begin our service by opening our hymn books to page one hundred and we'll all sing 'I'll Fly Away' together."

Alma Grace had heard better harmonizing but there was something about the way the congregation got into the hymn that melted her heart. The woman playing the ancient upright piano must have listened to quite a bit of Floyd Cramer because she sure put a lot of his type of runs into the music.

They were in the middle of the second song when someone touched her on the shoulder and she moved down the pew enough to let Jack Landry slide in beside her. "I'm late but I'm here," he whispered.

She pointed at the number on the hymnal page. Instead of reaching for his own book from the back of the pew in front of them, he nodded and shared with her. When that song ended, Darla Jean gave out another number.

Jack leaned over and whispered, "I guess you are here because you're pissed over that stunt about Easter. I heard they hid your wings and halo so you wouldn't take them back. They're out at the Prescott house. I'll shut down the police radio if you want to break in and get them."

"Shhh," Alma Grace said.

Small towns!

Especially Cadillac, Texas!

There weren't even enough cussing words in Josie's vocabulary to cover the way Alma Grace felt right then as she sang "When We All Get to Heaven." Damned old gossip vines anyway! Why couldn't people just accept things the way they happened and not talk them to death?

Darla Jean opened her Bible and read scripture about forgiveness. Then she shut it and started talking. Alma Grace heard the words. She believed them. But she dang sure wasn't ready to embrace them like a brother.

No, sir! If it hadn't been for all the gossip about Lenny cheating, Carlene for leaving him for it, those women for taking her prestigious position, and even Patrice for ruining a wonderful book, she wouldn't be sitting on the back pew of the CNC church that night. She'd be in her own place of worship singing in the choir and she wouldn't be sitting in the back row, either.

The clock struck eight and Darla Jean said, "We'll close with a word of prayer. We have refreshments laid out right over there for anyone who'd like to stay and have fellowship." She pointed to a table on the west wall.

Alma Grace bowed her head and planned to slip out the back door as soon as Darla Jean said "Amen."

Alma Grace glanced at Jack but he had his arms folded over his chest and his head cocked over to one side like he was thinking. He'd stepped into the Cadillac police chief's position back around Christmas time and he'd worn his uniform to the church services that evening. He looked good in it, too, but then Jack had always been handsome even back when she was still a gangly girl in junior high and he was a big tough high school football player. His brown hair was longer now than when he first came home from many years in the military but it looked good on him.

"You came straight from work, didn't you?" she said.

He nodded. "Had to work until the last minute but I like Wednesday night services so I try to make them when I can," he said. "You are here because you feel a need to be in church but you are mad at those women on the Easter committee, right?"

She nodded. "I'm not going to forgive them for a long time. Any of them."

"Can't say as I blame you. It was a mean trick. I go with Mama every year to see the Easter program. After what they did, I don't think I'll be there this year. Come on. Let's go have some cookies and coffee and visit. And remember, half of all the gossip you hear isn't true. Maybe those wings aren't at Violet Prescott's house after all."

"I left my car at the shop. I really should be going on back," she said.

"I'll walk you home if you're afraid of the dark," he teased.

Will you hold my hand? Will you kiss me good night? Will you push me out of the way when the angels throw lightning bolts at me for what I'm thinking right now? Questions dashed through her head like kids let loose after a long sermon in church.

"Okay, then," she said. "I could use a cup of coffee."

❧

Patrice unlocked the door to her two-bedroom house on the west end of town and threw herself on the sofa. She needed a glass of wine but she was too tired to go get it. If they had another three days like they'd just put in at the shop, she'd have to use a wheelbarrow to get the bank deposit to the bank. Who would ever have thought that pure old gossip could bring in more customers than high-dollar ads or even promotion gimmicks?

She leaned her head back and shut her eyes. But wait! What was that aroma coming from the kitchen and was that really a glass of wine on the coffee table? She sat up slowly and blinked but it didn't all disappear.

It almost smelled like the park did at the chili cook-off. Almost but not quite. She inhaled again and her mouth watered thinking about twenty different kinds of chili and all the beer that went with it. But it wasn't chili—it was something else that she couldn't identify.

"Did you get the bank deposit done and the statement balanced finally?" Carlene asked. "Supper is ready when you are. Your favorite. Lasagna and garlic bread. I stopped by Clawdy's and picked up half a peach cobbler for dessert and the lasagna is one of those frozen ones, but it's supper, right? Yancy came by and left a note on the bar."

"I haven't heard from him in three days," she said.

"It takes three days for you to calm down when you get that angry. It takes me a lot longer and it depends on how much Alma Grace prays as to how long it takes her. You fire up quick but it's a flash in the pan. I'm slow to burn but when I do, it lasts a long time. We're all different that way. Come on into the kitchen. You can read your note while we eat. I wanted some company tonight."

Carlene pointed to the dining room table when they went through the door. "That glass of wine is all you get so you'd best drink it slow."

"You can't tell me how much to drink," she protested.

"Tonight I can, because I poured half of what was left in your glass and half in mine. Your cabinet doesn't have another drop of liquor and there's no beer, so that's it," she said.

"It's six blocks to the liquor store," she reminded Carlene.

"And we are both too damn tired to go." Carlene cut a slab of lasagna and put it on her plate and pushed the aluminum pan across the table toward Patrice.

Patrice filled her plate, put a bite in her mouth, and rolled her eyes. She pulled a chunk of warm garlic bread from the loaf and laid it on her plate and sighed. "God, this is good even if it isn't homemade. We really should learn to cook, you know."

"If I knew how to cook I'd enter the chili cook-off just to piss Lenny off," Carlene said.

"That's for men only. Us mere old hardworking women don't get to play with the boys when it comes to the cook-off," Patrice said.

"What's the note say?"

Patrice opened it up and read it as she ate. "He says he's sorry. That he was a jackass and he wants to take me to dinner Saturday night in Dallas at my favorite Italian restaurant. Of course, I'm going to go so don't even bother asking. I love him and it was as much my fault as his that we argued."

"You going to tell him that?"

Patrice giggled. "Hell, no!"

"What was the fight all about anyway?"

"We either argued about which movie we were going to watch or we were fighting about buying more beer. I don't remember," she said between bites.

Carlene shook her head slowly. "That's a crazy thing to fight about."

"I know, but at the time my brain was pure mush," she said.

"You really love him?"

"Oh, yeah, I do. He's the one, Carlene. I know he is but I just got so damned mad that night."

"I understand the anger even if I don't understand the reason," Carlene said.

"I'm sorry. After what you've been through, it seems pretty trivial, doesn't it?" Patrice said.

Carlene used a paper napkin to wipe away the one tear that escaped. "We hardly ever had a fight. Maybe we should have. It might have shown him that I was a passionate woman."

Patrice reached across the table and laid her hand on Carlene's arm. "Darlin', don't you ever blame yourself for what Lenny did. This is his fault, not yours."

"Thank you." Carlene straightened her back and pulled the lasagna back across the table.

❧

Josie's phone was ringing when she got home that chilly evening. She left the front door standing open, set her takeout bag with a burger and onion rings on the kitchen table, and grabbed the receiver from the phone in the living room.

"Hello," she said.

"Mama, I've got bad news," her oldest son said.

"Do I need to sit down?" she gasped.

"No, it's not that bad but none of us can come home this weekend. We've got ball games starting up and they play on Saturday and the grandkids have a party to go to on Sunday. Will you be all right?" he asked.

Josie could barely keep the excitement from her voice. A whole weekend to do whatever she wanted. She could eat beans straight from the can or maybe live on cheesecake and beer all weekend. "I think I'll live," she said.

"We all feel terrible, Mama. And now more bad news. It might be a month or six weeks before we can get back up there. You really should drive down here on Friday nights so you won't be alone."

Josie clamped a hand over her mouth to keep the giggles at bay. "It's okay, son. I'm tired at the end of a long week of work. I'll rent a couple of movies and relax. Maybe in a couple of weeks, I'll drive down there."

"We'll call both days to make sure you are all right. You won't mope around and miss Poppa will you? We'll definitely be home in time for the chili cook-off if not before," he said.

"I'll be just fine. Give the kids a kiss from me and tell them good luck at their ball games," she told him.

She did the happy dance all the way back to the kitchen, twisting and turning with an imaginary salsa partner. She'd loved her husband with her whole heart, had mourned him when he died, but she was past the molly-coddling stage and ready to have some time to call her own. Spending time in her sons' homes was not how she wanted to spend it.

Her phone rang again and she dreaded answering it. Surely her youngest son wasn't calling to say that he and his family would sacrifice their time and come to Cadillac for the weekend.

"Hello," she said cautiously.

"Josie, are you sick? You sound like you are out of breath. Are you comin' down with the flu? It's going around up in Sherman and just over the line in Oklahoma," Beulah Landry said.

Josie rolled her big brown eyes toward the ceiling and hoped Beulah wasn't on a talking jag. "No, I'm fine. I just came home and was about to have supper."

"I won't keep you. I just called to see if you'd heard about the trouble down at my church. Thought you might want to know since you work at the..." Beulah stammered.

"Panty place," Josie said.

"It sounds so vulgar to say Bless My Bloomers, almost like a sacrilege," Beulah whispered. "Well, Alma Grace wasn't at church tonight so I asked her mama about her. Sugar told me that she might have had to work late, but when I got home, Violet called and said that Alma Grace was seen going into the CNC church. Did you know she was changing churches? I bet it's all over them changing the bylaws about the Easter program, isn't it?"

"I have no idea. I've always gone to church over in Tom Bean. That's where Louis went when we got married and I joined it," Josie said.

"She didn't mention it at the..." Beulah hesitated.

"She's old enough to make up her own mind about things so I reckon she can go to church wherever she pleases," Josie said.

The smell of a good old greasy hamburger wafted across the distance to her nose and her stomach growled. Beulah wouldn't be caught dead in Bless My Bloomers so she had to find out what she could over the phone.

"I guess she can but I'm real worried about Jack. He goes to that church and, well, I'd just die if he started going with Alma Grace.

She's religious and all but she's part owner of that place and I just don't know if my heart could take it. Last year when Prissy Parnell moved back to Cadillac after she got a divorce, I just held my breath for fear she'd go after my Jack. A divorced woman would be even worse than Alma Grace, I'm telling you," Beulah said.

Josie eyed the burger bag. "You've got the heart of a teenager and it's not givin' out anytime soon so don't worry. Jack and Alma Grace would be the most mismatched pair in Cadillac's history."

"Oh, thank you. I just knew you'd make me feel better. You've always had a knack for doing nice things ever since we were kids. Call me sometime. Bye now," Beulah said.

Josie was sure she'd rush right home every day and call Beulah to tell her all about Alma Grace and Jack. Jesus, Mary, and Joseph! She couldn't even imagine Alma Grace on the back of a motorcycle. Patrice, yes! Carlene, maybe! But not Alma Grace.

She took the phone off the hook and laid it to one side. In a few minutes the recorded voice telling her if she wanted to make a call, she should hang up and redial gave up and quit talking. Josie turned on the television and watched old reruns of *Law and Order* while she ate her supper.

❧

Carlene dressed in a short bright red tight skirt, black high heels, and a black-and-white color blocked sweater to go to her parents' house for supper. Her mama had said that her dad had finally calmed down and she'd put the keys to his gun safes back in his desk drawer.

She stopped at the convenience store for a gallon of milk her mother had asked her to pick up, and on her way out, there was Lenny leaning against the fender of her van, looking like a model for expensive champagne. He might be a jackass but he was a damn sexy looking one.

"What do you want?" she asked bluntly.

"To make up. To call Carson and tell him to forget about drawing up those papers. For you to come home where you belong so this damned gossip will stop. To have you back in my arms. You know you are my good luck charm for the chili cook-off. Ever since we got married, I've brought the trophy home," Lenny said.

"And what about Bridget?"

"You aren't going to forgive me, are you?"

"How would you feel if I'd been screwing around on you? Tell Carson to get the papers ready," she said.

"I'm telling you right now, you can keep your glorified underwear factory and that's all you'll get. I'm taking the house and everything in it." His voice was cold enough that it made her shiver.

"I don't want a damn thing in that house except my Granny Fannin's candlesticks. If you fight me over those, Lenny Lovelle, I'll get half of what you got if it takes every dime I've got."

His brittle laughter echoed through her ears. "You can have them."

"Well, that is real generous of you." She crawled into her van, slammed the door, and left rubber on the parking lot when she peeled out. Her hands shook but she wasn't crying another tear over that jerk.

Her mother met her at the door and gave her a brief hug, a kiss on each cheek, and led her into the den where her father already had a scotch on the rocks in his hand. Hank Carmichael owned enough oil wells in Texas to put him on those Top 500 Wealthiest Texans lists but he looked like a plain old rancher. His dark hair was always in need of a cut and Gigi often said that an Italian tailor could put him in the most expensive suit on the market and he'd still look like he'd just walked through a pasture.

Carlene loved him just the way he was.

He crossed the room and wrapped her up in a fierce embrace. "You want a drink, honey? And what do you want me to do about Lenny?"

She nodded and said, "Two fingers and neat. Don't be waterin' it down with ice cubes like you do yours. And I want you to ignore Lenny."

"I swear to God, you two are cut from the same bolt of denim. A woman should have a glass of wine, not two fingers of scotch," Gigi fussed.

"I bet she wouldn't like it if I had a beer, either," Carlene teased.

Hank handed her the drink. "Glad to see that my baby girl hasn't lost her sense of humor over all this."

She took a sip. "I'm glad to see that you haven't blown a gasket over it, Daddy."

"Damn near did there at first but I'm simmering down. He'd best stay out of my sight for a while longer though," Hank said.

Gigi poured white wine into a crystal flute. "I don't imagine that he wants to see you any time soon. And I expect that you'd best tell one of the Chili Kings that you aren't going to be on his chili cook-off team this year, either."

"Well, hell! I forgot about that. There ain't no way I'm going to be on his team ever again. I wonder if Yancy has told him that he's leaving," Hank growled.

"Where are y'all?" Tansy's southern voice carried down the foyer and into Hank's den. "We're here. Sugar said she and Jamie would be here soon as church let out and to save her some dessert. We are havin' pecan pie, aren't we? Hank, honey, are you all right? I swear Alex is mad enough to pinch Lenny's head right off and I'm not talking about the one on his shoulders. That boy is too stupid to know it but he done shit in his nest." She talked all the way to the bar where she poured half a glass of Jack Daniels and popped the top off a beer for her husband.

"You didn't tell me you were inviting the family," Carlene whispered to her mama.

"Times like this we need the support of family," Gigi said.

Alex took a long swig from the bottle and looked at Carlene. "Patrice says that he's wantin' to make amends. How do you feel about that?"

Her Uncle Alex had always been her favorite. A quiet man with thinning light brown hair, slightly overweight and broad shouldered, he'd always been like a big old teddy bear. But if anyone hurt one of the girls, as he called the three cousins, he went from teddy bear to angry grizzly in less time that it took to snap his fingers. He'd grown up on the Magee Ranch outside of Cadillac and had inherited the estate when his father died. Thousands of acres of Black Angus cattle and pumping black oil wells made up his *little spread*, as he called it.

"I'm not feelin' much love toward him right now but maybe he's about ready to stop giving me another chance at happiness. He's ready to take me to the cleaners now and, of course, it will be my fault if he doesn't get the trophy at the chili cook-off," Carlene said.

She felt strangely numb instead of mad. Maybe now that the anger was past, if she dug deep, she could find forgiveness in her heart. If she did, things would turn around with her cousins for sure. Patrice would be mad at her and Alma Grace would be crying tears of joy. It was a lose–lose situation that made her even sadder than a divorce.

Tansy tucked her chin and looked up at Carlene. "You should have taken a hammer to those damn trophies. What exactly does that mean about taking you to the cleaners?"

"I told him all I want from that house is Granny Fannin's candlesticks. I should have picked them up when I left but I was so damned mad I was seeing red, not crystal candleholders," she said.

"And?" Alex asked.

"He just laughed and said that I could have them."

"If he knows what's good for him, he'll have them delivered on satin pillows. Those were Granny Fannin's pride and joy. Her mama gave them to her for a wedding gift," Tansy said.

"Seven o'clock. Dinnertime," Gigi said. "Did y'all hear that Alma Grace pitched a hissy fit and is down at the CNC church tonight? That girl's finally growing a backbone."

Tansy laughed. "I heard that she's sitting in the back pew beside Jack Landry. Sugar is going to shit little green apples when I tell her. Hell, I might even wind up with her piece of pecan pie, yet."

"You can bet your sweet little southern ass that Sugar is praying about Alma Grace even going to that church. Jamie is probably having trouble getting her to hush," Hank said.

Gigi slapped at his shoulder then tucked her arm into his. "Hank Carmichael!"

He planted a kiss on her forehead. "It's the truth and you know it. I'm glad that I got the oldest Fannin sister and not the youngest."

"And I'm damn glad I got the middle child. Come here, Carlene, it will be my pleasure to escort two gorgeous women into the dining room." Alex held out his arm.

Carlene swallowed the lemon-size lump in her throat as she looped her arm in his. Her world might have crumbled but her family was pretty damned awesome.

Chapter 5

ALMA GRACE THREW UP both palms as she kicked the back door of Bless My Bloomers shut with the spike heel of her shoe. "I'm warnin' y'all, my patience is thin enough to give you a paper cut if you mess with me. It's amazing that everyone in town knows my business better than I do. It's enough to make a woman lose her religion."

Josie poured a cup of coffee and handed it to her. "Way I heard it was that Jack just walked you down the street to your car and you didn't even touch his motorcycle. That he kept his distance and y'all just talked like friends."

"Not me," Carlene said. "I heard that he roared all over town with you on the back and you were holding a longneck bottle of Coors in one hand and had the other one wrapped up around his chest. I heard that you were sleeping with him and that's the reason you got tossed off the Easter committee. And that you were wearing a short-tailed skirt with no under-britches up under it."

Patrice took a mug from the cabinet and poured herself a cup. "I don't give a shit what you did. I've got a date with Yancy on Friday night and I intend to have sex. The whole damn town can talk about it if they want to."

"Well, my kids aren't coming home this weekend, which means I don't have to cook, clean, or chase the grandbabies. I get to eat what I want, sleep as long as I want, and watch all four *Lethal Weapon* movies," Josie announced.

They looked at Carlene.

She shrugged. "Lenny was at the convenience store last night. He tried to sweet talk me into coming home. Maybe I should."

"Oh, Carlene, my prayers have been answered." Alma Grace almost swooned.

"You do and I'll put you in a straitjacket and haul you to the nearest insane asylum myself," Patrice declared.

Carlene got up and refilled her coffee mug. "I could go home, sleep in the same bed with him, but tell him there'll be no sex until he wins back my trust. If he really loves me like he says he does, he'll be willing for it, right?"

Patrice laughed so hard that black tears ran down her cheeks. "Damn you, Carlene, now I'll have to redo my makeup."

Alma Grace's smile lit up the whole kitchen. "Why is that so funny? I think it's a great idea. Y'all could read some marriage counseling books in the evening and there's still time for me to fly in the Easter program if you two reconcile."

Josie blew on the top of her mug and sipped it easy. "Might as well get Lenny's funeral planned. He's one of them who'd drop down graveyard dead if he didn't have sex on command."

"Josie!" Carlene exclaimed.

"Honey, I'm old but I do remember what sex is."

"Is that why he cheated? Because he has to have it every day and you were too busy, Carlene?" Alma Grace asked. "You know it's a woman's duty to satisfy her husband's needs, don't you?"

"Yes, Alma Grace," Carlene said acidly, "it was in my marriage vows. I vow to love, honor, respect, and screw Lenny Joe Lovelle at least three times a day and four on Sunday."

Patrice shot a dirty look across the table toward Alma Grace. "You've already tried my patience until it's frayed. I can't imagine how Carlene must feel with you talkin' like this."

Alma Grace threw her hand over her forehead in a dramatic gesture. "If those women hadn't been such bitches, I would never have gone to the CNC church last night, and if I hadn't I wouldn't have gotten to sit by Jack and he wouldn't have walked me back to my car. Besides the cookies were wonderful after the services and those people are very nice so don't bitch at me Patrice. I was just asking a question and reminding our cousin of her marriage vows. I just can't bear the idea of her sinnin'," Alma Grace fussed.

"Bullshit," Patrice said.

"Alma Grace said 'bitch,'" Carlene sing-songed.

Alma Grace's hand came down so fast that it was a blur. "Patrice has to put that sin in her book because she made me do it. Right now I'm going to put on my best smile and open the doors. Matter of fact, I'm going to smile all morning because Jack Landry sat beside me in church," Alma Grace said.

∽◦∾

Carlene and Josie had been adding lace, beads, rhinestones, and ribbons to a pale pink corset when a shadow in the doorway made them both look up. Lenny's mother, Kitty, swept into the room, pulled out a chair, and sat down across the worktable from Carlene.

Sweet Jesus, Carlene had always figured the woman had ice water in her veins but she was proving it that morning. She wore a black suit, black pantyhose, and high-heeled shoes. Even her hair had been recently dyed and was stovepipe black. Any other woman would be soaking wet with sweat, but not Kitty. She didn't even have a drop of dew on her upper lip.

"Well, what do you have to say about this problem you've created? The whole town is talkin' about you and it's getting ugly." The icy tone in Kitty's voice caused the temperature to drop ten degrees.

Carlene laid her needle down and took a sip of cold coffee. "What did Lenny say about this problem I created? Have you talked to him about it yet?"

If she picked up the needle and hurled it like a tiny miniature sword, could she do it with enough force to hit the jugular vein so Kitty would bleed out before the medics could arrive? She folded her hands in her lap to keep from giving it her best shot.

Kitty had never liked Carlene and didn't even bother to try to cover her feelings with a coat of fake sugar. Carlene was too tall, too big boned, too fat, too everything for Lenny, who had never done anything wrong—except for marrying Carlene—in his life.

Kitty sighed. "I should expect that someone like you could never take a joke. He told you it was a big April Fools' joke that he got one of his girls at the dealership to help him with. Bridget is just an office girl, for God's sake. But then I should've expected this from someone like you."

"Someone like her?" Josie raised an eyebrow. "What do you mean by that statement?"

"I don't have to spell it out, do I?" Kitty's narrow mouth pursed into a perfect little pucker. "Carlene Lovelle, enough of this. It's time for you to stop this nonsense and go home where you belong. The chili cook-off is coming up and you know what that means to Lenny. Those trophies are his pride and joy. And to think that you tried to destroy them. I'm ashamed of you. Have I made myself clear?"

Tansy pushed her way into the beading room and stood right behind Carlene's chair. "What are you doing here, Kitty? Apologizing for your son?"

"I'm trying my best to make Carlene see the error of her ways. Lenny loves her, though God only knows why, and I want my son to be happy. It was all an April Fools' joke and I have nothing to apologize for," Kitty answered.

"He's got a strange way of showing that he loves her. Even if it was a joke, which it wasn't, it was cruel and mean," Tansy said.

Sugar made her way into the room and said, "Carlene might go back but only after Lenny owns up to his mistakes and begs forgiveness from her and repents to God."

Carlene glanced toward the door.

Tansy read her mind. "Your mother is on her way. She had to park the car."

"He's got nothing to repent for or beg forgiveness for and he's going to file for divorce tomorrow if you don't go home tonight," Kitty said.

"That house is not my home anymore and I'm not going back to it."

Kitty pulled a brown paper sack from her purse and pushed it across the table. "Well, I guess there's only one thing left to do or say before I leave and never look back. Lenny sent your grandmother's candlesticks along for me to give to you. I understand that's the only thing you want from the house."

Carlene reached for it and heard the rattle of glass. She didn't know whether to weep or commit homicide when she looked inside the bag.

Tansy turned a strange shade of gray when Carlene poured the tiny pieces of sparkly glass out on the table.

Sugar gasped and threw her hand over her heart.

Kitty fished in her purse and tossed a tube of glue on the table. "Think of it as a puzzle that y'all can have so much fun putting back together."

Carlene whispered, "Why would he do this?"

"You falsely accused him. He only kissed Bridget and that's not adultery. He would never lie to me, Carlene. We tell each other everything. And besides, if it was a sin to kiss a woman after you were married, then Sugar, you could file for divorce from Jamie."

Sugar blocked her way. "And what is that supposed to mean?"

"It means that Jamie kissed me after we danced last year at the Jubilee and I had to put a stop to it or it would have gone even further, so maybe Sugar Magee should go find a lawyer," Kitty declared.

"Bullshit! Jamie wouldn't do that," Tansy said.

Kitty glared at Sugar. "Ask him."

Sugar's blue eyes filled with tears.

Kitty's smile bordered on evil.

Tansy was struck cuss-less, which was a first in her entire life.

Gigi stopped in the door. "I had trouble finding a parking spot. I swear the store is swarming with customers…what the hell is going on in here?"

Kitty rushed out into the hallway. "I was doing my damnedest to help this couple get back together. But your daughter is being stubborn."

"If you spread that rumor about Jamie, I'll tear you apart limb by limb," Sugar yelled.

"What rumor?" Gigi asked.

Kitty touched her hair and tilted her chin up to look Gigi in the eye. "Jamie kissed me at the Jubilee last fall."

"That's bullshit," Gigi said loudly.

Kitty shrugged. "It happened and lots of folks saw it happen."

Sugar melted into a nearby chair, put her head in her hands, and sobbed. "They broke Granny Fannin's candlesticks. That is just ugly and oh, my sweet Lord, Jamie kissed her…"

Gigi slapped a hand over her mouth. "Oh my God!"

Alma Grace rang up the sale for two pair of boy-cut panties decorated with ribbons and rhinestones and a lavender bra to match. She'd seen Kitty go back to the beading room. She'd seen her mama and Aunt Tansy come in not long after that, and then Aunt Gigi. Then Kitty practically ran outside and left rubber on the highway as she spun out of the driveway.

When her customer left, she hurried back to Patrice's office and crooked her finger.

Patrice pulled the earbuds from her ears but didn't turn off the MP3 player. "What? Is it lunchtime? I got so involved with the bank deposit that…"

Alma Grace whispered, "Kitty was here. Mama and Aunt Tansy and Aunt Gigi are all back there with Carlene and it's too quiet."

Patrice jumped up and beat Alma Grace across the foyer and into the beading room. "Holy shit! Why would Kitty come here?"

The only time Alma Grace had seen that expression on her mama's face was when Granny Fannin had died ten years before.

"Mama?" she whispered.

"Kitty said that your father kissed her at the Jubilee last year and that he wanted to have sex with her," Sugar said in a broken sob.

Tansy threw an arm around her younger sister. "That damn bitch always did lie. You remember when we were all in high school and she went after Jamie. If he'd have wanted to kiss her, he would have done it then when he was young and full of testosterone. He wouldn't do it now when he's past fifty."

Sugar shook her head. "She might be a bitch and she's definitely been waiting until the right moment to twist the knife in my heart. But it happened. I know it did. I've wondered why he was so sweet for the whole month after the Jubilee. He bought me a diamond and sapphire ring for no reason. It wasn't my birthday or Christmas."

"Daddy wouldn't kiss that woman. The devil himself would have to be blindfolded to kiss her," Alma Grace said.

Sugar wiped her eyes and straightened her shoulders. "He's going to have to pay for it."

"You're not divorcing Daddy over one kiss, are you?" Alma Grace gasped.

"Of course not, but he can't get away with it."

"Then what?"

Sugar pointed toward the ceiling. "I'm moving in one of those rooms up there until he convinces me that it will never happen again. And it's going to take a lot of convincing."

"I'm not leaving my house and I'm not getting in the middle of your fight, because I don't believe Daddy did it," Alma Grace declared.

"Of course you aren't. He's your daddy and he loves you and besides we will need someone to take messages between us," Sugar said.

❧

Gigi slid into a chair, put her palm on her forehead, and said, "She just said that because she's mad at Carlene because she won't go back to Lenny. Not that she gives a shit but you know how superstitious she is, Sugar. And Lenny has made no bones about you being his good-luck charm for the chili cook-off, Carlene. Kitty would do anything for him to win, even beg you to go back to him until the cook-off is over."

"I'm not leaving Jamie for good. I'm just going to live here for a few weeks until he repents. True repentance comes with fasting and prayer. Well, he can do without sex and pray real hard for forgiveness," Sugar said.

"You can live with me," Gigi said. "We've got three spare bedrooms at the ranch."

"Or you can stay with me," Tansy said.

Sugar shook her head emphatically. "No thank you. I'll be staying here and I'm giving my cook a paid vacation. He can't even operate a microwave so he will be fasting in more ways than one."

Fate was telling Carlene to go back to Lenny. Even living with a two-timing cheating son of a bitch wouldn't be as difficult as living with Aunt Sugar, who prayed every time someone sneezed or cussed. The sunlight sparkled against the bits of crystal dumped out on the table and Carlene decided Aunt Sugar's praying wasn't nearly as bad as Lenny.

"Which room do you want?" Carlene's heart grew heavier every day. Maybe she should just sell the shop to her cousins and move away.

"The biggest one. I'm moving all my bedroom furniture into it. Jamie can sleep on the couch or in the bathtub for all I care. Tansy, I feel a sinking spell coming on just thinking about kissing his lips after they'd been on Kitty Lovelle's. I need a good stiff shot of brandy," Sugar said.

"Mama!" Alma Grace raised her voice.

Sugar dabbed at her eyes with a tissue that Carlene handed her. "Don't you talk to me in that tone after what you did last night. Hurry up, Tansy, or y'all are going to have to scrape me up off the floor."

"We ain't got brandy in the house but I've got something that'll keep you from fainting." Josie disappeared from the beading room and returned in two minutes with a red plastic cup of clear liquid.

"Drink it down, Miz Sugar. Don't come up for air; just chug it right down," Josie said.

Carlene was dreaming. It was all a crazy nightmare. This wasn't happening. She pinched her leg and it hurt like hell. Aunt Sugar drinking? The world was coming to an end.

"Why would you bring me water?" Sugar asked.

"It'll help. I promise." Josie grinned.

Sugar turned it up and gulped three times. She slammed the cup down on the table and gasped like a fish out of water for a full minute before she could speak. "My God! That was not water."

"Nope, and you didn't faint. You might have a little trouble with your balance. Tequila does that sometimes, but you ain't going to faint," Josie said. "Now I've got to get back to work. Y'all clear on out of here and give me some room. I've had all the drama I can stand for one day. I'm an old woman."

Old, nothing. You're like Agnes. You'll be kickin' long after the world comes to an end. Carlene wished that she had the nerve to tell her Aunt Sugar that she could not move into one of the spare bedrooms in the same authoritative tone that Josie had sent them all out of the beading room. She couldn't refuse Sugar but maybe Uncle Jamie would be truly sorry by Monday. Surely three days would be enough fasting and praying. After all, he hadn't committed adultery.

How long would it take you to forgive Lenny? her conscience asked.

"Three days past eternity," she muttered.

"What's that about eternity?" Tansy asked.

Carlene raised a shoulder. "I was just thinking out loud."

"We're going to take Sugar to Clawdy's," Tansy said. "We need to talk about this over coffee until she settles down and you girls need to get back to work. But I'm swearing on Granny Fannin's Bible right now that this is not the end of that stunt with the candlesticks."

∽✧∾

Patrice whispered in Tansy's ear, "Try your damnedest to talk her out of this idea. Carlene sure don't need this in her life right now."

Alma Grace went to help a new bride who'd come in for fancy white undergarments. Patrice grabbed Carlene's hand and led her to her office across the hall from the beading room. She shut the door, motioned toward an overstuffed velvet chair in front of her desk, and pulled a bottle of scotch from a drawer.

"Sit," she said as she poured two fingers in a tumbler. She handed it to Carlene and said, "Drink."

Carlene did what she was told and then whispered, "She won't really move in here, will she?"

"If she stays very long, she'll find a cook. Aunt Sugar can't boil water and she doesn't like eating café food all the time. She'll either be gone by Monday or there'll be someone here to do the cooking and cleaning. You won't have to make a bed or worry about mildew in the toilet and we'll all gain ten pounds before Aunt Sugar decides that Uncle Jamie is forgiven."

"God hates me," Carlene said. "And I didn't do a thing but make that pair of red bikini underpants."

Patrice poured another drink and handed it to Carlene. "Lenny's Mama should have drowned him at birth. He's the cause of every bit of this. And to think that he smashed up Granny's candlesticks like that."

Carlene looked long and hard at the square bottle of scotch. "I'd have another if I didn't need to work all afternoon. Why would he do that, Patrice? It's the only thing I asked for and now Mama will hire Tip Gordon. I know she will."

Patrice perched a hip on the desk. "I hope she does. Hell, he's the best divorce lawyer in the whole state. Carson might be the best in north Texas, but Tip could sell a cigarette lighter to the devil."

"But why would he smash those candleholders?" Carlene asked again.

"Because some men are born stupid and Lenny is Kitty's son, isn't he? That gives him a double dose of dumb. Your punishment for marrying Lenny was having Kitty for a mother-in-law. I'm surprised you didn't poison her long ago," Patrice said.

"She sprinkles strychnine on her cereal like sugar. It's vitamins to her, so poison wouldn't do the trick. I'm not sure a stake through the heart could kill that woman." Carlene giggled.

Patrice smiled. Thank God for good scotch. It cured a multitude of problems. She had faith that her mama could talk Sugar out of moving into Bless My Bloomers. No one, not even Sugar, could out-talk Tansy Cordell. If worse came to worst, Tansy would start talking about her psychic powers telling her that Jamie had already repented. Yes, ma'am, Tansy would take care of it.

Customers arrived in a steady flow most of the afternoon—enough to keep Alma Grace busy but not enough that Patrice had to come out of her office to help wait on them. She peeked in on Carlene several times during the day but she hardly looked up from the table where she and Josie designed and decorated corsets all afternoon.

By four o'clock she had convinced herself that it had all blown over and that her mother had gotten the job done. Then the front door opened and Aunt Sugar's voice floated down the hall.

"Follow me, boys. I'll show you exactly where to set up the bed and put my things. Girls, I'm here. I only brought enough for one closet so I don't need your help. Y'all just keep on working. Carlene, honey, we'll get burgers for supper tonight and decide how we're going to manage without a cook after that."

Patrice's forehead hit the desk with a thud. The whole damn world had turned upside down. First Lenny whoring around and now Aunt Sugar moving into Bless My Bloomers. What next?

Chapter 6

ALMA GRACE STARED AT the bowl of cold cereal. "Daddy, what are we going to do?"

Jamie shook his head slowly from side to side. "Can you cook?"

"I can make ham sandwiches and open a can of soup."

"Then I guess we'll let Miss Clawdy's feed us breakfast and lunch and we'll eat ham sandwiches for supper. And just so you know, I did not kiss Kitty Lovelle. She kissed me and I backed away from her, left her standing right there in the middle of the street. I did not buy your Mama that ring to appease my conscience either. I bought it because I love her and the sapphires reminded me of her eyes," Jamie said.

"I believe you. Kitty is mad because Lenny isn't getting his way and she's out to destroy what she can. I'll talk to Mama."

"And until she comes to her senses, I'll worship at the CNC church with you. I'm not sitting in the same church with her and Kitty," Jamie said.

Alma Grace pushed the half-eaten bowl of cereal aside.

Dammit!

She didn't even bow her head and ask for forgiveness for thinking bad words. Instead she yelled it in her mind…*dammit, dammit, dammit!* There went any flirting with Jack Landry or sharing a hymn book or eating cookies with him. She'd have to sit beside her father and he'd insist upon sitting as close to the front as possible.

"Got to get to work. You have a good day and I'll see you at noon at Clawdy's," Jamie said.

"Should I bring Mama?" Alma Grace asked.

"Only if she's repented of accusing me of something I did not do and is ready to apologize to me," Jamie said.

Double dammit!

Sugar Magee had never admitted a sin in her life. Her wings didn't have the first sign of a smudge of dirt on them and her halo was so shiny and straight that even the angels envied her. There would be a foot of snow in Cadillac right in the middle of July before Sugar apologized to Jamie. It was going to be a long spring at Bless My Bloomers.

She fumed all the way to work that morning but when she arrived and the aroma of fresh-baked cinnamon rolls hit her, she smiled. Her mama had brought her cook so things were looking up.

"Maria?" Alma Grace looked around the kitchen.

"She's on vacation, remember? Sit down and have some cinnamon rolls. I got them over at Clawdy's this morning. How are you holding up, darlin'? Did your daddy send me any messages?" Sugar asked.

Her blond hair was tucked back behind her ears but the curls were fighting their way out of confinement. Her blue eyes searched Alma Grace's face for good news.

"Daddy said that you need to apologize for not trusting him. He says that the woman kissed him and he backed off from her so he didn't do anything and that he bought you the ring because the sapphires reminded him of your pretty blue eyes."

"I'm not apologizing for a problem I didn't create."

Alma Grace cut a warm cinnamon roll right out of the middle of the pan and poured a tall glass of milk. "Mama, you don't cook. Carlene only makes what she can heat up from the frozen section of the grocery store. You hate takeout food. How long do you think you can hold out like this?"

"Cinnamon rolls aren't bad, are they?" Sugar said.

Alma Grace took a deep breath and pulled out the big guns.

"Kitty finds out that you are making daddy fast in the bedroom, I bet what she'll be taking to the house won't be roast and potatoes."

"She wouldn't!" Sugar gasped.

"I think that she's proven that she would in a heartbeat," Alma Grace said.

❧

The aroma of hot cinnamon slipped up the stairs, through the crack under Carlene's door, and made its way through the feather pillow she'd crammed over her head to keep out the noise of Aunt Sugar's snores.

A week ago she'd packaged up a cute little bright red outfit and rang up the sale to Bridget who was going to Vegas with her sugar daddy. That little red pair of panties didn't have a tenth of a yard of fabric in them. Hell, they didn't have enough material in them to sag a clothesline and yet they'd turned her world, her family, and the whole town of Cadillac upside down.

She carefully removed the pillow from her head and got an even stronger dose of the cinnamon rolls. What would the scent of cooking do for sales? Would it make the customers hungry and they'd leave without buying anything?

She rolled out of bed, peeked out the door, and made a mad dash to the bathroom before Aunt Sugar claimed it. Mama said that Sugar always took two hours to get presentable in the morning. She didn't go to breakfast without checking for stray eyebrows and chipped fingernail polish, and saying her morning prayers. Carlene didn't know if Sugar prayed in the bathroom but she didn't have time to wait two hours before she went to work.

She passed Sugar on the landing on her way back to her bedroom. Fully dressed in a cute little sundress and sandals, her makeup was perfect, and her earrings glittered in the sunlight filtering in from a bedroom window.

"Good mornin', darlin'. Did you know that you snore?" Sugar asked.

"Yes, ma'am. And good morning to you, Aunt Sugar." Carlene smiled.

"You're runnin' a little late. Alma Grace and I've already had devotionals and I ordered cinnamon rolls from Clawdy's. Trixie was good enough to deliver them for me."

"Guess I'd better get on the ball if I want to grab one. Patrice loves cinnamon rolls and she'll eat them all," Carlene said.

"After morning prayers, I'll be back downstairs. Now you run along and get dressed in something pretty. If Lenny comes by again, you want to look nice." Sugar blew her a kiss.

Carlene dressed in a fitted bright blue dress with a scoop neck and long sleeves. It was Friday and the appointment calendar said that two wedding parties were coming from Sherman, so Alma Grace would need help. She picked up a necklace of chunky blue, yellow, and red stones wet with sparkling crystals between the different colors and fastened it around her neck, then added the matching bracelet and earrings. She carried her high heels down the steps and padded barefoot to the kitchen.

She took one look at the pan of cinnamon rolls and said, "Shit, Alma Grace! You can't take them right out of the middle. That's not playing fair."

Patrice caught the last sentence as she pushed the door open. "She's right. No taking them out of the middle. Did Aunt Sugar get up this early and get food already?"

"She gets up early every morning. We have devotionals before I come to work." Alma Grace ignored them and removed her second cinnamon roll from the center of the pan. "And she is always dressed with her makeup done and jewelry on, too."

Patrice cut two big rolls from the middle of the pan. "We'll treat this like a Scrabble board. I'm playing off Alma Grace's choice. So praying is done for the day?"

Alma Grace sighed. "Oh, no! Mama is upstairs doing her

morning prayers now. And Daddy says he's going to church at the CNC with me until she gets over her hissy and that means I can't sit beside or flirt with Jack Landry. Come on Pat-tee, help me out here."

"You call me that again and I'll smack you right in the mouth. You know I hate nicknames," Patrice said.

Alma Grace slid a nasty look toward Carlene.

"Don't look at me. I didn't make Jamie kiss Kitty or Kitty kiss Jamie or your mama move in here," Carlene said.

Patrice slapped Alma Grace on the shoulder. "Stop blaming Carlene for everything that happens. I swear if you got a pimple you'd figure out a way to make it her fault."

Alma Grace stuck her tongue out at Patrice. "But she promised to love him for better or worse."

Josie pushed her way into the kitchen. "This place smells wonderful."

"Alma Grace took hers out of the middle," Carlene tattled.

"She deserves it this morning, with what she's going through. Can't be easy for her mama and daddy to be at odds. This is a really nice treat this morning," Josie said.

Carlene smiled. "I could smell cinnamon all the way in my bedroom. I'm wondering if our customers will get a whiff of what's cooking and think they want to go to Clawdy's rather than buy under-britches."

"I can fix that," Patrice said. "I'll call over to Clawdy's and have Cathy make two dozen cookies every day and put them on the credenza in the foyer. Carlene, you call your mama and tell her to bring in that two-gallon crystal jar with a spout on the side that we used at your wedding for sweet tea and we'll put it out there, too. Feed the customers and give them something to drink and they'll stick around to buy more stuff. I can make sweet tea even if I can't cook worth a damn. I'll keep it full and pick up the cookies on the way in to work each morning."

Alma Grace slapped her forehead. "Why didn't we think of that before now?"

"You are a genius, Patrice." Carlene smiled.

"Hey, we could get some napkins printed with our logo on them, too, if this goes over real well," Alma Grace offered. "It's nine o'clock. Time to open the doors for business. Oh, there's Aunt Gigi pulling up at the curb."

Carlene shoved the last bite of her cinnamon roll into her mouth and followed Alma Grace to the door. Gigi slung it open and stepped inside just seconds after it was unlocked. The little bell at the top jingled but Gigi did not smile.

"Bad news," she said.

"Daddy didn't kill Lenny, did he?" Carlene held her breath.

"No, far as I know Lenny is still breathing but not because I want him to be. I smell cinnamon. Let's take this to the kitchen."

Carlene waited until her mother had rolls on a plate and a cup of coffee before she asked. "Okay, Mama, spit it out."

"I called Tip and he had a phone conference with Carson. Lenny is all hot air and shit, honey. He's spent every dime of y'all's savings on his trips with that bimbo and your joint checking is wiped clean," Gigi told her.

"Which means?" Patrice asked.

"Tip is going to fight for half the equity in the house. Lenny can either buy you out or he'll have to sell it and give you your portion but you're going to lose money when you consider that you put up the whole down payment on it," Gigi said.

Carlene sighed. "I don't care. He can have it. I just want my maiden name back and I don't want to have to sell Bless My Bloomers. I guess I should go start another checking account in my name only with my paycheck this week."

Gigi nodded. "Carson is proposing that Lenny keep the house and his truck. You keep your van and your wedding rings and the business."

"It's not fair," Josie said. "Not after that stunt with your granny's candlesticks. You need to figure out something else and hit him where it hurts. Tell him he can have those damned old rings and you'll take cash money for them."

"There's nothing short of shooting the bastard that would make him hurt," Gigi said.

"What does he prize more than anything?" Alma Grace asked.

"Duh! His women. But if we shot them all, the female population in Grayson County would be decimated," Patrice answered.

"The chili cook-off," Carlene whispered. "We could whip him at the chili cook-off next month. He'd just die if he lost to a team of women, especially if I was on the team. I'll sell my rings to buy what we need."

"There's never been women brave enough to enter that world. Some have talked about it but only in whispers and you aren't selling your rings for that. You can sell them and give the money to a charity," Gigi said.

"What world?" When Tansy entered a room, a force preceded her that said for everyone to take a step back and listen up.

"The chili cook-off. We're going to beat Lenny this year and take the trophy. Lenny prizes those five trophies on the wall of his man cave more than anything. Every time his team won the past five years, he gloated for days and days about it. Is there something in the rule book that says women can't enter?" Carlene said.

"They never have but I bet it's not in the rules," Gigi answered.

"Never have what?" Sugar breezed into the room and headed toward the coffee pot.

"The chili cook-off," Tansy said. "We're about to take Lenny to the ground at the chili cook-off."

"You know what people will say if you win, right?"

"Who cares what people will say, Aunt Sugar," Patrice exploded loudly.

Tansy took the stand and the room went quiet. "They're going to say that none of us can cook and we cheated. And Patrice, if you want a clean win, you'd better care. Lenny is going to say that we won because our husbands gave us the tips for good chili. I think there's still one of those cheap trophies in our attic somewhere from when Alex had a team. And Hank was on Lenny's team last year, remember?"

"Who gives a shit what he says or thinks? If we win, that means he loses. Didn't Grandpa Fannin make chili for the cook-off in his day? Hell, we can surely follow a recipe," Patrice argued.

Sugar nodded. "Yes, he did and I bet his recipes are in the attic at my house. I brought a lot of that stuff home with me when Mama passed on. Who all are going to be on our team?"

"Sisters, cousins, and Josie. That's seven and the limit," Gigi pointed at her sisters. "We're going to do this. We'll hit him where it hurts and take that trophy away from him."

"Whose kitchen are we going to use?" Tansy asked.

"Not mine. I'm living right here," Sugar declared.

"Well, there's a kitchen here and it's never used for much so we'll make our chili right here. The girls can run the business and we'll test recipes until we find just the right one to whip the Chili Kings," Gigi said.

"We can't have the smell of chili in the store while we're trying to sell merchandise," Carlene argued.

"Then we'll pick out our recipe, shop for the ingredients, and make it in the evenings. By morning, the smell will be gone," Tansy said. "I've got an idea. Gigi and I will take that other bedroom upstairs so that if it gets late, we can stay over. I'll call the house and have some furniture brought in today."

"Sounds good to me," Gigi said.

At the reality of what the Fannin sisters were planning, Carlene shot a desperate look toward Patrice. She'd be living with all three of them for six weeks until the cook-off was over. One little suggestion had turned into a full-fledged mission. That was enough to put her on her knees in prayer without a word from Alma Grace.

Patrice caught the expressions on both her cousins' faces at the same time. Poor little darlin's, didn't they remember that their faces could freeze like that? It wasn't often that the youngest got to take the reins and make decisions, but today belonged to her.

She held up a hand and snapped her fingers to get everyone's attention. "Okay, ladies, here's the way we're going to handle this. Mama, you go on and sign us up for the chili cook-off today. We need a name for our team. Lenny's is the Chili Kings. We could be the Chili Queens."

Josie shook her head. "Oh, no! That is not the name you girls should use. He'll say you stole the idea from him." You should be the Red-Hot Bloomers. That'll rub salt into Lenny's wound real good when we beat the hell out of him with the panty squad."

"I like it," Gigi said. "Put us down as the Red-Hot Bloomers Team when you go enter us in the contest, Tansy."

Alma Grace looked like she was about to cry. "So you are all going to have rooms upstairs with Mama until the cook-off is done. Uncle Alex and Uncle Hank aren't going to like that a bit."

"It's not every night. Just when we work late on our chili recipe," Gigi said. "It's not like we're leaving them. We'll be home with them all day, have supper with them, and then come here when the shop is closed to start experimenting with the recipes."

One stray tear found its way down Alma Grace's cheek. "I don't know if I can be on this team. It would be working against Lenny and Carlene ever getting back together and I'm not sure Jesus likes that idea. He wants us to forgive and forget, not split a marriage apart with a chili cook-off."

"Oh, stop it!" Carlene said.

Sugar patted her daughter on the back. "Honey, do you remember in the scripture when David desired another man's wife and he sent that man out into the front lines of battle just so he would be killed?"

"What's that got to do with a chili cook-off?" Alma Grace asked.

"Think about how mad God was at David for that stunt. He punished him. Maybe Carlene and Lenny will get back together someday but not before Lenny is punished. This is a lot less punishment than David got."

Alma Grace looked up into her mother's eyes. "Are you sure, Mama?"

"If I'm going to help develop the recipe and learn to cook chili, then I expect you can be on the team," Sugar said.

"You can't cook," Alma Grace reminded her.

"I'm about to learn to make the best chili in Grayson County, Texas. And I can do anything I want to do. I never wanted to cook and your daddy said I brought enough to the marriage with my beauty and..." Sugar blushed.

"And what she takes to the bedroom." Gigi laughed.

"I'll be on the team but I'm not going back to our church until after Easter because I'm still pissed," Alma Grace said.

Sugar shook her finger at her daughter. "Alma Grace Magee! You are talking like Tansy."

"Well, I am and I'm not having any more devotionals with you until you and Daddy both quit acting like teenagers," Alma Grace said. "And if Jack Landry asks me, I'm going to ride on the back of that motorcycle with him."

"You, young lady, are the one acting like a teenager. I suppose the next thing you're going to tell me is that you're going to move in with that renegade Jack Landry, since you are so angry." Sugar groaned.

Patrice snapped her fingers again. "Whoa. Put away the butcher knives and guns. Aunt Gigi, you and Mama will be staying part-time upstairs with Aunt Sugar. Carlene and Alma Grace are going to stay at my house. I've got two extra bedrooms and if y'all can live together for a few weeks, then we can. But the three of you have to realize, we do have a business to run in the bottom half of this house. No loud noise. No stomping around during the day. We don't give a shit what you do at night. You can have a prayer meeting or get drunk or brew chili. But during the day, you will behave, understood? Aunt Gigi, you won't even have to bring any furniture since Carlene's bedroom can be yours."

Carlene poked her cousin on the leg and mouthed, "What about Yancy?"

Patrice shrugged and whispered, "I'll manage."

"Can I move in tonight?" Alma Grace asked.

Patrice nodded. "And so can you, Carlene."

"Thank you, Patrice, but I'm too tired to move tonight. I'll do it after work tomorrow," Carlene said. "Now let's get to work. Josie and I've got underwear to design. This place won't run itself and thank you for letting me live at your house."

"I've got quarterly tax forms to take care of." Patrice picked up her coffee and headed to the office.

The door's bell jingled and Alma Grace hurried off toward the store.

Patrice laid a hand on her shoulder as they passed in the foyer. "What you do in your bedroom is your business. I don't give a shit when you come in at night or when you leave in the morning but I will not have morning devotionals with you. Understood?"

Alma Grace saluted sharply. "Yes, ma'am."

❧

"What in the hell have we set loose?" Gigi said when they were alone in the kitchen. "Thank God it's not football season. Hank and I have never missed a Longhorn game in our lives and we always go together."

"It'll be fun. We haven't lived together like this since we were teenagers," Sugar said. "We've each got a room and we're going to learn to make world-class chili. What more could we ask for?"

"More than one bathroom." Gigi shook her head. "Hank is going to pitch a helluva fit."

Tansy smiled. "Alex won't like it either but it's for a good cause. And I read the cards this morning. My bird was happy and I knew it would be a good reading. Guess what they told me? They said that nobody will expect us to come up with a prize recipe since everyone knows we can't cook and it will surprise the hell out of everyone when we win. This is going to be fun."

"Oh, we've got to plan our tent and our logo to go on the little bowls to serve our chili and the recipes." Sugar rubbed her hands together. "Josie, do you have any good recipes we could start off with?"

She shook her head. "Oh, no! Louis never liked chili so I didn't make it very often."

"Well, shit!" Tansy moaned.

"That's what I just said." Josie grinned. "I'm going back to work, and don't worry. There's recipes by the dozens for every kind of chili in the world on those cooking sites on the computer." She headed out of the kitchen.

Gigi clapped her hands. "I'll bring my laptop and we'll hunt up the best recipes and then get busy, but first Tansy's got to go to the Chamber of Commerce and register the team. And we've got to go to Sugar's house while Jamie is out and go through the attic where we just might find the last recipe Daddy made before he passed."

Sugar whispered, "I can't go home until he apologizes and repents. Y'all will have to do it. I'll go register the team and use the company laptop to look at logos while you're gone."

"Is that big old heavy cooker that Daddy made chili in every year in your attic?" Gigi asked.

Sugar's eyes twinkled. "Yes, and I put a lot of loose recipes in it when I took it from Mama's house. I bet somewhere in there is a recipe for his prize-winning chili."

"But that was his recipe. We need to have our own," Tansy protested.

"It will be ours when we add our own special touches. Gigi, you do make chili for the family gatherings sometimes. What's your secret?" Sugar asked.

"It's my special secret that I don't share." She wasn't telling her sisters that her chili came straight out of a gallon can she bought at the store and added a teaspoon of liquid smoke and half a cup of Worcestershire sauce after it started to boil.

She wasn't one damn bit excited about spending so much time with her two bickering sisters either. Or sleeping alone on late nights. Or eating takeout for supper most of the time. She'd gain ten pounds for sure, yank her hair out by the roots in an attempt to keep peace on the second floor, and holy shit, she'd have to share a bathroom with a saint and a psychic.

Tansy reached across the table and laid one hand on Sugar's and the other on Gigi's. "I see a gold plastic trophy in our future. I see Lenny madder than hell and our husbands all being really nice to us for a long time after the next six weeks and begging us never to enter the contest again. I see women in Cadillac throwing down roses for us to walk on because we are entering a world where women have never trod before."

Gigi pulled her hand back. "I hear bullshit, Tansy. You are not a psychic. Women are going to throw rotten tomatoes at us for ruining the chili cook-off and our husbands might even divorce us. So by damn, with stakes that high, y'all had best help me find a recipe that will win this contest."

Sugar held up her hand. "I'm on the decorating committee. That means I'll take care of the shirts, the tent, and the logo. Y'all have to find the recipe."

"Hell, if you will," Tansy said. "I'm not wearing a shirt with Red-Hot Bloomers plastered across the front and a Bible verse on the back. You don't order a damn thing without our consent and that means all seven of us, not just a nod from Alma Grace. I do give you credit for your sermon that convinced her to at least join the team, though."

"I was thinking of 'Vengeance is mine, saith the Lord,' or something like that. It wouldn't have to be in big letters." Sugar pouted.

"No religious stuff," Gigi said. "We'll beat Lenny without the help of the angels."

Chapter 7

GIGI TALKED AND HANK sipped his scotch with his long legs propped up on a hassock in front of his favorite chair and didn't interrupt one time as she talked and talked and talked.

"Well?" she asked after a full minute had elapsed at the end of her speech.

Had he not heard a word she said? She'd worried all day about how to approach him with the idea and he hadn't butted in one single time. It damn sure wasn't the time for him to daydream about oil wells and cows.

"Sounds like your mind is made up," he said.

"Lenny has to pay," she answered.

"Wouldn't it be easier to just shoot him?"

"Then he'd be dead. This way he'll have to live with the fact that he's a loser," Gigi said.

"That's asking a lot for a little revenge."

"It's not for me or even for Sugar. I can't say it's even for the broken candlesticks, although I figure my mama is sending some karma out from the grave and Lenny is in deep shit. Don't tell Tansy I said that or she'll be saying that Mama was a psychic, too. This is for Carlene. Kitty came to the shop today and called her fat," Gigi said.

Hank jumped up so fast that he was a blur. "Kitty Lovelle said what?"

"She said that she never understood why her precious son married a fat woman," Gigi said.

She'd fussed and fumed around with arguments about why she'd be gone so much in the evenings for the next few weeks and all it took was one sentence and one three-letter word—F-A-T—to do the trick. Carlene had always been built just like Hank's grandma, whom he adored. Tall, big boned, never skinny even in high school—but she'd been the president of her class all four years of high school, on the debate team, played basketball and volleyball, and as her senior picture above the mantel portrayed, had been a beautiful woman. He didn't see Carlene as anything other than his gorgeous daughter.

"You can go to Mexico and learn to make the hottest damn chili in the world. I'll pay for the cooking lessons myself. That woman and her son have to be taught a lesson," Hank said.

Shit! Why hadn't she thought of going to Mexico? She and her sisters hadn't been on an all girls' vacation in two years and they were due one. But they couldn't give Lenny the satisfaction of having professional chili makers teaching them how to cook. No, sir, they had to win fair and square. And he couldn't have even one excuse when it was all said and done.

"Lenny would say that we didn't invent the recipe ourselves if we did that. That's why we aren't going to ask our husbands to help us out with recipes. We want to do this on our very own," Gigi said.

Hank grinned. "And I'll pay for a double-page spread in the center of every newspaper in Grayson County to show off your trophies when you do. Hell, I hope he comes in fourth. That way he won't even get a ribbon."

She crossed the room and looped her arms around Hank's neck. "When it's over, I will plan a whole week at the beach just for us."

Hank tipped back her chin and kissed her solidly with hunger and promise. "I'll do the plannin' and I'm thinkin' an Alaskan cruise would be nice."

"With lots of seafood, no relatives, and no chili."

He swept her up in his arms and started up the stairs with her snuggled down close to his chest. "You got it, darlin'."

❧

Tansy handed Alex a beer when he walked through the door. He took one look at the suitcases sitting beside the door and rolled his eyes.

"It's true then? Y'all have entered the contest?" he asked.

"Patrice called, didn't she?" She answered his question with one of her own.

He nodded. "She's not looking forward to the arrangements either. Hank and I were all smug feeling sorry for Jamie because Sugar moved out until he does proper repentance. But we didn't even kiss Kitty Lovelle and our wives are moving out."

"You damn sure better not kiss that hussy. It would be the last lips you kiss if you ever do and we're not moving out. I'll just be in and out of the house. If we are working on the chili late at night, we'll stay at the shop. If not, I'll be home, and nothing says you and Hank can't stop by and have a drink with us in the evenings," Tansy said.

"You really think you can beat Lenny at the cook-off? Wouldn't it be easier to take him down another way? Like burn down his business or get him fired? Hell, I'll buy the car dealership and fire his sorry ass, myself," Alex said.

Tansy kissed him on the cheek and pushed him backward until he was forced to sit on the sofa. She straddled his lap and cupped his cheeks in her hands. "I love you, and I'll be home part of the time and I'll never leave you again once this cook-off is over. If I can live with my sisters above a lingerie shop and learn to make world-famous chili, you can live with me just popping in and out for a few weeks. And remember that's just one suitcase over there. If I was planning on spending all my nights at the shop, there would be a dozen. Dinner is being served in the bedroom tonight.

Your bath is already run and I'm wearing absolutely nothing under this kimono."

Alex grinned. "I knew I married the right Fannin sister!"

◦◦◦

How in the devil did Uncle Jamie sleep with Aunt Sugar? Evidently he used earplugs or he'd wander around in a daze from lack of sleep all the time. Carlene finally turned on the bedside lamp and sat up in bed. It sounded like a chain saw fighting its way through a truckload of hogs across the hall. She should have moved in with Patrice that night like Alma Grace had done, and she would be sleeping soundly.

She eased out of bed and made her way downstairs to the kitchen where she downed two shots of scotch. She eyed the bottle as she started out of the room but decided against drinking enough to pass completely out. She had to work the next day and there were appointments on the books for three weddings. Maybe they should attend bridal fairs and promote a bridal line of lingerie for the bachelorette parties as well as weddings.

She'd been working on a fancy white lace corset that afternoon so she flipped on the light in the beading room. Brides, in their rose-colored glasses, were downright stupid. She'd been one and she'd had the perfect wedding five years before. Now look where she was. She'd trusted Lenny with her heart and he'd broken it every bit as badly as he had Granny's candleholders.

Tears streamed down her face as she sat down in a gold velvet vintage rocker pushed back in the corner. She pulled the quilt from off the back and wrapped it around her body. Was the fact that she was a plus-size girl what drove Lenny away? He'd seen her naked before they married, so if he didn't like curves, then why did he propose? If he wanted a tiny-size trophy wife, why did he marry a woman who bought her clothing from the plus-size store?

Using the back of her hand to wipe the tears, it came to her in a flash that she'd been his security blanket. *He couldn't leave his poor dumpy wife because she'd kill herself without him, but he would if he could. And they felt sorry for him right into those big round beds on the trips that didn't have a damn thing to do with the car dealership. No wonder he doesn't have a pot to piss in and he's spent all my money along with his! He's probably had dozens and dozens of women. And he told them all he'd leave his fat wife if he could.*

She set the rocker in motion and then realized that she couldn't hear the snoring anymore. The tears disappeared and she was smiling when she fell fast asleep.

⚮

On Saturday morning, when a cattle trailer brought a load of Gigi's furniture, the crackle of gossip flying through the air was almost audible. Every woman in Cadillac and the surrounding areas suddenly needed a new bra or pair of under-britches. By the time the trucks unloaded Gigi's bedroom furniture and suitcases, both sides of the street were lined with cars and trucks of every description. If Tansy hadn't pulled right in behind the last truck, she'd have had to park three blocks away and pull her suitcase up the street.

"Where's the paparazzi? I should at least get to shield my face when I sneak in the door with my suitcase," Tansy fussed when she opened the car door.

Yancy quickly rounded the front of the car and held the door for her. "I brought Patrice some chocolate cupcakes. I understand you are moving in today. If you'll pop that trunk lid, I'll be glad to carry your things upstairs for you."

Tansy flashed a brilliant smile. "Thank you, Yancy. I've just got one suitcase but I'll sure be glad for you to carry it for me. Is it as crazy in there as it looks from out here?"

"Yes, ma'am. I didn't even get to talk to Patrice. The store is jammed full of women and more are in the foyer eatin' cookies and drinkin' sweet tea. I'm not so sure that feedin' them is a good idea. You feed a stray dog and it'll just keep coming back for more." Yancy carried the heavy suitcase without huffing and puffing one bit. "If you'll shut the trunk and open the door for me, I'd sure appreciate it."

She followed behind him, admiring the way he filled out those tight-fitting jeans. Her daughter had a keeper there if she'd just wake up and realize it. "This is the only day they'll get fed, trust me. Patrice will see that two dozen cookies won't last five minutes and all the profit will go across the street to Clawdy's. She's a better business woman than that."

Someone swung the door open before she could touch it and Yancy proceeded up the stairs without a hitch. Tansy, on the other hand, was bombarded with questions.

"Is it true that the Fannin girls are entering the chili cook-off and you've left your husbands? Women don't do that," one lady said.

Agnes Flynn, who lived two doors down from the shop, looped her arm in Tansy's. Agnes was well past eighty and great-aunt to Cathy and Marty Andrews, who ran Miss Clawdy's Café. She was the most outspoken woman in Cadillac and nobody messed with her.

She pulled Tansy up on the first stair and said in a loud voice. "Granny Fannin would be so proud of you girls for what y'all are doin'. This is as big as marchin' on the White House for women's rights. All us women are proud as hell of y'all. I'm here to tell you that if y'all needed someone for your team, I'd gladly throw my lot in with you but since you got enough, I'm pledgin' a thousand dollars to the cause for y'all to buy the tent." She whipped a brown paper bag out of her purse and shook it open. "My check goes into this bag. It'll be settin' over there on the credenza beside them cookies. Donations are welcome but don't be tryin' to tell the Fannin girls how to make chili. Their Mama was a fine cook and they'll be makin' the winnin' potful at the cook-off. Oh, and I've got five dollars to bet that they win. Anyone wants to bet, Patrice will be our bookie."

"Bettin' is against the law and it's immoral," Violet Prescott said from the doorway into the store.

The noise went from raising the roof to dead silence in less than a second. Tansy whipped around to see what Agnes would say or, worse yet, what she'd do. She and Violet had been arch enemies for years. The previous year at the Fourth of July festival they'd gotten into a fistfight and wound up in jail.

Agnes ignored Violet and went on. "Like I said, Patrice is our investment banker. I'm buying stock in the Red-Hot Bloomers Team. When they win, my stock will pay off damn good. I'm figuring that Violet will buy stock in Lenny's team since his mama is her friend. Now remember, there are about eighteen more teams on the roster so you can bet on any one you want. Y'all see Patrice between now and the day before the cook-off if you want to buy stock in any team you think might win the cook-off this year. I'm throwing a party at Clawdy's on Mother's Day afternoon to celebrate the big win from the team I'm bettin' on. Anyone who joins the Red-Hot Bloomers Team has an invitation."

At first there were a few whispers and then slowly the noise level rose. Agnes winked at Tansy and said, "That ought to keep them busy for a few days. Lord, I love it when there's excitement in Cadillac."

"Have you talked to Patrice about this?" Tansy asked.

"Hell, no! But she'll take care of it because we all want to whip Lenny's cheatin' ass. Never did like that boy or his mama. If I have to sabotage his chili by putting a dead rat in it, fur, tail, asshole, ears, and all, he will not beat Carlene." Agnes slapped her fist into the palm of her other hand with every word.

"Oh, no!" Tansy declared. "We've got to win fair and square, with no doubts."

Agnes patted her on the arm. "Then I'd say y'all better put on your aprons and get to work. I'll do my part in keeping Kitty away from your husbands while you are over here."

"How can you do that?"

Agnes flashed a grin that bordered on crazy. "Honey, I'd tell you but then we'd both wind up in prison."

"Dear God!" Tansy exclaimed.

As she headed up the stairs to unpack her suitcases, Tansy made up her mind that if Cadillac was still standing after the cook-off, she was going to a party at Clawdy's and she would buy more than five dollars' worth of stock in the Red-Hot Bloomers Team. If she had to make chili every night for six weeks, then she would at least make a few dollars with her *stock*. Kitty would put money on Lenny and it would be so sweet to take it from them. Things were looking up for sure.

∾✦∾

The store looked worse than a Chicago dump ground when the doors finally closed at five o'clock that afternoon. Carlene melted into a chair beside one of the messy dressing rooms and threw the back of her hand over her forehead in a dramatic gesture.

"My God, what a day," she said.

Alma Grace sat down in the middle of the floor. Her face was a picture of bewilderment as she looked up at Carlene. "Please tell me it's over. Do we have a bra left in the stockroom?"

Patrice joined Alma Grace on the floor and leaned against a dressing room doorjamb. "There are bras left but there's not a cookie out there or a drop of sweet tea. Our mothers escaped off to look in the attic for Grandpa's chili recipes. If it's in the Fannin family, they say it's not cheating. I need a drink, a cupcake, and sex, in that order."

"There's whiskey in the kitchen but Alma Grace already moved in and I'm packed and ready to move tonight. Your privacy is gone. Where are those cupcakes that Yancy brought?" Carlene asked.

"They're in the bottom drawer of my file cabinet. I swept them away in a hurry. And honey, Yancy has a house, too. I'll have my drink now and then I'm going to his house. If y'all are still awake when I come home later tonight we'll have cupcakes as a reward for surviving this day," Patrice said.

Alma Grace whined as she removed her high heels and rubbed her feet. "Do you think the worst of it might be over? If not, we'd best hire some help, ladies."

Carlene's giggle was giddy. "The cash register is bulging and poor old Josie was dragging when she left. I'm glad tomorrow is Sunday."

Alma Grace stretched out on the floor, not even caring that her spandex skirt rode up to the bottom of her panties. "My feet and my back hurt and I've side-stepped so many damn questions about you and Lenny that I am dizzy."

Patrice kicked off her shoes and wiggled her toes down into the carpet. "You said a cuss word. You been prayin' and cussin' more than usual. I wonder if that's a sign that if you should stop prayin' those naughty words will stop comin' out of your mouth."

Alma Grace slapped a hand over her mouth. "I did, didn't I?" She looked up toward the ceiling and fluttered her eyelashes. "Forgive me, Lord, for saying an ugly word. Put it in Carlene's heavenly book, not mine. She's the one who got all this started. Amen. And for your information, I will not stop prayin' for Carlene, Patrice."

Carlene looked up at the ceiling. "Go ahead, God. Slap it on my page. It's already messy and Alma Grace's whole book is spotless clean. But don't put your pencil up because you are going to need it since she's flirting with Jack Landry and he's pure old sin on a stick."

"I am not and he is not!" Alma Grace said quickly.

"You are, too," Patrice said. "And every girl in town has had the hots for Jack at one time or other. What do y'all say we go home and come back tomorrow afternoon to clean this up? We can drive out to the Rib Joint and get some barbecue for supper and have one of my cupcakes for dessert."

"I thought you were going to Yancy's," Alma Grace said.

"Sex can wait. I want ribs and beer," Patrice said.

"We'd better hurry up. Our mamas went upstairs to change into their cooking aprons. If we aren't gone when they come back down, they'll guilt us into helping," Carlene said.

"Hey." Josie poked her head in the door. "I figured it would look like a tornado struck in here. Need some help before I go home?"

Patrice shook her head. "I thought you were gone."

"I was all the way to the car and forgot my keys," Josie said.

"We're not cleaning up tonight. We're comin' in tomorrow and taking care of it."

"I'm not coming in here tomorrow. When I walk out that door, I'm not coming back until Monday morning, so speak now or forever hold your peace," Josie said.

"We'll take care of it. Enjoy your day without a bunch of company," Carlene said.

"Oh, there's a paper bag in your office, Patrice. It's got some checks in it from folks who want to help bankroll the Red-Hot Bloomers Team. Did Agnes talk to you about being our stockbroker?"

Patrice nodded. "I've got a bank bag and a spiral notebook full of the folks who are buying stock on both sides of the fence. I hope to hell we win or else Agnes and Violet might wind up in jail again."

"Or Mama," Patrice said. "How much does it take to bail a woman out of jail for fighting? Mama won't put up with Kitty saying too much more about Aunt Sugar."

Josie nodded seriously. "I'm going to the convenience store for a slushy. Y'all want me to bring you one on my way home? And I have no idea how much it'd take to get Sugar out of a jail cell but we'd best find out and have the cash ready. Tansy really would whup that hussy just for upsetting Sugar and truth is she'd enjoy doing it. She and Agnes might even get to share a cell. Not to put any pressure on you about the cook-off, but Alma Grace, you'd best stop prayin' for Carlene and start prayin' they learn how to make one helluva world-class bowl of hot chili."

Carlene held up her hand. "Patrice, I'll take a hundred dollars worth of stock on Aunt Tansy if she and Kitty get into a good old catfight but you'll have to extend me some credit until I build my checking account up again."

"Put me down for a hundred on Aunt Tansy and a hundred on Mama. You can bet that Mama will want in on that catfight," Alma Grace chimed in.

They all looked at Josie. "Don't look at me. I'm the one who's going to hold that mean-spirited bitch down while the Fannin girls snatch her baldheaded. And Alma Grace you can save your self-righteous looks for your cousins. I'd like to see her get her smart ass kicked twice for the stunt she pulled with the candlesticks and glue. I could have called her something a lot worse. Good night girls. Maybe next week will be normal."

Normal!

They wouldn't see normal until after the cook-off, if then.

Carlene yelled up the stairs. "We're leaving, Mama. Y'all don't look at the mess in the store. We'll take care of it tomorrow."

"Is Alma Grace going to church in the morning?" Sugar hollered.

"CNC if I go," Alma Grace shouted.

Carlene had the doorknob in her hand when someone pounded on the front door of the shop. "Someone probably left their purse. Hope we can find it among all this mess," she said as she made her way to the door.

She slung it open and gasped.

Lenny took a step forward and glared at her. "What the hell do you think you are doing, entering the chili cook-off? That's not for women. Are you crazy?" Lenny was yelling so hard that the vein in his head looked like it was about to pop wide open.

"Are there rules that say women can't enter? If so, we are going to protest that the contest is sexist and shut down the whole cook-off," Carlene said.

"Not written down but it's understood. This is for men only," Lenny said.

"Not anymore," she said.

"You won't win. You'll just make a fool of your whole family," he argued.

"We'll see about that. You worried that you won't win the trophy this year?"

"Oh, I'll win. I always win, but this year will be real sweet, especially since you tried to break all my trophies," he growled.

"But darlin'," Carlene said in her best sugary-sweet sarcastic voice, "you always said I was your good luck charm, remember?"

"I just said that to make you feel important," he said.

"If you win, you send Bridget on down here and I'll give her a brand-new pair of red panties. Her choice of bikinis, thongs, or maybe she'll want some maternity under-britches," Carlene said.

"You aren't funny," he said hoarsely.

"It sounded damn funny from my end. Has the April Fools' joke done a one-hundred-eighty-degree turn to bite you on your sorry ass, Lenny?"

"Go to hell." He stormed off the porch.

Carlene turned around to see both her cousins standing beside the credenza. "Now we really have to win the contest."

Chapter 8

GIGI PULLED A BIG pot from a box that she'd used to haul ingredients from her house. The laptop waited on the table with the first recipe they intended to try that night. First thing she had to do was open two big cans of chicken broth and there was no electric can opener. She searched in the drawers and finally found a handheld one but none of the three knew how to use it.

Someone knocked on the back door and Tansy opened it. "Hello. Come on in. What can we do for you?"

A red-haired lady with a face full of freckles stepped into the kitchen. "Y'all might not remember me. I was in grade school when y'all were up in high school but I remember the Fannin sisters real good. And I brought this Mexican casserole over for y'all's supper. My ex-husband has a team at the chili cook-off—the All My Exes Team, since the guys are all divorced. I just want you to know that I hope you beat the shit out of them and if you need any help in any way, you just call me. My name is Betsy Wilder."

"You know how to operate a can opener like this?" Tansy asked.

"Yes, ma'am. Show me the cans you want opened and I'll do it for you before I go on up to the nursing home in Sherman to work," she said.

"Thank you and thanks for the casserole," Gigi said when Betsy finished and headed for the door.

"Y'all are welcome. Good luck and that is a disposable pan. You just enjoy the casserole and throw it in the trash," she called back over her shoulder.

"That was awful sweet of her, wasn't it? Now, we have to put the ground beef into the stock which is to be poured into the pan," Gigi said.

Tansy carefully poured the yellow liquid and then waited. "I didn't remember Betsy but I do remember the Wilder family. Now what do we do?"

"Well, I'm not putting my hands in that raw meat and it says that it should be crumbled up. I can turn on an oven so I'll heat up the casserole. It sure smells good," Sugar said.

"Oh, hell, give me the ground beef. I'll do it," Gigi said.

"Then we have to cut up that big red onion and the garlic," Sugar said.

"Your job. I touched the meat," Gigi told her.

"I can do that if you two will measure out all the dry spices in one bowl and the liquid spices in another," Tansy offered. "But you'd best not tell a soul if my mascara runs."

"This is going to be some awesome chili." Sugar measured honey, molasses, liquid smoke, and lime juice. "Wouldn't it be something if we found our winning recipe right here at first?"

"Wait until we taste it. I swear, I never heard of putting molasses in chili before," Gigi said.

"That's it. Easy peasy. Put it all in the pot and let it simmer two hours. It'll be ready by bedtime," Tansy said. "What are we doing the rest of the evening?"

"We're setting up the electric cooker and getting our chicken to cooking for tomorrow's recipe," Gigi said.

"I'm not touching a dead bird. It would be sacrilege to Dakshani," Tansy said.

"You have to touch the raw meat, Gigi," Sugar told her.

"Okay, okay, I'll do it. I don't know how Mama ever cooked all those years," Gigi said. She put two chickens in each of two crock pots because tomorrow they were making enough to fill Grandpa's big cooker.

"Who's going to taste all this shit? We're going to have enough chili to feed an army," Sugar asked. "I decided to turn off the oven. We can heat up what we want of the casserole in the microwave."

"We'll find someone to taste it for us. Hey, we should get Patrice to make us some little suggestion and comment cards so we can see what people like the best," Tansy said.

Gigi's nose curled as she removed the wrapper from the chickens and slid them into the crock pots. The minute she finished she rushed off to the bathroom to wash her hands with that disinfectant soap the girls kept in there.

While she was gone, Tansy's phone rang. She took it out into the foyer so she could talk to Alex privately. And that's when Sugar realized that no one had even opened the cayenne pepper. She twisted the lid off and found a tablespoon measure, filled it up, and dumped it into the pot. When she stirred it up, it didn't smell nearly as hot as the chili she'd sampled at the cook-off in previous years so she put in another tablespoon.

"Please, Lord, let this be wonderful so we don't have to cook anymore," she prayed.

Gigi came back, pulled a bottle of tequila from the cabinet, and poured two fingers in the bottom of a glass. "Don't you look at me like that and don't you dare start praying," she told her sister. "I've got to get the taste of that raw meat out of my mouth."

"You didn't eat any of it, did you?" Sugar was appalled.

"No, but I smelled it and it's in my mouth now," Gigi said.

"Well, I've done my part. I'm going up to take a bath. You keep watch on the pot and stir it every fifteen minutes. I'll take my turn while you take a bath," she said.

Gigi stirred and smelled, then reread the recipe and frowned.

She'd watched Sugar measure all the ingredients into the bowl except for cayenne pepper.

"Well, shit! I bet that's what gives it the heat. It'll be bland as oatmeal without it." She picked up the tequila, tossed the rest of it back, shivered, and then checked the recipe. It said a tablespoon but Sugar had put all the measuring utensils into the dishwasher. She found a fourth cup measure and it didn't look so big so she filled it up, poured it into the chili, and stirred it well. Then she poured another two fingers of tequila and carried it toward her bedroom. She still had things to unpack. Tansy could damn sure watch the chili and talk at the same time.

"Stir every fifteen minutes. Tequila and bourbon is on the bottom shelf above the stove," she said as she passed Tansy.

Tansy nodded and headed toward the kitchen. She listened to Alex telling about a new colt born on the ranch that day and ran her finger down the recipe. Damn it! The cayenne pepper was sitting right there. Sugar had put up the spices as she measured them so she wouldn't get confused. Evidently she forgot to put that one in the mixture.

It said a tablespoon but Tansy couldn't talk and measure, too, so she shook a little in the pot, smelled, and shook a little more, and then be damned if that little cover with the holes in it didn't pop right off and the rest of what was in the bottle got dumped.

"Oh, well, that should be just about enough to make it good," she said. "No, I'm not talking to you. Sugar forgot to put the cayenne in the chili but I took care of it. Now tell me more about the new colt."

They met in the kitchen at ten o'clock that evening ready to taste their first pot of chili. Sugar had taken on the last job of stirring and already had three plastic bowls on the cabinet waiting when Gigi and Tansy arrived.

"It smells good," Gigi said.

"Y'all sit down and I'll serve it up." Sugar smiled. "But first we say grace."

No arguments so she bowed her head and thanked the Lord for the wonderful meal they were about to partake of and then she filled three bowls and put them on the table.

"I just know this is going to be heavenly," Sugar said.

"Okay, on three we all put the first bite in our mouths, chew slowly, and then we'll pass judgment," Tansy said.

"One, two, three," Gigi said.

The chili went in.

Gigi ran to the kitchen sink, spit it out, grabbed the tequila, and sucked on it like a starving baby.

Tansy spit it out on the floor and turned up the bottle of bourbon and gulped a dozen times.

Sugar chomped twice before the fire hit her mouth and she spewed it all over the wall, fell out of her chair, and clutched at her throat, gasping for air. She didn't even hesitate when Gigi handed her the tequila. She just turned it up and downed what was left in the bottle.

"Damn!" Tansy said. "That is some hot shit."

"Ha….ha…hot as hell." Sugar's breath still came in short gasps.

Gigi slid onto the floor next to Sugar and started to giggle. "We've got to get rid of it. Nobody can ever know about that recipe."

Tansy sat down with them. "You are drunk. That bottle of tequila was almost half full."

"I might be but so are y'all. Even Sugar."

Sugar fanned her mouth and her words were slurred. "Mouth feels like I ate fire. Pour it out in the backyard for the wild animals."

Tansy giggled. "What the wild animals ever do to you?"

"Jamie says coons will eat anything." Her head bobbed around with every word.

"I'll do it," Gigi said.

Using two potholders she carefully carried the chili out the back door and dumped it off the edge of the porch. The night breezes wafted the chili up to her nose and it started to run. A stray dog came running up, licked at the edge, and took off with his tail between his legs, howling like he'd been struck by lightning.

Gigi had trouble focusing but she could tell that wasn't a cat but a skunk coming from around the corner of the lilac bush. She backed up a step. The skunk sniffed the air and a black and white blur went running toward the back of the lot.

"Y'all think we should call out the hazardous waste people?" she asked as she carried the pot to the sink and ran water in it.

Tansy pointed. "It took the paint off the wall. We might have invented a biological weapon."

Sugar giggled. "God almighty but that shit was hot."

Tansy used a chair to steady herself when she finally stood up. "The tequila or the chili, which one was hotter?" Her words came out in slowly slurred bits and pieces.

Gigi sunk into a kitchen chair and stared at the spots on the wall. "That damn chili was hotter. Wasn't it, Sugar?"

"Damn straight."

❧

Patrice pulled the blanket up over her and Yancy and scooted close enough that she could feel his body warmth. He kept the porch swing going with the heel of his boot and his right arm tightly around her shoulders. His left held her hand in his lap and his thumb made sexy little circles in her palm.

"Thank you for helping Mama into the house today," Patrice said.

"You are very welcome. I called Lenny this afternoon and resigned from the Chili Kings."

"Oh, my sweet Jesus. I forgot that you were a member of his team."

"*Was* being the word here, darlin'. He was mad as hell but he can find another team member. Actually he has to find two more because Carlene's dad resigned, too. I promised I wouldn't give you any of our secrets but he said he had perfected a new recipe for this year and it didn't matter anyway," Yancy said.

Patrice kissed him on the cheek. "I'm sorry, darlin'."

"Don't be. I'd much rather make love to you than make chili with Lenny and the guys. Now tell me about your day. I was worried that Agnes and Violet would come to blows right there in the foyer so I stuck around until they'd finished bickering."

She stretched enough to kiss him hard, teasing his lips open with her tongue and tasting beer and pretzels. "The store looks like a dozen women had a major catfight. Agnes set up a support fund for the Red-Hot Bloomers Team. And she made me the investment person, which is a glorified name for bookie, so everyone can… quote"—she brought both hands out from under the quilt to make imaginary signs in the air—"'buy stock in whichever team they think will win.' When Lenny's team loses, then whatever stock they have is given to the winning team and Agnes is throwing a victory party at Clawdy's."

Her hands went back under the quilt and she unbuttoned his shirt.

He clamped a hand over hers. "God, that feels good. I'm so glad you came over tonight. I'm lost when I don't see you for a whole day and night."

"Me, too," she mumbled.

He chuckled. "I'm wondering, if I am involved in a sexual relationship with a bookie, could I lose my job."

"If you lose your job, we'll give you one selling underpants at Bless My Bloomers. I bet we'd have record sales with someone as sexy as you in the shop. All you'd have to do is make a suggestion and the women would buy anything."

Carlene laced her hands behind her head and stared at the television in still another new bedroom. Hopefully Alma Grace had not inherited her Mama's snoring gene. Carlene was on the verge of too tired to eat when they'd gotten to Patrice's house. And then she had to unpack six boxes of clothing and put it all way. Aunt Sugar, Aunt Tansy, and her Mama, bless their hearts, had packed her things and they were organized so well that the unpacking didn't take long.

From the noise in the bedroom right next to hers, Alma Grace wasn't having much luck with her unpacking job. She wasn't cussing but she was sure doing a lot of very loud grumbling. Any minute now Carlene expected to hear desperate prayers asking God to zap down more closet room and maybe an extra chest of drawers.

Her phone rang at the same time the one on the rerun of *Golden Girls* did on the television set. "Blooper." She pointed at the TV, and then she realized that Blanche was talking and the ringing noise was coming from her nightstand.

She rolled over and grabbed the phone. The caller ID said it was coming from the Cadillac police station. Holy shit! Had Aunt Sugar and Kitty squared off already?

"Hello," she said breathlessly.

"Carlene? This is Jack Landry. How are you this evening?"

"I'm fine. What's wrong?"

"Nothing is wrong, Carlene. Why would you ask that? Oh, the thing with Sugar and Kitty, right? Or was it Agnes and Violet?"

"Either or both,' Carlene said.

"Jail is empty and town is quiet. I do believe we're safe for the night." He chuckled.

"Well, that's a relief," she said.

"I wanted to tell you that I'm sorry for the mess you are in."

"I'm not giving up the contest," she said bluntly.

"I don't think you should. I'm just glad I'm not on the police team because I'd like to see you girls whip Lenny's ass. I hear there's a betting pot at the lingerie shop and I'd just love to put fifty on the Red-Hot Bloomers but, honey, I'm afraid to be seen coming inside. If I met you at the Cadillac Café tomorrow for lunch and slipped the money to you, would you buy me that much stock? And Cathy, Marty, and Trixie will be buying stock, too. Trixie says that she's going to turn a hundred dollars into five hundred." He chuckled.

"Gossip brought out the whole town today and we've got to clean the shop up tomorrow afternoon but thanks for the invitation," she said.

"Okay, then Carlene, let me put this a hell of a lot plainer. I've had a crush on you ever since high school but when I came home from the army you were married. I know you are going through a helluva divorce but I'd like to date you. I'm willing to wait until the divorce is filed and you've moved on past that," he said.

Alma Grace is going to kill me, was her first thought.

Her second was, *How long will he wait?*

"Well, are you going to say anything?" Jack asked.

"I'm not sure I know what to say."

"It's too early for you to date anyone. I realize that, but I don't want to be left in the backseat a second time so I decided to be like Rhett Butler and speak my piece."

"You've seen *Gone with the Wind*," she gasped.

"Three women are my best friends. Yes, I've seen *Gone with the Wind* about a dozen times. And I figure if Rhett can declare himself to Scarlett while she is still in widow's weeds, I can tell you that I've had a crush on you before you sign the divorce papers," he said.

Carlene had always thought Jack Landry was downright sexy

but he was two years older and he never even looked at her, or did he?

Alma Grace is going to hate you even more than she does for getting a divorce and ruining her Easter program, that niggling little voice in the back of her head sing-songed away.

"You think it would be all right if I call sometime during the next few weeks? Maybe until after the chili cook-off? We could just talk about our day and how things are going."

"I guess that will be okay." Carlene wondered if she'd said the words out loud.

"You going to church tomorrow?"

"I'm sleeping in after today."

"I've got night shift so I won't make it, either. I heard that your mama and your aunts were up in the attic lookin' for your grandpa's old recipes today. Lenny ain't got a chance in hell if they find the real one. My granny said that your grandpa's chili was the hottest damn stuff in the whole state."

Alma Grace likes him. You can't do this. Besides, you aren't even divorced yet, the voice screamed.

"Looks like I've got another call. Saturday night drunk probably needs some help getting home. Good night, Carlene. Don't work too hard tomorrow."

She looked from phone to television when she heard the rap on her door. Blanche was talking to Rose and Dorothy in the kitchen so it wasn't coming from there.

"Carlene, you still awake?" Alma Grace asked as she knocked again.

"I'm awake," Carlene said.

Alma Grace didn't wait for an invitation. She marched in and sat down on the edge of the bed. "Do you think God will hate me if I don't go to church tomorrow morning? I started to set the alarm and I'm so tired that I just want to sleep in. Besides I don't want to be there if Daddy and Jack are both there. It would just be too awkward."

"Don't ask me. You're the one who can quote scripture and verse. Didn't even God rest on the seventh day or something?" Carlene said.

It was the perfect time to tell her that Jack wouldn't be in church, but how did she do it without saying how she knew?

Chapter 9

Tansy, Gigi, and Sugar were sitting at the table with recipes spread out around them and takeout coffee cups in their hands, instead of margaritas and magazines. Clarice stopped in her tracks and got a whiff of greasy hamburgers with onions and something that smelled horrible. The trash can had the remains of a casserole in a disposable pan. Was that the culprit for the rancid odor?

"Hello." Sugar's eyes looked like she'd been crying. "They found a whole raft of recipes inside Mama's old electric cooker. You can't buy these old heavy metal ones anymore. The new ones are lightweight and cheap plastic."

Alma Grace pushed inside the kitchen behind Clarice and gasped. "Mama, you are still in your pajamas."

"But I have my makeup on. I didn't go to church this morning. I did have a little prayer and meditation time in my bedroom. I just couldn't bear to sit in that pew without your daddy beside me," Sugar said defensively and shot both of her sisters a dirty look.

"I'm only dressed because I had to drive down to the café and get hamburgers," Gigi explained when Carlene looked her way. "We stayed over last night. Tonight I have a date with my husband to go to dinner and we'll begin our cooking tomorrow night."

Patrice was the last one inside the house and she just shrugged and said, "Good mornin', Mama and Aunties. What is that foul smelling shit out there beside the porch? It's killed the grass for a foot out around it and even the fire ants are making a detour around it."

"Sugar still snores like she did when we were kids," Tansy tattled.

"I was here first so live with it." Sugar looked up at Alma Grace and asked, "Which church did *you* go to this mornin'?"

"Neither one. I'll be dam…hanged…if I go to our church." She slapped the top of the cabinet. "I'm still pissed at the whole committee and I'm pretty mad at Kim, too, even though she used to be my friend."

"Alma Grace! One day away from church and you're talkin' like Tansy," Sugar scolded.

"Well, I *am* pissed. I could pitch a hissy I'm so mad, so that's pissed. They stole my job, my halo, and my wings and I'm not going to go back to that church until I've forgiven them," Alma Grace declared. "I hope every one of them but Barbara Culpepper gets laryngitis the day of the program. If she has to carry the whole program, everyone will be holding their ears."

Tansy shut her eyes and crossed her chest with her hands. She leaned back and raised her head toward the ceiling and said, "I have a vision of someone tying a knot in the ropes and instead of Kim floating from balcony to pulpit gracefully, she gets about halfway and just hangs there in the harness, waving back and forth like alfalfa in the wind."

"Are you going to figure out a way to tie that knot, Mama?" Patrice asked. "And how did you have a vision right here in Bless My Bloomers. Your cockatiel is your muse and he is at home. You have to have that damn bird close by to get visions or see things in dreams. And no one told me what that shit is beside the porch. It's awful."

"My precious Dakshani lit on my shoulder just before I left yesterday so his spirit is still with me, and besides, Mama sometimes visits me in a vision or in a dream and it's her spirit that I feel this morning, not my bird's." Tansy moved one hand from her chest and waved it over the top of the recipes. "Mama has promised me that she will take care of Alma Grace's pain for being fired and Carlene's pain over being cheated on. You don't mess with Mama or her offspring."

"Tansy Fannin Cordell, you are full of shit," Gigi said.

Tansy's brown eyes opened and she dropped her head dramatically to her chest. "This psychic business takes the energy out of a person. Carlene, make us a pot of coffee to give us a boost."

Aunt Tansy playing psychic always lifted Carlene's spirits. "Sounds to me like y'all have had enough coffee. How about I make a big pitcher of sweet tea instead?"

"Anything, darlin'. I always have a sinking spell after a vision," Tansy said.

Gigi tucked her chin into her chest and said, "Well, my sister, you'd best rise on up out of that sinking spell because we've got work to do."

"Oh, my God. Y'all tried to make chili last night and that's what's out there, isn't it? What in the hell did you put in it?" Patrice asked.

"Too much cayenne pepper," Sugar said honestly.

"It was so hot that Sugar drank tequila to get the fire out of her mouth and a sweet lady came and brought us a casserole for supper. We had enough that we finished it off for breakfast. She showed us how to open cans with that thing in the drawer," Tansy said.

Patrice shook her head slowly. "And y'all are going to find the prize-winning recipe for us to win the cook-off?"

"Don't you doubt us for a minute. Our first attempt might not be right but we'll learn," Tansy said.

"Well, try Granny's recipe and follow it to the letter," Carlene said. "Granny would have put the chili recipes in the cooker because that was probably the only time it ever got used. Lenny kept his cooker in the closet in his office. It's like the Holy Grail. He probably bows down to it three times a day starting the week before the cook-off. And his recipes are in his gun safe. He changes the code regularly so I can't get inside."

"*Duh*, Carlene," Gigi said. "It wasn't his recipes he was protecting. It was his little black book and maybe even pictures of all his women. He was protecting his sorry ass by keeping that safe locked up."

Patrice giggled. "You got that right, Aunt Gigi. Good thing she didn't know the code or there might have been buckshot holes in Lenny in the dealership that day. I'm talkin' real bloodshed, not just holes in a Corvette."

"Well, if she ever does shoot the bastard, she'll take care of it with one shotgun shell. I taught her not to waste ammunition just like my mama taught me," Gigi said.

"I can't believe my mama got drunk," Alma Grace whispered.

"It was drink the tequila or lose all my precious teeth," Sugar told her defiantly.

∽⚬∾

This was hell.

Alma Grace stopped inside the door to the store, putting her elbows on the checkout desk and her head in her hands. She shut her eyes and prayed that when she said amen it wouldn't look like a tornado had hit the lingerie racks.

God said no!

"Why? Why? Why?" Alma Grace whined.

"Might as well stop questioning and get to work," Patrice said.

"Ask and ye shall receive," Alma Grace groaned. "I forgot to ask for the cleaning fairies last night. I was too busy praying that you didn't get pregnant when you went over to Yancy's place. That's all we need right now."

"Well, thank you so much but I'm a big girl and I don't give a rat's ass about what people say," Patrice said.

A sneaky little doubt found its way into Alma Grace's mind, causing her to frown. Had God said no about Carlene and Lenny? Was she praying selfishly because she wanted to be right?

Oh, no, she thought, *get thee behind me Satan. This message is not coming from heaven.*

Carlene giggled and picked up a corset from the floor under a round rack. "Shit! A thread has come undone and there's at least a dozen beads gone. Inspect as you clean and put all the ones that need repairs on the counter. Josie and I'll have our work cut out for us tomorrow."

"I'll start in the dressing rooms," Alma Grace said.

Patrice drew a virtual line from cash register to the back of the store with her finger. "I'll take the left side. Carlene, you do the right. We might get it all done by supper time. Our treat is going to be fried chicken from the convenience store for supper. We'll be too tired to cook anyway."

"Cook? You mean microwave frozen burritos, and we can't get takeout for supper. I miss mama's cook." Alma Grace sighed.

"You'll live." Carlene smiled.

"Why don't you ask God to deliver a home-cooked meal to our door tonight?" Patrice smarted off.

"You are mean," Alma Grace said.

"It makes as much sense as all that prayin' you've been doin' wanting Lenny and Carlene to get back together," Patrice said.

Alma Grace threw a wave over her shoulder and pulled back the fancy satin curtain into the first dressing room. "I'm going to ignore you, Patrice. It looks like hogs have been rooting around in here. I swear my daddy's pig pens look better than this. It's horrible."

She checked each piece of lingerie and made two piles on the bench along one side of the small space. One needed repairs; the other could be returned to the rack.

Her phone vibrated in her hip pocket and she pulled it out, checked the ID, and laid it on the bench. She didn't want to talk to Kim; she was still royally pissed. And according to Uncle Hank, that was a step worse than being just plain old pissed.

The floor was cleared and she was busy putting lingerie back on the hot-pink velvet hangers when Patrice pulled back the curtain. "Phone is for you. Guess yours is turned off."

Her cousin's eyes were sparkling and the grin on her face said she was up to no good.

"Who is it?" she asked.

"I don't know." Patrice shoved the phone toward her.

She answered it. "Hello?"

"Turn on your phone, Alma Grace. What if somebody died or had something real important like I do to tell you and there you'd be in the dark. I'm your friend, girl," Kim said. "I know y'all are in there cleaning up from yesterday because I drove by and saw your vehicles parked in the driveway. And your mama wasn't at church this morning. Is she sick nigh unto death? That's the only thing that would keep Miz Sugar from services."

"Mama is fine. We didn't want lightning to strike the church building and we would have been hypocrites if we would have been there. We're both pissed at the way I've been treated. That Easter program has grown into a big production under my care and you know it."

Kim's sigh came through the phone as loudly as if she'd been standing right next to Alma Grace. "Oh, honey. I hate to be the bearer of bad news."

"Bad news?" Cold water replaced the blood in Alma Grace's veins. "Is my daddy all right?"

"Of course, he's all right. He was down at that CNC this morning sitting right up near the front. I bet he put a big check in the plate because our offering total was down by hundreds this morning. That's not the bad news."

Alma Grace could visualize Kim's nose rising exactly three inches. It always did when she was miffed, which was just a religious form of pissed.

"I know that Jack Landry walked you home after you forsook us and went down to the CNC on Wednesday night. I heard that you were flirting with him and that you even said you wanted to ride on his motorcycle. Well, I've got a cousin who has a cousin who works as dispatch at the police station on the night shift," Kim said.

"And? I don't suppose either one is a sin, is it?" Alma Grace said coldly.

"No, but he does go to the CNC even though his mama, bless her heart, prays that he'll come back to our church. He's been on the prayer list for weeks and weeks and he's not even sick. She's afraid he won't go to heaven if he gets killed in the line of duty since he was baptized in our church."

Alma Grace considered throwing the phone over the top of the petition separating the dressing room from the one next to it.

"Well, anyway…" Kim dragged out the words. "To make a long story short, Jack called Carlene last night. My cousin's cousin said that she just accidentally hit the wrong button and heard it all. He said that he'd had a crush on her since high school, but by the time he got up the courage to tell her that, he was in the military. When he got home, she was already married to Lenny but he said that he was going to be like Rhett Butler in *Gone with the Wind*. You know when he told Miss Scarlett that he was in love with her right after her husband had died. Well, Jack said that he realized the divorce hadn't even happened but he'd be waiting in the wings when it did, and she gave him permission to call her on the phone between now and that time."

Alma Grace saw red flashes dancing in the dressing room.

Kim went on. "You poor thing. He was just walking you home in hopes of learning more about Carlene. I'm so sorry but friends tell friends when something is going on and I had to call. I should've come by but I didn't want to tell you in front of Carlene."

Alma Grace hung up the phone without saying good-bye or

thank you. The woman had just shattered her dreams so why should she thank her. Red dots were still flashing in front of her eyes when she marched right up to Carlene and popped both hands on her hips.

∞

Steam boiled out of Alma Grace's ears, her hands were on her hips, and she looked like she was going to shoot first and pray later. "When were you going to tell me? I had to hear it from Kim."

"What are you talking about?" Carlene whispered.

"Kim's cousin's cousin works at the police department. And she listened in to the conversation between you and Jack last night. Does the part about *Gone with the Wind* ring a bell?"

Patrice stopped working and, in a couple of long strides, joined her cousins in the middle of the store. "What about *Gone with the Wind*? Did y'all rent it? I'm not watching that damn show ever again so tell me right now and I'll go to Yancy's until y'all are done watching it. It makes me cry when Bonnie dies."

"No, we didn't rent it. Carlene is Miss Scarlett and Jack is Rhett Butler and he's declared himself to her. Her, Patrice, not me! He was just using me to get close to her." Every word got shriller until the last one was little more than a squeal.

Patrice slumped down in a chair beside the cash register. "Tell me more."

Alma Grace set her jaw. "She knew I liked him."

"And he likes her. She can't do anything about that, Alma Grace. Except tell him that you like him so she can't be seen with him or he can't call her because it will upset you," Patrice said.

The hands left her hips and hung limply. Her hand went to her mouth. Her blue eyes widened. "She can't do that! It would be so embarrassing. I could never look at him again."

Patrice disagreed but she did it without saying a word. She'd looked at Lenny and Carlene together for years and she'd had drunk sex with Lenny on her twenty-first birthday. With all the other notches on his bedpost, she doubted that Lenny even remembered it but she still couldn't look at Carlene right then.

"Then cool your heels. Carlene has always been the sensible one of us. She's not going to ride down Main Street on the back of his cycle and flip off Kitty Lovelle. She's just going to talk to him on the phone," Patrice said.

"I can be mad because she didn't tell me." Alma Grace pouted.

Patrice nodded. "We both can be mad about that but I swear if you start prayin' about it, I'll slap the shit out of you."

Carlene threw up her hands. "I'm sitting right here. I can hear you! I wanted to tell you but I didn't want to break your heart. I haven't even signed those damned papers yet. The lawyer told Mama that they'd probably bring them out here to me or send them by registered mail by the end of the week. It can't be too soon but I'm not going to jump from frying pan to fire. Believe me, it hurts like hell to get burned."

Alma Grace plopped down in a chair and sighed.

"I recognize that self-righteous look. If you start praying, I really will throw you out in the yard and lock the door," Patrice said.

"Promise?" Alma Grace finally smiled.

Carlene shook her head slowly from side to side. Was this blasted arguing between them going to go on until the crack of dawn? "Oh, hush, and get back to work, the both of you."

"Hey, when y'all want a break in there, come on to the kitchen. A nice lady whose husband is on the Blazing Saddles Team just brought us a wonderful rum cake. She says that she and her sisters are getting a team up for next year if we do well this year," Gigi yelled.

❧

The day lasted a whole week. No, it lasted two weeks and it was dark when they left to pick up some fried chicken from the convenience store for supper. Grieving was done in steps. Carlene knew that. Divorce had to be as traumatic as death, right? She'd had the flash of anger, the denial, and the little voice in her head filling her with doubts that Lenny was right in saying that it was her fault.

After she paid for the chicken, she finally got past the idea that she'd caused Lenny to cheat. She might have been busy and not given him one hundred percent of the attention he wanted, but she didn't make him cheat. That was on his list of sins, not hers.

Somewhere between the time she started the car engine and drove out of the parking lot, a white-hot fire started burning inside her heart and soul. Lenny was wise to keep his codes to that gun safe secret because she still had a key to the house. She could waltz in there and kill him in his sleep. Orange was one of her best colors and she'd always heard that prison jumpsuits were very comfortable.

In Texas the liquor stores were closed on Sunday but convenience stores could stay open twenty-four/seven and they were allowed to sell wine and beer. Carlene wasn't a beer drinker like her cousin, Patrice, but she did like good cheap wine. She whipped into the parking lot of the convenience store on the outskirts of Cadillac but the guilt came back when she picked up a bottle of blackberry wine. She tucked it firmly under her arm and carried a six-pack of Diet Coke and a gallon of milk to the front of the store. That was heavy enough to ensure a paper bag with handles.

Alma Grace would never know that she was buying wine on Sunday, so she wouldn't have a reason to preach at her for it.

She parked her van behind Alma Grace's cute little red Prius and Patrice's white Cadillac SRX. If they didn't need the van for the business, she'd trade it in next week for a motorcycle. She might buy a cycle anyway and roar up and down the street that Kitty lived on every night.

A soft drone of phone conversation was coming from Patrice's bedroom. Were she and Yancy having phone sex because she was too tired to go to his house that night?

She snuck the milk and soda into the fridge, left the paper bag sitting on the cabinet, and tucked the wine into her purse. She opened the cabinet doors to find a gorgeous stemmed glass and carefully stuck it upside down in her purse. She felt like she'd won the lottery when she locked her bedroom door. Quiet, blessed quiet. She loved her mama and the aunties. She loved her cousins, even when Alma Grace prayed. But she craved quiet, and if the wine did the right job, she'd have peace of mind and soul to go with the physical quiet surrounding her.

She kicked off her shoes, left her jeans and shirt lying on the floor beside her bed, unfastened her bra and threw it toward a rocking chair in the corner, and donned a faded old gray nightshirt with the Texas Longhorns logo on the front. She poured a glass brimful of wine, sipped, and lounged against the pillows propped against the headboard of her bed.

Two glasses later, the bottle was nearly empty. The rage had subsided and the doubts began. Maybe Alma Grace was right after all. The truth was that Jack had walked Alma Grace a block down the street after church. Rumors told a whole different story. Carlene would never believe that story about an April Fools' joke but maybe other than that one indiscretion Lenny had been faithful. Perhaps they could work on their marriage and it would be even stronger than it had ever been. She needed to talk to him and it couldn't wait until morning.

She parked at the curb and padded barefoot up to the door. When she finally got her key into the doorknob, it wouldn't work, so she leaned on the bell, listening to it ring and ring for a good thirty seconds. When he didn't come to the door, she started knocking and kept it up until the door swung open.

There he stood with pajama bottoms riding low on his hips and a grin on his face. She'd always loved that grin and the sparkle in his eyes. Maybe that's what Alma Grace meant when she said to find something she loved and work forward in baby steps from that. He wasn't one of those men who had a dark shadow by five o'clock but by this time of night he did have enough scruff to add to his sexiness.

She started to reach across the distance and touch his cheek but everything suddenly started spinning and she used the hand to grab the doorjamb.

"Well, well, look who has come dragging back home at the eleventh hour. So I guess you are ready to apologize?" he said. "And by the way, darlin', you look like hell."

"Well, thank you, Lenny Joe. And your ego is still as big as the whole state of Texas," she said. "I came here tonight to talk to you, civilly, like adults, without mud slinging, but I see that I've wasted my time and yours."

"I'll talk. You'll listen. If you want to come back to me, there's a new set of rules. I like being married but I like playing around. It's as simple as that," he said. "And I'm not changing, Carlene. I'll be discreet."

"Holy shit!" she muttered. "Does that mean if I'm discreet I can screw other men, too?" she whispered.

He shook his head emphatically. "A woman doesn't have the needs that a man does. Some of us are not one-woman men. You will apologize to my mother and I'll take this visit as your apology to me and we'll go right back to our old lifestyle. You won't ever find anyone else who'll want you, anyway. This way you can have a husband and a family."

"Why wouldn't anyone else want me?" she asked.

"Darlin', you are too tall, too big, and too much woman. It takes a man like me to handle you," he said.

She sighed and pushed away from the door. "Good night and good-bye, Lenny." She turned around and even though it took every bit of her concentration, she made it to the car without stumbling.

She got all the way to the shop before the tears flooding her cheeks blinded her and she pulled over to the curb.

"That was the absolute most stupid thing I've ever done," she yelled.

The words were still bouncing around inside the van when the voice inside her head said, *Okay, Carlene, you listened to Alma Grace's advice and it brought closure like nothing else could. Go home and listen to your heart. Not Alma Grace or Patrice or anyone else.*

❧

Patrice was on her way down the hall when she heard Carlene crying in her bedroom. It didn't take a mathematical genius or a degree in advanced psychoanalysis to know that she was crying about Lenny.

She rapped lightly on the door. When there was no answer, she turned the knob to find it locked. That was a very minor setback. She'd opened doors with ice picks, hairpins, and even a toothpick one time. A quick trip to the kitchen netted an ice pick and the door swung right open.

Patrice burst in to the room to find Carlene with a glass of wine in one hand and an empty bottle in the other.

"Where did you get that wine?"

"At the convenience store." Carlene slurred a couple of words.

Patrice plopped down on the edge of the bed. "You are one drunk girl."

"No, ma'am, I am not, but if you'll go get us another couple of bottles of wine, we could be by midnight," Carlene said.

"Drunk, who's drunk?" Alma Grace asked from the doorway.

"I am but don't preach at me for drinking. Besides, Jesus drank wine," Carlene said.

Alma Grace crossed the room and sat down on the bed beside Patrice. "What happened? I was going up the hall to see if we had any milk."

"I just bought a gallon so, yes, we have milk. I talked to Lenny, face-to-face," Carlene said.

"Oh, did it go well?" Alma Grace held her breath.

Patrice took the bottle and the glass from her hands, sat down on the bed, and wrapped her arms around Carlene. "What did he say? Spit it out."

Between gulps she told them the story and how she'd had to stop on the way because she couldn't see for the tears. "It hurts but I'm truly done with the man. No more chances. No more thinking about it."

"This might just be a minor setback. Every therapist knows the first visit in marriage counseling is sometimes rocky and it's just a baby step at a time," Alma Grace said.

Carlene wiped tears from her eyes.

Alma Grace sighed. "I'm going to my room to pray. The Bible says that God hears the fervent prayers of the righteous."

"You're wasting your time," Carlene said.

"Tell God to send lightning bolts to kill Lenny Lovelle," Patrice said.

Chapter 10

THE SISTERS ARRIVED JUST as the shop was closing on Monday afternoon. Sugar met them in the kitchen and handed each of her sisters a little bibbed apron printed with roses and edged with lace that matched the one she already wore. Gigi wore a hairnet over her updo and the other two had on ball caps. Sugar's curly ponytail, pulled out of the hole at the back of the cap, looked like a ball of twisted yarn, and Tansy's didn't look much better even if it was a little bit longer.

"So you are trying chicken chili tonight, I take it?" Josie said.

"We found Mama's recipe for it. The chicken is already cooked," Gigi said.

"Which one of you handled the cold, dead bird?" Josie asked.

Gigi raised her hand. "I did."

"And she didn't even put oven mitts on her hands," Tansy said.

Josie looked up at Gigi's hairnet. "Goes real well with your longhorn earrings but the apron clashes with your orange jersey."

"They made me put the hairnet on," Gigi said.

"Well, I was wondering." Josie smiled.

"Y'all about to get busy?" Patrice asked.

"Yes, we are. You want to stick around and taste our product?" Sugar asked.

"No, ma'am. I'll taste it at the cook-off." Patrice pulled her platinum hair up into a messy ponytail and secured it with a rubber band she pulled from the pocket of her snug-fitting jeans.

"How about you, Carlene?" Gigi asked.

"Carlene has had a hangover all day. She'd upchuck if she ate chili," Patrice told them.

"I do not!" Carlene said right behind her. "I've got a wine headache and I took four aspirin and it's wearing off."

"It's Lenny's fault. She wouldn't drink so much if he hadn't riled her up," Josie said.

Patrice nodded in agreement. "She went to the house and talked to him and finally figured out there is no future with him."

Josie threw up her hands. "I heard all about it this morning at the convenience store. I'm glad you've figured out what most of us knew all along, honey. Now let's get on with the job of running a business and beating the shit out of him in the cook-off."

A hard knock on the kitchen door sent Tansy to open it.

"Floral delivery for the Fannin sisters," the man said.

"I'll take it. Thank you," she said.

"Have a nice day." He nodded.

Tansy set a lovely arrangement of yellow daisies, white mums, and purple-tipped baby carnations on the kitchen table and opened the envelope with the card. "I bet it's from our husbands."

Sugar and Gigi were suddenly glued to her side.

"Well?" Josie asked.

Gigi took the card from Tansy. "She don't have her reading glasses. It says: *We are all proud of you for entering the cook-off and we're rooting for you even though our husbands are the Wildcat Team. We hope you teach the whole bunch of those male chauvinists that women can do anything a man can.*"

"I'll be damned," Josie grinned.

❧

Alma Grace was the last one to come trailing into the kitchen. She sat down at the table. "That smell is going to get into our lingerie. Nobody wants to buy panties that smell like chili."

Gigi slapped her leg and laughed loud and hard. "They would if they knew that chili turns a man on more than perfume."

"If it still smells like this in the morning I will be duct taping the door shut, all around it. I think I'll go by the store and buy potpourri to set on the credenza and some candles to burn in the store just in case," Alma Grace said.

"It'll all be out of the house by morning but who is going to taste for you all?" Patrice asked.

"Agnes is taking care of that," Sugar said.

Patrice shivered. People tasting something that the Fannin sisters cooked? That was a scary thought. It might even get poor old Agnes thrown in jail.

❧

Alma Grace was about to load her cart with candles that evening when she noticed the plug-in air fresheners with replaceable units. She mentally went through the store, the beading room, the office, and the foyer, counting all the places where she could plug them in and bought several. Lavender scent for the store, rose for the office, gardenia for the foyer, and plumeria for the stockroom. Surely to goodness, that would knock out the smell of chili.

She turned the corner and there was Violet Prescott—and the woman actually smiled at her. Alma Grace immediately looked out the plate-glass windows at the front of the store to see if it was snowing or if the sky was falling fast toward the earth.

"Alma Grace," Violet said sweetly.

"Miz Prescott." Alma Grace nodded.

"Darlin', I'm so glad that our paths have crossed today."

No lightning bolts and the sky only had a few big white clouds floating around.

Violet opened her handbag.

Alma Grace looked around frantically for a place to hide if the woman brought out a gun.

Violet pulled out an envelope and shoved it toward her. "This is cash money and the names of the people who are donating to Lenny's party fund which will be held at my plantation."

Alma Grace shook her head and clasped her hands behind her back. "No, ma'am, I will not take that from you. You will have to put it in Patrice's hands yourself. If there was a discrepancy in the amount that reached the shop, you could blame me."

Violet shoved the envelope back in her bag. "I should have known that even you with all your righteous ways are still kin to Carlene."

"Yes, ma'am, and blood runs thick in the Fannin family." Alma Grace quickly pushed her cart toward the checkout counter but she could feel Violet's eyes boring holes in her back the whole way. She might not agree with Carlene or with Patrice, but by golly, they were kin folks. Violet Prescott wasn't.

❧

The next morning Alma Grace beat everyone to the shop, sniffed as she walked in, and swore she could smell a faint hint of chili. It didn't take her long to plug in all her new floral-scented room fresheners. Then she slipped into the kitchen and checked inside the refrigerator. Sure enough there were several large containers of the chili that had been made the night before.

"This place smells like a flower shop," Patrice said.

Alma Grace jumped and slammed the refrigerator door on her fingers. "Dammit! That hurt. And better that it smells like flowers than a chili factory. Do you see all that stuff in there? What are we going to do with that much chili every day for weeks on end?"

"Feed the poor people. Maybe Preacher Isaac down at the church can take it to the soup kitchen in Sherman."

Alma Grace scanned the whole kitchen before she spoke. "You think that's safe?"

Patrice laughed. "Probably not but it's a way to get rid of it. That first batch is still killing the grass out in the yard. If we could figure out how they made it, we could sell it as weed killer and make millions."

Carlene and Josie arrived through the back door at the same time. "Wow! It smells nice, not at all like chicken chili. Where is last night's cooking?"

"In there. Patrice slammed my finger in the door," Alma Grace said.

"There's a rubber seal. It might smart but you won't die," Josie said bluntly.

"Will you taste it and tell us if it's decent enough to go to the soup kitchen in Sherman, Josie?" Patrice asked.

"Not for a million bucks," Josie said. "Carlene, you make a pot of coffee and we'll get busy. We've got lots of work still to do after that business on Saturday."

※

"If you are going to lounge in here, you could pick up a needle and help us," Carlene said to Patrice in the middle of the morning.

"You don't want me to do that. I'd have blood all over everything. I can't sew on a button without poking my fingertips. Besides I'm the bookkeeper and fill-in salesperson, which is what I'm doing until Alma Grace gets back. There's no customers right now so I'm taking a break."

Alma Grace breezed into the room, opened up a big bag, and poured a dozen more fresheners on the table. "I didn't plug any into your office, Patrice, or in this room. Y'all can do that. I checked upstairs. Mama is praying and the other two rooms are empty so I guess Aunt Gigi and Aunt Tansy went home last night. This isn't such a bad setup after all, is it?"

"So we smell like a funeral home instead of a panty shop," Josie said.

Patrice shook her head slowly. "A flower shop, not a funeral home. Now tell us about the gossip you heard over the weekend."

"First weekend I get to have peace and quiet and my damn phone rings all weekend long. Beulah called to tell me that Kitty has put a restraining order on all three of you because she says that you threatened Lenny," Josie said.

Carlene ran her fingers through her hair. "I didn't threaten him."

"I know that but Kitty is just being her own bitchy self, honey," Josie went on. "And then Agnes called, laughing her fool head off to tell me that you and Jack Landry are getting married as soon as the divorce is final. Gossip has it that you've been seeing him off and on since y'all were in high school on the sly and it didn't stop when you married Lenny."

"Oh, my God! We didn't ever date and he's only called me one time," Carlene said.

"And Alma Grace is in tears and only time will tell if she is pregnant with Jack's baby after they spent the night together in the store among all the sexy underwear after church on Wednesday night," Josie said.

Alma Grace blanched and slumped down in a chair across the table from Carlene.

"Patrice is the only one that is in the clear so far, but there's talk that Yancy might break up with her over all this. You girls are pretty wicked. It's a wonder an old woman like me can even work with you," Josie said.

Patrice laughed until it echoed off the walls. "Alma Grace might be needin' to do some 'fessin' up. You did get pretty perturbed yesterday about Jack calling Carlene."

"He only walked me to my car. He didn't even kiss me," Alma Grace sputtered.

"I'm not finished," Josie said. "Poor Beulah had to increase her heart medicine when she thought Alma Grace and Jack might get involved. After all, y'all do own a place that promotes sex with all your fancy unmentionables. Now that he's interested in Carlene, why, that's a divorced woman as well. She's just sure when she goes to see Doc Hardison this morning that he's going to increase her blood pressure medicine, too. She's probably wrung the threads out of ten hankies this weekend."

All three cousins waited for a full minute.

"Any more?" Patrice finally asked.

"Kitty is deciding how to go about taking all your fathers to bed so that she can break up marriages to pay Carlene back for cheating on Lenny. I believe that's all. I'd rather have my kids and grandkids at the house as talk on the phone all weekend," Josie said.

"Mama will shoot her graveyard dead if she even winks at Daddy," Carlene said.

"She'll have to stand in line behind Tansy Cordell and Sugar Magee if she makes a play for any of our fathers," Patrice gasped.

∽✖∼

The bell rang before Alma Grace could voice her opinion. The day couldn't get worse. She told herself that right up until the time that she saw Kim waiting in front of the cash register.

"Good mornin', Alma Grace. I have a corset put back and I've come to pick it up," she said cheerfully.

Alma Grace rifled through the layaway box under the counter and laid the white bag with the shop logo imprinted on the side on the counter. She peeled a ticket from the handle and rang up the sale.

"So now that the divorce is final, you're going after Lenny, right? I think that the story I heard was that you were a notch on his bedpost and you'd like another turn?" Alma Grace said icily.

Kim nodded and then shook her head from side to side. "Yes, I did say that but I've changed my mind. I'm going to use this cute little thing to seduce Isaac."

Alma Grace almost choked. "The preacher."

"Yes, ma'am. That damned Floy got mad at me when I told them we should at least reimburse you for the wings and halo that you bought with your own money. I'm just a little bit superstitious and I didn't want to take a chance on wearing them if they were stolen outright. So now I'm sitting in the back row of the choir and I've been fired from the Easter program, too, and they're going to let Macy Bardeen be the angel because she's about your size," Kim said.

"But what has Isaac got to do with that?" Alma Grace asked.

Kim shrugged. "Not a damn thing. I guess I'd better learn to curb my cussin' if I'm going to be a preacher's wife."

"A preacher's wife!" Alma Grace stammered.

"Nobody, not even Floy Gastineau, will put the preacher's wife in the back row of the choir. And next year I will be the president of the Easter program. Those dumb changes they made will be changed back and you can be the angel if you want to be. That'll teach them to mess with me. Now I'm off to the beauty shop to get my nails done in a color to match the corset. Tonight begins my seduction."

"You are wearing that on the first night?" Alma Grace whispered.

"No, darlin', but I want him to get used to me wearing pink. First the fingernails and a teary confession that I was the one who stole your wings and halo and I'm so sorry. What does he think I should do? Yes, of course, I'll bring them home to you and the church ladies can buy another set if he thinks that is the right thing." She wiped an imaginary tear from her eye. "Then it'll be dinner at my house to repay him for listening to me. After that he'll ask me out and we'll go from there. Three weeks from now the corset will come out of the tissue paper."

"A lamb to the slaughter," Alma Grace said.

"Exactly. It might take a year but that's okay. Floy needs to suffer that long and she will come close to a heart attack when she sees me with him." Kim smiled.

Alma Grace barely got the story told in the beading room when the doorbell declared that there was another customer. When she saw Violet Prescott standing there with a scowl on her face, she yelled for Patrice.

❧

"Good mornin', Miz Prescott. I've been expecting you. Alma Grace said that you had some money to invest in the chili cook-off?" Patrice's tone dripped with sugary sweetness.

She held out an envelope. "The money and the names are all in here."

"Well, then you just follow me back to my office," Patrice said.

"Why? I just want you to take it and put it on our side."

"Because we will count it together with Alma Grace as a witness. We will both sign a waiver stating the amount each party involved donated and Alma Grace will witness it for us so there are no future problems. We can't have it said that we cheated anyone with the party money," Patrice explained.

Violet's high heels clomped on the hardwood floors and her huffs left no doubt that she was steaming. "Did you make Agnes and her cohorts do this? Ah, ah, ah-choo!" Violet sneezed.

Josie was coming out of the ladies' room and stepped back in, rolled off a fist full of toilet paper, and handed it to Violet on her way across the foyer. "Bless you."

"Excuse me. Place smells like plumeria and I'm allergic to it. Answer me, Patrice; did Agnes have to sign her name?"

"Yes, ma'am. We made her sign in blood."

"Don't you make fun of me." Violet's eyes disappeared when she squinted.

It took several minutes to count the money and then they were a dollar short of the amount written on the envelope.

"See, that's why we have to count it together," Patrice said.

Violet took out her wallet and handed Patrice a dollar bill. "Now does that make everyone happy?"

Patrice sounded like she was explaining the process to a six-year-old. "You might want to go over it one more time just to be sure about what you are signing."

"It's a donation list, not a court document," Violet fussed.

"Hey, Carlene, would you take care of that?" Alma Grace yelled across the room when the bell rang on the door.

∽⁘∽

Carlene laid her needle down and found Agnes sitting on the staircase. "Well, good mornin', Miz Agnes. What can I do for you today?"

"Why does this whole place smell like a flower shop?"

Carlene sat down beside her. "Because Alma Grace is afraid the chili smell will linger."

"I came to tell y'all that I've told everyone in town that as soon as the shop closes tonight to line up at the back door for a chili tasting. Patrice can give everyone a little comment card and we'll write on it," she said."

"I'm sure Mama will be glad for all y'all to have a bowl of their chili but I got to warn you, they never have cooked much."

"They've got your Granny's recipes and any blind fool can follow directions. And they're usin' your grandpa's cooker so they can't go wrong. I told everyone that they'd better come early because there was only one cooker full. So tell them to get it heated up. Startin' at five o'clock, they can pass it out the back door as long as it lasts every evening," Agnes said. "And folks can leave their comment cards in a coffee can on the porch."

As soon as Agnes was gone, Carlene headed to the shed at the back of the lot, grabbed a shovel and a big black garbage bag, and cleaned up the chili that had been dumped. Her nose ran. Her sinuses were wide open and her mascara was running down her face by the time she got the bag into the dumpster. She just hoped that it didn't burn a hole plumb through the plastic before the garbage collector came the next day.

She'd barely locked the front door that evening when the cars started lining up at the curb. The Fannin sisters were ready with their first cooker of chicken chili and Agnes got the first bowl, carried it to the back porch, and leaned against the post. Everyone that got in line heard her ranting about what wonderful chili it was and that it was just the first attempt. Tomorrow's batch would be even better.

Gigi smiled at her sisters. "I'm glad I laid in a stock of red plastic bowls."

People were everywhere. Some of them were sitting on the back porch, some on the park bench, and some ate standing up. The front porch soon filled up and in forty-five minutes the chili was all gone.

"Am I too late, darlin's?" a big booming masculine voice called out at the back door.

Gigi stuck her head out of the kitchen and squealed. "Tip Gordon! Yes, you are too late for a bowl of chili. But I've got a glass of sweet tea left and we'll be making chili again tomorrow. I'll save you some if you'll come back. Tonight we're making pork chili instead of chicken."

"Just my luck. Hank Carmichael steals the prettiest girl in all of Texas right out from under my nose and now I can't even get a bowl of chili. That's too bad but I came for two reasons. One to get a bowl of chili and the other to donate some money to the cause." He handed her a folded check. "Put some black lace on your tent and frill it up all fancy. When Lenny goes down, I want it to be hard."

"Why?" Carlene slipped out into the foyer.

"It's that damned Carson Culpepper. He's struttin' around like a banty rooster tellin' everyone that he whipped me in a big settlement divorce. I can't say a word because if I do, Lenny might come after your shop, so I'll pluck a few feathers out of his tail this way. I hear there's going to be an after-party when y'all win this thing. Why don't you have it at the Denison Country Club? I keep a membership there. The girls at Clawdy's can cater it and we'll have a grand old time."

Gigi smiled. "You are a politician, Tip. What's in all this for you?"

"I get a lot of people to see that I backed the right team. I get to do a little stumping for that judge's nomination that's coming up and Carson Culpepper gets to eat a little bit of dirt," Tip grinned.

He was a handsome man at sixty with thick white, wavy hair that he combed straight back. He was Texan from his expensive eel boots to his big belt buckle and Stetson hat that he held in his hands.

"Sounds fair to me," Gigi said. "Miz Agnes wants to have the party at Clawdy's but nothing says you can't do some stumpin' over there and there'll be more people come if it's locally held."

He settled his hat back on his head, tipped it toward the ladies, and swaggered back outside, making sure to stop and talk to the last of the chili tasters on the way.

◆

Patrice was on her way out of the shop when Kim stepped up on the porch. She wore a white sundress that looked good against a dark tan. Her dark hair was held back with a pearl clip, and pink toenails peeked out from the ends of her white sandals.

"Did the corset not fit after all?" Patrice asked.

"Oh, no, it's perfect and I love it. I've got something I thought Carlene would want to know."

Patrice wasn't sure Carlene could stand knowing much more in one day's time but she called her to the front. Alma Grace left straightening a rack of bras to see what Kim wanted. They all met in front of the cash register and looked at Kim.

"It's about Lenny," Kim said.

"Please don't tell us someone really burned down his house," Alma Grace said.

"What?" Kim asked.

"Rumor has it that he took out a restraining order on all of us because I threatened to burn down his house. I'd feel terrible if someone really did it," Carlene said.

"It's even worse than burning down his house."

The color left Carlene's face. "Is he dead?"

"No, he's alive and kicking and trying to talk his way around a catfight that went on in his office this afternoon. Viselle, who owns that little flower shop up on Main Street in Sherman, is my friend. I stopped in there today and she told me the story. Lenny's secretary called this morning and told her to send that big bouquet that she advertised in the paper at Valentine's. Remember it? Well, it has a dozen roses in it and all that pretty baby's breath and ribbons and all and it's more than three feet tall. I wanted someone to send it to me but I didn't even get a single rose." Kim paused.

"And?" Carlene asked.

"The secretary said for Viselle, who admits that she's sent dozens and dozens of flowers to women for Lenny and even has his business credit card numbers on something like speed dial in her computer, to send them to Macy Bardeen who works in the office at the dealership. She was to sign the card with a big open heart and Lenny's name. I guess Macy was so flattered that she ran straight into Lenny's office. He was sitting in his chair so she threw herself into his lap, wrapped her arms around his neck, and kissed him smack on the lips. That's when Bridget snuck over to her office and found the card, and when she got to Lenny's office, there they were all tangled up together." Kim grinned.

Carlene giggled.

Patrice roared.

Alma Grace asked, "And what happened then?"

"Well, the secretary swears to God that she didn't send it and Bridget jerked Macy out of Lenny's lap and the catfight was on. What is it they say about hell hath no fury like a woman scorned?"

Alma Grace sighed. "I'd hoped he was ready to repent."

"Repent, hell. He's worse than ever. Just thought y'all might like to know that before you go home. Lenny's pretty mad and since everything is Carlene's fault, he might be throwin' a fit at you. Now, I'm off to cry on Isaac's shoulder. Wish me luck." Kim was gone before they could gather their thoughts into a coherent sentence.

"Whoever did that deserves a medal," Josie said.

"Agnes?" Carlene asked.

Patrice made the sign of a phone receiver, putting her thumb in her ear and her pinky near her mouth. "Hello, Viselle, darlin'. This is Fay Ann at the car dealership. How are you today? Well, that's so nice. We're havin' such lovely weather for spring, aren't we? Yes, ma'am, I'm so ready for Easter. Now honey, could you please fix up that big old flower arrangement you advertised in the paper and take it to Macy Bardeen? Sign the card with an open heart and Lenny's name. I know, honey, he does have a way with the women but then it's good for the flower business, isn't it? And could that delivery go out today? Just charge it to Lenny's credit card."

She hung up the make-believe phone.

Carlene's mouth dropped. "You sounded just like her."

"I went to school with her and she's got this nasal twang that's easy to mimic," Patrice said.

"But why?"

"Because Macy Bardeen has Alma Grace's wings and halo and she's going to sing Alma Grace's part at the Easter program. And even though I'm mad at her for the way she's acting toward you, she's still kin. And because we said we were declaring war, I started the fire. And I did not break the restraining order's rules about how close we can get before we start setting him on fire," she said with a shrug.

Alma Grace dropped her head and her mouth moved in silent prayer.

Patrice touched Alma Grace on the shoulder and whispered, "God is telling you no! Listen to Him. Even He doesn't want Lenny in our family anymore."

"How do you know what I'm praying for? Don't judge the book by the cover or the back blurb," Alma Grace snapped.

Carlene hated this bickering. Patrice shot looks toward Alma Grace that should have knocked her to her knees but somehow she caught them midair and sent them back with enough force that Carlene could feel the chill.

If she prayed as much as Alma Grace, she'd ask that they could have a three-way hug like they used to do before the divorce. She missed that so much.

❧

The lighting was perfect. The weather wasn't so hot that it would melt her makeup but it wasn't raining, which was a good sign. She hated doing off-site interviews and stories in the rain. It wasn't a big story but it would give her some real television time. She nodded for the camera operator to flip on the recording light and started.

"The Red-Hot Chili Cook-Off brings about lots of competition but this year it's gone up a notch here in Cadillac, Texas. I'm standing on the church lawn and behind me are twenty cookers all lined up in a row. Wait a minute, turn off the cameras. There's a skunk sniffing around the last cooker," the reporter said.

"Makes for good footage." The camera operator grinned.

"If it sprays we'll be in trouble," she said. "Give it a minute to leave and we'll reshoot."

Besides, she had an audience. At first it was just Police Chief Jack Landry leaning on his patrol car and then a pickup pulled up behind it, talked to him for a minute, and pulled a cell phone from his hip pocket. Now there were no less than fifty people standing out there pointing and laughing. Evidently, they knew something she didn't and she intended to find out what it was before she did the thirty-second news story the second time.

She talked to several men and one red-haired elderly woman while the skunk crawled up in the last cooker in the long row like he was riding in the last car in a parade.

"Okay, I've got it," she whispered to the camera operator. "If I stand right there beside the church sign, will the skunk be in every second of the footage?"

He nodded and zeroed in on the church sign that gave the times for services, and in small letters across the bottom were the words "Free chili samples at Bless My Bloomers every evening after five. Comments appreciated."

She fluffed up her blond hair and nodded. "The famous chili cook-off in Cadillac is coming up soon and the competition has begun. As you can see, one contestant is giving away free samples." She did a sweeping motion toward the church billboard. "But it appears that this year someone has taken it a step further and has stolen every single contestant's cooker along with the trophies won by Lenny Lovelle for the past five years. Is it a statement that his cooker is the last in the row? We only know that it's his because his trophies, filled with what appears to be fresh bull manure, are in the cooker along with a skunk that has joined us for this interview. Antics will happen when there are this many contestants. What will happen next in Cadillac, Texas?"

She was prepared to stop with that but the camera operator gave her a sign to keep going. She smiled and smoothly went on.

"Police Chief Jack Landry says the first call about missing cookers came at midnight. He was at the Magee ranch outside of town playing cards with his friends. The last call came at six this morning. A reliable witness says that the skunk and the fact that

Lenny Lovelle's cooker is last in line might be karma. For what? We'll have to wait until the cook-off to find out. Meanwhile, it appears that there are several recipes inside those cookers. Could they be the winning recipe from days gone by?"

The camera operator held up ten fingers to designate ten more seconds.

"The mystery might never be solved but if you're in the area, go on by Bless My Bloomers and get a free sample of chili. And don't miss the cook-off where all twenty of these cookers will be filled with more than bull manure and skunk."

The camera operator held up a closed hand and the recording light went off. He touched the button on the phone twisted around his ear and said, "Station called in. They're airing the whole thing at six. You did a great impromptu job."

"Thanks, Richie." She smiled. A skunk in Lenny Lovelle's cooker was the icing on the cupcake. That would teach him to screw her and not call, send flowers, or even a box of candy. Paybacks really were hell.

ᘓᘗ

"I swear on Mama's Bible, Sugar," Gigi said after they'd watched that part of the six o'clock news four times.

"Thank you, darlin'"—Tansy smiled at Gigi—"for having the good sense to record that so we could see it over and over. I just know that it's an omen that our cooker is the one at the front of the line and that bastard Lenny's is at the back with a skunk and bullshit. I wish I'd thought of doing that."

"Swear again," Sugar said.

"Okay, I swear that I talked to Hank and he says that Jack, Alex, Jamie, and he were playing poker all evening at your house. You'd rather Jamie was playing poker as kissing Kitty or stealing cookers, wouldn't you?" Gigi said.

"But who else could get into our kitchen, take our cooker, and not touch anything else?" she asked.

"They took our first recipe. Too bad we didn't readjust that cayenne pepper, then we'd know who they were at the cook-off when people started rolling around in the grass like they were having some kind of fit," Tansy said.

"That's only because the recipe was right beside the cooker," Sugar said.

"I wish I knew who did that and I damn sure wish they would have invited me to go with them." Tansy sighed.

"I just wish I was a little mouse in the corner when Kitty and Lenny have to clean out those trophies." Gigi giggled.

Chapter 11

A DEPUTY FROM THE Grayson County Sheriff's Department, in uniform and with a gun on his hip, looked out of place in Bless My Bloomers. Alma Grace made sure the curtains were drawn all the way on the two cubicles with customers inside before she went to the front counter. Her father and her uncles had been at the jailhouse playing poker with Jack Landry. Surely they hadn't put any stock in that vicious gossip about her, Patrice, and Carlene. She could almost feel the cold cuffs around her wrists when her lead-filled knees carried her from the back of the store.

He looked as nervous as the devil at the Pearly Gates and was most likely shopping for a last-minute birthday or anniversary present for his wife. They'd had male customers before but none that looked at the ceiling rather than the merchandise.

"Could I help you, sir?" Alma Grace asked.

He wasn't tall but he was well built, had close cropped brown hair and gorgeous blue eyes. He nodded and his Adam's apple bobbed up and down a couple of times.

"I hope so, ma'am. I'm Patrick Kelly from the Sheriff's Department but folks call me Rick." He pointed to the badge on his shirt. "Are you Carlene Lovelle?" His voice was deep and steady and his eyes were fixed on Alma Grace's forehead.

"No, what is this about?" Alma Grace said.

"I have something I have to put in Carlene's hands," Deputy Rick said.

Alma Grace rounded the end of the counter and brushed past the man as she headed toward the beading room. "Hey, Carlene, someone to see you."

When she turned around, she ran smack into Rick Kelly's chest. He instinctively put his arms out to keep her from knocking them both to the floor, turned bright red again, and took two steps to the side.

"I'm so sorry. I didn't realize I was that close to you but I had to get out of there. It's so…" he stammered.

Alma Grace looked up at him, her blue eyes locking with his. "So what? So sexy? So girly? Do you have a problem with that, Officer Rick?"

"No, ma'am. I just have a problem with me being in the middle of it all," he said.

"What can I do for you?" Carlene asked.

He blinked and looked away from Alma Grace. "Are you Carlene Lovelle?"

"Yes, sir, I am. I suppose you are here to serve me with divorce papers?"

He nodded and pulled a yellow envelope from his hip pocket. "Yes, ma'am. Consider yourself served. And you ladies have a good day." He hurried toward the door in a blur.

"You come on back to see us when you need the perfect present for your wife," Alma Grace called out, giddy with relief that it was divorce papers and not an arrest warrant.

What's the matter with me? I don't want her to get a divorce. I've spent hours praying for reconciliation. I can't change horses in the middle of the stream.

"I'm not married," he threw over his shoulder.

❧

Carlene laid the envelope on the beading table, picked up her needle, and went back to work. A year ago, she and her cousins quit their jobs, pooled their savings, got a bank loan, and opened the doors to Bless My Bloomers. Did that really have anything to do with the papers lying there beside a bright red bra with rhinestone straps?

Lenny had given her several chances to change her mind the past two weeks. What would have happened if she had?

Josie stood up and stretched. "Don't look back. If you'd given him another chance, when it happened again, it would have been easy to give him another one. Pretty soon, you would have had no self-respect left."

"How did you know what I was thinking?" Carlene asked.

"You wouldn't make such a good poker player. What you think is written on your face. Now let's talk about the theft of the cookers. I'm surprised that Kitty hasn't been in here screaming that you did it," Josie said.

"Mama figured that she might so she talked to Tip and there's a restraining order on her and Lenny. They can't come near me or the shop or Patrice's house. She's tried to call but I put a block on her phone number. I don't want to talk to her," Carlene said.

Josie threw back her head and guffawed. "Them red panties sure did set the whole town on its ear."

Alma Grace slid into a chair across the table from Carlene. "Whew! I just knew that deputy had an arrest warrant for you."

"But we were all three together all night at Patrice's. Why would anyone think I'd do something stupid like break into twenty houses?" Carlene asked.

"It wasn't just houses. The bank and the fire station and the convenience store owners. They all enter the cook-off. And Lenny's cooker was at the end of the line and it did have his trophies in it. I was so happy that you weren't arrested that I went into a dressing room and gave thanks to God," Alma Grace said.

Gigi pulled up a chair and sat down beside Carlene. "So you've been served. Alma Grace, I thought you'd be weeping and moaning because the divorce is real."

Alma Grace raised her chin a notch. "I'm still praying for reconciliation but I am glad that Carlene wasn't taken off to prison."

Carlene ignored her cousin. Nothing short of a miracle or Aunt Tansy's magic would make things right between them all again.

"Should Tip look at it before I sign?" she asked.

"Might be best if he did. He's in the county courthouse today. I'll give him a call and bribe him with a bowl of chili to come by here," Gigi said.

"It's surreal, Mama. How does a person go from married to divorced in only two weeks?"

"Honey, you went from married to divorced in five seconds. Today is just the day that the paperwork gets started," Gigi told her.

They'd just closed the front door when people started lining up at the back one. Carlene and Josie waited in the beading room, the papers still in the envelope when Tip poked his head in the door.

"You are a brave man to eat chili that the Fannin sisters made," Josie said.

"I've eaten lots of chili. It's my favorite food. In my opinion there ain't no bad chili. Just good chili and better chili," he said.

"I'm sorry Tip but we ran out. I went to get you some and the cooker was empty. I promise next time I'll put a bowl back for you," Gigi said.

"I understand y'all made pork chili today and it's my favorite kind. It's never won the cook-off but I still like it because that's the kind that Mama made. I expect you to try it again before you quit making it altogether. Now let's look at these papers." He picked them up and flipped through them. "It's pretty much what Carson discussed with me that first day."

"I read it. I get my maiden name back, a check for the down payment I made on the house, my van, my wedding rings, and my business. Right? I wonder where he's getting the money to repay me for the down payment," she said.

"It doesn't matter as long as he does it. I told Carson there was no way you were losing that." Tip sipped the sweet tea that Gigi set in front of him. "I heard that he did a nasty little trick with your grandmother's candlesticks."

Gigi narrowed her eyes. "Oh, he's going to pay for that when we win the chili cook-off. We plan to work for the next six weeks on perfecting our chili. Tomorrow we start making it from beef. We've decided the chicken or the pork is not the recipe to win."

Tip nodded. "I agree. The winnin' recipe has always been made from beef or venison. So I'd put my money on that."

Carlene pulled the papers toward her and signed her name at the bottom with a flourish. "Guess that's it, then. I'm Carlene Carmichael again and the past five years have been erased."

Tip shook his head slowly from side to side. "Honey, experience is what you get when you didn't get what you wanted. And every experience in life gets us ready for what's comin' at us in the future. So don't count it as wasted. Count it as a lesson learned and, next time around, learn from it and maybe you'll get what you wanted all along."

Josie sneezed and grabbed a tissue. "Excuse me. I'm finished with that last bra. I hope I'm not coming down with the flu. Man, that stuff is awful this year. Sweet little young married woman that moved in next door to me got it this past week and she's been sick as a dog. I took chicken soup to her over the weekend. She's missed work all week. She said her husband is away on a business trip and she's hoping he doesn't come home until she's over it."

"You had time to make chicken soup while all that was going on?" Carlene asked.

"It was in the freezer. Leftovers from the last time the kids were all home. Chicken tortilla soup. Guaranteed to cure the flu." Josie sneezed again. "And speaking of gossip, Kitty Lovelle is giving her son the money to reimburse you for the down payment. She bragged about it at some meeting Beulah was in and she told me. Kitty says that it's a small price to pay just to get rid of you. Beulah doesn't cuss or say bad words but I think that Kitty's real words were to get your fat ass out of her son's house and life."

"Well, thank you, Kitty," Carlene said.

"Are you going to buy another house here in Cadillac?" Josie reached for another tissue.

Carlene shook her head. "Not for a while. After the cook-off, the mamas will go home and I'll have the upstairs of this place to live in until I make up my mind. There's too much going on with our mothers in the kitchen, all this chili stuff, and trying to keep up with the sales right now for me to think about a house."

Josie picked up her coffee mug and headed out the door. "Want me to put yours in the dishwasher on my way out, too? My throat is dry so I'm stopping up at the convenience store for one of those slushy things."

"No, I've still got coffee in my mug. I'll just finish it and talk to Mama for a little while before I go. I feel pretty empty right now and it doesn't have a thing to do with hunger. Have a good night. See you tomorrow," Carlene said.

"It will pass, child, and you'll move on with your life just like Tip said. And you aren't divorced until Lenny signs the papers and they are filed. You are lucky you don't have to go to court and face him with a judge looking at both of you. Since you are agreeing, you won't have to do that." Josie sneezed again.

Carlene looked at her. "Are you sure you're not getting the flu?"

"Not me. I'm healthy as a horse." Josie waved the comment away with the back of her hand like it was a pesky gnat.

Carlene went to the bathroom, slid down the back of the door, and put her head in her hands. Her family and Josie were supportive and wonderful beyond words, but she was the first Fannin ever to have a divorce. She felt like it had been written in indelible ink across her forehead, branded there for the whole world to see that she had failed. Tears washed mascara down her cheeks in long black streaks as her heart broke one more time.

Vows in one hand. Self-respect in the other. Alma Grace still on one side. Patrice firmly on the other. Would her world ever be whole again?

∽ᘛᘚ∼

Lenford Joseph Lovelle II, aka Lenny Joe Lovelle, signed the papers before him with a flourish and handed them to Carson Culpepper.

"I'll need that check before I file them so that everything is on the straight and narrow," Carson said.

He was a short, rotund man with a rim of brown hair circling an otherwise bald head. Even though he wore custom-tailored suits, somehow he always looked like he'd slept in them and had just climbed out of bed.

Lenny reached into his desk drawer and handed the check to Carson. It riled him to have to pay Carlene a single dime but it couldn't be helped. Like Carson told him, he would have spent that much refurnishing the house if she'd contested and demanded her part of the contents. His mother, bless her darling heart, had given him the money with no strings attached.

Her words had been, "Take it, honey. When I die, it'll all be yours anyway. And it's worth it to me for you to finally be rid of that fat-assed woman. You've always deserved better."

"Looks like we're done, then. And Kitty has already taken care of my bill but I'd have almost done this for free just to get to whip Tip Gordon at something. That bastard thinks he's so damn good." Carson waved from the door as he waddled out to his car.

Lenny was a free man or at least he would be in a few months. In the state of Texas the petition is filed and sixty days later the divorce is granted if neither party decides to contest the petition. So in two months he would be absolutely free. Then there would be the thirty days waiting period before he could remarry. Basically he had three months before Bridget could have a wedding. However, she would start planning it tomorrow now that the petition was on the way to the courthouse.

He didn't want to marry Bridget. Sex with her was all right. Nothing spectacular but all right. After that kiss that Macy planted on him when she received the flowers, he'd been taking a closer look at her. She'd brushed past him at the watercooler twice now and Lenny was an expert at knowing when a woman was ripe for the plucking.

Macy definitely was. She'd do just fine to have a fling with so that Bridget would break it off with him. And the vibes floating around her certainly weren't from the angel singing the final song at the church services on Easter, either. Maybe she was one of those business women that didn't think about wedding cakes and white dresses three minutes after the first time they had sex.

Lenny just plain did not want a wife, not ever again.

Mistress, yes.

Changing mistresses as often as he pleased, definitely.

Permanent commitment, no.

In the beginning Lenny hadn't wanted to marry Carlene but she wasn't like other women. She wasn't clingy; she didn't have to talk to him every day. She was confident, mature, and in the end it was Lenny who was begging for a wedding.

His mother had warned him that he was making a mistake the day of the wedding. Kitty had been right. Bless his sweet little mama's heart; she had tried so hard to make Carlene feel like a Lovelle because she'd wanted a grandchild. Not two, not a dozen;

just one and it had to be a boy. They'd name him Lenford Joseph Lovelle III and call him Ford. Lenny had liked the idea but now he was glad that he and Carlene didn't have children.

He laced his hands behind his head and stared at the ceiling.

Bridget barely knocked before she entered. She shut the door, drew the blinds shut, and straddled his lap.

"Are they signed, darling?" she asked.

"Signed and on their way to the courthouse."

"I'm the happiest woman on earth. Can we go look at rings tonight?"

"Mother says that we'd better wait the full sixty days for the final decree before we do that. It would be bad for business if we rush things," he whispered into her hair.

She locked her lips on his, unbuttoned his shirt, and ran her hands across his broad, muscular chest.

He pretended he was kissing Macy, and her soft little angel hands were on his chest. His fantasy soon made him very uncomfortable, especially the way Bridget had hiked up that short little skirt, leaving so much soft thigh for him to touch.

His desk phone rang and he quickly reached around Bridget to answer it. "Sherman Autoplex. Lenny Lovelle speaking," he said.

"Lenny, I think I'm coming down with the flu so I'm going home early and taking tomorrow off. I sure hope you don't get it. Don't eat any of the cake in the lounge. Bridget sneezed in there today and she might be getting it, too," his secretary said.

"Get well and we'll hope it's just allergies," Lenny said.

He picked Bridget up and set her to one side. "Are you sick?"

"No. I had a little sneezing fit in the break room but I'm not sick. My skin is warm because I'm hot as hell for you," she giggled. "I'll make supper for you tonight at your house. I've got a great recipe for clam chowder and we can eat it naked in the middle of the living room floor. I'll pick up wine to celebrate your divorce."

Lenny had always been quick on his feet when it came to fabricating a good lie and he was so sincere about it that it came off as gold-plated truth. "I'd love to, darlin', but Mother has planned a dinner at her house. And since she's given me the money to get rid of Carlene, I really do owe her."

"I could come with you," she suggested.

"That would be wonderful but Mother thinks we should be very careful until the final decree is done. But won't it be fun to sneak around?" he said seductively.

Bridget giggled. "We're professional at that, aren't we? Oh, well, the weekend belongs to me. We are going to just hole up at your house and play role games until Monday morning. I've got the cutest little nurse outfit and you are going to be my patient."

She sneezed twice and she barely covered her nose with her hands. Lenny reached for a tissue and handed it to her and ushered her right out into the showroom.

∽◦∽

Candles provided the only light in the living room and takeout Chinese had been shared from the coffee table. Patrice popped the cork on the bottle of wine and poured two glasses. She looked at Alma Grace who shook her head from side to side.

"I cannot, in all good faith, celebrate the divorce that I've been praying so hard would not come about," she said with her chin tilted up a notch.

Patrice shot a dirty look across the square coffee table. Lord God Almighty, Sweet Jesus, and the angels! Didn't praying open her eyes to understand a damned thing?

Carlene raised her glass and clinked it against Patrice's. "To a bright future. May we all three find happiness within ourselves."

"Hear, hear!" Patrice said.

There was a faint knock on the door and Yancy threw it open

before anyone could even yell "Come on in." He kicked off his boots and sat down on the sofa beside Patrice.

"Mind if I join the celebration?" he asked.

Patrice handed him her glass of wine. "We'll share."

He sipped the wine and said, "I understand that the papers are filed and Bridget is already after Lenny to go look at rings."

"You've got to be kidding me. Is he going to get engaged on the very day he gets divorced?" Alma Grace gasped.

Carlene slowly shook her head. "He'll feed her some line of pure old bullshit. Speaking of which, I understand that Kitty sent his trophies off to a professional place to have them fumigated. He's not going to marry her. I doubt if he ever gets married again. The only reason he stayed with me was because I gave him an excuse not to marry his women. Now it'll be some other reason. Probably that his mother needs him. Too bad he didn't think of that one before he married me."

"You got that right. Bridget told her friend that they have to be very secretive until the whole thing is final." Yancy chuckled.

Carlene glanced at Alma Grace just in time to see her raise her head from a silent prayer.

"And I heard that he's already sending flowers to another girl at the dealership," Yancy said.

"I did not go within fifty feet of the dealership. I did it all with cash money out of my own pocket." Patrice poked Alma Grace on the arm. "You want to try to top my stunt."

Alma Grace put on her prissy, pious face. "I most certainly do not!"

Chapter 12

No one was in the kitchen.

The aroma of Clawdy's pancakes or omelets did not come from the direction of the trash can in the corner. There was no bickering or giggling among the Fannin sisters. There was a balloon bouquet tied to the back of a chair. Carlene stopped and read the card. It was from a lady in Sugar's Sunday school class who had a son-in-law in the Smokin' Bobs Team whom she did not like. She was sending her best wishes for the Red-Hot Bloomers to win the cook-off.

One thing for sure, their all-woman team had a hell of a lot of support. Carlene wished that Alma Grace supported her as much as the women in town were showing love to the Fannin sisters and their team. She put the card back in the envelope and heard footsteps, running not walking; the bathroom door opening but not shutting; groans and loud whining.

Dear Lord, either Gigi or Tansy had died in the bathroom, and Sugar had found them. They'd better hope they were already talking to St. Peter because if they came back to life and told a single person what Sugar looked like with no makeup, she'd finish them off for sure.

Carlene's foot was on the first step when her phone rang. She pulled the phone from her pocket and answered, hoping it was her mother saying that they'd all overslept or that maybe they'd celebrated her divorce and all had hangovers.

It was Josie and she sounded like hell.

"It's the damned flu. I won't be in today. Hopefully, I'll be better by Monday if they let me out of the hospital tomorrow. Don't come up here. They won't let you in without a mask," Josie said.

Carlene stopped and sat down on the steps. "Hospital?"

"Crazy, ain't it? I passed out from the car to my house and my sweet little neighbor called 911. They brought me to the emergency room and admitted me. Said I was dehydrated but I'm beggin' y'all. Don't come see me. I'm contagious. I just hope no one there gets it. That damned Violet Prescott sneezed when she came to give Patrice money the first of the week. She probably infected me." Josie's voice was weak and she didn't even use one Mexican cuss word, so she had to be very sick.

"I'll call this afternoon and evening both to check on you. Should I call your kids?"

"Hell, no! I'll be out in a day or two. I don't need them hovering over me. Don't call them unless the doctors say I'm dying and then call my preacher instead of the kids. And tell Patrice and Alma Grace that Violet sneezed on them, too."

"Okay, call me if you need anything and I'll bring it up to the nurses' station. Promise?"

"I promise. Here they are with more medicine. I swear the nurses are even wearing masks. Hope it's an easy day at the shop. Bye now." Josie's cough sounded like she was trying to bring up her toenails.

❦

Alma Grace stopped right in the middle of the kitchen and stared at the empty table. Where was her mother? She was always up with her makeup on and her devotional book in front of her by this time. All right, so nowadays, it was recipes instead of godly advice but still she was up and ready for the day.

She heard footsteps upstairs and hurried out into the foyer. Maybe her mama had forgiven her father and they'd all gone home. That would be a glorious answer to a prayer.

Or would it? That would mean she'd have to go back to her house and she really liked living at Patrice's place.

"Carlene?" she asked.

"Josie is in the hospital with the flu and she says we're not to come visit her because it's contagious."

"Should I send flowers? I'll definitely put her on the prayer list down at the church," Alma Grace said.

"I don't know about flowers. They might not let her have them if she's really sick. And Alma Grace, I'm really, truly tired of all this praying shit. Mama, are y'all awake?" Carlene yelled up the steps.

"Don't you dare take another step," Gigi hollered down in a weak voice. "We've all got the flu up here and we've been taking turns in the bathroom all night. We are feverish and achin' all over and there's nothing left to throw up. We don't want you to get it. We'll be fine. Just call the pharmacy and…"

"She's gone to the bathroom," Sugar said. "Alma Grace, are you there?"

"Yes, Mama."

"Call your daddy and tell him he's forgiven. If I die, I don't want him to think I left this earth without telling him," Sugar said weakly.

Alma Grace quickly jerked her phone from her hip pocket and called her father. "Daddy, Mama has the flu and so does Aunt Tansy and Aunt Gigi. And they've put Josie in the hospital with it, so it's serious. Yes, sir. I agree."

Tansy's feeble voice floated down the steps. "We'll be fine soon as this wicked diarrhea and vomiting stops."

⤚✤⤙

Patrice heard voices and didn't even stop in the kitchen. She went straight to the foyer and raised an eyebrow. "What in the hell is going on in here?"

Alma Grace pointed upward. "They have the flu and so does

Josie. Josie is in the hospital with it and our mamas think they can scare it off with something from the pharmacy. Daddy is on the way to get Mama. He says Mama is going home today."

Patrice stood at the end of the staircase and raised her voice. "Mama, do you have a fever?"

"Patrice Cordell, don't you come another step. Sugar sweated off all her makeup and doesn't have the energy to put more on. If I die, my will is at Tip Gordon's." Tansy's voice was barely a whisper.

Patrice flipped open her phone and called her father.

Carlene did the same.

And they said in unison, "Daddy, we need you to come to the shop right now."

When they finished talking, they stared at the phones.

"We did get our flu shots at Walmart that day, didn't we? I'm not just dreamin' it, am I?" Alma Grace asked.

Patrice nodded slowly. "Yes, we did and I hope they work."

"We did?" Carlene frowned.

"Remember? We ran into you there. You were with Lenny and we were in line for the flu shot and we talked you into it but Lenny has always been afraid of needles." Patrice reminded her.

"Just like his mother. Yes, I remember it well, now. I teased him about not taking care of him if he got the flu since he was too big of a baby to take the shot. But I was just joking. I would have taken care of him. I wouldn't now but I would have then," Carlene said.

There was a knock on the door and Alma Grace opened it to find Kim on the porch. "You don't want to come in here. Mama has the flu and we're stalling opening the doors to the shop until Daddy gets here to take her home."

"I've had the flu shot but I won't take long. I just wanted to tell your mamas they might not want to make chili today or for a few days. Folks are dropping like flies so they won't be interested in tasting it for them. I've got a cousin who works in admissions at the emergency room…"

Was the girl kin to someone in every working environment in the whole state? Alma Grace wondered.

"…and she said that Violet Prescott and Agnes both showed up at the same time. They only had one room and Agnes said she'd die before she shared it with Violet. So they moved the flu patient out of Josie's room and put Violet in there and put Agnes with the lady who'd been in Josie's room. You think the hospital will still be standing with all three of them in there? Tell your mamas to go on down to McKinney if they get too bad because there are no hospital rooms left in Sherman. They say there are two kinds hitting people. One kind is fever, vomiting, and diarrhea and lasts about twenty-four to thirty-six hours and the patients are weak for a few days. The other one is worse and lasts longer and is a lot more serious."

"Dear God Almighty," Alma Grace whispered.

"Who died?" Patrice gasped.

"Nobody, but Violet is in the same hospital room with Josie. Agnes refused to share a room with her."

"Lord, help us all," Carlene said. "Josie says Violet sneezed on her and gave her the flu. She's liable to poison the woman."

Jamie pushed his way into the place without a word. His face was ashen and his long legs took the steps two at a time. He was a blur and there was no arguing when he told Sugar she was leaving. He carried her out, wrapped like a baby in a big quilt with the top edge flipped down over her face.

"Don't take her to Sherman, Daddy. Kim says they're full and sending people to McKinney," Alma Grace said.

"She's going home. I called a private nurse on the way over here and our doctor will make a house call every day that she is sick. I'll be in touch as soon as he tells me what we need to do."

"Did you see her face?" Patrice asked.

"I didn't even try," Alma Grace answered.

෨෭ඌ

When Hank arrived he stopped long enough to drop a kiss on Carlene's forehead. "Gigi, get your shoes on. You are going home," he shouted as he started up the stairs.

"I am not. You get your ass out of here, Hank Carmichael. I'm not leaving."

"You can walk or I'll take you out over my shoulder like a bag of chicken feed. Your choice. God, you look like hell, woman."

"You don't want to catch this. Go home."

"I got a flu shot, remember? You refused to get one because you and both your sisters are afraid of needles."

"Mama, they put Josie in the hospital and Violet and Agnes, too," Carlene yelled.

"My God!" Gigi said.

"That's where you belong but Jamie hired a nurse who's going to make the rounds among the three of you. So shoes or over my shoulder?" Hank asked.

"If you put me over your shoulder, I'll throw up again. I can walk if you'll just hold on to me real tight."

"I didn't know they hated needles," Patrice said.

"Neither did I." Alma Grace wiped away a tear. "I thought they were all ten feet tall and bulletproof."

"Well, we aren't," Gigi said. "And you'd better not tell a soul how bad we look, either."

෨෭ඌ

Alex Cordell whizzed through stop signs and both red lights on Main Street. If anything happened to Tansy, he was holding Lenny Lovelle responsible. Damn that sorry bastard's hide anyway. Every bit of the past two and half weeks was his fault. He was stupid from the bone marrow out to his skin. Hell, even his aura, as Tansy talked about when she was spouting off her pseudo-psychic abilities, was probably stupid.

He slammed on the brakes and slid into the empty driveway beside the house. He'd gotten the call when he was out in the horse stables rubbing down his favorite animal after a long morning ride across his land. His boots were dirty and his jeans faded but he didn't give a damn. Tansy was sick and all he could think about was that he hadn't seen her in two days.

The door flew open when he crossed the porch and he hugged Patrice. "Where is she?"

Patrice glanced up. "Uncle Jamie and Uncle Alex have already rescued Aunt Sugar and Aunt Gigi. I don't think she'll give you much sass."

"She had better not give me any sass," Alex said.

"I can't leave," Tansy whined. "What about the cook-off?"

"Right now you are my top priority. Now get out of that bed," Alex said.

"I can't. I'm too weak to stand up," Tansy said.

"Well, darlin', we can damn sure fix that problem."

She went out just like Sugar had, minus the quilt.

"I'll come see about y'all this evening after work," Patrice yelled. "Mama, listen to the doctor and nurse, and behave."

"You stay away from the house until it's not contagious anymore," Alex called out as he loaded Tansy in the car and drove away.

❧

Carlene inhaled deeply. "Now what?"

"I vote that we put a note on the door that says we are closed until Monday and start wiping everything down with a disinfectant. I'll get on the Internet and see how long the flu germ lives in the air.

I think it has to be transmitted by sneezing, kissing, and that kind of thing," Patrice said.

"I'll go to the store and get supplies," Alma Grace offered.

"Thank goodness the house came with a washer and dryer. We'll be doing laundry all day," Carlene said. "I'll start stripping beds."

"I'll gather up towels for the first load," Patrice said.

Carlene opened a window to let fresh air into the bedroom to replace the sick smell filling her nostrils. She stripped down the bed, tossed the whole bundle down the stairs, and went to Tansy's room to repeat the process. When she finished there, Patrice had gathered up the first bunch and the landing at the bottom was free so she hurled another bunch downward.

She had Sugar's bedding raised over her head, ready to throw, when Alma Grace breezed across the foyer. "Whoa!"

"Stand back. I'm going to let it fly and then you can come on up," Carlene said.

Alma Grace wore a cute little short skirt, high heels, and a top that fit like a second skin. She'd clamped her curly hair up into a ball of springy tendrils, part of which fell around her perfectly angelic face.

"Set the cleaning supplies on the table and go to Patrice's. Put on some sweats and a work shirt. And look in the bottom drawer of my dresser and bring me some of the same. I bet Patrice wants some, too. This is going to take all day and we're closed so we might as well be comfortable."

Alma Grace whined like a sick kitten. "I have never cleaned in my life. Can't we call in a fumigation company or cleaning ladies?"

Patrice tapped her on the shoulder. "Move and let me pick up the last of the laundry. And we're not calling a cleaning service. They'd be afraid to set foot in here just like any customers will be. You can bet your sweet little ass that the whole town knows our mamas have been taken home and not a single person is going to come in here until the first of the week. Hell, we probably couldn't even pay someone to steal the chili cooker again."

"By Monday the women in town will be so hungry for gossip that they'll be willing to brave the flu bug." Carlene laughed. "Y'all think we can rent these rooms out if business ever goes bad? They look pretty spiffy the way our mamas have fixed them up."

Alma Grace sighed. "I'll go get work clothes. Y'all want me make a trip to the store while I'm out and get stuff for lunch? Once I've changed, I'm sure not going back out in public, not even down the street to Clawdy's. And you'll have to tell me what to do. I've always had a cleaning lady."

"Yes," Patrice said. "Sandwich stuff, chips, soda pop, and some cookies. Lots of cookies and a gallon of milk. And you might not be able to afford a cleaning lady forever so consider this Cleaning 101. If you pass, we'll train you in the fine arts of Bathroom 102."

Alma Grace sighed again.

"And praying will not get you a passing grade," Patrice said.

❧

Alma Grace pulled her smallest suitcase from the closet and carefully packed her oldest pair of jeans. She didn't own a pair of sweatpants and didn't ever intend to own them. They were baggy, unbecoming, and what if she were to get in an accident on the way back to or from the shop wearing such horrible things. She wasn't sure St. Peter would even let her look through the gates in such attire. She folded a shirt that was missing a button from the cuff and her running shoes that had never walked on anything but the treadmill in her mother's indoor gym.

She opened the bottom drawer of Patrice's chest to find a tangled mess of sweat bottoms, socks, and underwear—unfolded and rolled up together like she'd taken them straight from dryer to drawer. Her tongue made noises like a mad wet hen as she gathered what Patrice asked for and folded it neatly into a pile. The closet floor wasn't a bit better with high heels, sneakers, boots, and house shoes all thrown in a big pile. No wonder she was late getting to work every morning.

Carlene's organizational skills were a little bit better but not much. Her shoes were lined up neatly but her dresser drawers were jumbled up with nightshirts, sweats, and T-shirts all stirred up together. She held up a faded nightshirt and clucked a few more times. If Carlene was wearing that pitiful thing to bed with Lenny…well, it did make her wonder.

She packed it all into her suitcase and carried it out to the car. Maybe they'd have the cleaning all done when she got back. The car engine started up with a purr and she backed out of the driveway and pointed the car in the direction of the convenience store. Cadillac hadn't had a real supermarket in years. The one where the CNC now stood had been put out of business when the big supermarkets and Walmart went in up in Sherman. It just couldn't compete with the prices.

Then it hit her like a tornado. Who was going to make chili for the cook-off since the mamas were sick?

"But we've got four weeks until we have to present the winning pot of chili and they've all gone home so when they get well, they could work out of any one of their kitchens. They'll be over the flu in a week and they can figure out the recipe then." She brushed a lonesome tear away from her cheek.

Kim pushed out of the store as Alma Grace started in.

"Were you talkin' to me?" Kim asked. She wore hot-pink sweats with rhinestones spelling out "cowgirl" down the side of one leg, a pink zipped-up hoodie that stretched across her boobs, and her brown hair was still damp from a fresh cut at Stella's place.

"No, I was just whining to myself. My mama is sick with the flu," Alma Grace said.

"Oh, honey, I heard that Jamie already got a private nurse to go back and forth among the three of them and that the doctor is making house calls. Have you heard anything more from Josie? Can I help in any way?"

Alma Grace shook her head. "Not a thing but I've had my flu shot so I'm going to visit her whether she likes it or not. We are disinfecting the whole house and the shop. You want to help clean?"

Kim's hazel eyes glittered. "I would but I've promised to help Isaac straighten the Bibles and hymn books and clean out those little places on the back of the pews where they go. People put things like gum wrappers and leave toys in them and they have to be cleaned every week. But promise you'll call me. My cousin can't go in the room. She's just a receptionist and we're all just dying to know what's going on in there. A nurse told my cousin that Josie made them pull the curtain between her and Violet and refuses to even look at her."

"Well," Alma Grace said slowly, "Violet sneezed on her and she says that's what made her sick."

"Didn't any of those old gals get their flu shots?"

"I don't know about Violet and Agnes but Josie said she wasn't takin' no flu shot, that she hadn't been sick in forty years, not since she was ten years old and got the chicken pox," Alma Grace said. Maybe if she talked longer, she wouldn't have to clean as much.

Kim leaned in and whispered, "I heard that Kitty Lovelle didn't take it and neither did Beulah Landry. But Jack is taking her to the clinic right now and making her get one. She came out of her house wearing a surgical mask a while ago and got into the car with Jack. I bet none of them bypass it next year. Don't forget to call me on your way home from the hospital. And tell Josie hello for me. I'd send some cookies or food but I guess she wouldn't want to eat anything."

"I'd wait until she gets home and take her some kind of light soup," Alma Grace suggested.

"Good idea," Kim said. "See you tomorrow in church?"

"Sure but I'm not singing in the choir," Alma Grace told her.

"Me, neither." Kim giggled. "Want to do lunch afterwards?"

"Have to take a rain check on the lunch. I'm going to see about Mama soon as services are over," Alma Grace answered.

"Give her a hug for me. We'll miss her in church."

Alma Grace had two bags in each hand when she pushed her way into the kitchen. A load of towels, still warm from the dryer, was piled on the table. The washer was running and the dryer humming with sheets, and still the floor was covered with more laundry waiting to be done.

Patrice called down from the second floor. "Is that you, Alma Grace?"

"Yes, it is."

"Start folding and keep the laundry going. I looked up the flu bug and it can live forty-eight hours on slick surfaces and twelve on porous surfaces. We're wiping down everything up here with those disposable wipes you brought," she yelled down. "And you did good getting the ones that say they'll kill flu viruses, even if they were more expensive."

"I'll change and get right on it," she yelled back. "I'll put the suitcase with y'all's sweats in it at the bottom of the stairs."

Forty-eight hours.

They should be in fine shape to open up for business on Monday.

Forty-eight hours. Maybe Macy would get it and be too weak to sing at the Easter program.

Chapter 13

PATRICE DRESSED UP IN her best jeans and a cute little jacket with rhinestones on the pockets and across the back yoke.

Carlene had already left to spend the day with her mother. Hopefully, the flu vaccines they'd all had would keep them well through the epidemic plowing right through Grayson County with the heaviest count being right from Cadillac.

The doctors said Josie might come home on Monday. Alma Grace promised that she'd come sit with her a spell that evening and that she'd bring her a slushy from the nearest convenience store.

Patrice raised an eyebrow when Alma Grace stepped into the living room. "You going to church or are you speaking at the local hooker organization?"

She wore a bright red short dress that fit like spray paint, red high heels, and clunky silver jewelry. A perky little red hat with a fluffy illusion bow at the back sat at a jaunty angle on top of her curly hair and big silver hoops dangled from her earlobes.

"I'm not singing in the choir but I want Kitty and Lenny Lovelle to know that I'm in church. I'm sitting on the front row this morning where they can see me real good. And where are you going all dressed up?"

"To Yancy's family reunion. I was going to cancel but Daddy says that I should go because all Mama is doing is sleeping a lot. Why are you sitting on the front row and not in the choir?"

"It's a secret but I want them to know who did it and not be able to prove a thing. You'll know when it happens." Alma Grace smiled.

"You'd better get going. It takes at least five minutes to drive there, five minutes to park and get in, and it's getting close to eleven o'clock," Patrice said.

A sly grin tickled the corners of Alma Grace's cute little bow mouth. "I want to walk in right in the middle of the first song."

"A hint?"

"Not even a whisper of a hint. Now it's time to go. See y'all tonight. Don't wait up. You going by to see Aunt Tansy when you come home?"

"I'm going by before we go. I'm leaving Yancy in the truck. I sure don't want him to catch anything since he did not get the flu shot."

∽✽∾

Timing was everything.

The choir was standing. With her back to the congregation and waving her hands around, the choir director didn't even know what was going on behind her. Alma Grace did not slip in and quietly slide into a back pew.

Both wooden doors swung open and she used the center aisle like a fashion runway, singing in a beautiful soprano voice all the way to the front pew. She slowed her walk so that she sat down on the last note of the song and crossed her legs.

The choir director turned, saw Alma Grace, and suddenly spiky horns replaced her imaginary halo and her angel wings disappeared. At least, that's the way Alma Grace saw it.

For several minutes she didn't say a word and then she cleared her throat. "We'll go on to sing"—she looked down at the program and coughed—"to sing, I'm sorry, this is when the choir will sing a special number and then Brother Isaac will speak to us."

Yes, sir, timing was everything.

Alma Grace recognized the prelude to "Satan's River." After the first line that said Satan had a river that was deep and wide, she stood up, turned around to face the congregation, raised her arms toward the ceiling, and began singing with the choir.

Not everyone in the church had heard the gossip about her being ousted from the Easter program so they took that as a sign they were supposed to stand up and sing along. The rest of the congregation sure wasn't going to be left sitting, so up they popped, also. When the lyrics said that big yachts were sailing on Satan's river and never stopped to think about God's golden rule, the congregation was clapping and singing to the top of their lungs, drowning out the choir.

Before she sat back down, she blew kisses at the congregation and looked up with an angelic smile into the preacher's face. From the pew right behind her, Kim touched her on the shoulder and gave her a thumbs-up sign.

"Well, now I'd say that was lively singing this morning." Isaac smiled. "Thank you, Alma Grace, for getting in the spirit. Before I begin my sermon, I'd like for us all to take sixty seconds to pray silently for the members of our congregation who have contracted this horrible flu. All of the Fannin sisters have come down with it and our prayer angels will be meeting an extra day this week to pray for the sick. So if you are interested in joining them, please contact Floy after church today."

He bowed his head and everyone did the same.

Alma Grace shut her eyes and prayed that God would heal her mama and her aunts and that she would hear an okay to the plans she would set in motion that day. It didn't take a whole minute so she looked up to find Macy Bardeen glaring at her from the second row in the choir.

Alma Grace graced her with a beautiful smile and a little toodle-oo wave.

Isaac raised his head, leaned forward until his lips were practically kissing the microphone, and said in a loud booming voice, "Vengeance is mine, saith the Lord!"

Well, shit! Pardon me, Lord, but that just pisses me off, Alma Grace thought and then looked around to be sure she hadn't said the words out loud.

Isaac backed away from the microphone and dropped his voice to a whisper. "It doesn't matter how mad we are at our neighbor or our brother, even if he or she is riding down the Satan's river on that big yacht. Not even if the yacht has pretty flashing lights, plenty of fun and liquor, and he or she is breaking a multitude of the commandments, vengeance does not belong to us. Revenge is a disease and it cannot be let run rampant or it will consume us as Christians."

Can't I change your mind, Lord? She's a real turd and just this one time, won't you look the other way, God? I already bought the bottle of wine and do you know how much trouble it was for me to get it out of the convenience store without anyone seeing? Alma Grace argued with her conscience.

Isaac grabbed the microphone and held it close to his mouth. If Grandpa Dean was snoring in the back pew, he was rudely awakened when Isaac yelled, "God said no! You are not to be a vengeful person."

Alma Grace sighed. *Okay, then, God, you can't talk much louder than that. I won't do it but I expect to see some results. It's your job. I did my job and prayed about it. You said no, so get on with it. I'll slip the wine up in the cabinet tonight and my cousins will think the other one bought it. What if I don't actually send it to Lenny but just leave it on his porch? Then it would be up to him whether or not he actually drinks it, right?*

Isaac went on. "God will never say yes to someone who wants revenge. He is a kind and loving heavenly father who cannot put his seal of peace upon a heart like that."

Alma Grace pasted a smile on her face but there was a frown in her heart. *Okay, okay! I get it. No is no and it won't ever be yes no matter how much I pout and beg.*

The sermon went on and on but Alma Grace had lost interest.

The answer had been given and the promise made and God could probably rain down coals of fire much hotter than she had in mind, anyway. She just had to have a little faith.

She stared at Macy, making her so uncomfortable that she either looked at the back of the church or the ceiling. Then she turned her gaze on Floy, already glowering at her with so much fire that Alma Grace was glad there was a back door in the church. If that old witch set fire to the pew with her mean looks, then Alma Grace would lead the stampede through the back door.

When services were over, the back row folks filed out first, shook Isaac's hand, and made a beeline for the café down on Main Street for Sunday dinner. Those on the front rows had to wait their turn and often had to wait for a parking place and a table when they finally got to the café. But Alma Grace didn't mind a bit because the choir left by way of the back door, hung up their black and white robes, and then came back out to wait in line to have a word with the preacher.

Since she sat on the front row and since Macy and Floy were the first ones out of the choir room, they had no choice but to fall in behind her.

"What you did when we were singing was unforgivable," Floy whispered.

Alma Grace turned around and hugged her. The woman tried to fight her way out of the embrace but Alma Grace hung on like a Saturday night drunk that didn't want to fall.

"Don't push me," she whispered.

"Let go of her," Macy hissed.

Alma Grace did and hugged Macy even tighter. "I will forgive you because God says I have to, but I don't like you for stealing my wings and halo," she whispered. "You will never know how lucky or unlucky you are. I guess it's all in how you look at it and how you study it after it happens."

She didn't need to shake Isaac's hand or to tell him that the sermon was great that morning. It wasn't all that wonderful, anyway. Even if God took care of the vengeance, she had wanted to teach Macy a lesson. Now, she wouldn't be able to take a bit of the glory.

Alma Grace had barely gotten past Floy's evil looks when the woman sneezed like an overweight elephant, blowing it right in Macy's direction. She quickly grabbed a bottle of disinfectant wipes from her purse and cleaned her hands. "I'm so sorry. That came out of nowhere. I usually don't sneeze like that."

"She sure doesn't," Alma Grace said. "She always sounds like a mouse. Clean those hands good! You wouldn't want to give Macy or the preacher the flu," Alma Grace said.

"It's allergies. I haven't been sick in years," Floy said tersely.

Alma Grace looked up at the ceiling. "Yes, sir, what you promise, you do deliver. Thank you for allowing me to see your glory. Amen."

"You are thanking God for my allergies?" Floy frowned.

"Yes, ma'am, I am. Y'all have a wonderful day, now."

She kicked off her shoes when she got into her car, fastened the seat belt, and was about to turn the key when someone tapped on her window. She looked up into the eyes of the deputy who had delivered the divorce papers.

He made a motion for her to roll down the window. "Alma Grace Magee?"

"Yes, sir. Did I park in a wrong spot or something? Please don't tell me you think I stole all those cookers."

He smiled. "No, ma'am. A sweet little thing like you couldn't lift all those heavy cookers and I don't think your conscience would let you break into businesses and homes. I'm in uniform because I just finished a shift but I'm off duty. I don't have your number but Jack Landry had Carlene's and she said that you'd be here right now." It came out in a rush as if he couldn't get the words out fast enough.

"Okay," she said.

"I'm a deputy sheriff but I'm also a youth director over in Luella. I've planned a wiener roast tonight and we'll be making s'mores, too, out beside the farm pond at my folks' ranch. I was wondering if you'd like to go with me," he said.

A date after nearly a year of famine? And Floy had sneezed on Kitty and Lenny, too?

Life was good. God had not forsaken her completely.

"I'd love to," she said.

"Good, I don't know where you live. Directions please? I could pick you up at six thirty."

She told him how to get to Patrice's place.

"Wear jeans, a jacket, and boots. My truck is in the shop for repairs so we'll have to go on my motorcycle. Is that a problem?"

Alma Grace gulped. "It isn't a problem at all."

Even if the gossip burned down the town, she would be sitting behind a sexy off-duty deputy on his motorcycle that very evening.

She drove straight to Gigi's house and barely knocked before she pushed the door open. Carlene and her Uncle Hank were sitting in the living room, each with a beer in their hands. "How's Aunt Gigi? And who gave you permission to tell people where I am? That deputy came right to the church. Everyone in the parking lot saw him tap on my window. I bet they're already spreading tales that we really stole those cookers and Jack was covering for us."

Carlene patted the sofa beside her. "Sit down. Have you had lunch? There's stew on the stove. It was that last batch of chili that made so many people sick but it'll only last a couple of days. Don't you dare tell anyone but the doctor says they've got food poisoning, not the flu like Agnes and Josie have contracted. Mama would just die if anyone knew. Now tell me about the deputy. I hope he asked you out on a date. He was sexy and sweet both."

"Yes, he did and I bet our mamas sure don't want to make chili for a few weeks. If worse comes to worse, Aunt Gigi can drag out her old family recipe and make the tried and true recipe for the cook-off. It's better than any I've ever eaten so I bet it would win. My mama would just die if she thought she'd made people sick. We can't tell them. Promise me that it will be our secret," Alma Grace said.

Hank looked up from the sofa. "I agree."

"How did it happen?" Alma Grace asked.

"I'm telling Patrice. We don't keep secrets like that from each other and our fathers know," Carlene said.

Hank finished off his beer. "I put a bunch of outdated ground pork on the cabinet to throw out. Gigi grabbed it instead of what was in the freezer and they made pork chili out of it. And Patrice should know but your mothers can't. Y'all really could make her old standby chili but I'm not so sure it would win the contest. It's not nearly hot enough or original enough," Hank said.

"It could win if we tinker with the recipe. Okay, then, we have a plan, and when the Fannins have a plan, all is right with the world. Are you on your way to see about Aunt Sugar?" Carlene said.

"Yes, and then I'm taking a slushy to Josie. I'll wear the mask and after that I'm going with Rick to a wiener roast with his church youth group. Don't wait up for me." Alma Grace giggled.

"Oh, honey, I'll be on the sofa when you get home. No way am I going to let you heat up wieners and not hear about it. Hell's bells, I might even pray that you want to go to bed with him and he's too righteous to have sex after the prayers you've been sending up on my behalf," Carlene said.

"You have a dirty mind."

"No, darlin', I have a sexy imagination. Have fun. And tell Aunt Sugar to listen to her doctor. Daddy says that she's been arguing about her medicine. She thinks prayer can heal her," Carlene said.

"Oh, dear," Alma Grace groaned.

Violet Prescott valued her gold fingernail on her right forefinger more than any of her vast collection of jewelry. Once a week she had her nails done at Ella's Beauty Shop. Kayla, the fingernail expert at Ella's, always carefully removed the fingernail, manicured and polished her nails, then replaced the gold nail with special adhesive. Violet simply *had* to get out of the hospital on Monday or she would miss her appointment.

The curtain drawn between Violet's part of the room, on the side toward the windows, and Josie's, on the side beside the door into the hallway, did not filter out the whining about that damned gold fingernail. The aide sighed when she came in with a lunch tray and disappeared with it on the other side of the curtain.

"This soup is lukewarm," Violet said. "And I couldn't possibly eat a baked potato. I need toast and tea."

The aide rolled her eyes as she passed the end of Josie's bed. She returned with Josie's tray and moved the bedside table over Josie's lap.

"You need to eat, honey. If you don't, you won't go home. Try the chicken soup and drink the broth if nothing else." The aide smiled.

Josie managed a weak grin. "I don't think it will stay down."

"The potato is pretty good after all. I think I can eat part of it," Violet said.

The aide went out into the hallway and brought back a nurse. "I'll put a shot of anti-nausea medicine in your IV, Josie. That should help."

"Thank you," Josie said.

"Hey, y'all over there. I'd like another potato and when are you coming to change these sheets. They are wrinkled up under my body and causing pain. They are rough and I feel like I'm lying on sand," Violet yelled.

The aide leaned down and whispered, "I have to write down what and how much you eat and I'm serious, ma'am, if you don't eat, you have to stay longer."

"Okay, I'll do my best. If I don't get out of here soon, I'm going to strangle that woman in the other bed," Josie whispered.

The aide whispered, "If you do, I'll open the window for you and toss her out of it. And if you tell anyone that I said that, I'll get fired."

"Thank you, Esmeralda." Josie read the Hispanic girl's name tag.

"You are very welcome, Miz Josie. I don't know how you stand her constant whining."

Josie was napping when she heard the door open again. There was no rest for the dying in the hospital for sure. If they weren't taking vitals, they were drawing blood or bringing food that wouldn't stay down.

She barely opened one eye. "Who in the hell are you?"

Alma Grace giggled. "You look like hell."

"Well, you don't look much better in that paper robe and mask. Hell, I thought they were coming to take me to surgery. I told y'all not to come up here. I can be sick and the store will still run. If y'all get sick, it's a different story."

Alma Grace pulled a slushy from behind her back. "I've had the flu shot so I'm protected. I brought you a prize. I even went to the store that makes lemon-lime so it wouldn't upset your stomach."

Josie reached for it.

"Your hands are shaking. I'll hold. You sip," Alma Grace said.

"That tastes so good. Thank you, Alma Grace. Who would have thought when I left work Friday that I'd be laid up and you'd be looking like shit in that getup? How are you all? No one else is sick?"

"I've got a date with that cute deputy who brought Carlene's divorce papers," Alma Grace whispered and pointed at the curtain. "I don't want her to know. He's the youth director at the church over in Luella and the gossip will start soon enough without her knowing."

Josie took another sip from the straw and motioned the cup away. "And the other girls? I've been so worried that I infected the whole lot of you."

"Carlene is with Aunt Gigi. Patrice is at a family reunion with Yancy. She was going to cancel but Uncle Alex said for her to go on, that Aunt Tansy was sleeping most of the time anyway. She'll be spending the evening with her mama so her dad can have a break."

"Oh, my God!" Violet screamed.

Josie shut her eyes. Anyone with that much volume and who could eat two baked potatoes should be catapulted out of the hospital, not wheeled out in a chair by a good-looking orderly.

"Nurse, nurse! Where's my call button? God Almighty! It's gone."

"Should I go over there?" Alma Grace asked.

"Hell, no!"

Alma Grace peeked around the curtain and quickly dropped it. "That was not a pretty sight. They really should put backs in those hospital gowns or else she should wear panties."

Josie shivered.

"It's gone. I can't find it. I'm going to faint," Violet screamed.

Two aides and a nurse darted past Josie's bed like marathon runners.

"Miz Prescott, what are you doing out of bed? You're going to rip your IV out. Settle down now and we'll get you squared away again."

"It's gone! I tell you, it's gone. It was there after I ate so I know I didn't eat it. But now it's gone!"

"What is gone?" Esmeralda asked.

"My gold fingernail. It has to be in the bed somewhere and you've got to find it. My son gave it to me for Christmas years ago," Violet screeched.

Alma Grace clamped a hand over her mask to keep the giggles at bay.

Josie didn't even try to keep quiet. Though weak, her laughter filled the room.

The curtain flew open and Violet glared at Josie. "Don't you dare laugh at me! I caught this at your store. You probably gave it to me."

Josie sat up so fast that her head spun and she had to grab the rail. "You sneezed on me!"

Esmeralda grabbed the curtain and swung it shut. "Settle down Miz Prescott before you yank that IV right out. They hurt going in, remember? You cried and yelled with the pain when we had to stick you so you don't want to go through that again. I'm thinking that your fingernail probably fell off into the other sheets when I changed them after lunch."

Violet whined. "Then go to the laundry room and find it."

"Miz Prescott, that's not even a possibility," the nurse said. "There are hundreds and hundreds of sheets and towels in the laundry with dozens of washers and dryers going around the clock. We will not waste a single work hour looking for one gold fingernail."

"I will have your job," Violet hissed.

"Honey, I'll be glad to give it to you, especially this week," the nurse said seriously.

Josie laughed again but the curtain didn't even flutter. "Give me that slushy. I can hold it now. I'm much stronger."

Alma Grace pulled up a chair and handed the cup to her. "Carlene says if you're still here tomorrow night, she'll be up to see you. And if you get to go home, she'll bring you food and slushies every day until you are well. Patrice says that she'll bring tequila so you can make that wicked green stuff. She says that if it will cure a hangover, it'll be death on the flu."

"She's a prophet." Josie sighed.

Chapter 14

PATRICE PICKED UP THE remote and turned off the ten o'clock news when she heard the motorcycle in the driveway. "Sounds like she's home."

Carlene raised an eyebrow.

"No, we won't peek out the curtains. She's old enough to date, to kiss, and to even have sex, and besides, he's a youth director, for God's sake. I bet he doesn't even kiss her." Patrice answered the unasked question.

"And if he does and we miss it?"

"We'll know, believe me." Patrice's eyes danced.

Alma Grace floated into the living room, a smile on her face, cheeks all aglow from being close to a bonfire and lips bee-stung from kissing, not once but many times.

"Kissing on a first date?" Carlene asked.

"Did you both ask God if that was all right?" Patrice asked.

"Yes, we did kiss and, no, we did not pray about it. And I'm not discussing it because it will jinx the whole thing. But yes, I like him a lot."

"I bet we can get her to tell us everything that happened. Every single little detail, like if there was tongue and did he get to second base?" Patrice said

"If she drinks this, I bet we really can." Carlene held up a bottle of Boone's Strawberry wine.

Alma Grace shook her head emphatically as she plopped down in a chair. "Not even if I drank all of that."

"Want to tell us why you bought it?" Patrice asked.

"What makes you think I did?"

"Well, neither one of us drink it so we wouldn't buy it," Carlene said.

"Okay, if you'll leave me alone about Rick, I'll tell you about the wine."

Patrice held out her hand.

Carlene put a five-dollar bill in it.

"What's that all about?"

"I bet her five dollars you'd fold and tell us about the wine. She didn't think you'd own up to it even if we preached a sermon about how drinking was vile and wicked or if I started praying," Patrice said.

"You praying? That'll be the day," Alma Grace said. "How'd you really find out about the wine?"

"I ran into Floy in the store when I went for Popsicles and she asked me why you were seen buying wine yesterday. I guess her neighbor's daughter works in the convenience store," Carlene explained.

Alma Grace threw the back of her hand over her forehead in true Scarlett O'Hara style. "Do we ever do anything that isn't broadcast all over town?"

"Not in my twenty-plus-years in this place," Patrice said.

Sitting up, Alma Grace sighed heavily. "Patrice, you said that flu germs live on slick surfaces for forty-eight hours, remember?"

Both cousins stared at her as if she had two heads and only one eyeball.

"I was going to take the wine bottle into Josie and Violet's room today and hopefully one or both of them would cough on it or sneeze on it. It's got a slick surface," she explained.

"You wouldn't make someone sick. Not over fake wings and a tinsel halo. You are too sweet for that," Patrice declared.

"Yes, I would. It's Macy's favorite kind of wine and I planned to leave it on her front porch so she'd get the flu. I wanted her to cough for weeks and not be able to wear my wings and sing in the choir. So there."

"You pray that Lenny and Carlene will get back together and then you give him the flu? What if she gives the flu to Lenny by kissing him and then Carlene did let him kiss her? It would be all your fault if your cousin died," Patrice said bluntly.

Alma Grace clamped a hand over her mouth. "Oh, my sweet Jesus. I didn't think about that. I was just trying to make Macy sick. I forgot that she'd been flirting with Lenny."

"What changed your mind?" Carlene asked.

"God said no and didn't leave a bit of wiggle room when He did. He said that revenge belonged to Him and I was to back off."

"Well, shit!" Patrice exploded. "I wish you would have fixed it so she got the flu and Lenny died with it. And since when do you listen when God says no? He's been tellin' you that ever since Carlene and Lenny split but you don't listen to him on that issue."

Alma Grace held up a finger.

"Listen to me. Floy sneezed all over Macy. She swears it was just allergies. God can't expect me to pray for her after what she did so I will not feel guilty when she comes down with the flu or when Macy gets it. Honest, right hand to God, I wouldn't have done it if I'd thought Carlene would get sick."

"Well, thank you, Alma Grace." Carlene smiled. "Now tell us about Josie."

"I'd rather hear what happened on the way home from that bonfire. Did you have sex?" Patrice said.

Alma Grace blushed scarlet. "We did not! But the funniest thing happened at the hospital."

She went on to tell about Violet's tantrum over the fingernail, not leaving out a single detail.

"Does Agnes know?" Carlene asked between hiccups.

"Oh, honey!" Alma Grace said. "Do you think I'd leave the

hospital without checking in on her? That would be unchristian of me. Besides I was already decked out in mask and gown and"—she leaned forward—"Josie made me promise I'd go see her before I left."

"What did she say?" Patrice asked.

"She laughed so hard she got a coughing fit and I wished for the wine bottle just in case God changed his mind. I told her about it and she said that she would have licked the damn bottle if I'd brought it."

"Well, Tansy!" A familiar voice said behind her.

Alma Grace clapped both her hands on her head and ducked. "Where is it? Tell me it's a big joke y'all are playing on me. You know Aunt Tansy's bird hates me."

Patrice had been giggling with Carlene but now she pointed to the corner where a cockatiel paced back and forth along a four-foot rod attached to a four-foot stand. "Mama was terrified that Dakshani would get the flu from her so she made me bring him home. Mama made me bring his exercise bar and even his jewelry. She was afraid that he'd be lonely without his things."

Alma Grace removed her hands and sat up straight. "He's roped down to that bar, isn't he?"

"By a very expensive rhinestone leash attached to his leg," Carlene said.

"And you won't let him off it when I'm in the house?"

Patrice crossed her chest and held up two fingers. "I promise."

"Why couldn't a black cat or a cute little poodle help her psychic powers? They wouldn't light on my head every time they got a chance." Alma Grace said.

"Well, Tansy!" Dakshani squawked the only two words he knew again.

Carlene laughed. "Maybe he thinks your curly hair looks like a nest."

"Well, Tansy!" Dakshani yelped louder.

Patrice pointed at the bird. "Hush!"

He turned his back and splattered his answer on the newspaper below the bar, fluffed his feathers, and tucked his head under his wing.

"Now," Patrice said, "I've got gossip. Hopefully, it will take the heat off us at the shop for a few days and we can get things back to normal. Cathy Andrews is taking a week off from Clawdy's. She and John from out at the Rib Joint got married at the courthouse Friday and they've gone on a honeymoon."

Alma Grace unzipped her boots and removed them. "It's about time. She's been living with him for months."

Patrice held up a hand. "She's pregnant. Trixie says that she's over-the-moon happy."

"Think Marty will ever settle down?" Alma Grace asked.

Carlene yawned. "I wish Lenny would ask Marty out. She'd teach him a thing or two."

"Marty only dates cowboys. If it ain't got boots and a Stetson, Marty don't give it the time of day and believe me she wouldn't go out with him after the way he's treated you." Patrice giggled and fished her phone from her jacket pocket. She hit a couple of buttons and waited. "Hi, Kim. I'm just calling to check on you, make sure you didn't get the flu. Yes, Alma Grace is home from her date and, yes, she did have a wonderful time."

Patrice nodded. "Why, yes, I did hear about Cathy Andrews."

A pause and then, "Oh, honey, we shouldn't judge. That little baby might grow up to be a minister in our church but I heard that Marty might be hearing the tick of her biological clock. I'd sure hate to see her go out with Lenny."

Alma Grace gasped.

"Oh, please don't repeat that. I'm not even sure I heard it right but it won't happen anyway. It's probably just a rumor but why else would he be looking at a pair of boots and a Stetson? Marty has never gone out with a feller that wasn't a cowboy."

She winked at her cousins. "Don't tell anyone about Marty. Talk to you later."

"Why did you do that?" Carlene asked.

"It'll make Bridget and Macy both mad if they think he's lookin' at Marty," Patrice said. "I might be mad at Alma Grace for not supporting you the way she should but I'll still take up for her sorry ass."

"Well, thank you, I think. But Marty don't deserve that," Alma Grace argued.

"Ah, she'll shoot him down so fast that he'll wonder what in the devil hit him. It's not as good as the flowers and it'll take some heat off of us," Patrice said.

"But you lied," Alma Grace whispered.

"I did not lie. I'm sure at some time in his life Lenny looked at boots and hats. How could he not? Macy wears boots to work every day and Lenny's boss wears cowboy boots."

They'd both shut their bedroom doors and Patrice was changing the newspaper scattered under Dakshani's bar when she felt a presence behind her. A peek over her shoulder revealed Yancy sprawled out on her sofa in Longhorn lounging pants and a thermal shirt. He'd slipped in the door and she hadn't even heard him.

Yancy adjusted a throw pillow under his neck and covered up with a throw from the back of the sofa. "Skunk sprayed under my house and I didn't deserve his attention the way that Lenny did. Do you mind if I crash here until morning? I'll be out of the house before y'all even wake up. I'll call Jack tomorrow morning and he can send out animal control to take care of the skunk."

Patrice dropped a kiss on his forehead. "You don't have to sleep on the sofa. You can sleep with me."

"The sofa is fine. What is that thing in the corner?"

"That is Mama's psychic bird, Dakshani. He's roped down and roosting for the night."

Yancy set her hormones to humming when he smiled. "So I'm sharing the room with a psychic bird? Will he tell me my fortune in the morning?"

Patrice kissed him—hard, long, and lingering. "I can tell your fortune right now. You are hot as hell and you are going to bed with me."

"Yes, ma'am." He cupped her face with his hands and kissed her again—hotter, longer, more passionate. "But you'll have to be quieter than usual or else take a ribbing tomorrow from your cousins. I love you, Patrice."

"I love you, too, and, darlin', I can be quiet," she said.

"It'll be the first time."

❧

"Well, Tansy!" Gigi said.

"That makes me miss Dakshani. I swear it's your voice that he talks in," Tansy said.

"Carlene says the bird is fine. They've got him set up in the corner by that window and he's prancing from one end to the other squawking at the neighbor's cat," Gigi reassured her.

Sun poured into the room through floor-to-ceiling windows in the sitting room at Tansy's house. She lounged on a plush brown leather love seat with end tables and a coffee table in front of her. Gigi had claimed one of the pale yellow, buttery soft recliners that made up the sitting arrangement. A pitcher of sweet tea, a silver bucket of ice, and three glasses were set in the middle of the coffee table.

Tansy poured two glasses and propped herself up on the throw pillows. "There's no way that cat can get in the house, is there? Poor Dakshani would have a heart attack if that cat chased him."

"Of course not. Now tell me, are we going to live and get even with Violet for giving this to us?"

"Of course we're going to live. We have to win the chili cook-off. The woman in the mirror scared the hell out of me this morning. I think I had the flu worse than you did. Where is Hank? I sent Alex off to work just to get him out of my hair. He's smothering the hell out of me. The nurse said my fever broke but I still feel weak as a kitten."

"That's what the nurse told me this morning, too, so I sent Hank to work, too, and then I made Carlene drive me over here. If I had to stay in that bedroom another day I'd climb the walls."

Tansy set her glass back on the table and slung her legs over the side of the love seat. "While I was drifting between this world and the next, all I could think about was chili. Even without Dakshani here, I had a vision about the cook-off. Of course we won. Oh, and look what I got in the mail today." She handed Gigi a lovely get-well card. "Read the note inside."

"I'm enclosing my great-grandmother's recipe for war-time chili. It only calls for a cup of meat and lots of kidney beans. My husband is on the Money-Maker chili team and he refuses to even look at it. Since you all have opened a door to us women, we are planning to form a team next year and I'll be serving war-time chili for sure. Thank you, Millie Donavan."

"Looks like we really did open the way for a new bunch of teams. There might be enough money in a couple of years to build a brand-new fire station." Gigi handed the card back to her. "Now tell me about your dream."

"I was wearing green beads like a Mardi Gras necklace only it had seven little chili peppers hanging on it. And we were all stirring a pot of chili," Tansy wheezed.

"Was it a big black cauldron and we all showed our boobs so we could get more necklaces?" Gigi asked.

"Don't make fun of me. I'm telling you about my vision. You are the necklace, Gigi. You make the basic chili that we all like and then we all gather round the pot and put in one ingredient. We'll write it down and put it in your jewelry safe. When we win, then we'll make it the same way every year."

"What kinds of ingredients?" Gigi was suddenly interested.

"Tell everyone to study recipes and bring their secret to your house the weekend before. We'll make several pots all the same way and freeze it, then have it ready for the cook-off so we'll have plenty. That's what I got from my vision but believe me it had meat in it. It wasn't vegetarian," Tansy told her.

"You just might have an idea."

Tansy nodded. "If I feel better tomorrow I'm going to tell Patrice to bring Dakshani home. I know he's missing me and my powers are getting weak without him here. And just for the record I'm taking two flu shots next year," Tansy said.

Gigi popped up the footrest on the recliner. Two days of hanging by a thread between life and death took its toll on a middle-aged woman. She wasn't sure that she hadn't been on her way for an up close and personal talk with St. Peter until that morning when the nurse declared that she could get dressed and go to Tansy's house.

"Hello." Alma Grace's voice floated from the foyer. "I brought Mama. Are you in the sunroom?"

"Yes, we are," Tansy said.

Gigi motioned toward the other chair. "Good mornin', Sugar, darlin'."

"Ah, that sweet tea does look good." Sugar melted into the chair and pulled a fluffy throw over her legs. Her hair was pulled back with a wide red headband decorated with rhinestones. Dangly diamond earrings flashed in the sunlight and her makeup was perfect but her eyes looked tired.

Alma Grace quickly filled the remaining glass with ice and tea and handed it to her mother. "There you, go. Sweet tea will make you feel better."

"Honey, you'll have to get another glass if you'd like something to drink," Tansy said.

"Don't have time. We're opening the shop again. You girls have a good time. Daddy says that he'll check on you at noon," Alma Grace said.

"You tell Jamie that we'll be fine. My cook is making us a light lunch and we've got lots to talk about. We're going to discuss the cook-off. If we decide we need a nap, we'll help your mama up to the bedrooms or else we'll rest right here," Tansy told her.

"I know the secret to the winning chili!" Sugar said.

"Well, y'all enjoy your day." Alma Grace disappeared out into the hallway.

"We've been talking about it, already," Gigi said.

"You know how Mama always said that all the secrets of life were in her Bible? Well, I had Jamie go get it for me from the credenza down in the foyer when I thought I was going to die and I've been lookin' through it this morning. I found a Hershey wrapper marking the place where Jesus fed the thousands with just a few fishes and loaves of bread. I think she was telling me to put chocolate in the chili but not to use too much."

Gigi smiled. "I'm surprised it wasn't tucked in beside the Ten Commandments."

"Why?" Tansy asked.

"That's where it says not to commit adultery."

Sugar nodded in agreement. "You've got a point. Mama wrote the directions on the back side of the wrapper. According to what she had there, we should use one half a bar. It didn't say chili but I just know in my heart that the chocolate is Daddy's secret."

Tansy fluffed her pillow and shifted to the other end of the love seat. "Maybe you should put chocolate in the chili for your ingredient," and went on to tell her about her vision.

"I think that's what Mama is telling me. I thought I caught a glimpse of her when I was floating up close to heaven yesterday, and I remembered what she said about the secrets being in the Bible."

Gigi felt cheated. She didn't go to the Mardi Gras or to talk to her mama when she was sick. And she sure didn't think about chili. Lord, just the thought of it even two days later made her gag. But then she'd always been the grounded sister whose vice was simply Texas Longhorn football.

That was it. They were the eccentric Fannin girls who'd bring chocolate and probably bird feathers to the chili but she'd make the basic recipe. Yes, sir, Gigi was the grounded, completely normal sister.

✺

The shop had been fairly quiet most of the day. Kim came by at noon and she and Alma Grace had a whispering session over near the plus-size teddies. Patrice had been holed up in her office all day.

Josie called in the middle of the afternoon to say that she was getting out of the hospital but that her son had driven up from Austin and was taking her home with him for a week to recuperate. She actually sounded happy about the idea, which surprised Carlene.

Just as she was sewing the last bit of expensive lace to the corset, Carlene heard the bridal party in the foyer. She set it aside and joined Alma Grace in the shop. The bride and her friends squealed when they saw the panties, bras, corsets, and fancy hose with wedding bells embroidered around the top. The squeals got louder when Alma Grace brought out the frothy white peignoir adorned with French Chantilly lace around the edges and hem. The bride, who was six feet tall and wore a size eighteen, whipped out a credit card and paid the enormous bill.

"It's just what I wanted. Everything is perfect. I'm going to be beautiful," she said breathlessly. "Carlene, I'm so glad that you put in a shop for us gals who aren't a size four."

"Hey, now!" one of the bridesmaids said.

"Nothing against you tiny girls but it's so exciting for us plus-size women to find pretty things, too."

"Yes, it is," Carlene said. "I'm glad you are pleased."

And I'm sure glad Josie finished whipping up that peignoir on Friday, Carlene thought.

She went back to the designing/beading room feeling a lot better about the day. It was great to be appreciated and needed. But the good feeling surrounding her like a nice warm jacket on a cold rainy day didn't last long. She felt the chill even before Kitty Lovelle stormed through the door uninvited and cussing worse than Josie.

Her face was scarlet; her expression right out of a horror film; her mouth set in a firm line and her jaws working; she looked like she could kill Carlene with her bare hands.

"You caused this. I know you did just like you've caused that ruckus between him and Bridget by sending that hussy flowers. And you were involved with that horrible, mean trick with the cookers. I know you did it so don't look so innocent. Well, are you happy now?"

Carlene stared, wide-eyed, at the woman. Any minute she was going to fall on the floor and commence frothing at the mouth and all Carlene could think about was the yards of Venice lace on the table. She hoped that Kitty didn't pull it off when she went to squirming around like a worm in hot ashes.

Should she call 911 right then or wait until her former mother-in-law stopped breathing and then call? She was wondering if she could claim the phones didn't work, when Kitty stomped her foot.

"Listen to me. I'm talking to you, girl. He's sick. Real bad sick with the flu and I know that you are the cause. He's run down because of the way you've treated him and acted and he didn't have the good health to fight it off. Before he married you…" Kitty threw her hand up and took in the whole room.

Lenny hadn't married the shop or the whole family. Hell, he wiggled his way out of every family function that he could and he hated the shop. He wouldn't even help with the renovations for it.

"Before he got tangled up with the likes of you, he was never sick. So it's your fault," Kitty screamed.

"You aren't supposed to be within fifty feet of this place or my house or any of our homes. Didn't you take out a restraining order on my family? But since you are here, I can tell you that Lenny was never sick when he was married to me. It's probably the fact that he's busy chasing after every skirt tail in the whole county that's got him sick. Is he in the hospital?"

"I don't give a damn about a restraining order. They aren't worth jack shit. And no, he's not in the hospital. He's at home and Bridget won't even let me in the front door. And Macy has it, too, and she might not even be well in time for the Easter program. I'm never forgiving you." Kitty stormed out in the same foul mood that she'd brought with her when she arrived.

Patrice looked around the edge of the door. "Do you give a shit if she forgives you?"

Carlene shook her head.

"Do you give a shit if he has the flu?"

Another shake.

"Then let's lock up. It's after five and we still have to run by and see Agnes and our mamas before we go home. They're over at my mama's so we can see them all at once. They've been talking about chili all day and Aunt Sugar says she's found the secret to the winning recipe."

Alma Grace met them in the foyer. "Who was screaming in here? I was getting the dressing rooms straightened up and thought it was sirens until I heard someone leaving."

Patrice threw her arm around Alma Grace. "Lenny has the flu. Bridget won't let Kitty in the house and she's mad as hell. And Macy has it, too."

Alma Grace blew a kiss toward the ceiling. "Thank you, Lord."

Chapter 15

Not rain, snow, sleet, or PMS could keep the Fannin sisters from the United Daughters of the Confederacy committee meeting that week. Even if the sickness had killed them, their spirits would have still hung on long enough to hover over the meeting. It was the one where they discussed putting Confederate flags on the graves of the fallen on Confederate Veteran's Memorial Day during the last week of April. And this year they were voting about whether to buy the next size bigger flag.

Sugar dressed in a cute little pink spring suit with a pencil-slim skirt, floral blouse under a matching fitted jacket, and gold jewelry. She hadn't felt up to going down to the Yellow Rose to get her hair done so she'd arranged for Stella to make a house call. And then she'd invited Gigi and Tansy.

Hair done.

Stella gone back to the shop.

Tansy in one bedroom getting dressed.

Gigi in another one.

Sugar sat down in a rocking chair and sighed. Dressing tired her out, and even though they'd argued, she was glad that Jamie had insisted on them having a driver that day. She simply had to get her energy back because after lunch with the committee in Sherman, they were going to stop by the grocery store to purchase ingredients for the first batch of new chili. After that they had to attend a meeting at the church concerning the annual Cadillac Easter egg hunt. After the way those hussies had treated Alma Grace, there was no way she was missing that meeting, either.

Floy had gotten the flu a day after Sugar and her sisters and there was no way she'd have the energy to fight them on every single solitary issue like she usually did. If Sugar played her cards right, she might even dethrone that old girl this year.

Gigi sat down on the blue velvet vanity bench with her back to the mirror. She wore chocolate brown slacks with a sweater set in off-white that looked great with her champagne-blond hair. A scarf with orange and yellow swirls put some color in her face and her signature Texas Longhorn earrings sparkled every time she moved her head.

"Who would have thought getting dressed would be such a chore?" she said.

"Turn around and put on some more blush. You still look like death warmed over," Sugar said.

"Blush isn't going to help. I need fresh air and sunshine on my skin," Gigi argued.

Tansy yelled from the hallway on her way to Sugar's bedroom. "Patrice said if I'm able to go to two meetings then she's bringing Dakshani home on Saturday. Poor baby will be glad to get back in his room where he's got a place to fly and play." She crossed the room and sat down on the edge of the bed. "Y'all as wore out as I am?"

She fluffed out her tiered gauze skirt in a swirl of red, white, and blue. Her royal blue blouse with billowing sleeves caught up at the wrist with wide cuffs was belted at the waist. The buckle, a Confederate flag, was done up in rhinestones and silver.

Sugar nodded. "That which does not kill us will make us stronger. We've got to talk the committee into bigger flags and this is our one chance in a million to boost Floy Gastineau off her throne at the Easter egg meeting. It's time for us to bite the bullet and start buying plastic eggs and stuffing them with candy. Kids don't eat real eggs anymore and they're a pain in the neck to dye every year but you know how set in her ways Floy is."

"Honey, they are a pain in the ass, not the neck. I'm with you on the plastic eggs but who is going to stuff those six million fake eggs? And is this really the year to fight for more change after we've turned Cadillac on its ear by entering the chili cook-off?" Gigi asked.

"We're in hot water so we might as well fight for the plastic eggs while we're at it. On Saturday before Easter, everyone can bring a casserole for lunch and we'll make a day of putting candy into plastic eggs. We can make an assembly line," Tansy said.

"Did you have a dream about it?" Gigi teased.

"Hell, no! My bird is over at Patrice's. He's my muse and the only dream I had while he was gone was the one about the chili. I'm sure his spirit was still in the house or I wouldn't have had that one," Tansy flared up.

"Hey, don't get your panties in a wad," Gigi said. "We got to save our energy and go in as a united front if we're going to get our flags and our plastic eggs both today."

Sugar stood up. "Alma Grace called and said if we weren't too worn out to come by the shop after the church meeting. They've picked out a tent and some stuff for the cook-off that they want us to look at."

Gigi groaned when she pushed up off the bench. "My bones feel like they are a hundred years old."

"Stop your bitchin'. Those that endure until the end shall be…" Tansy said.

"Saved," Sugar finished for her. "I can't believe you're quoting scripture."

"Hey, I have a Bible somewhere in the house and I go to church. But I was thinking something more like those that endure until the end shall be called angels."

Gigi led the way to the door. "Us, angels? You must've been really sick."

"Speak for yourself," Sugar snapped.

⌒⌬⌒

Gigi didn't give a rat's ass whether they put flags on the graves or not, whether they were faded and small, or whether they were big as king-size bedsheets and brand-spanking-new. Tansy was the one who'd followed in their mama's footsteps in the Daughters of the Confederacy, had served as president of the organization for two years, and had kept her sisters involved.

At least once a month, when they had a committee meeting to discuss whatever the hell was next on the calendar, they had a nice lunch in a decent restaurant. But that day Gigi hoped they still had potato soup on the lunch menu. Her stomach wasn't ready for anything heavy, not after that horrible illness.

Tansy looked up in the rearview mirror and caught Gigi's eye. "It's time our daughters stepped up and joined the organization."

"Good luck with that," Gigi said. "Carlene is going through a divorce and running a business. Can't you just see her getting all dressed up in something halfway conservative and going to a lunch in the middle of the week?"

Sugar looked out the side window from her place in the backseat of the minivan. "Don't look at me. Alma Grace is still fuming over the Easter program at church. I'm not even sure I can talk her into stuffing plastic eggs with us after she gets off work on Saturday. This is not a good time to approach her about joining anything."

Gigi touched Sugar on the shoulder. "Didn't you hear about Sunday?"

"If you or Tansy didn't tell me, then no, I didn't hear about Sunday."

"Have you seen Alma Grace?" Gigi asked.

"Every day."

Tansy snapped her fingers and shook her head at Gigi. "Maybe that's Alma Grace's story to tell, Gigi."

"If that's so, then she should have told her mama before now. Did she tell you about her date with that cop?" Gigi asked.

Sugar raised her chin a notch. "And I'm real glad that she listened when the good Lord spoke to her and told her that she could not take vengeance upon herself. Me, I'd have cracked that wine bottle over Lenny's head and then went to work on Kitty with the broken end."

Tansy gasped.

"Don't be so shocked. I would have repented and promised to never do it again," Sugar said.

Their driver parked the van right in front of the doors and hurried around the front to open doors for the ladies. "Y'all going to be about an hour and a half, right?"

"That's right, Larry. You can go do whatever you want and come back and get us if you don't want to wait," Sugar said.

"I'm going to go to the hospital and have lunch with my wife in the cafeteria there. She works in housekeeping and it'll be a great surprise for her." He smiled.

"Don't worry if you're a little late, and…" Sugar pulled a bill from her pocket and handed it to him. "Lunch is on us. We appreciate you driving."

"Well, thank you. You are so sweet, Miz Sugar."

"Don't be thinking that little gesture will win you any favors with those old barracudas waiting for us," Gigi told her sister as they made their way inside the restaurant.

"God rewards those who are kind," Sugar quipped.

✦

Tansy ordered spaghetti with marinara sauce but after two bites she pushed her plate to one side and sipped sweet tea. She scanned the table for eight. Three were Fannins so she needed two more votes to carry the proposal. She couldn't count on Edna Green because she was friends with Floy and she'd vote against anything that Tansy suggested. The president already said that she didn't think they should spend any unnecessary money that year. That left three fairly new members on the committee that she might sway.

The president stood up and led the discussion against buying new flags because next year would be the 150th celebration of the end of the Civil War. In her opinion their money should be spent on a big blowout that year. They could approach the idea of new and bigger flags at that time. Until then the old ones would hold up one more year.

She ended with, "We need to have a serious membership drive. Two of us have been responsible for going to the cemeteries alone for the past ten years and putting the flags up for our holiday. Those of you"—she cut her eyes around at Tansy—"with daughters should be grooming them to take over their inherited responsibilities."

"So Tansy, unless you are planning to buy the flags and put them out yourself, then I suppose we are ready for a vote," she said.

Tansy stood up slowly. "Those flags are a disgrace to the Confederacy. They're faded and torn. Why should our daughters be inducted into an organization that cares more about a damned Valentine's dinner than buying decent flags for the cemetery on our Memorial Day? Now we can vote."

Tansy was disappointed when the vote didn't go her way but by damn next year Patrice would be a member. They'd think they'd done gone to battle with a buzz saw when she made up her mind about flags or parties.

"One down, one to go. We didn't do too hot in that one. Hope we do better with the plastic eggs," Gigi said as they made a side trip to the ladies' room at the end of the luncheon.

The president of the organization was coming out when

Tansy opened the door. "Oh, pardon me. A word in private, Gigi," she said.

"Whatever you've got to say to me, they can hear," Gigi said.

"This has nothing to do with the Confederacy but I wanted to congratulate y'all on entering the chili cook-off. My husband is a member of the Beefeaters Team. Next year the wives of the Angus Association plan to get up our own team since y'all have broken the ice."

"Why couldn't you say that in front of all of us?" Gigi asked.

The woman pulled a hundred-dollar bill from her pocket. "I wanted to give this to you anonymously to put toward your campaign and I don't want the Beefeaters to know about it," she said sheepishly.

"Thank you," Tansy said. "And it will be kept a secret."

"I'll see to it that she's not president next year for the big celebration. We'll be voting in the fall and I'm making sure Patrice is a member before election," Tansy said.

"How many years does a person have to be inside before they can be president? I forgot," Sugar said.

"No one's ever been voted in right after joining. It's a big job," Tansy said.

"Then put me up for the vote. When Edna finishes her term, I'll be president and I'll install Patrice as vice president and we'll sit back and watch her bring this business to the modern world standards and thinking," Gigi said.

Tansy nodded seriously. "That could work. And we'll have a lot of clout because word will get around about the plastic eggs and the fact that we were the first women to enter the chili cook-off."

"And win it," Gigi said.

❧

If Carlene had anything to do with fashion, baby-doll pajamas would be back in style that spring. She had updated the old seventies style, complete with bloomer bottoms, and she'd whipped up six pair to test the waters. She'd just finished creating one in bright yellow with a flowing, see-through top with spaghetti sequin straps. The bloomers had matching sequins scattered on them to glitter and flash in soft candlelight.

She looked up at the clock and laid all her things to one side. It was almost time for the church Easter egg committee and she was a member even though she was sporadic about attending. If her mama and aunts could go after being sick, there was nothing that she could use for an excuse not to be present.

Her mission was twofold. Someone had to be there to keep Aunt Sugar from scratching Kitty's eyeballs out. And to vote with her mama and Aunt Sugar to use plastic eggs filled with candy. She hadn't liked real eggs when she was a kid and that was twenty years before. With all the hype about bad eggs causing everything from salmonella to ingrown toenails these days, mothers would rather their kids got bad teeth from too much candy.

Alma Grace caught her in the foyer. "I'll go to the church on Saturday and help stuff plastic eggs if you can help vote out those nasty real eggs."

"I'm holding you to that," Carlene said.

Alma Grace nodded seriously. "You've got my word and that's as good as gold. And we'll guilt Patrice into helping us."

Larry was sitting on the church porch, leaning against a porch post with his cowboy hat pulled down over his eyes, when Carlene arrived.

"You driving today?" Carlene asked.

He tipped up his hat with one finger. "It's a tough job but someone has to do it." He grinned. "Your mama said to tell you to come to the back door. They're meeting in the fellowship hall."

"Thanks." Carlene stepped around him.

Floy sat at the end of a long table with her minions all lined up on the left side. On the right side were the three Fannin sisters, Kim, and Agnes. Carlene slid in beside her mother. The whole place had the feeling of a funeral about it—quiet, cold, and stiff.

Floy stood up and said, "Okay, we are here to decide on a time for the Easter egg hunt on Sunday afternoon. We've always had it out at Violet's Plantation but she's not feeling up to that many people since she's been so sick. So do I have any suggestions for another place?"

Agnes snorted. Granted it was barely more than a grunt but it was big enough to classify as a snort.

Violet snarled at Agnes. "You don't even have a right to be here. You haven't been in church since last fall."

"I beg to disagree," Agnes said. "I've been in church every Sunday and most Wednesday nights. It just hasn't been in this church. However, I have not legally moved my membership and I have been on the Easter program and egg committee for fifty years so I do have a right to be here. Y'all can have the Easter egg hunt in my front yard if you want to."

Kitty's head looked like a bobble doll when she wiggled it around. "That is not big enough for an Easter egg hunt, and you know it Agnes Flynn."

"You can have it at my house. We have a twenty-acre backyard of rolling hills. Jamie and the hired hands will set up a tent with refreshments. Tell everyone to bring lawn chairs and blankets," Sugar said.

"That is so sweet," Beulah said. "It'll be like that last scene in *Steel Magnolias*. I always loved that part of the movie. I vote that we have our egg hunt at Sugar Magee's place. Anyone second it?"

Carlene raised her hand. "I'll second the motion."

Floy's words came out through gritted teeth, "The motion has been made and seconded. This year's egg hunt will be at Sugar and Jamie Magee's. The announcement will be made on Sunday morning and we'll put it in the local news section of the newspaper this week to let everyone know that it is for the whole community. Now who's up for making cookies for refreshments?"

Sugar raised her hand. "I'll take care of that and the sweet tea and coffee. I'll call Clawdy's tomorrow and get them to cater it for us. The ranch will provide all refreshments."

Floy's smile was more like a grimace. "Okay, let the minutes show that Sugar has volunteered to do the refreshments this year as well as have the egg hunt at her place."

Sugar pushed back her chair and stood. "I'd like to make a motion that we have the hunt at my house every year and let the minutes show that I will take care of the refreshments every year, also."

Violet jumped up so fast that her little beady eyes had trouble keeping up with the motion. "You are just trying to run the whole church like your daughter did the Easter program but it's not going to happen, Sugar Magee."

"I second the motion," Tansy said above Violet's yelling.

Floy clapped her hands. "Quiet. This is a business meeting, not a free for all. Since we have a disagreement we will have a vote. All in favor of moving the egg hunt permanently to Sugar's, please raise your hand."

Beulah's hand shot up quickly and the expression on her face said that she knew she'd done the wrong thing immediately. It was seven to five, with her vote swinging the decision to move the egg hunt permanently.

"Thank you, Beulah," Agnes said.

Beulah put her hand down slowly like a little kid who, without thinking about the consequences, had just shot his teacher the bird.

"It does make more sense," she whispered.

Agnes leaned across the table and said, "You might as well move on over here in our camp."

Violet pointed but the gold fingernail was gone and somehow her authority had gone with it. "Oh, hush, Agnes."

"And now for the controversy over the eggs." Floy raised her voice over the noisy comments that had started. "In my opinion we should keep the old ways and dye real eggs. That's what makes it an egg hunt. The other way should be billed as a candy hunt."

Carlene raised her hand. "I'd like to point out that plastic eggs and candy do not cost more than real eggs. When y'all raised chickens and gave the eggs to the church for the egg hunt, it was one thing, but now you have to buy them, throw away what gets broken in boiling, and deal with the big job of dying them. And then you have to be so careful hauling them to the hunt. Plus mothers won't let their kids eat them because they might contract salmonella from eating eggs that have been cooked that far in advance."

"That's bullshit," Kitty said loudly. "We boil them, color them, and refrigerate them until time to hide them."

"Would you let Lenny eat one?" Sugar asked.

She and Kitty locked gazes and neither one of them blinked.

"Lenny has been very ill. Only today has he been well enough that I could even leave his side. I wanted to take him to the hospital but he is such a big strong man that he would have none of it," Kitty said.

"That's not what I asked," Sugar said.

"No, of course not. He couldn't eat a boiled egg today. But if he was a little boy, I'd let him eat one," Kitty countered.

The noise started again with everyone either expressing their concern for Lenny or else talking about plastic eggs. Carlene hit the table with her fist and the room went as quiet as the calm before a tornado. "You wouldn't let him eat something that made him sick, Kitty, not even to get back at me."

"Lenny is not a part of this." Kitty looked at Floy. "I make a motion that we use real eggs and keep our old traditions and it has nothing to do with how much I dislike you."

"I make a motion that we use plastic eggs so the kids won't get sick and so that the eggs aren't ground into the earth when they step on them in their rush to hunt them," Sugar said.

"I second Sugar's motion," Tansy said.

"I second Kitty's motion," someone else said.

"And I'm the president and you are supposed to wait for me to ask for someone to second a motion." Floy raised her voice again.

Kitty glared across the table at Sugar. "You just want to keep those nasty smelling eggs out of your yard."

"Point proven. Nasty smelling eggs, folks. Out of her mouth, not mine," Sugar said.

"Jury can't decide." Agnes laughed. "Call the preacher."

Kim pulled her phone out of her purse. "I'll take care of that. I do believe he is in his study so this shouldn't take long."

Isaac arrived in a couple of minutes. His light brown hair was wet with sweat, his glasses slid down on his nose, and his khaki shorts had grass stains on them. "I was mowing, ladies, so forgive the way I look. Now what is this problem?"

Carlene stole a look at Kim and got a slight blush and a smile in return.

"We have a locked vote on whether we should have real eggs or plastic ones," Floy said. "I think we should stick with the old traditions and stay with real eggs."

"And Sugar?" Isaac looked at her.

"I think that we shouldn't waste our money on eggs that the kids wouldn't eat anyway and that their mothers won't let them eat for fear of having sick kids. We can buy the plastic eggs and fill them with candy. Tansy has offered to foot the bill for the eggs and Gigi will buy all the candy to fill them. We just need the whole committee plus any other volunteers to help stuff them on Saturday. The men and teenage boys can hide them just as well as they can real eggs," Sugar said.

Isaac glanced at Kim and said, "My vote is for the plastic. I sure wouldn't want one of our children to come down ill from eating tainted eggs. Is the issue settled then, ladies?"

Sugar smiled. "Thank you, Pastor Isaac."

Isaac pushed up his glasses and nodded. "You are very welcome. I expect you will all be here to help on Saturday. If you are going to be here at lunchtime, each of you could bring a casserole. I'll even tell the men's Sunday school class to come around and lend a hand, too. Good day, ladies. I've got to get back to my mowing. Springtime means the grass is green and healthy."

"Yes," Agnes said under her breath.

"You old fool. You just ruined Easter," Violet said.

"No, I just made it the best one ever for the kids. Hell, maybe we'll even get more kids out to the hunt when they find out they ain't huntin' eggs that they have to throw at my mailbox," she said.

"Y'all going to be here Saturday?" Kim asked. "If you're not, then I'll take over as president for you that day."

Floy raised her hand. "I'll be here. The day that you take over my spot is the day I'll be knocking on heaven's door."

Kim leaned over and whispered in Carlene's ear, "I told you that corset would do the trick. She might want to go to heaven but she's not ready to crawl up in a casket just yet, and by this time next year, I'll be the preacher's wife. We'll see how much power they all have then. But you know what the crazy thing is? I started off to get even with them and I've plumb fallen in love with Isaac. Now tell me about the chili cook-off. Can I do anything to help y'all out with it?"

❧

Gigi waited until they were in the van to explode. "I volunteered to buy the candy?"

"And I'm buying all the eggs?" Tansy asked.

"Yes, you are and you'll get blessed for doing it. Besides it's a tax write-off and I needed Pastor Isaac to see that we were a united front. I think he's afraid of us when we stand together," Sugar said. "Larry, here's my ranch credit card. When you take us to Bless My Bloomers, I want you to go to Walmart and wherever else that sells plastic eggs and bags of small individually wrapped candy and buy…" She looked at Gigi.

"We usually make thirty dozen eggs but that's just when the church kids are invited. We always wanted them to have at least eight or ten each," Gigi said.

"Then get eighty to a hundred dozen plastic eggs and enough candy to fill them up. This has to be the best hunt ever," Sugar said.

"Okay," Gigi said.

"That'll only be about a hundred dollars for each of you to cough up. I'll spend five times that amount on cookies, tarts, sweet tea, and coffee and it'll be worth every single dime," Sugar said.

A knock on the window beside Sugar put an end to the argument. They turned to see Kim standing there waving a bill. Sugar pushed the button to roll down the window and Kim handed her the fifty through the window. "The lady who gave me that to give to you as a donation to the Red-Hot Bloomers Team wants to remain anonymous and I can't tell you her name but her husband is on the Stingers Team and she's mad at him this week."

Larry dropped them at the back door of Bless My Bloomers and said he'd be back in an hour and a half. The supply catalogs were already spread out on the kitchen table and all three of the mamas sunk into chairs.

Alma Grace poked her head in the kitchen and gasped. "My God, y'all look like the wrath of Lucifer hit you. You should all three be home taking a nap, not here."

Carlene came through the back door and sat down with them. "You could have ridden back here with me."

"We needed to talk to Larry and send him to buy eggs and candy," Sugar said.

"Get us some sweet tea. We've all got a faintin' spell after fightin' for new flags, buyin' stuff to make our first batch of chili, which by the way we will be serving Saturday at the Easter egg–stuffing party, and then winning the war against real eggs," Tansy said.

"What happened?" Alma Grace asked.

Gigi picked up the catalog while Sugar told the story. She turned the page and there was a hot-pink canopy with frilly black lace around the top. It advertised Precious Penny's Escort Service in black letters across the top and showed it with three ladies sitting behind a six-foot table covered in a hot-pink and black-striped cloth.

"This is the one," Gigi said.

"Mama, we are the Red-Hot Bloomers. Don't you think it should be red?" Carlene asked. "And that is a canopy, not a tent."

Tansy held the page open with her forefinger. "I agree with Gigi. That is the one. Order all of it, the canopy, the cloths for the tables, and the tiebacks for the sides. And spend the extra money for that thing." She pointed to a picture on the adjoining page that showed an easel with a picture in a gold gilt frame. "They've used a picture of their staff and we will use a picture of all of us in our T-shirts. We're buying seven. One for each of us and one for Josie. We might not all be on the team but we all support it."

Tansy nodded. "Pink for the first all women's team. You think Josie will like it?"

Josie stuck her head in the back door. "That's the one I picked out before I got sick so it's got my vote. I think our T-shirts ought to keep with the same theme. Hot pink with bold black letters."

"You're back. I can't believe you are back. You don't have to do a thing but just be here," Carlene squealed and rushed across the room to hug her.

"I dropped by to tell you I'll be here Monday morning." She pulled out a chair and sat down. "Looks like four of us have stared the grim reaper in the face and outran the sorry sucker. All these smart-ass folks who are betting against us are going down hard. If it's true that what don't kill us makes us stronger then the Fannin sisters and I are all four made of steel."

"You got it," Tansy said.

Chapter 16

PATRICE STOPPED SO QUICKLY inside her living room that evening that Carlene and Alma Grace plowed into her back. She had to grab the wall to keep from falling flat out on her face. Something gritted under her feet and Alma Grace squealed at the same time.

A broken crystal vase made Patrice glad that she hadn't kicked off her high heels in the car. Something brushed against her leg and the neighbor's big yellow cat made a flying leap toward the window, bounced off it, shook himself off, and made a beeline down the hall with all three women behind him.

Patrice slapped a palm over each cheek when she realized the bird wasn't on his perch. "Dakshani! Where are you?" She raced to her bedroom, dropped down on her knees, and lifted the bed skirt. There was the cat, crouched down, with feathers hanging out of his mouth.

She rolled back on her butt and put her head in her hands. "Shit! He ate Dakshani."

"How did he even get into the house?" Clarice sat down on the edge of the bed.

"Are you sure he ate him?" Sugar whispered.

"He's got gray feathers hanging out of his mouth."

"We'll go to Dallas right now and buy another one. Cockatiels all look just alike," Alma Grace said.

"Well, Tansy!" Patrice quipped.

"A new one wouldn't talk," Carlene explained. "And it wouldn't have the rhinestone leash around its leg. Aunt Tansy had that made special at the jewelry shop."

Patrice looked under the bed again. "He's got part of the leash dangling out the side of his mouth."

"It must've been a helluva fight. Curtains are ripped and snagged, stuff is knocked off and broken everywhere I look," Carlene said.

"Mama is going to cry," Patrice said.

"The first thing we've got to do is get that cat out of here. Someone had to have put it in the house because I locked the door," Alma Grace said.

"Kitty!" Carlene said.

"I know it's a kitty cat did it but it's not my fault," Alma Grace said.

"No, Kitty Lovelle. She is so mad about us joining the chili cook-off and winning the fight for the eggs that she did it and she's blaming me for that cooker theft. I know she did," Carlene said.

Carlene noticed the open window just as the cat scampered out from the other side of the bed. He jumped through it and a flash of yellow took off around the house. She pulled back the sheers and jerked the mini blinds up. "It wasn't a cat that scratched his way in through the screen. That thing has been cut all the way around. I'm tellin' you, Kitty did it. It's payback. She knows I'm allergic to cats. She stayed with us while her house was getting painted and brought her cat. I had to take allergy pills every single day."

"But Dakshani?" Patrice asked.

"She had no idea there was a bird in the house. It's just payback for me," Carlene said.

"Well, Tansy!"

"You don't have to keep reminding me. Carlene already told me," Alma Grace said.

"Well, Tansy! Well, Tansy! Well, Tansy!"

They all looked up at the same time and there was Dakshani, his little orange cheeks, topknot, and beady eyes barely visible as he peeked out over the top of the bowl-shaped light fixture up next to the ceiling.

He craned his neck in every possibly direction, flew down, and lit on Alma Grace's head.

She stiffened her shoulders and shivered. "Get him off me."

"It's just a bird," Patrice said. "Come on, darlin'. Mama is going to be so upset that your pretty tail feathers are gone." She talked baby talk and sounded just like Tansy. Dakshani hopped onto her finger and left a yellow and green blob on the carpet at her feet.

Alma Grace raised a hand and then stopped midair. "Oh, shit!"

"You got that right." Patrice giggled.

"Patrice, check my hair. See if that bird left anything in my hair," Alma Grace whined.

"I've got to get him in his cage. I don't have time to see if he crapped on your head. If he did, take it as a sign from God that you been prayin' too much," Patrice said.

"I hate birds. I really, really hate them."

"Bend down here. I'll check your hair," Carlene said. "And then I'll get some paper towels and clean up the carpet. Patrice, you just make sure the bird is safe.

Patrice baby-talked to him all the way to the cage. When she opened the door, he hopped inside and pecked at a special bird biscuit hanging on the side.

"Well, Tansy!" he said but he kept a wary eye out for cats.

❦

Alma Grace was in luck. Nothing was on her head. Carlene headed toward the kitchen for paper towels but before she took two steps Alma Grace squealed.

"There he is."

A big yellow cat had jumped up on the outside windowsill. He licked his lips as he watched every movement that Dakshani made.

"That's the neighbor's cat, isn't it? That one has a white patch on his head. The one that was in the house was darker and didn't have any white," Alma Grace said.

"It was a stray that Kitty rounded up from somewhere. I know that woman and I know she did it," Carlene answered.

The neighbor's son looked through the window, grabbed his yellow cat, and took off.

Carlene took off for the front door, being careful not to step on any glass. She slung it open and yelled, "You stop right there! Don't you take another step, young man, or I'm calling the police."

Ronnie set the cat down slowly, dropped down on his knees, and put his hands behind his head. Kids watched too much television these days. An eight-year-old boy shouldn't even know to do that.

"Have you seen anyone around the house today or anytime this past week?"

"Please don't be callin' the police. My mama will skin me alive."

"Ronnie?" Patrice leaned out the window.

Tears streamed down the little boy's face when he saw Patrice. "Miz Lovelle give me ten dollars and she said if I don't tell she'll give me ten more if I'd check all the windows every mornin' to see if any of them would open." He fished around in his jeans pocket and brought out a ten-dollar bill, wadded up into a ball. "Give it back to Miz Lovelle and tell her that I don't want it."

Carlene reached out and took it from him. "You did the right thing, Ronnie. But from now on, you don't do anything that you'd be ashamed for your mama to know, okay?"

"Yes, ma'am, and I'm sorry. Can I go home now?"

"Yes, you can."

He turned and disappeared around the side of the house.

Carlene and Alma Grace went back inside and shut the door behind them.

"Kitty would have thought finding an unlocked window was perfect timing after the Easter egg thing," Carlene said.

"What are we going to do about this?" Patrice asked.

"Pray," Alma Grace said and dropped her head before either cousin could say a word. "Dear Lord, I'm grateful for this lovely spring day and such beautiful weather that you have given us. I give thanks for my cousin, Carlene, because she took care of me today when she made sure my hair wasn't crapped on, so bless her with something real nice. I'm glad that Dakshani is alive even though I have fussed about not liking him in the past. You have saved Aunt Tansy from heartbreak by giving birds wings so they can escape cats. Now Lord, you have proven to me that vengeance is yours so now I come to you asking that you rain coals of fire down upon Kitty Lovelle's head for being so mean. I realize that we pulled some pranks but you didn't tell us no. I've got a feeling Kitty didn't even ask for your opinion before she put a cat in this house with Dakshani."

Carlene bowed her head at that moment and shut her eyes.

Alma Grace took a deep breath and went on. "Please give Aunt Tansy the grace not to shoot Kitty, but if she does, help her to aim straight and to make it quick so that Kitty does not lie in pain and misery."

Patrice's eyes went shut and she bowed her head.

"And be with the sisters, Mama and Aunt Gigi, at the church tomorrow. Help them to realize that the house of God is not a place to snatch Kitty Lovelle baldheaded or to burn her at the stake out in the yard. Help them to understand that the yard is also consecrated ground and to remember to take her to the field on down south of the property where there are plenty of sticks lyin' around to use for kindling. And Lord, I'm trying to forgive Carlene for doing all this right before Easter but it's pretty tough so I need more strength. In the name of your sweet son, Jesus, I ask these things and beg forgiveness in the same name for the times when I have sinned. Amen."

"Amen," Carlene and Patrice said in unison.

"I'm taking Dakshani home right now and y'all are coming with me. He's not spending another night in this house. We've been invited to Aunt Sugar's for supper but we'll take the bird home first," Patrice said.

"You going to tell her?" Alma Grace asked.

"Yes, ma'am. She'll find out anyway so we might as well tell her right up front. Kitty will brag about it to Violet. She'll brag about it to Beulah who can't keep a damn thing so she'll tell Agnes who will tell Mama. And then I'll catch hell for not being honest. Ronnie isn't the only one that has got a mama that he's afraid of."

Alma Grace giggled. "I didn't know you were afraid of anything."

"Not even the devil scares me like Mama," Patrice said. "We'll clean up later. Help me load up that bird and all his equipment and let's go."

"Why did you even ask if Patrice was going to tell? Don't you want her to?"

Alma Grace set her mouth in a firm line. "Oh, yes. If she didn't tell, I would. I hope she rips every one of those dyed black hairs out of Kitty's head and lets Dakshani peck her eyes out. She deserves it for letting that cat in here."

"Ah, how sweet of you." Patrice smiled.

"Sweet, nothing. That bird almost crapped on my head."

༄

Tansy almost went into heart failure when she saw poor Dakshani's tail but Gigi reminded her that he could have been supper instead of just de-tailed. Even that didn't make her laugh. Patrice had never seen Tansy so mad. If bad auras could be hurled through the air, Kitty had best be ducking and dodging like a pro boxer.

Patrice sincerely hoped that Alma Grace's prayer did not get stuck on the ceiling, and since she'd done such a good job, she didn't even begrudge her going off to the Rib Joint to have a glass of tea with Rick instead of back home with her to help with the cleanup. And she couldn't fuss at Carlene for dashing off to the shop to put the finishing touches on a cute little peignoir set that a woman had ordered to wear on the cruise celebrating her twenty-fifth wedding anniversary.

Still, Patrice hated to face all the havoc that one yellow cat and a bird had created in her house. She'd be cleaning until midnight and then getting up the next day and going back to work to finish up quarterly tax forms.

Doorknob in hand, she was about to push inside and tackle the job when the door flew open and there stood Yancy. The house smelled like chocolate brownies and two wine glasses sat on the counter.

"You and the cousins have a little argument in here?" he asked.

Patrice kicked off her shoes and wrapped her arms around Yancy's neck. "Bless your heart. You've cleaned it all up. I love you, Yancy."

"And made double-fudge brownies with cream cheese icing, and bought a bottle of wine so you could tell me all about it. Have they moved out?"

"No, and we didn't have a fight but you are the most wonderful man on the earth," she said.

He led her to the sofa and sat down beside her.

"Wine first," she said.

"Then the story about how someone had a field day with china and tried to rip your sheer curtains to shreds? I trashed them. They couldn't be repaired," he said.

Patrice told what had happened between bites of three brownies and two glasses of wine, finishing with taking poor old Dakshani home and how her mother had almost fainted when she saw him.

"You are shittin' me," he said when she finished. "We should make sure that Jack Landry knows what has happened. The only thing that'll be left of the church is the bell and that's only because it's made of metal and can't be torn apart. Women are vicious."

Patrice shrugged. "If you could have heard the prayer that Alma Grace sent up, you'd be even more worried. And honey, Alma Grace did show the side of her that wasn't so sweet today. I didn't know she had it in her." She did her best to repeat the prayer word for word.

"Holy hell!"

"I know and I even said 'amen' when she finished."

Yancy drew her close to his side and kissed her forehead.

She snuggled down closer into his arms. "It's been a rough day. Everyone is gone for a while. Let's go to bed."

"Your wish is my command." Yancy grinned.

⌒∽⌒

Rick was sitting in a back booth when Alma Grace arrived at the Rib Joint. Cathy waved from the counter where she worked a couple of nights a week at her second job. Alma Grace wiggled her fingers in that direction and thought about going to the counter and congratulating her on her recent marriage but then her eyes locked with Rick's and the rest of the world disappeared.

He said something but she couldn't hear over the loud jukebox music. She leaned forward and said, "What was that?"

"Let's get out of here. I can't hear my own thoughts."

She nodded.

He ushered her out the door with a hand on her lower back. Heat flowed from his fingertips, through her blouse, and right to her skin. It was so hot that come morning she'd still have a red spot in the shape of his handprint.

"My place is about a mile up the road, on the outskirts of Luella. I've got sweet tea there," he said.

"I'll follow you so I don't have to come back for my car," she told him.

She shushed the crazy voice in her head that said she shouldn't be following him home like a little lost puppy. She reminded it that she was well over the legal age of twenty-one and that Rick was a youth director, for Jesus' sake. He wasn't a serial killer and she was perfectly safe.

The little white house had roses in full bloom twining around the porch posts. The flower beds were well kept and the lawn had been mowed recently. He held the door open for her and the living room was well lit. Serial killers didn't grow lovely roses or turn on the lights.

He shut the door behind her and motioned toward the sofa. "Coffee, tea, hot chocolate, or soda?"

"Tea is fine," she said.

"Make yourself at home."

He poured up two glasses of sweet tea and carried them to the coffee table, sat down beside her, and drew her close to his side. "You are so beautiful, Alma Grace, both inside and outside."

"I bet you say that to all the girls." She smiled up at him.

"Oh, no! I'm pretty shy when it comes to girls. I've dated some but the last couple of years I've devoted myself to the church youth group. I couldn't believe it when you said you'd go with me to a bonfire with a bunch of unruly kids," he said.

"I've devoted myself to the church choir. I couldn't believe it when you…"

He cupped her face in his big hands and lowered his lips to hers. Every single nerve ending in her body tingled. Her hormones set up a whining noise like a buzz saw and her hands wrapped around his neck. Prayer was the last thing on her mind when she moaned and hoped that this was the beginning of something that would end in the bedroom.

It did not end in the bedroom. It ended right there on the sofa with clothing tossed all around them and a fluffy throw with the Lord's prayer printed on it creating a cocoon for them to cuddle inside.

"I'm not…" she whispered.

He put a finger over her lips. "I know, Alma Grace, darlin', I know."

"But," she managed before he kissed her again.

"Can I tell everyone that I know that we are officially dating and you are my girlfriend?" he asked.

"Are you sure?" she asked.

"I've been sure since the first day when I walked into your shop and stuttered and stammered like a teenager," he said.

"I thought that was because you were in a lingerie shop."

"I have five sisters, darlin'. I know what panties and bras look like. I grew up with them in the bathroom, in the laundry, and everywhere I looked. I kept visualizing you in all those pretty things and well…" he said. "So can I tell the whole world we're a couple?"

"Can I tell everyone?" she asked.

"Oh, yes, ma'am."

"Can I tell first?"

"You better hurry because I'm going to start yelling from the housetops in the morning that my girlfriend is Alma Grace Magee. I'm calling my mama first."

"And where does your mama live?" she asked.

"Saint Jo. I was raised over there on a ranch north of town."

"Guess we've got a lot to find out about each other." She snuggled tighter against him.

"And what fun it will be. Dinner tomorrow night?"

"Okay," she murmured as her eyes closed. She hadn't heard a word about divorce, chili, birds, or plastic eggs for the whole evening. God had rained down blessings upon her head for sure.

Carlene came in through the back door, turned on the kitchen light, and made her way to the beading room. The fancy little silver peignoir was almost finished. She just needed to work a few more beads into the Venetian lace border on the hem of the gown. She sat down at the table, picked up where she'd left off, and started to work. As usual, when she worked with her hands, her mind thought about other things.

Aunt Tansy, bless her heart, had been so upset over the bird and then so mad at Kitty that the famous Fannin vein in her head had come nigh to exploding. If adrenaline cured food poisoning, neither the Fannin girls nor their daughters would ever be sick again.

She finished the job at hand, hung the matching gown and robe on a velvet hanger, and turned out the lights, locked the door from the inside, and closed it. She was almost to her car when she realized someone was leaning against it.

"Holy shit! Jack Landry, you just shocked five years off my life," she said. "What are you doing here anyway?"

"I'm here on official business," he said.

"Well, I figured that much since you're in uniform and since…" She clamped her mouth shut before she said "since you haven't called me since that first time."

"I haven't changed my mind about going out with you. I'm being patient even if it isn't easy," Jack said.

She bit her lip to keep from smiling. The divorce wasn't final and she wasn't actually free but that didn't mean that knowing she was attractive to someone didn't make her feel special and good about herself.

"Thank you for that."

"Yancy called me a while ago right before I finished my shift at the station. He told me about the cat. So you are allergic to cats? How about dogs?"

She shook her head. Official business was finding out if she was allergic to dogs?

"Good because I've got a couple of big old golden retrievers living in my backyard and house. We have a pretty good friendship going and I'd hate to have to get rid of them." He grinned.

She backed up a few steps and sat down on the porch step. "Love dogs but not those little yappy things."

He crossed the yard and sat down beside her, carefully keeping a foot between them. "So you reckon there should be police presence at the church tomorrow?"

"Depends on whether Aunt Tansy brings Granny's old sawed-off shotgun."

Jack rubbed his square chin. "You think she might?"

"Depends on whether Mama and Aunt Sugar hide it good enough she can't find it and whether Uncle Alex locks the gun safe. She was pretty damn mad about her bird."

"Kitty shouldn't have done that but I can't let Tansy shoot her even though it seems like the right thing to do. You know that, don't you?"

Carlene could feel sparks hopping between them. How in the hell did a woman leave one man and feel like that about another in less than a month? Alma Grace would say that she was sinning. Patrice would give her some long-winded explanation about the body having sexual needs. Right then, she would rather listen to Patrice.

"I wouldn't want you to get all mad at me if I had to step between them to protect Kitty," Jack said.

"Honestly, I don't think she even knew there was a bird in the house. She used a bedroom window, probably hoping it was my bedroom, and shoved the cat inside through it. The bird was in the living room. It was a mean trick but she didn't set about to get Dakshani eaten or his tail feathers plucked," Carlene said.

"Mama says that Kitty moved in with Lenny. Said she wasn't leaving until he was completely well and that he couldn't go back to the dealership until she said so," Jack chuckled.

Carlene clamped a hand over her mouth but the laughter exploded between her fingers. "That is the best revenge in the world. She'll smother him to death," she said between giggles. Then she got a case of hiccups. "What…about…Bridget?"

"Kitty threw her out. Told her that she didn't have enough sense to take care of Lenny. I'm surprised she didn't get the flu but I did hear through the grapevine that he's got his eye on someone else at the dealership who did get it so he's probably messing around on Bridget already. That bother you, that he's doing that?" Jack asked.

Carlene shook her head.

Jack leaned in like he was going to kiss her and immediately the hiccups stopped. "Well, now I know three things, in addition to the fact that you are beautiful. You've got a lot of sense, you like dogs, and if I act like I'm going to kiss you, it scares the hiccups right out of you."

"It didn't scare me. They just stopped. I'm not scared of anything, Jack Landry, and to answer your question, it should bother me that he's chasing women, shouldn't it? I was so mad and so hurt at the first, but then when I was honest with myself, I figured out that I must have been in denial for a long time. I had to have known, Jack. Down deep inside my heart, I had to have known that he was up to his old tricks. I just didn't want to do anything about it. Sometimes even a cold nest beats no nest at all."

"I understand, Carlene. I really do. I had a relationship not long ago and I wanted her to be the one so bad but my heart said no. So I know where you are coming from. But enough about that. Let's let the past be the past and forget about it. Y'all got a plan for the cook-off? What with your mamas getting sick and Josie going to the hospital, has it thrown a monkey wrench in the works?" Jack asked.

Carlene stood up. "We've got it covered. How'd you get here anyway, Officer Landry?"

"Motorcycle is parked out behind your car. I'm off duty but not out of uniform yet."

"Well, how about that? Don't suppose you'd give me a ride home on it, would you? I'm staying at Patrice's but then I bet you knew that from the grapevine, right?"

"What about your car?"

"I reckon I can ride to work with one of my cousins," she said.

"You sure about this, Miss Carmichael?"

Oh, yes, Carlene was a Carmichael again and she was ready for a motorcycle ride.

"I am sure."

"Okay, then just hop on the back and put your arms around me and I'll take you home, Cinderella."

"I'm not a princess, Jack," she said.

"To me, you've always been a princess. Don't go messin' with my image of you, darlin'."

Chapter 17

THE CHURCH PARKING LOT looked like a used-car dealership when Carlene and Kim pulled their vehicles in side by side. Carlene recognized her mother's car so evidently her dad was letting Gigi drive now. Right beside it was Tansy's Cadillac and then Sugar's Lincoln.

"Looks like we've got lots of help." Kim waved as she got out of her vehicle. "Wait just a minute before you go in. I hear Agnes's old Ford. Let's wait on her to go in with us. She might save your life. After last night they might be waiting for you right inside the door with rocks to stone you to death."

"What did I do?" Carlene asked.

"You are a hussy, a bad one bordering right up there beside a hooker." She lowered her voice and whispered the last word. "You rode down Main Street on the back of Jack Landry's motorcycle. Honey, next week you might be runnin' a whorehouse."

"Holy shit!" Carlene said.

"Hey, I got the news at midnight and I wasn't the first one on the list of who to call if something juicy happens."

Carlene leaned against the van and raised an eyebrow. She dressed conservatively that morning since she had to come to the church: pink slacks topped with a yellow and pink swirled print cotton sweater, yellow platform heels, and a pink silk scarf.

Agnes crawled out of her old Ford and waved. She wore a pair of stretch jeans and an oversized T-shirt with Clawdy's logo on the back. Her red hair hadn't seen a brush that morning but she had applied lipstick that ran into the wrinkles around her mouth.

"Maybe I should just slink in on my knees praying for redemption," Carlene laughed. "I rode less than a mile with him and said good night without even kissing him on the cheek."

"You'll pay hell," Agnes said

"Maybe Agnes can protect us both. I'll be guilty by association just walkin' in with you two renegades." Kim laughed.

Agnes looped her arm in Carlene's and pulled her forward. "I damn sure can. Come on. We're going in with our heads held high. You've signed the papers to divorce that sumbitch, Lenny Joe Lovelle, so if you want to ride on Jack's motorcycle with him, you can do it even if it constipates Kitty. And if she acts up, I'll pull that scarf from around your neck and strangle her with it."

Three tables were set up with the one in the middle holding bags and bags of plastic eggs and small individually wrapped candy pieces. Kitty and her posse of five had already taken up residence at the table closest to the door with the Fannin outlaw sisters sitting at the table at the other end. The line was drawn, not in the sand, but in the middle of the fellowship hall.

Carlene slid into an empty chair beside her mother and Agnes took the seat at the head of the table. Kim sat right beside Carlene.

"Y'all will tell me if they start throwing knives or spears, won't you?" Kim asked.

"Don't worry about them. If I wink, you just dive under the table and don't get in my way," Tansy said.

Isaac came into the fellowship hall from the church, talking as he crossed the room. "Good afternoon, ladies. I'm afraid I couldn't talk the men's Sunday school group into helping you stuff eggs but I did get them to volunteer to help finish spring-cleaning on the grounds. I understand the Fannin sisters have brought a big cooker of chili for us to eat at lunch. Jack Landry will be by in a little while to lend a hand. There's lots of help out in the yard so I thought he and I could keep you supplied with eggs and candy. With our big clumsy hands we wouldn't be much good at filling those little old eggs."

Jack waved from the door and went right to the table, picked up an armload of plastic bags, and delivered them to Carlene's table.

"Feels kind of tense in here," he whispered for her ears only.

His warm breath on her neck made her want to hug more than his back.

"You got that right," she said.

"And these are for you ladies," Isaac said cheerfully as he brought supplies to the other table. "With all this help, we'll be done in no time. Miz Sugar has also provided these cute little stickers to put on the eggs once they are filled to keep them from popping open. As you finish, put them in the paper bags beside your chairs. The guys who do the hiding will have them all ready to go that way."

By noon the center table had been cleared off. All the paper bags were filled with eggs ready to be hidden the next day and there had not been a single word of fraternization between the two tables. The aroma of freshly cut onions, corn chips, and chili filled the fellowship hall as a dozen men filed in the door ready for lunch.

"Guess it's time to start serving," Alma Grace said.

Carlene's insides were jacked up to the boiling point but that had more to do with Jack than it did with the tension in the fellowship hall. Adrenaline and guilt did not make good bed partners. If she had truly loved Lenny, she couldn't be looking at another man with lust in her eyes before the ink was hardly dry on the divorce papers. Yet, she had loved him and she was. It was so confusing that she wanted to throw plastic eggs at the ceiling and watch candy fall like confetti.

She shoved her hands in the pockets of her slacks and wrapped her fingers around a crumpled up ten-dollar bill. Should she give it back to Kitty right there?

No time like the present, her conscience said. *Besides, you're in church. Nothing will happen here other than she'll stutter and stammer and deny that she gave that money to Ronnie.*

"Hey, Kitty," she called out as she rounded the end of the table where Agnes was still sitting. "Ronnie, the little boy next door, asked me to give this back to you."

Carlene laid the bill on the table and Kitty popped up like a jack-in-the-box. She grabbed the bill and shoved it into her purse and turned on Carlene.

"You have the audacity to even speak to me after cheating on my son? You are a…"

"You might want to be careful what you call me considerin' you are in church," Carlene warned.

"I wish that cat had eaten that dumb bird and I hope you get pneumonia from your allergies and die," Kitty hissed.

Gigi's head whipped around. "You are talking to my daughter."

Kitty shook her fist at Gigi. "Well, your daughter was seen with Jack Landry last night, flaunting herself on the back of his motorcycle."

Gigi started across the room. "She's signed the divorce papers. Your son was still married when he was stupid enough to leave his bimbo's under-britches in his briefcase."

Tansy had been talking to Kim when suddenly she looked at Agnes. "What did she just say?"

"She said that Carlene signed the divorce papers," Agnes answered.

Tansy stood up and swept her skirts to one side. "Before that? Did she say she wished that cat had eaten Dakshani?"

A wicked grin stretched the wrinkles around Agnes's mouth so the lipstick looked just right.

Tansy started toward Kitty. "You bitch. I don't care if we are in church. I'm going to pull every one of those dyed black hairs out of your head."

Kitty came out from around the table and met her halfway, bowing up into her face. "Don't you talk like that in front of Isaac."

Carlene wasn't sure whether to hold Sugar back or turn her loose to support her sisters. She had to make a decision quickly because the look on Sugar's face said that Kitty had already gone too far and if she mentioned Jamie's name, she might end up toothless as well as bald.

"Ladies, ladies," Isaac said. "This is the season of resurrection. Forgive. Forget and move on."

Violet took a step toward Kitty and pointed at Agnes. "I'm not in a forgiving mood. Agnes Flynn shouldn't even be here. She hasn't been in this church in months."

Agnes reached down into her bag of eggs, picked one up, and hurled it like a baseball. It hit Violet right between the eyes, bounced once on the table, rolled across the floor, and didn't even break open.

Damn, those were some good stickers, Carlene thought.

Violet instinctively grabbed one of her eggs and launched it at Agnes. Agnes caught it like an outfielder, drew back, and let it fly across the room, binging Violet in the nose that time.

"Agnes Flynn, you have gone too far," Violet screamed.

Agnes took off in a run to meet Violet halfway across the room. "I don't mind going to jail again."

How in the devil did two old women move so fast? Carlene wondered.

Agnes managed to slap Violet once before Tansy, Gigi, Sugar, and Carlene dragged her backward.

Violet had her fists doubled and was flailing at Agnes when Jack and Isaac forced their way into the melee. She landed a right hook in Isaac's eye and a left undercut in Jack's crotch, putting both men on their knees.

"See what you caused?" Violet snapped at Agnes.

Beulah came out from around the table and slapped Violet on the other cheek. "I've put up with a lot from you, Violet Prescott.

But if you've ruined my chances at grandchildren, I will never forgive you."

Kim rushed to Isaac's side. "Darlin', come on with me and I'll get an ice pack for that eye."

"Darlin'?" Floy hollered. "You are dating that hussy? I'll see to it you are fired as soon as the vote comes up."

Carlene knelt beside Jack. "What can I do?"

"Nothing," he huffed. "Just give me a minute."

Isaac managed to get to his feet and threw his arm around Kim. "Yes, we are dating. Yes, she is my girlfriend. I'm going to get this tended to and then we're going to have lunch and you are all going to behave like civilized adults who do not sling insults about firing the preacher."

Everything went so quiet that it was eerie. Finally, Alma Grace dropped her chin to her chest and started to pray. "Father, as we partake of this chili that has been prepared by the future winners of the cook-off, please let us do it gracefully even if we don't like each other. Amen."

Everyone stared at her but no one said a word.

"My cousins and I will serve the chili. Y'all come right on in and enjoy lunch. We're anxious to know what you think of this new recipe. Does it need more chili powder or maybe more beef? We are up for suggestions and little suggestion cards are stacked up beside the chili pot."

Like always, food brought even enemies together, even if there was a separation of the two factions when they sat down to the tables to eat.

Agnes threw off Tansy and Sugar's hands and whispered, "You are all welcome."

"For what?" Tansy asked.

"It was getting out of hand, Tansy Cordell. Another minute and you and Kitty would have been on the floor scratchin' eyeballs and a snatchin' hair. Then Sugar would have jumped in and Gigi was already spittin' mad. So it would have been three against one and even though I didn't give a shit if y'all whupped Kitty Lovelle, I didn't want her hurt and in the hospital." She paused, took a deep breath, and whispered, "She's moved in with Lenny and I think that's the best punishment he can get for his sorry-ass deeds so let's keep her healthy, girls. Hell, I might even take her a pie next week."

"Thank you, Agnes," Carlene said, and she meant it from the heart.

Agnes smiled and whispered to Beulah, "It was two birds in one shot. I was thinkin' about throwing an egg at Violet the whole time I was puttin' candy in them. When she gave me a good reason, I did it. I still got a damn good throwin' arm. I enjoyed that so much that I'm comin' to church here tomorrow just to pester the shit out of Violet. Sorry about what she did to you, Jack. Next time we get into it, you'd do well to get behind me so I can protect you. And Beulah, honey, he's going to have to do more than ride down the street with Carlene to make grandbabies. Now let's get into this chili. I think it needs some more onions and maybe some more chili powder. What do y'all think?"

Alma Grace sat beside her mother and father in the crowded church. The sun was out that morning with not a single cloud in the pale blue sky. The meteorologist had declared it a perfect Easter Sunday with temperatures predicted to hit seventy-five degrees. Not bad unless there were lots and lots of bodies that registered 98.6 on the thermometer. And they were jammed up tight shoulder to shoulder in the church where the air conditioning had gone out during Sunday school.

Windows had been thrown open but there wasn't a breeze to be bought, borrowed, or stolen between the Gulf of Mexico and the

Red River. Alma Grace was glad that she'd bought a cotton sundress with a bolero type sweater for the day and that she hadn't had time to shop for new shoes, so the ones on her feet were broken in.

Violet sat across the aisle from them. Makeup couldn't cover the purple bruise around her eye. Isaac sat on the bench behind the podium with a matching light purple tie and eye. At least it was Easter and they were all the right pastel color, Alma Grace thought.

Agnes was right behind Violet. She winked at Alma Grace when she caught her eye. Lord, those two old women were going to their graves fighting and feuding.

Carlene slid into the pew next to Alma Grace and picked up a cardboard fan from the back of the pew in front of them and started fanning. "What happened to the air conditioning?"

"It's broke. Where's Patrice?"

Carlene fanned wider so the air would catch Alma Grace. "She and Yancy are on the way. He's coming to dinner," she whispered.

"Is Jack coming, too?" Alma Grace

"Hell, no!" Carlene said.

"Shhh," Sugar fussed. "The program is about to begin. Floy is taking her place."

Patrice and Yancy slipped in at the last minute beside Carlene. "Where's Mama and Aunt Gigi?"

Alma Grace leaned around Carlene and pointed to the front. "They're on the front pew so they can make Kitty uncomfortable. She and Lenny both are in the choir this morning."

Isaac took his place behind the podium. "Today we are having our yearly Easter musical program. The Easter committee and the choir have worked very hard on this program. So y'all enjoy it and have a wonderful Easter. The entire offering today will be going to our Easter fund for next year's production. So when the plate is passed, be sure to dig deep into your pockets."

Dig deep in her pockets, her Texas posterior. Alma Grace

had already donated wings and a halo. That's all they'd ever get from her.

Somewhere behind her she heard a noise like ripping cloth. And then off to the side, a bubbly noise that left no doubt there was some major farting going on in church. Thank God the choir was singing loudly or the next one would have rattled the windows. What in the devil was going on?

She caught Patrice's eye and they each clamped a hand over their mouths like little girls trying to keep back the giggles. Then Carlene's face said that the smell had hit her nose and she quickly looked at both her cousins.

"Yesterday's chili," Patrice sighed.

"I'm glad I didn't eat any of it," Alma Grace whispered to Patrice.

"The deacons did and look at the wiggling on their pews behind the pulpit. I bet the choir is getting a noseful…" Patrice giggled.

Violet and another lady jumped up at the same time, right in the middle of the choir's rendition of "Amazing Love" and trotted down the center aisle toward the bathroom.

No one in the congregation smiled as Macy's glittery wings and lovely halo turned her into a floating angel above the congregation. Some were already leaving, hunting for fresh air. The brave souls who hung on had an expression of pure misery on their faces. Heat rises and with it went the aftereffects of spicy chili. Macy gagged, coughed, covered her mouth, and completely lost her voice during her solo.

Alma Grace looked up, winked at the ceiling, and said a fervent, if short, prayer of thanksgiving.

❧

Carlene was in the yard gasping for air when her father draped an arm around her shoulders. "Happy Easter, baby girl. Your basket is on the kitchen table at home. What in the hell was that smell in there anyway. Did a sewer pipe break loose or something?"

"Daddy, I'm twenty-seven years old. That's too old for an Easter basket and the smell was pure old farts. I think it came from the chili our mamas served at the church yesterday," she said.

"I don't care how old you are. You'll always be my little girl even if you don't have blond pigtails and those little fancy white shoes on today. So after the dinner at Sugar's, you'll come by and get it?" Alex asked.

"Chocolate?" she asked.

"One big Easter bunny is chocolate but the fluffy little stuffed bunny isn't." He grinned.

"Solid or hollow?"

"That hollow shit ain't real chocolate," he said.

Gigi popped him on the arm. "Don't say bad words in church."

"Well, your mamas turned the whole Easter program into a fart machine and it smelled like shit in there so I don't see that saying a few bad words is so wrong. So that's why Macy couldn't finish her song. This is the best Easter ever!"

He squeezed Carlene's shoulders. "See you at Sugar and Jamie's. Oh, and just so you know. Your mama invited Agnes and Beulah. And Sugar felt sorry for Jack and Isaac so she invited them. And Alma Grace invited Kim. So it's turned into a big party."

Carlene swallowed hard. "God…"

"…is good." Alex's grin got even bigger. "Drive safe now. Lord, it'll be good to get out of this damned hot church and get this tie off. It would have been a good day for Isaac to preach on hell bein' seven times hotter than earth or about the stink when God sent down the plagues."

Alma Grace looped her arm in Carlene's and dragged her off toward a side exit. "I don't need to shake hands with Isaac. Let's get out of here. I was feeling pretty angry that everything went so well, then the chili hit bottom and I found something to be downright happy about."

"Alma Grace!"

"Well, I did."

⚬⚬

Patrice propped her feet on a chaise lounge on the patio where dinner had been served buffet style with all the traditional Southern foods, starting with baked ham and candied yams. Tulip centerpieces blooming in pastel-colored pots were on the center of the tables covered with pink, yellow, and blue plaid cloths. It was all very much in tune with the Easter holiday and now the guys, including Yancy, had all followed Uncle Jamie out to the horse stables to look at a new colt born just that morning.

"Got to admit when that motorcycle pulled up in my driveway last night, I figured it was Alma Grace. I ran to the window and peeked out but be damned if it wasn't Carlene. Y'all want to know what happened?" Agnes asked.

Gigi set her bottle of beer on the table. "I'm listening."

"Mama!" Carlene exclaimed.

Beulah blushed.

Agnes patted her hand. "Don't go havin' a heart attack. They didn't make grandbabies even though after the way Violet tried to un-man him, it might have been a good idea."

"Jack walked her to the door. I had to hustle to get to the living room window to see what happened next," Patrice said.

"And?" Tansy asked.

"He slowly brought her hand to his lips, kissed her fingertips, and left. It was the most romantic thing ever." Patrice sighed.

Beulah changed the subject. "Is Violet invited out here today?"

"The whole town is invited," Sugar said. "It's a glorious Easter and we will put away our differences so the little ones can all hunt their eggs."

"Speak for yourself," Agnes said.

"Can I grow up and be just like you?" Patrice asked.

"You sure can, honey."

"Agnes Flynn, I'm mad at you," Beulah said.

"What the hell for?" Agnes asked. "I got you the right to hit Violet. Why should you be mad at me?"

"It's not fair that you get a grandbaby and I don't," Beulah said.

"It's not really my grandbaby since Cathy is my niece, not my daughter. And if you'd gotten started when you were twenty instead of waiting until you were almost forty to have Jack, you might have a dozen by now," Agnes told her.

Beulah worried about everything and everyone so Patrice was surprised when she drew her eyes down at Agnes.

"I wish I had and I wish I'd had five or six kids instead of one. You girls pay attention to me. You're all looking thirty in the eye. Believe me, it'll be here before you know it. It's time for you to settle down and have babies. You'll regret it when you are my age and don't even have grandchildren," Beulah said.

"You listenin' to her?" Yancy bent over and kissed Patrice upside down.

"Yes, I am. Are you?" she answered.

Yancy kissed her again. "The guys have arrived and they're getting ready to hide eggs. You sweet ladies just sit right here and we'll do this job. Jamie says to tell Sugar that the caterers have the refreshment tables all ready. Y'all look like a picture from a Southern magazine all sitting around drinkin' lemonade."

Gigi held up her beer bottle. "Darlin', this is not lemonade."

"And it's not five o'clock but my lemonade has a little kick to it. If you'd like some, it's in the green pitcher," Tansy said.

⁂

Folks began arriving in droves one thirty. Carlene had never seen such a turnout to an Easter egg hunt in her entire life. The whole yard and gardens behind Sugar's house really did look like a picture from a Southern magazine. Women had tossed piecework quilts down around the edge of the hunting field and the elderly were sitting in lawn chairs.

"Think I could hit Violet with an egg from here? I don't know why she came. She doesn't have any little kids. That weird son of hers and his new wife have told her that they aren't planning on a family," Agnes whispered.

Josie pulled up a chair next to Carlene. "That was a fine dinner, Miz Sugar. I'm getting my appetite back. How about y'all?"

Gigi held up her beer. "Not much for food but Coors sure does taste good. Would you look at that?"

"Well, y'all did put it in the paper that the whole community was invited," Josie said.

Kitty threw out a quilt about ten yards from the patio for her and Lenny. Bridget joined them but Macy's quilt was only six feet away. Bridget couldn't keep her hands off Lenny; Macy couldn't keep her eyes off Lenny. Poor man had two women vying for his attention and his mama living with him. It must be pure hell. Agnes was right. That was the best punishment ever. Maybe Carlene would make her a pie and take it to the house, too.

"I can't believe she is here," Gigi gasped. "And Lenny? Lord, we had to practically pay him to come to anything the family had when y'all were married and now he's showing up?"

Jack pulled up a chair and sat down beside Carlene. "I got my eggs all hid. It looks like a plastic factory exploded out there. The dentist business is going to be booming."

"Better dentists than some of them dying with botulism," Sugar said.

"Salmonella," Agnes told her. "Botulism is what they get from green beans that haven't been cooked right."

"You think Kitty would like a green bean casserole?" Tansy asked.

Jamie's big booming voice came through a bullhorn. "Okay,

kids. It's one minute until I shoot this gun. Get ready now. Don't cross the line until you hear the shot and then get after it. My advice is to take it slow and easy and not run. Oh, my goodness, would you look at that? The Easter bunny is here!"

"Where is Yancy?" Patrice asked.

Jack pointed. "Costume fit him. Did y'all really think we were looking at a colt? Jamie said whoever looked best in the costume had to wear it."

A giggle escaped from behind the hand that Carlene had clamped over her mouth. "You're kidding me!"

"He must love you a lot, Patrice," Jack said.

The Easter bunny was pink with a big head and pink ears. He carried an oversized pink basket filled with little chocolate bunnies and he hopped up and down the line dropping one in each basket.

"You better latch on to that man," Tansy said. "Look at the way Macy has turned her attention from Lenny to him."

Alma Grace patted Patrice on the arm. "We'll double team her if she starts flirting with your man."

Jack leaned over and whispered to Carlene. "If it makes you nervous for me to be here, with Lenny right there and all, I'll go up there with your dad and the guys."

Carlene reached over and laced her fingers with his. "I'm just fine. I might need you to keep Agnes and Violet out of trouble. Or Aunt Tansy and Kitty."

"I'll do what I can if Tansy and Kitty get into it but, darlin', I'm lightin' a shuck out of here if Agnes and Violet do. Those two can fight until one of them is dead before I step in again," he said.

Agnes cocked her head to one side. "Did I hear my name over there?"

"Yes, ma'am. I said if you and Violet have a little altercation, I'm going to start runnin' and I ain't stoppin' until I'm safe in my jailhouse," Jack said.

"Smart man, Carlene. You'd do well to make Beulah some grandbabies with him," Agnes said.

Beulah rolled her eyes and threw up her pudgy hands. "Agnes Flynn!"

Agnes shrugged toward Beulah. "Honey, welcome to the world of being old and sayin' what you think. It feels real good."

The Easter bunny finished giving the kids the candy and hopped over to the patio. He pulled an envelope from his basket and handed it to Sugar. "Found this in the bottom with your name on it."

She carefully opened it and read the note: "Dear Miz Sugar, this is a donation for the Red-Hot Bloomers Team and a thank-you for a lovely party today. My brother is on the Hellfire Team and he gives me grief about women never being able to make chili like he can. Next year I'm proving him wrong and want to thank you for paving the way for us girls."

Sugar tucked the money into her pocket along with the note. She'd share it with her sisters, later, but right then she wanted to watch the children pick up all those lovely plastic eggs.

⟳

Dusk was setting when Patrice kissed Yancy good night on the front porch. "You made a cute Easter bunny."

"Did you want to pull my ears or my tail?" he asked.

"Oh, honey, I wanted to tear that costume right off you and pull something else altogether," she said.

"Then I'll make arrangements to rent it sometime. I love you, Patrice. Today was fun. I told Jamie that I'd be the bunny again next year. Next up on the agenda is the cook-off. You won't be too disappointed if you don't win, will you? That chili your mamas brewed up was some wicked stuff." He strung kisses down her neck, her shoulder, and all the way to her fingertips.

She watched him drive away until the taillights disappeared, then grabbed the doorknob only to have it swing open from the inside. Carlene handed her a glass of sweet tea and motioned her toward the sofa.

"Let's talk chili cook-off now that Easter is done," she said.

"But shouldn't Alma Grace be here?"

"She doesn't deserve it. Didn't you see the way she's been all happy for the first time in a year and not once today did she offer to pray, not that I'd have stopped her after those last two prayers. God, that was beautiful," Carlene said.

Patrice set her glass down on the end table and threw her head back on the sofa. "That witch is having sex, isn't she? She's the religious one of us and she gets to have sex today? What's wrong with this picture?"

"Evidently, God loves her more than us."

"How long has it been for you?" Patrice asked.

"Three months before I left so right at four months."

"Three months. Shit! What was going on?"

Carlene took a deep breath. "I thought it was because I'd gained ten pounds and was totally unattractive to him. I made new lingerie and paraded in front of him in it. I asked him outright finally and he said that he'd been so busy that he was tired."

"Well, that was the God's gospel truth. He was too busy banging other women," Patrice said.

"I'll always wonder if it was my size. Both Bridget and Macy are little women."

"Did you not see the way Jack looks at you? Honey, your size don't have a damn thing to do with it. Lenny likes them small so he can feel big."

Carlene didn't say anything for a while and then she said, "Thank you."

"Are you crying?"

Carlene dropped her head into her hands. "Kitty hated me

because I'm a big girl. Beulah isn't going to like me because I'm divorced and run a panty shop."

"Who gives a shit?" Patrice asked.

Carlene's tears dried up, and she smiled.

"What are you thinking about?"

"What Agnes said, but right now I'm changing the subject and we're talking about the chili cook-off," Carlene said.

"Don't you dare tell me you're thinkin' of pulling out of it."

"Hell, no! Aunt Sugar told me that letter Yancy handed her was from yet another woman who wants to have a team next year. We've really started something. I'm just hoping we can make the best chili in the whole state," Carlene said.

"Honey, it's not all the chili. It's the package it comes in. Our mamas have taken fried chicken to lots and lots of funerals but they took it out of the box from the KFC store and put it on a fancy platter. And folks thought it was the best damn chicken in the world. They're all three professionals at what they do. Have some faith," Patrice said.

"Now you sound like Alma Grace," Carlene told her.

Patrice threw a pillow at her. "That little shit! Don't bring up her name. She's over at Rick's getting laid and we're talking about chili!"

Chapter 18

TWO WEEKS LATER THE mamas were still perfecting their chili recipe and sending it up to the soup kitchen in Sherman. They didn't get many suggestion cards but Isaac assured them that the homeless folks loved every variation they came up with.

Dakshani had a new tail feather and Tansy declared it a family holiday. The yellow cat with the rhinestone tooth jewelry was last seen sitting on Lenny's front porch with a can of freshly opened food in front of him. Patrice swore with a grin on her face that she had no idea how he got there.

Carlene could hardly believe that a month had passed since she signed the divorce papers. One more and it would be finalized. Thirty days after that, Lenny would be free to remarry.

Alma Grace looked perfectly miserable when she sat down across the table from Carlene that morning. Josie was working on a white peignoir with fluffy white boa feathers around the edge of the dressing robe and her sewing machine didn't even slow down. Carlene was busy drawing an intricate W initial on a black and hot-pink corset and didn't look up until Alma Grace sighed the third time.

"Okay." Carlene laid the garment down.

Josie took her foot off the pedal and the sewing machine stopped.

"Mama wants me to move back in my little house on the estate. She misses our morning devotionals and having me around," Alma Grace said.

"It is your home and it's only another week until the cook-off when Patrice is going to boot you out of her house anyway," Josie said.

"Did I hear my name?" Patrice asked from the foyer.

Alma Grace motioned with a backward wave. "Come on in. It concerns you, too."

"What?" Patrice leaned on the doorjamb.

"Aunt Sugar wants her to move home," Carlene said.

"And I don't want to."

"Rick?" Josie asked. "They've met him, right?'

"We've been busy with the church group on Sunday and I work days and he works different shifts so…" She shrugged.

Josie mumbled something under her breath in Spanish and Alma Grace looked at Patrice for translation.

"I couldn't hear her," Patrice said.

"I said that you're afraid she'll know you are spending every free minute in bed with Rick. And that you'd rather be having sex with him than prayin' with your mama," Josie said.

Alma Grace sighed again. "I know it's not right but I'm bein' truthful."

"You can buy a house in town or you could just move in with Rick. He's got a house," Patrice said.

Two spots of crimson dotted Alma Grace's face. "Mama would die if I moved in with him and it wouldn't be a good example for the youth group and…can I please take one of the rooms upstairs? You'll be moving back into one pretty soon, Carlene. Patrice really will want us to leave after the cook-off so she and Yancy…well, you know. She's been patient but after all we are interfering with her life. Our mamas left furniture up there so it would be an easy move for both of us."

"No men in the house after closing hours. Gossip is one thing but knowing without a doubt is another." Josie laid down the rules.

Patrice nodded. "Amen. Your boyfriends can pick you up at

the back door or at the front door. You can stay out as late as you want, come and go as you please. We've proven that gossip is good for business."

Alma Grace frowned. "Said from the woman who jumps in the bed with her boyfriend every chance she gets."

"In my house. In his house. In the barn. But not in my office at Bless My Bloomers," Patrice said.

"I don't have a problem with that rule. I'm not planning on taking anyone to bed until my divorce is final and I damn sure wouldn't do it at the shop," Carlene said.

They all looked at Josie.

She shrugged. "That's all. I spent a week with my kids and I learned right quick that I do not want to lose my job because that would mean I'd have to move in with them. So I'm going to protect the business."

The sewing machine began to purr again.

Carlene picked up her tailor's chalk.

Patrice went back to the office.

Alma Grace pushed back her chair. "I'm moving in tonight and telling mama that I'm not coming back to the estate."

Carlene said, "But remember we're meeting at my mama's house every night this week to make batches of chili. Bring your secret ingredient. They've got the basic recipe down to a fine art now, they said. I just hope the hospitals haven't had too many homeless in there with food poisoning."

"Rick is working the night shift until Saturday so we've only got tonight and then we'll be apart for a week anyway," Alma Grace said.

❧

Gigi left her car at home and drove Alex's ten-year-old work truck out of town that Monday morning. She wore a scarf over her light-colored hair, jeans, boots, and a faded chambray shirt that she left hanging on the outside of her jeans. She left her Texas Longhorn jewelry at home and applied very little makeup. Hopefully anyone seeing her leave town would think she was the wife of one of the hired hands.

She paid particular attention to any cemeteries she passed on the way. A flicker of red when the warm breezes blew but for the most part she couldn't even see the Confederate flags that had been put on the graves the week before. It was a shame, as Tansy said, that they weren't bigger so they'd catch everyone's eye and the holiday would be remembered.

The next generation couldn't be expected to carry the banner of Confederate history and even Texas history with pride when all they had to work with was those little bitty faded things. Oh, yes, she was definitely crawling on the soapbox with her sister and things were going to change next year. She'd see to it if she had to donate the money for bigger flags from her own charity account.

She could have gotten what she needed in Sherman but Gigi Carmichael wasn't taking any chances, not when she needed so much. Not when her daughter's reputation and happiness were on the line. Not when she could teach Lenny Lovelle not to mess with a Carmichael or a Fannin. She'd gladly drive the extra miles to McKinney in a truck with no heater or air conditioner. At least it wasn't raining and there wasn't even the faintest hint of a tornado boiling up to the southwest. It was actually a very pleasant day with the windows rolled down, and the radio worked just fine.

She turned up the volume until the folks in Fort Worth could have heard the country music playing on her favorite radio station. She tapped her fingers on the steering wheel as Alan Jackson sang, "Livin' on Love." The lyrics said that it sounds simple but love could walk through fire without blinkin'. Well, her daughter had walked through fire tryin' to live on love and it hadn't worked. But there was always next time and Jack Landry would make a better father to her grandchildren than Lenny Lovelle. She could see Carlene and Jack in a porch swing when they were old just like Alan sang about and she would damn sure do her part to start the process right after the chili cook-off.

"Shit, I'm seeing visions like Tansy." She giggled.

Speaking of Tansy, her sister had better be creating a big diversion that would have the whole town of Cadillac gossiping because if anyone found out where she got her chili recipe Lenny would do his damnedest to get them thrown out of the contest.

❧

Tansy had driven a Cadillac ever since Patrice was born. Jamie bought her a brand-new white one to bring the baby home from the hospital in and it was still in pristine condition parked in her garage. When Patrice had her first baby, hopefully with Yancy and in the near future, she would inherit the car to use to bring Tansy's first grandbaby home.

That day she drove a brand-new bright-red Caddy with a vanity plate that read TANSY-20. It had nothing to do with her age. That was simply how many brand-spanking-new vehicles she'd driven off the Cadillac car lot in Sherman. She never had done business with Lenny's place and now she was damn glad she hadn't.

As she parked next to the curb in front of Lenny's house, she got mad all over again. Kitty Lovelle was eating from that fancy set of china she'd bought her niece for her wedding gift and using the sterling cutlery that Sugar had bought. That put even more spring in her step as she stomped up to the door and rang the bell.

Kitty took long enough to get from wherever the hell she was that the anger had time to simmer a little longer. When she opened the door, Tansy was taken aback for just a minute.

The woman was green. Not with envy, but really green. Green fluffy terry flip-flops, green terry robe, green towel turban-style around her head, and green on her face.

"What in the hell are you doing here?" Kitty hissed.

"Why in the hell do you look like that?" Tansy asked.

Kitty tilted her chin up slightly.

Shit! She was green all the way to her boobs!

"Well?" Tansy asked.

"It's not a bit of your business but I have a masseur who makes house calls and also does mani-pedis. I've just gotten my mask on so he can remove it during my face massage. I wouldn't have even opened the door but I thought it was him. You've got to the count of five to state your reason for disturbing me. One."

Tansy stuck her foot in the door so that it couldn't be shut.

"Two."

"I'm here for the rest of my bird's leash. I paid a fortune for it and I'm taking it back," Tansy said.

Sugar, darlin', I will never doubt the power of your prayers again. You said that you would pray that I'd catch her at her worst and be damned if it hasn't happened.

"I don't know what you are talking about," Kitty said.

A big yellow cat sashayed across the floor and rubbed around her ankles.

Kitty pushed at it with her toe. "Go back to your room, OJ."

"As in Simpson."

Kitty reached down and picked the cat up. "As in Orange Juice."

Tansy could see the rhinestones dangling out the side of his mouth. "That's the sorry bastard who tried to eat my bird and that's the rest of my leash. You take it out or I will." She removed a set of needle-nose pliers from her purse and took a step forward.

"Don't you touch my cat with those things," Kitty screamed. "Get off my property or I'll call the police right now."

Yes, ma'am, Sugar, you do have a direct line to heaven. This is working great!

"Give me that miserable cat. I'm getting my leash back," Tansy yelled as she grabbed for the cat.

OJ let out a high-pitched meow that rivaled both the women's shrill screaming. He clawed Kitty on the back of the hand and darted out the door where he dived under a rosebush and growled like a mountain lion.

"Come here." Tansy took off after him. "You are as stupid as Lenny. I'm not afraid of you. I'll yank every one of your teeth out."

That brought Kitty outside like a shot, chasing after Tansy. "Don't you talk about my son like that. The only stupid thing he did was marry your fat niece."

Tansy stopped chasing the cat and turned around so quick that Kitty ran into her, bounced backward a step, and fell flat on her ass on the green lawn.

"What did you say?" Tansy asked.

"I said he married your fat niece," Kitty yelled.

Tansy put a foot on Kitty's thigh and clicked the pliers toward her face. "You will regret saying that. Since I can't catch that sumbitch cat, I'll just take a couple of your miserable teeth."

"Help! Help! Call the police," Kitty screamed. "This woman is trying to kill me."

Keep prayin', Sugar. God is listenin'.

The masseur's van drove up and the hunky man behind the wheel pulled out his cell phone on his way to break up the fight. Tansy waited until he was on the way and grabbed Kitty by the shoulders and rolled with her.

"Help! Get off me, you bitch. I just wanted my leash back. God Almighty, why are you trying to kill me?" Tansy yelled.

Kitty pushed away from her and stood up. She started for the house but had only gone two steps when Tansy reached out, grabbed her by the ankles, and brought her down again. Sirens brought every neighbor on the block out of their houses. Jack bailed out of the police car. And that's when the sprinkling system came on, soaking Kitty's terry robe and shoes. She stopped dead, stomped her foot, and screamed.

"I am going to kill you, Tansy!"

"What is going on here?" Jack asked. "I got a call there was a fight and I was only a block away."

Tansy tossed the pliers under the rosebush, hitting the cat on the tail, and it ran back in the house. She jogged away from the sprinklers. Getting wet was a small price to pay and besides she looked a helluva lot better in her wet jeans and shirt than Kitty did with green beauty mask goop running down her face.

"She's crazy, Jack. She said she was going to kill me. You heard her. I just came over here to get my bird's leash out of her cat's mouth and she chased me outside and threatened me."

"She threatened to pull my teeth out with those damned pliers," Kitty wailed.

Tansy held up both hands. "What pliers? Take her to jail. She's ruined my clothes and she attacked me."

"She said she was going to pull Lenny's cat's teeth out to get that stupid leash. He loves that cat and he never could have one when his fat wife lived here," Kitty yelled. "And then she attacked me. All I did was call Carlene fat. That's my opinion. It's not against the law to state my opinion and I'm not going to jail."

"You're both coming to jail with me right now. We can straighten this out without an audience," Jack said.

"But my masseur?" Kitty wailed.

"He can come back another time. Are you getting into the car without cuffs or do I need to bring them out?" Jack asked.

"I'm not sitting in the backseat with her. She might scratch my eyes out," Tansy said.

"Put her in the front seat, Jack. She's got pliers somewhere on her. I swear to God she does," Kitty told him.

Patrice was working on an order when she got the call from Jack. At first she thought it was a prank but when he assured her that her mother was in a jail cell right next to Kitty Lovelle, she grabbed her purse and ran out of the shop.

It was only three blocks to the jail but she drove like she only had five seconds to get there. Jack wouldn't tell her a thing except that she needed to come get her mother and that Lenny was on his way from Sherman to do the same. They'd both been charged with disturbing the peace, and if she wanted to pay the fine, she could take Tansy home.

Jack was sitting behind his desk, a big grin on his face. "Some days, ladies, this job is a hoot."

Patrice shook her head in disbelief. "Daddy is going to pitch a fit. Why didn't you call him instead of me?"

"She said to call you. Come with me. I'm not sayin' another word. I want to see the look on your face." Jack chuckled.

Tansy was sitting on a bed in a jail cell filing her nails, her hair in limp strands, her clothing wet and plastered to her hide. She stuck her tongue out at Kitty Lovelle, sitting in the next cell. "See I told you my child loves me more than yours loves you. If he lets you sit in jail, he can get on with his stupid womanizing. I bet he's screwing Macy right now, maybe even in your bed."

"Don't you call my son stupid and he's seeing Bridget, not Macy," Kitty said.

Patrice turned to look at Kitty and was instantly struck mute.

Was that really Kitty Lovelle or had the Jolly Green Giant produced an offspring in Cadillac, Texas?

"Told you," Jack said. "Are you willing to pay your mama's fine?"

Patrice nodded.

"I sure will. This is priceless."

Jack unlocked the cell door. "Tansy Magee, I'm going to release you but only if you promise you'll stay away from Kitty's house."

"Yes, sir." Tansy smiled.

"And Lenny's house," Jack went on.

The smile faded. "I want my leash back and her cat has it."

"Kitty?" Jack said. "You are going to get that leash out of that cat's teeth and bring it to me. I will give it to Tansy."

Kitty brushed blades of grass from her robe. "It will fall out on its own sometime when's he's eating."

Tansy marched out of the open jail cell. "And what if he swallows it? You can just pay me for a new leash. I'll expect one hundred twenty-nine dollars in the mail next week. I won't make you pay the tax or shipping costs."

Kitty rattled the door. "It'll be a cold day in hell when I send you a thin dime and your Carlene is still fat."

The grin faded from Jack's face and his jaws worked like he was chewing gun. He led the way back to his office and sat down behind his desk.

"I'm sorry she keeps sayin' that about Carlene," he said softly.

"How much?" Tansy opened her purse.

"Not one dime if you don't tell Gigi what she said," he whispered.

"My lips are sealed," Patrice said.

Tansy drew her eyes down in a serious frown. "I'll gladly pay double what the fine is if you'll give me five minutes in that cell with her. She'll think fat when I get done."

Lenny rushed into the office and stared at Tansy glaring at him while Patrice giggled. "What in the hell is going on here, Jack? Are you declaring war on us because of Carlene—and what in the hell is so funny anyway?"

"Your mama is green." Patrice's giggles turned into guffaws.

Jack shrugged. "Your mother attacked Tansy Magee. You can take her home if you want to pay the fine for disturbing the peace."

Jack pulled out his wallet. "How much?"

"One hundred and twenty-nine dollars," Jack said with a straight face.

"But if you let her sit in the cell, you can have an evening free to entertain your women," Patrice whispered. "I'd think about if I was you."

Lenny hesitated for only a second before he pulled out his wallet and started counting bills.

ᘏᐧᘏ

Gigi parked the truck as close to the kitchen door as she could and hurried inside. She removed the scarf and sunglasses and tossed them on the cabinet. Tansy handed her a glass of sweet tea and Sugar pushed a platter of cookies her way.

"Okay, Tansy, tell me if we've had a big enough diversion to keep anyone from trying to figure out our secret recipe."

Tansy giggled. "I guaran-damn-tee that I started enough gossip to put our chili on the back burner for the whole week. You could have bought all that stuff in Walmart at Sherman and talked to Violet on the way out, it worked so well. I even managed to sneak a picture with my cell phone. Jack didn't make me give up my purse when he put me in the cell."

"Jail. Dear God, what did you do?" Gigi asked.

"I had a little scuffle with Kitty. She shouldn't have put that damn cat in the house with my precious Dakshani," Tansy said.

"Help me get this stuff in the house and under lock and key and then tell me the whole story. Did you already tell Sugar?" Gigi asked.

"No," Sugar pouted. "She said that she was only telling it one time and I've been on pins and needles waiting for you to get home."

They'd barely gotten the food inside and put into the pantry when they heard the rattle of an old truck stopping outside, a knock on the back door, and Agnes yelling as she entered the kitchen. "I figured y'all would be here together. I came to celebrate with you."

"Celebrate what?" Gigi asked.

"Did you tell them?" Agnes looked over at Tansy.

Tansy smiled. "What did you hear?"

Agnes picked up a cookie. "That you've been in jail for fightin' with Kitty Lovelle. Beulah is wringin' at her hanky because Jack likes Carlene and Lenny might do something crazy."

Gigi hiked a hip on a bar stool and asked, "Now why would Jack do anything? This is Tansy and Kitty's fight."

"I heard the fight was over that damn cat that almost ate Tansy's bird and that Tansy called Lenny stupid and then Kitty called Carlene fat and they really got into it," Agnes said. "Anyway Beulah is afraid that Jack will wind up losing his job."

"Jack is a smart man and the town is lucky to have him as chief of police," Gigi said. "If he loses that job, Jamie will make him head of security for the entire estate."

Agnes laughed. "Can I tell people that?"

"Not this week, darlin'. Wait until after the cook-off," Gigi said.

Tansy made her way to the television, plugged her phone into an apparatus on the front, poked a few buttons, and turned around.

"You might want to be sitting down for this," she said.

Agnes claimed a rocking chair, Sugar sat on the arm of the sofa, and Gigi curled up on the far end of the sofa.

Tansy held the control in her hand and nodded at Sugar. "Your praying helped."

"Of course it does. Now show us the pictures," Sugar said.

"You sure that it's big enough that the whole town is talking about it?" Gigi asked.

"No one gives a shit what the Fannin girls are doing today or what they are buying. The whole town is talking green and it's not about the environment, either."

She hit a button and there on a fifty-inch screen, bigger than life was Kitty in living green color, sitting in a jail cell.

Sugar gasped. "I'd die if I got caught like that. Bless her heart!"

Gigi roared so hard that she got a coughing fit. "We could be brewing moonshine out here and we wouldn't even make the back page of the gossip vine. You did send it to Patrice, didn't you?"

Tansy tilted her head to the right and then to the left. "It was even better when she had the green towel all done up like a turban. And yes, I sent it to Patrice but I goofed and hit the send all button and I'm afraid everyone on my mailing list got it. Oops!" Tansy said sweetly.

"It don't get no better than that. Serves her right for calling Carlene fat. Kitty isn't off the hook yet," Gigi said.

The big yellow cat ran down the stairs when Lenny opened the door. It rubbed around his legs and purred, the rhinestones hanging out of its mouth like a lip ring on a rock star. He loved cats and had been the one who brought him in the house when he found him on the front porch. Now he wished he'd taken the thing back to the shelter where his mother had found him.

Kitty had stomped out of the jail with no sign of an injury but now she limped up the sidewalk.

"You okay, Mama?" Lenny asked.

"I'll be fine, honey. Don't you worry your head about me. You're just gettin' over the flu and trying to work. I swear, a lesser man would have still been laid up in bed. You just go on back to work. Me and OJ will hold the place down. I'm going to take a shower and rest the whole afternoon and then I've got a committee meeting tonight at Violet's," she said weakly.

He hurried back outside, cupped her elbow, and led her into the house. "I'm not going to let you drive anywhere tonight. You are much too nervous and you could hurt yourself. I'm sending Bridget to spend the rest of the afternoon with you. She can take you to your meeting and stay with you until I get home this evening. I've got some after-work appointments so I'm going to be late."

"That is so sweet of you, darlin'. I've been wrong about Bridget. If you love her, then I'll be nice to her. She can be my guest tonight at the meeting," Kitty said. "Now you get on back to work. They have such a hard time runnin' that place without you."

"Yes, ma'am." Lenny dropped a kiss on her forehead. "I'll see you late this evening. What time will you be home?"

"About nine," Kitty answered.

"I'll be home by ten. Keep Bridget here with you, okay?"

"Don't you worry about me, honey. She and I'll be fine. I might even get out the family picture album and show her your baby pictures. You were so cute and grew up so handsome." Kitty smiled through the splotchy green goop.

Lenny brushed a few wilted blades of grass from the passenger's seat of his car when he got inside. He'd barely cleared the driveway when he hit the speaker button on his phone and called Bridget's number.

"Hello, darlin'. Is everything all right?" she asked.

"Oh, Bridget. I'm so worried about my mother. This is terrible on her nerves. I've got late appointments tonight and…" He let the sentence hang.

"What can I do?" she asked.

"Nothing, darlin'. It's just that I hated to leave her alone when she is so torn up and she has a meeting tonight. And I've told you how she is about her club thing. If she doesn't go, the sky will fall and the whole world will end." He chuckled.

"I really didn't like her when she moved in and kicked me out but I'm changing my mind. I'm sure I'll feel the same when we have our son. It's just a mother's love for her child that makes her so possessive," Bridget said.

"Thank you. You'll never know what that means to me, just hearing you say those words," Lenny told her.

"Since you've got late appointments, why don't I go sit with her? I didn't take a lunch break so I could leave now," Bridget offered.

Lenny's smile showed gorgeous, even white teeth. His eyes twinkled and he winked at himself in the rearview mirror. "Oh, honey, I couldn't ask that of you, not the way that she treated you when she moved into the house. I mean, kicking you out like you were sinning and telling you that you weren't taking care of me right. No, no! That's just too much for you to do."

"I insist," she said. "Your poor mother needs me. I heard how Tansy treated her. She needs a woman to talk to and to understand how mortifying it was to be put in jail in her robe."

"Well, it's so hard for me to say no to you. Are you sure?"

"Never been surer in my life. I'll finish these papers I'm working on right now and be gone when you get here. That way she won't have to be alone very long. And you are so right. She doesn't need to be driving herself in her condition."

"I can never thank you enough," he said. "But I'll damn sure try. Tomorrow is lunch at the Hampton hotel in Denison. You bring the cheese and I'll pick up the wine and we'll take a two-hour lunch in our favorite room."

Bridget giggled. "The one with the beach chair on the picture beside the door."

"That's the one. Our special room. You can pick up the key for Janie Smith at the desk," Lenny said.

"I can't wait."

Lenny counted to twenty very slowly and then poked the familiar buttons to Macy's phone. She answered on the second ring.

"Hello, darlin'. Are we clear for tonight?" Macy asked.

"Meet me at the Hampton in Denison at five thirty. I'll pick up takeout and a six-pack of beer. You just bring your sexy self. There will be a key for Janie Smith at the desk. I'll be waiting."

"All evening?" Macy asked.

"Until nine thirty. I need to be home at ten. Mother has had a terrible day and I couldn't be out a minute later."

"Poor darlin'. I heard what happened in Cadillac. You are such a darlin' for taking care of your sweet mama," Macy said.

Lenny did a mental happy dance. "Thank you. I just wish she wasn't so attached to Bridget but right now in her frail state of mind, I just can't break up with Bridget or she'd go off the deep end."

"The right time will come along," Macy said. "See you in an hour then at our special little Hampton room with the beach chair picture on the wall beside the door."

"And we'll pretend we're lyin' naked on the beach, eating fried chicken and drinkin' beer," he said smoothly.

❧

Rick lugged several suitcases to the back door of the shop. Alma Grace pulled them inside, pulled the door shut, and laced her fingers in his. He led her back to his truck and opened the passenger door for her. Before he buckled up, he reached across the seat and brushed a kiss across her lips.

"I still can't believe that you are dating me. I'm the luckiest man alive. I hate it when you leave me in the middle of the night. I know you can't be seen leaving my house at daybreak but what if we got a hotel room tonight? I'll be on night duty for the rest of the week and you're going to be tied up with the chili cook-off. Let's sleep together tonight. I want to wake up with you in my arms tomorrow morning," Rick said.

"Sleep?" Alma Grace asked.

He smiled. "After we do other things." He fastened his seat belt.

"I'll get you home in time for work tomorrow, I promise. I just want to hold you all night in my arms."

"I didn't bring an overnight bag," she said.

"We don't need anything but each other."

"Then let's do it," she said.

∽৵৹

A few hours later she awoke with a start. It took a few seconds to get her bearings and realize she was in a hotel, not her bedroom at Patrice's house. Rick was sleeping right next to her. He looked so peaceful with those thick lashes resting on his cheeks. She couldn't imagine being without him for a whole week.

A noise startled her. Someone was rattling the door handle and cussing outside her door. She eased out of bed and tiptoed to look through the fisheye but all she could see was a couple of distorted people making out across the hall. She could still hear swearing so she opened the door a crack, leaving the safety chain in place. A drunk was trying every door on the second floor. When his key wouldn't work, he tried the next one and then the next one.

A giggle took her attention back to the couple across the hall. The man had the woman pressed up against the door whispering something in her ear.

Alma Grace gasped when she recognized Lenny and Macy, kissing and trying to open the door at the same time. Neither of them whipped around to see where the noise came from and she was very glad since she only had a sheet around her naked body. But there was no doubt about it; that was Lenny and Macy over there.

Damn that sumbitch! She'd taken up for him, prayed for him, and asked God to make him see the error of his ways so that Carlene would reconcile with him and there he was with Macy. God had been telling her no all along and she'd been too stubborn to listen, too eager to prove Patrice wrong. And now she had to backtrack.

She'd gone against her blood kin for him and he'd been a bastard all along. Patrice was right and Carlene was right and she'd been wrong. Well, by damn, he wasn't getting away with another thing.

She had dropped her purse right inside the door when Rick had backed her into the room, stringing kisses all over her face, so she fished inside, brought her cell phone out, and stuck it out the door. Two snaps later she had pictures, grainy but there was no doubt who was hugged up together beside that cute little beach chair.

"Don't go," Rick mumbled when she got back into bed.

"I'm right here, darlin'."

"I love you, Alma Grace," he whispered in a half-sleep state.

She hugged herself and snuggled down to go back to sleep. She dreamed of a time when she, Patrice, and Carlene were all just little girls. They were dressed in their Easter dresses and were having tea at the little table on the patio. She awoke with a smile on her face. Those were happy times and they'd have them again, by golly, with no contention between them ever again. From now on, if God said no, she intended to be listening real good.

Chapter 19

THE JALAPEÑO JUBILEE, PROBABLY the biggest event in Cadillac, Texas, was held every fall right after the Texas State Fair and ended a long, hot summer. Easter brought on spring and the whole town looked forward to the program at the church and the egg hunt. And then they started talking about the chili cook-off.

Folks were excited when the tents started going up that Friday morning at nine o'clock sharp. It was always held the Saturday before Mother's Day and folks for miles and miles around marked it on their calendars. If they weren't coming home to Grayson County or adjoining Fannin County to see their mamas, then they loaded their mothers up in vans, trucks, and cars and brought them to the cook-off as a treat.

Rule number one said that the city park was roped off on Friday morning at nine o'clock; the tents and tables or however the contestants wanted to display their chili could begin at that time. The displays surrounded the park, facing inward, creating a small, colorful open-air festival with picnic tables and a kiddy carnival in the middle. Contestants had their chili ready for the judges to taste at ten o'clock sharp on Saturday morning. At eleven o'clock the gate was opened to the public. At four o'clock the judges rendered their rulings and the street dance began at eight sharp.

Rule number two stated that the seven-member teams had to work alone in setting up their work space and that no outside help could be solicited. That came about back in 1993 when a team brought in a professional service to build a structure for them.

Number three said that every team was responsible for its site. The cook-off committee would not police the area after the tents, tables, etc., were in place. That rule was put into the contract when one team spray-painted graffiti on another's display in 1979.

Bless My Bloomers had a sign on the door that said "Closed for the Chili Cook-Off Friday and Saturday." Patrice didn't figure they'd have enough business those two days to pay them to turn on the lights anyway.

Patrice drove her father's flatbed truck to the site, parked as close to their assigned space as she could, and all three cousins bailed out. Tansy parked her Caddy behind the truck and the mamas and Josie crawled out of it.

They wore jeans with matching hot-pink T-shirts that had their logo splashed across the back in black: Red-Hot Bloomers. Above the words was a printed clothesline with bikinis and thongs pinned to it. A red bowl of chili was below with red, yellow, blue, and pink flames licking upward toward the words. Those were their Friday shirts.

The official shirt that they would wear on Saturday was similar but it sported lace around the legs of the bikinis and sequins on the thongs, enough sparkle on the flames to make them look hot, and the wording was done in red sparkly letters. And they'd be wearing them with designer jeans and hot-pink high heels. Josie refused to wear high heels but she had invested in hot-pink running shoes that lit up around the soles with every step.

"Woo-hoo!" Agnes yelled from a lawn chair from across the street. "Lookin' good!"

Carlene waved at her. "Tomorrow is better. What are you doing here so early?"

"Overseeing my investment," Agnes said.

The tent was in a long box that took all seven of them to tote to their site. Alma Grace whipped a box cutter out of her hip pocket and made short order of the cardboard without leaving a single gash on the hot-pink and black material. She closed the tool, put it back in her pocket, and picked up the directions.

"I'm mechanically challenged," Sugar said.

"That's what they're all depending on so don't say that out loud. We need for them to think we are meaner than junkyard dogs," Gigi whispered.

Alma Grace handed the directions to Carlene. "This woman can do anything. I have lots of faith in her."

"Really?" Carlene asked.

"Oh, yes, I do." Alma Grace smiled.

"Well, thank you. It's very simple. First we set it up with the back leg on the east end."

They all gathered round and helped her hoist the eight-foot-tall metal sticks to that corner. "Patrice, you hold this leg and I'm going to take this one to the other side." She walked twelve feet across the back of their site. "Mama, hold this leg, while I go forward with one."

In a few minutes the basic tent was up with all the metal pieces locked in place to hold it together. "See, I told y'all it was worth putting out a few more dollars to get it partially assembled and not just a bunch of bolts and nuts and pieces of steel," Josie said.

"Now we bring in the tables," Tansy said.

"And then comes the big jobs," Sugar moaned.

They set up two picnic tables end to end at the back. Those would serve as a workstation and a place to sit and sip iced tea between customers. The eight-foot table in the front would hold the chili, bowls, corn chips, sweet tea, and condiments for sale.

"We'll get the freezer," Alma Grace said when Tansy started toward the truck.

"What do you need a freezer for?" Lenny asked.

"What are you doing here?" Alma Grace asked right back.

"I'm on my way back to my truck for a screwdriver. Y'all cheated. You should have to put up a real tent rather than a pop-up."

Carlene smiled sweetly. "Then put that in the rule book next year. Tip read the directions and said our tent was fine."

"You still didn't answer my question. What do you need a freezer for?"

"It's a big, big surprise," Carlene said.

"It better not be against the rules or I'll see to it you are thrown out and laugh the whole time you are packing up to leave," Lenny said.

"How's your mother?" Tansy asked.

Lenny gave her a go-to-hell look and strutted off toward his truck.

"Good job," Josie said and held up her hand for a high-five with Tansy.

"I'm disappointed in the lace around the top," Alma Grace said. "It should be sparkly."

The freezer wasn't much bigger than a dorm-size refrigerator but it would hold two hundred Dixie ice cream cups and when they ran out, they'd send Kim back to the shop to get more. The rule book did say that the team had to stay on-site the whole time and that they could have one person to replenish supplies when needed.

Alex told Patrice that the amendment came about back in 1987 when tent sites looked like a wrestling tag team with guys running out to get more beer or even hamburgers for lunch.

The multi-outlet plug would be full by the next morning but the freezer was the first thing in the line. When it cooled down, they'd bring in their ice cream cups wrapped in unmarked brown paper bags and put them inside. Lenny could just wonder all night long what they had up their sleeves.

Patrice and Carlene brought in two more boxes and set them on the picnic tables. One held the drapes to enclose the tent and tiebacks if they wanted breezes to flow through, the banner for the top, and the tablecloth and banner for the serving table. The latter wouldn't go up until morning but all the others had to be in place that day.

"One cooker of chili on the tables getting warmed up and ready, the other at the front being served, switch when the front one is empty." Gigi checked off her list as she talked.

"I like it," Agnes hollered.

"Doin' good, Lenny," Violet yelled from ten yards down the road from her.

"Lord, what have we done?" Sugar whispered.

"We're winning a cook-off and making a statement for all the women who want to enter in the future. Agnes and Violet are at it like always. Hell's bells, Aunt Sugar, if it wasn't this, it would be something else. They love to fight so we're making them happy," Patrice said softly.

∿⚬∽

Carlene stirred the last batch of chili in the big pot at her mother's house. They'd even had Tip go over the rule book, line by line, word by word, and not one thing was there about opening gallon-size cans of chili and then adding their own special touches. It was a revelation to find out that all the years they'd had hot dog cookouts and chili suppers Gigi's special recipe had not started with beef or venison.

"What did you do with the empty cans?" Tansy asked.

"I peeled the labels off and put them in a garbage bag and gave them to a dumpster last night after midnight," Gigi said.

"What dumpster? And what did you do with the labels?" Tansy asked.

"The one behind the Chinese takeout store in Sherman and the labels went through the shredder in the office," she said.

"Good job," Josie said.

"Okay, time to add our own stuff one last time." Carlene pulled the tab on a can of beer and slowly poured it into the chili, stirring the whole time.

Gigi put in a half a cup of Worcestershire sauce and four table-spoons of liquid smoke.

Tansy added two cans of chili beans and Patrice donated eight ounces of chopped jalapeño peppers. Alma Grace spooned six tea-spoons each of chili powder and Cajun seasoning. Josie opened up a gallon bag of cooked hamburger meat and dumped it in the pot.

"I know the rules didn't say we had to start with meat but it makes me feel better knowing that it's in there," she said.

"It's boiling again," Carlene said.

Sugar removed the wrapper from a Hershey bar, broke it into sections, and tossed it into the pot. "Mama wouldn't have left that candy paper in the Bible if she hadn't meant for us to put it in the chili. It's our biggest secret ingredient."

"Anyone want to taste it?" Carlene asked.

"Hell, no!" Patrice threw up her hands. "That first night was enough for me."

Josie smiled and said, "You are all a bunch of pansies. A little jalapeños never hurt anyone. It might be the very reason me and Agnes have lived as long as we have."

"We are not pansies," Patrice said.

Carlene handed the spoon to her mother. "Speak for yourself. After I ate a bowl of the recipe on Tuesday night, all I could think was *come on ice cream*."

Josie nodded seriously. "Even if we don't win, the judges won't forget our hot chili or the ice cream that they'll get after they taste it."

"Oh, we're going to win," Tansy said. "I know we are."

"Did you have a dream, Mama?" Patrice asked.

"I did every night for a whole week. Lenny might as well tear down his stupid tent with a crown on the top and go home. His reign is over! That trophy is ours this year. And I don't even care if we never enter again, but this year belongs to us," Tansy said.

Carlene sucked air. "Aunt Tansy, you did not buy off the judges, did you? I want to win this fair and square."

"I don't even know who they are," she answered.

"I do," Josie said. "Floy's husband is one. Cathy's new husband, John, is one. The Mayor, of course, is one. Y'all's preacher Isaac is one and he says that next year he and Kim might have the first mixed team for the church so this is the only year he's judging. Brenda Culpepper and Tip Gordon are the others."

"Shit!" Gigi slapped her thigh. "I should have thought about buying off the judges."

"I did my part in getting Isaac's vote with the Easter egg hunt and I have been praying," Sugar said.

"Right now, we'll take all the help we can get," Carlene said. "As long as it's legal and we win without cheating. I really, really want that trophy."

"Who gets to keep it?" Josie asked. "We going to farm it out to a house a month and then start all over."

Gigi turned off the cooker and put the lid on it. "I was thinkin' it should go on the credenza in the foyer of Bless My Bloomers."

∽৵৹

Carlene had agreed to take the first watch and stay at the tent until eleven when Alma Grace would relieve her. She'd brought a romance book and a book light to read by, but it didn't interest her. She had five hours with nothing to do and she wasn't good at being still. She checked everything, making sure that the sandbags were in place if a strong wind kicked up, everything was secure on the tent, and the freezer was plugged in. Heaven help them if they gave the judges melted ice cream.

The banner with their logo shimmered in the moonlight but the lace was blah, just like Sugar had said. If she'd had time, she would have dressed it up with sequins and shimmering hot-pink beads.

"Glitter spray!" She jumped up and pulled a box out from under the table. Patrice had thrown it in the box just in case they wanted to make the table banner sparkle. Digging around in it, she found three cans of iridescent spray. The folding step stool they'd brought with them earlier put her high enough that she only had to tiptoe a little to put the spray exactly where she wanted it.

She worked on six feet of lace then moved the stool. When she put her foot on the bottom step the leg fell into a gopher hole and Carlene landed square on her back. She was looking at the stars one second and Lenny's face the second.

Holy shit! She'd died in that two-second fall and gone straight to hell.

"You okay?" he asked.

"Am I alive?" she asked.

"Your eyes are open," he said.

She sat up. Nothing hurt except her pride. "I thought I was in hell when I saw your face."

Lenny chuckled. "Welcome to the club."

"What are you doing here?" she asked.

"Just leaving. My watch is over. I'm going to win this, Carlene. I know you want to win to make me suffer but all this fluffy shit won't win a chili cook-off. You should stick to the jubilee and making jalapeño banana muffins rather than chili. That's a man's job, not a woman's."

Carlene scooted away from him. "That's sexist."

He yawned and stretched. "Maybe it is but you're just making a big ass out of your whole family."

"Are you implying that I have a big ass?"

He smiled but it wasn't a bit nice. "Well, there is that, but no, I was not. I was speaking the truth. How are you going to feel when they call my name to come get the trophy and you've lost…again?"

She frowned and stood up. He didn't offer to help and if he had she would have slapped his hand away. She didn't need anything from Lenny, not even a helping hand.

"Again?" she asked.

"You lost me because you just couldn't hold on to me. You lost your marriage because of your temper. And you are going to lose this cook-off because of your anger. I'd wish you good luck but it would be wasted so I'll just say good-bye," he told her.

"I kind of like that idea. Good-bye, Lenny," she said.

Just like that she was free of him. She wasn't a loser. She'd won already because he was gone from her heart.

She checked the step stool each time before she put a foot on the bottom stair and had just finished spraying all the lace when a hand came out of the shadows to help her off the stool.

"Jack Landry, what are you doing here?" She put her hand in his and felt immediate heat from the inside flowing outward all the way to her cheeks.

"I thought I'd come by and see if everything was quiet. Didn't know if Tansy and Kitty might be taking the same watch." He dropped her hand, folded the stool up, and set it behind the freezer.

"We want the mamas fresh for tomorrow so us girls are doing the watch. I'm taking first shift. Alma Grace is going to take over at eleven and then Patrice is coming in at four in the morning."

"Want some company?"

"I'd love company," Carlene said. "Want a beer or a glass of sweet tea?"

"I'm off duty so beer is good."

He wore jeans and a white T-shirt, scuffed boots, and his hair still had water droplets, proving that he'd been in the shower not long before. She inhaled and got a whiff of his aftershave, something woodsy and tantalizing that was so Jack Landry.

She opened two beers, handed him one, and sat down at a picnic table. He took a swig and sat down across from her, his long legs stretched out and knees touching hers under the table.

"I didn't hear your motorcycle," she said.

"Came in my truck in case I had to haul Tansy and Kitty back to the jail."

"Why'd you come back, Jack? I always wanted to get away from north central Texas. It was my dream to live anywhere else on the planet. You got away and saw the world but then you came back to Cadillac. Why?" she asked.

"It's home, and if you had left, you'd have been drawn back just like I was. It might not be perfect but it's home. You still dream of leaving?"

She shook her head.

His knee put out enough heat to take care of half the planet in the dead middle of a cold winter. The night breeze was pleasantly cool but not chilly. She couldn't imagine how it would feel if his bare skin touched hers when pure old blistering heat flowed through two pair of jeans.

"No, I'm settled here now. I've got the shop and my family and I'm not leaving," she said.

Jack sipped his beer again. "Not even if you don't win tomorrow?"

"Winning will make me very happy but it's not the end of the world if we don't win. Of course, I'm speaking for myself, not Aunt Tansy. You might do well to bring backup to the judging announcements if she doesn't win after what Kitty did with the cat." She smiled.

"Will you go to dinner with me next Friday night?" he asked.

"Will you come to Mother's Day dinner with me at Mama's on Sunday?" she asked right back.

He grinned and she wanted to kiss him so bad that she had to down a third of her beer just to keep busy. "I will if you will."

"Deal." He reached across the table to shake hands.

She put hers in his and said, "Jack, I'm not rushing into anything. I want you to know that."

"It's still a deal. Thanks for the beer. I'd better make the rounds and check on everyone else."

"Thought you were off duty," she said.

"I am but…" His phone rang and he reached inside his hip pocket for it. "Jack Landry, here."

He was standing by the time he put it back. "Got a catfight going at the convenience store. See you later."

"Fannins and Lovelles?" she asked.

"Agnes and Violet," he hollered back at a dead run.

⤛⤜

Alma Grace showed up at exactly the right time.

"The lace looks so much better! How did you do that? It even shines in the moonlight. Just wait until the sunlight hits it tomorrow. It'll look like it's been sprinkled with diamonds," she beamed.

"Little bit of glitter spray did the trick. Did you catch a nap?"

Alma Grace shook her head. "I finished unpacking my things and put the rest of Mama's things in my suitcases. They're loaded in my car to take home to her on Sunday."

"There's a pillow in the back of the van and the seats are down. I'm not sleepy. Go get a nap and when I can't keep my eyes open I'll come wake you. It's parked right behind the tent. You can duck under the tape," Carlene said.

"Are you sure? It's my turn," Alma Grace said.

"I'm sure. I've been doin' a lot of thinking and now I'm settling down to read a while. You could sleep at least an hour or two."

"I'm not going to argue," she said.

She'd gotten to the first sex scene when a shadow covered her light and she looked up to see Jack again. "Must've been some catfight."

He sat down at the picnic table. "Not really. By the time I got there Ethan had shown up and had Violet cornered and Trixie was in the car with Agnes beside her."

"What set it off this time?"

"You know how they are." Jack shrugged. "Got another beer?"

∽✿∾

Jack Landry wasn't about to tell Carlene that Violet had made a rude comment about Carlene being too fat to dress the way she did and that Agnes threatened to black both her eyes. He'd never understand why Kitty or any of those women thought Carlene was fat. She was tall, yes. She was curvy, oh God, yes! She was sexy as hell with all that gorgeous blond hair and those big green eyes. Her complexion was so smooth that he wanted to touch her face just to see if it felt like silk. Her stomach was flat; no fat rolls showing on her back beneath a skin-tight shirt that he'd like to peel off so he could kiss her from belly button to lips. But fat? From his standpoint, those women had an acute case of bullfrog-green jealousy.

He also wasn't going to tell her that he'd settled the catfight, seen to it that both women were safely on their way home, and that afterward he'd gone home. He'd tried to watch television. He'd tried to read a brand-new mystery book by James Lee Burke. Nothing worked so he'd finally driven back to the park to check on Carlene.

"Alma Grace runnin' late?" he asked.

"No, she's sleeping in the back of the van. She looked worn out so I told her I'd take it another hour or two," Carlene explained.

Jack sat down beside her, shoulders touching, backs against the table, legs out and crossed at the ankles. "I heard that Rick Kelly is keeping company with Alma Grace. He's a good man and a fine police officer."

"She likes him a lot. They'd make a good couple," Carlene said.

"Good match. Both got that religious bend to them and come from good solid backgrounds."

She laid her book down. "You ever think about getting married?"

"Is that a proposal?" He grinned.

"No, it is not!"

He put his arm around her. She fit well there, like a woman should. "I've had a couple of serious relationships but I was in the service and always moving around. Since I've been home there was one that might have been serious last fall but it just didn't work out. Remember I told you about her. Why?"

She laid her head on his shoulder. It felt right, like it should be there. "Did you ever feel like you were in limbo or that maybe you were moving too fast, either one?"

Her hair smelled like spray paint and coconut shampoo mixed up together. "Yes, to both. Those first two years I was home felt like limbo. I had Trixie and Marty and Cathy but they were like sisters. Darla Jean was like my cousin. Good friends, all of them, but I wanted a relationship. Then I found one and it moved too fast, burned out, and was over all in a few months."

"How is Cathy?" she asked.

"Great. Excited about the baby. Excited to be married to her best friend. I feel like I'm going to be an uncle," he answered.

"You like kids?"

"Oh, yeah. Love them."

"What about chili? I mean really, really hot chili?" she asked.

He laughed out loud. "Now that was a change of the subject."

"I know but I've had enough serious talk for one night," she said.

Carlene Carmichael would never be dull, that was for absolute sure.

"I like chili and I like it hot."

But there isn't any chili in the world as hot as you are, she thought.

She didn't know when she fell asleep on his shoulder but when she opened her eyes, Patrice was standing there with a twelve-cup coffee pot, water and coffee in a bag, and a dozen donuts.

"Where's Alma Grace?" Patrice whispered.

Jack pointed to the van and put his finger over his lips. "Coffee looks good."

"Anyone try to sabotage us?" she asked.

"Been pretty quiet except for a few pretty loud snores," Jack answered.

Carlene yawned. "What time is it?"

"Gettin' close to daybreak. You can go home and get dressed. I brought my things to change in the van before the judges come around," Patrice said.

"You stayed and let me sleep?" Carlene asked.

Patrice patted him on the shoulder. "You are a good man, Jack. I'm not going to have to work with sleepy, bitchy women all day. Remind me to buy you lunch someday."

"I'll do that," he said. "But I think right now I'll get on home and catch a few winks before the gates open. I have to be in uniform then."

"We'll try to keep Mama and Kitty on opposite ends of the park," Patrice said.

"I'll deputize you both if you can do the same with Agnes and Violet."

Patrice poured water into the coffee pot. "Honey, those two old buzzards love to argue. It's what keeps them young and alive."

"At least stick around and have some coffee. Your shoulder made a fine bed," Carlene said.

"No, thanks. See y'all sometime around noon. Good luck." He kissed Carlene on the forehead and disappeared into the darkness.

Patrice opened her mouth to say something but Carlene shook her head. "Not a word. Not a single word. It was wonderful and I like him."

"If we win because he kissed you on the forehead, just think what'll happen if he really plants one right on your lips?" Patrice smiled. "Go home and get a couple of hours of real sleep. Your mama said you and Alma Grace are to be at her house at nine sharp to help bring the chili and the rest of the supplies out here. And you are to be dressed and have your hair done. And you're not going to believe it but Alma Grace told me that she was wrong to pray for you to reconcile with Lenny. I don't know what happened to change her mind but she had tears in her eyes when she told me."

∞⚬∞

Alma Grace awoke in the back of a moving van and thought she'd been kidnapped. She had her phone in her hand and the first two numbers of 911 hit before she heard Carlene humming.

"Where are you taking me?" she yelled over the rumble of the wheels and the wind whipping through the open windows.

"Home. It's almost five o'clock. Patrice is taking care of the site now. We both slept."

"But…"

"Jack came along and I rested on his shoulder."

She crawled up into the passenger's seat. "That rotten Lenny or his mama didn't do anything to our tent?"

"No, and I didn't do anything to theirs. Can't speak for what Patrice might do between now and daybreak, but I was good."

"Well, crap!"

"What does that mean?"

"It means that I wanted a reason to get even with him. I was wrong all along, Carlene, and I apologize. I'll get down on my knees under the red light on Main Street and beg if you'll forgive me. You were right to leave him and not to listen to me about going back to him. He's a rotten old rat that doesn't even deserve a woman like you."

"Well, thank you, Alma Grace. What changed your mind?"

In that moment, Carlene's world tilted right back to normal. Her heart shook off the heavy feeling and everything was right again for the first time since that morning when she found those red underpants.

"No thanks necessary. Just say that you'll forgive me. I'm so so sorry and I've seen the light, believe me, I saw it up close and personal and I'll tell you later about what changed my mind," Alma Grace said.

"You are forgiven and I love you," Carlene said.

"Thank you," she whispered. "I'll show you later today what I'm talking about even if God doesn't give me a sign to let the whole world see. I promise."

"I don't care if I never see, Alma Grace. I'm just glad we're okay," Carlene said.

Alma Grace had been looking for a sign from above about those two pictures of Lenny and Macy on her cell phone all week. She just needed something to show her the way. Something that said she should delete them or something that said it was all right to show them to Kim, who would definitely tell the right people to cause a great big hullabaloo between Bridget and Macy, and Lenny would be left with no one but his mama in his life.

She was hoping that he or his minions would try to sabotage their tent, or that they'd do something really mean like set fire to it and then she'd have her sign, but she had nothing.

It was enough to make her want to cuss like Patrice!

Chapter 20

CARLENE STIRRED THE CHILI one more time so the aroma of their special blend would fill the judge's noses before they ever tasted it. Six judges lined up in front of the Red-Hot Bloomers stand, laid their clipboards with a blank page covering the stack of entries on the table, and eyed the whole display from back to front.

Alma Grace opened the freezer and removed six cups of ice cream with six special little wooden spoons on top imprinted with "Red-Hot Bloomers thank you." She set one in front of each judge's station.

"Good morning," Patrice greeted the judges with her best smile. "We realize that you are only allowed to taste the chili, itself, but in appreciation for all your work, we have an envelope for each of you. Inside you'll find a coupon redeemable anytime today for a bowl of chili with or without chips or condiments, a free glass of sweet tea, and another cup of ice cream." She laid them on top of their clipboards as Josie carefully measured one fourth of a cup of chili into each hot-pink plastic bowl with the team logo printed on the side.

Isaac looked down the row and nodded. They all scooped up a spoonful and put it in their mouths.

"Holy smoke, that's hot!" Isaac grabbed the ice cream and shoveled two bites into his mouth before picking up his clipboard and writing.

"I taste a bit of Cajun. I like it," Floy's husband wrote on his clipboard before he opened his ice cream.

Tip ate the whole sampling, pulled a snowy white hanky from his hip pocket, and wiped his brow. "Now that is some damn good chili."

John, the owner of the Rib Joint, tasted, thought a few minutes, and tasted again. "I'd put chili on my menu with this recipe. Fine job, ladies."

Barbara Culpepper, bless her heart and God love her soul, couldn't get to the ice cream fast enough. Steam rolled out her ears and she fanned her face with her clipboard, all the while reaching for a bottle of water in the shoulder purse hanging across her chest.

"Ice cream, darlin'." Gigi opened it for her and stuck the little spoon in the middle. "It coats the palate and takes away the burn."

Mayor Jim Burdette tasted, wrote on his clipboard, nodded at the ladies, and left his ice cream sitting on the table.

"Good luck to you," he said as he moved to the next exhibition.

Carlene waited until they were at the next tent before she sat down at the picnic table. "Well? Aunt Tansy, you're the psychic. What do you think?"

"I'm not a bit worried, darlin'. We're having a party at Clawdy's this evening at seven o'clock. We'll all get our money from Patrice and Monday morning the newspaper from Sherman is coming to take one final picture…of the seven of us at Bless My Bloomers when we hang that picture of us over there above the credenza and set the trophy right below it. It's in the bag. Stop worrying now. In less than an hour the gates will open and we're going to get our ten points on the sheet for selling the most chili. We will completely sell out of all four batches," Tansy said.

"Alma Grace, your opinion?" Carlene asked.

"Well, I think that after eating that chili, Barbara Culpepper may sing a little better come Sunday morning," she said.

Carlene looked at Josie. "Mayor was on the fence. I wouldn't even play poker with him on a good night. Can't read his face a damn bit."

"No strings of Spanish?" Gigi asked Josie.

"Not today. Today it's press one for English."

Patrice sat down beside Carlene. "They're going to taste twenty kinds of chili and there won't be a nickel's worth of difference in any of it, but they won't forget ours or our tent. Mama, what were you talking about? Ten points?"

Gigi picked up a blue folder and waved it. "Seventy points for the chili. Ten points for the overall look of the tent or site. Ten points for keeping the site friendly and presentable, and the judges will be milling around individually all day to check on things like that. Ten points for how much money each tent makes to give to the fire and police department."

"Does it say that we have to charge five dollars a bowl?" Sugar asked.

"Yes, it does," Gigi read aloud from the folder. "No booth or exhibitor can charge more than five dollars per serving but each booth or exhibitor can add drinks, condiments, or other items to their sale to make it more appealing. I do not intend to break a single rule and get disqualified. We are breaking ground for women of the future even though I will not do this ever again. One trophy is enough for me."

Agnes waved from the tape at the back of the tent. "Hey, y'all! You been judged yet? I'd duck under this tape but that sorry ass Lenny might say that you had more in your tent than seven and get you thrown out."

"We've been judged, Miz Agnes. Heard you had a little mix-up last night," Sugar said.

"Violet don't have any idea when to shut her mouth. I swear that woman's got a magic mirror in her house and when she looks in it she sees Marilyn Monroe or Betty Boop instead of an old, chubby woman who's trying to outrun wrinkles and age," Agnes declared.

❧

"You want a glass of sweet tea, Miz Agnes?" Alma Grace asked.

"I'd just love one. It'll get me through until I can get through the gates. I've got my car parked across the street and my lawn chair out beside it."

Alma Grace scooped ice into a hot-pink cup and filled it with sweet tea. She carried it to the back of the tent and handed it across the yellow tape.

"Thank you, honey."

"Now what was it that caused the mix-up last night?" Alma Grace asked.

Agnes crooked her finger for Alma Grace to come closer. When all that separated them was six-inch-wide yellow plastic tape, Agnes cupped her hand over Alma Grace's ear and said, "She called Carlene fat. Crazy old bitch is so round if I ever knocked her down she'd roll all the way to Mexico so what right has she got to call anyone fat. It came straight out of Kitty's mouth and Lenny said the same thing from what Violet said."

"Oh, really!" Alma Grace said.

Agnes backed away and nodded very seriously. "I disagreed and I said so and that damn store clerk called Jack."

"Well, thank you, Miz Agnes. I disagree, too," Alma Grace said.

"I'll be seein' y'all soon as they open the gates. I got to keep an eye on my investment today," Agnes said.

"Darlin', you might want to set your lawn chair somewhere between us and Lenny's team's site. Wouldn't want you to miss something wonderful when they announce the winner," Alma Grace said.

Agnes gave her the thumbs-up sign.

God had given her the sign she'd been waiting on. She wasn't expecting it to arrive with red hair, wearing a pair of faded stretch jeans and a Clawdy's T-shirt. But then God most usually worked in mysterious ways, just like he had when she wanted to take vengeance in her own hands.

Alma Grace dug her cell phone out of her purse, held up a

finger, and stepped outside the tent. "Kim called a few minutes ago and I didn't have time to talk. I'm going to step outside and call her back," she said.

She propped a hip on the bar holding the teeter-totter and pushed the buttons. Kim picked up on the third ring.

"Sorry, darlin', that I didn't have time to talk earlier but I had to get all dolled up for this affair. We just had our judging and now we're waiting for the gates to open," Alma Grace said.

"No apology necessary. I've been on the phone with my mama. She heard that Lenny was downright rude to Carlene last night. Kitty was bragging about it," Kim said.

"Oh, really," Alma Grace said.

Thank you, sweet Jesus, for giving me another sign. You're just putting them out there like politicians' banners on election year and I'm truly grateful, Alma Grace prayed.

"Kitty thought it was funny but Mama is just livid. And did you hear that Agnes and Violet got into it again over someone saying Carlene was fat. Lord, I'd give anything to have her curves. Hell, I wouldn't mind wearing a sixteen if I could look like her," Kim went on.

"Ain't it the truth? I'm about to send you a couple of pictures. You do what you see fit with them. I just do not want them to trace back to me even if you have to work them through a dozen people." Alma Grace held the phone out from her ear and presto they were immediately in Kim's phone.

"What am I looking at?" Kim asked. "Oh. My. God! Is this what I think it is? How did you get this?"

"Like I said, send it through at least a dozen people. It is date and time stamped and that little picture of the beach chair by the door should tell them what hotel it's in," Alma Grace said.

"Oh, honey, I know just where to start this bit of news. It should hit Bridget's phone by one o'clock at the latest, right before it gets to Macy's."

Yes, sir, Agnes deserved to have ringside seats when the shit hit the fan.

❧

Jack and his officers removed the plastic tape at eleven o'clock and the gate was opened by cutting a bright red ribbon across two poles that supported the Cadillac City Park sign. People poured in and children took off for the playground equipment. Old folks set up lawn chairs with coolers beside them. Those who didn't eat chili might want a bologna sandwich for lunch. No one wanted to miss the fun or the visiting.

The day was beautiful. The sun was bright. The television meteorologist had promised high eighties on the thermometer. A few fluffy white clouds floated around but not a single dark rain cloud threatened the day.

Patrice started fidgeting when, five minutes after the public was allowed in the park, they still didn't have a single customer. She stepped outside the tent and looked around. "No one is buying from any of the vendors. Why would they line up, fight over parking spaces and walk from three blocks away, and not buy?"

Violet walked past and stuck her nose up in the air, went straight to Lenny's Chili Kings' tent, and bought the first bowl of chili sold that morning. She carried it right past the Red-Hot Bloomers and told Patrice, "It will give me great pleasure to announce that Lenny has won this afternoon. His chili, as always, is flawless."

Patrice turned around to face her six team members. "I'd forgotten that she gets to announce who wins."

"Well, ain't that nice," Agnes said.

Patrice jumped. "You aren't supposed to sneak up on me like that, Miz Agnes."

"I didn't sneak up on nobody. I come to buy chili. I want it with corn chips, onions, and mustard squirted over the top. And I heard that y'all are givin' away ice cream with yours. Nice touch." Agnes pulled five dollars from her pocket and laid it on the table. "How much did you bring?"

"Of what?" Patrice asked.

"Chili. Lenny's got three big cookers full. I done got the count on all of the vendors. They all got three cookers but the Bank's tent right straight across over there. They've got four. So how many did y'all bring?"

"Four," Gigi said. "Should we have brought more?"

"Four is good. Lenny might sell out before you but don't get excited if he does. You're going to make more for the cause because you got more to sell."

Josie fixed Agnes a Frito chili pie in a bowl with a spoon stuck in the middle, refilled her tea glass, and handed her an ice cream cup, all on a sturdy plastic tray with a napkin and wooden spoon for her ice cream on the side.

"Now that's service. Y'all are doin' a knockout job. You'd think you'd been at this for years. Hell, next year I might put in a site just to pester Violet. I could get Cathy and the girls and Jack to help me," Agnes said. "Get ready for a rush here in about ten minutes."

A few people stopped by to speak to Agnes and, just like she said, in ten minutes not only did the Red-Hot Bloomers have a rush, the line reached ten yards out into the park. In thirty minutes the first cooker was half gone and all seven of the team worked furiously.

Patrice took the money.

Alma Grace put an ice cream cup, napkin, and wooden spoon on each tray.

Gigi scooped ice.

Sugar poured sweet tea.

Tansy kept the table restocked with chips and the mustard bottle filled.

Josie refilled onion and relish bowls.

Carlene dipped chili.

At noon they'd emptied the first cooker and were working on the second. Another batch had been poured up and was heating. Gigi stirred it often to keep it from sticking and filled cups with ice in her spare time.

There was a lull at a few minutes past one. Patrice swiped the sweat from her forehead with a paper towel and took stock of the remaining supplies. They were working on the third cooker of chili and the last one was heating. They'd sent Kim for the last batch of ice cream to put in the freezer. It looked like maybe they'd gauged things just about right. Half the napkins were gone and they were down to a little less than half the chips. Josie had chopped way more onions than they needed and they'd have enough mustard to last through the next hundred years.

The next round hit before she had time to sit down, and at two thirty, they were completely sold out.

"Now what?" she asked.

"Now, according to your father, who had a team for years, when you sell out, you take your money to any one of the judges so he can mark your paper that you've had a sell-out. Then you are free to tear down your serving table, clean up your site, pull a picnic table out to the park, and relax until judging is done," Tansy said.

Alma Grace kept a close eye on the crowd but she didn't see Macy or Bridget. She'd seen the signs but patience was not one of her better virtues. Still if God gave her the signs, she trusted Him to produce the results.

She helped box up the leftover plastic items and paper goods. Carlene and Patrice took the empty containers and the cookers to the van and the whole place was tidied up without even a wadded-up paper towel on the grass. Gigi and Tansy folded up the table they'd used to serve from and the three mamas carried a picnic table down to where Agnes was sitting under the shade of a big pecan tree.

"I see you are cleaned up, so I'll collect the money," Isaac said.

"Patrice has it." Alma Grace kicked off her shoes and buried her feet in the cool green grass. She was wiggling her toes and thinking about how good it felt and almost missed Bridget when she stormed past Agnes and stepped on her toes.

"Hey, watch where you are going," Agnes yelled after her.

Bridget didn't even turn around, much less apologize like a southern lady should.

"Shhh," Alma Grace whispered to Agnes. "The show is about to begin and you don't want to hold her up. She's the star."

Agnes's eyes twinkled. "I knew you was the one to tell. I just knew it."

Bridget marched right inside the Chili Kings' tent, poked Lenny in the chest, and started ranting. "So you're off screwing with Macy while I'm at home babysitting your mother."

"What are you talking about? Have you been drinking?" Lenny asked.

Bridget yelled to the top of her lungs, "I am sober as a judge with my eyes wide open. Damn you, Lenny Lovelle. Granny told me if I could steal you away from your wife then someone could take you away from me, but would I listen, oh, no! Well, we are done and I don't ever want to hear from you again."

She put both hands on his chest and pushed with all her might, sending him backward into the team's preparation table. His team members caught the table before it spilled everything onto the ground but a few napkins fluttered away on the breeze. Folks who'd been oblivious to the argument turned to see where the golden napkins were coming from.

"Well, shit," Agnes said. "I could pitch a better fit than that and I'm over eighty. Girls these days just don't have much spunk."

Bridget picked up a plastic bowl and hurled it at him.

He caught it like a Frisbee and said, "Go home, Bridget. We'll talk later. You are making a fool out of yourself."

"Fool! You are calling me a fool? What about you, getting caught in a hotel with Macy when I'm babysitting Kitty, who you say is feeble and losing her mind."

"I am what?" Kitty yelled from ten feet away. She left Violet's side and the people parted like the Red Sea, giving her room to plow her way through the crowd to the Chili Kings' tent.

Lenny tried to soothe Kitty before she ever made it to the tent. "Mama, she's lying. She's heard some false gossip. And y'all need to get on out of here because you'll cause us to get disqualified. Only the team members can be behind the table."

"I paid for this freakin' tent and everything in it so I will damn sure come inside it if I want to. So I'm feeble and losing my mind? Is that right, Bridget?" Kitty asked.

"Yes, ma'am. He said he had to work late but look at this." She flipped her phone around for Kitty to see. "Date, time, and place where he and Macy were in the Hampton hotel while you and I were going to a club meeting. He coerced me into staying with you. Hell, I even begged him to let me stay since he made you out to be totally helpless after that fight with Tansy."

"Now it's getting better," Agnes said.

"Holy shit!" Carlene whispered. "He's done the same thing to me a dozen times. Not with his mother but manipulated me into believing he had to work late. I wonder if he keeps a room at the hotel."

"Shhh," Agnes said. "It's fixin' to get better."

Alma Grace pointed at Macy making a beeline for the tent.

"You hussy! How did you get that picture? Floy is mad at me and says I can't even sing in the church choir and that I'll never be an angel in the Easter program again. My mama is throwing a fit because Violet is liable to kick her out of the jalapeño club." She slapped Bridget across the face.

Bridget screamed as she drew back her fist and landed a good right hook to Macy's eye. "It wasn't me and if you hadn't been there, you wouldn't be in trouble."

Lenny got between them and flying fists from both women landed a few blows on his torso but not a one reached his face. Not until Kitty picked up a gallon jug of tea and coldcocked him up beside the head.

"Losing my mind, am I? Well, you can damn well take care of yourself from now on, Lenny," she said.

He instinctively put out both hands when he fell forward and one brushed the last cooker of chili right off into the grass. Two of his buddies were quick enough to grab him before he hit the ground and dragged him to the backside of the tent where they stretched him out on the ground.

The three women looked more than a little bit lost to Alma Grace now that Lenny was laid out like a corpse. Then Kitty threw up both hands and wailed, "My baby, my poor, poor baby boy. Look what you two bitches have caused. If he's dead, I'm going to kill both of you before they take me to jail." She tied into them slapping and hitting until they ran outside the tent.

Macy slipped and fell ass over sparkly jeans in the green grass. When Bridget started around her, she got tangled up in Macy's feet and fell forward landing right on top of Macy. When she came to a stop and sat up, Bridget realized she had the advantage, took a deep breath, and drew back to hit Macy again but Jack's big fist closed around her hand.

"I'd say we've had enough excitement, ladies. Y'all want to walk out of here on your own or do I need to get out the cuffs?"

"What did Bridget have on that phone, anyway?" Gigi asked.

"It's a dirty picture of Macy and Lenny at the Hampton." Agnes pulled her phone out of her pocket and held it up. "I got it about ten minutes ago. God bless technology. Gossip has risen to a whole new level."

Bridget stormed out by going between the Chili Kings' tent and the one next to it. Macy left the way she arrived. Straight out through the gate.

"Best damn cook-off we've had in years," Agnes declared.

"Could have been better if one of those girls had hit Kitty with a jug of tea," Tansy said.

"Maybe next year, darlin'." Agnes patted her hand.

"Or if Kitty had killed Lenny," Gigi said. "Look, that son of a bitch is already sitting up with a bag of ice on his cheek and Kitty is kissing him on the forehead."

"Now that ain't never goin' to happen. He's stuck with her for life. You don't know how lucky you are, Carlene," Agnes said.

"Yes, I do." Carlene laughed. "Win, lose, or draw, I'm the luckiest woman in the park today."

Alma Grace touched her arm.

"I don't know how you stayed with him as long as you did. He's a real son of a bitch and that's not a cuss word; it's an honest statement," Alma Grace said.

Carlene raised one perfectly arched eyebrow. "I told you earlier, you are forgiven. It's okay so don't you dare start praying."

"I realize that it's all a bigger plan than I could foresee. If you hadn't left Lenny, then Rick wouldn't have brought the divorce papers and I wouldn't have met him. We wouldn't have entered the chili cook-off and the mamas wouldn't have moved into the house making us move in with Patrice, which gave me the courage to move away from Mama's place. We've all grown closer, mamas, daughters, and friends because you left and besides he's a rotten bastard."

"That he is not. His mama and daddy were married," Carlene said. "And to think it was all over little red bikini under-britches."

"Amazin', ain't it?"

At four o'clock sharp, Violet took the stand behind the microphone in the center of the park. Her gold fingernail with a brand-new rhinestone at the tip sparkled in the sun as she tapped the microphone a few times to get everyone's attention.

"If you will all quiet down, the judges' scores are in. First of all, let's give a big round of applause to the six judges who helped us today," Violet said.

The clapping went on for fifteen seconds before she tapped the microphone again. "And another round for all the wonderful contestants, the folks who came out and supported our fund raiser for the Cadillac Volunteer Fire Department, and the fire department itself for all the good it does."

She only let that last ten seconds before she hit the microphone with an ink pen. "And now for the moment we've all been waiting for. Third place goes to the Money-Maker Team sponsored by the Cadillac Bank. Congratulations. And at this time I'd like to announce that this year we brought in almost twice as much as we did last year."

Agnes cupped her hands over her mouth and yelled, "That's because there was a women's team. Next year it'll be even better."

"Amen, and they had the best chili in the whole park," another elderly woman hollered.

Violet tipped her head up so high that all three of her chins showed. She gave everyone time to get through applauding and opened the second envelope. "Second place goes to the Fire Engine Team, which is run by the fire department. Congratulations."

She held up the third envelope and waved it in the air. "And now the moment we have truly waited on. First place..." She opened it and didn't even look down. "...for the sixth year in a row goes to..." She held it up, saw the name, and turned scarlet. "I'm sorry. First place goes to the Red-Hot Bloomers Team for their first win. If one of the team members will come forward for your trophy..."

Alma Grace had never seen seven women move so fast. Six pair of high heels grew wings and flew and Josie's shoes sparkled the whole way to the center of the park. Cameras flashed as they all gathered round and let Carlene hold the trophy high in the air.

"Daddy, we won!" Alma Grace screamed.

"I see that, baby girl. I'm so proud of all of you," Jamie said.

"I'll see y'all at the party at seven and bring that trophy with you," Agnes called out.

"Yes, ma'am," Alma Grace said.

❧

Hank hugged Carlene tightly. "You did it. Does it feel good?"

"Yes, Daddy, it does. Winning always feels good when you work as hard as we did but I was a winner before Violet even said our name. I've got family, friends, and a happy life ahead of me."

"I heard that Lenny called you a loser," Hank said. "Want me to do what his mama couldn't?"

"No." Carlene laughed. "I want to forget all about him and the past and jump into the future like diving into the deep end of the swimmin' pool."

Gigi came over and made it a three-way hug. "Did you see Lenny? He was already coming across the park to get the trophy when Violet realized she should have looked at the paper in her hands instead of assuming."

"No, I was looking at Agnes. Her expression was priceless. Let's get ready for the party," Carlene said.

❧

Alex picked Tansy up and spun around with her until they were both dizzy. "I think I'm happier than any of you. I sure thought Lenny had it in the bag even after that fiasco in his tent. But it was funny the way that Violet screwed up. We won, darlin'! Next year…"

Tansy put a finger over his lips. "There might be a Red-Hot Bloomers next year but I won't be a part of it. Only red-hot bloomers I'll have is the ones I wear to the bedroom for you," she whispered.

"Well, I sure like that," Alex said.

❧

Jamie hugged Sugar close to his side. "You going to save that sexy shirt for next year?"

"Not me. I'm so sick of chili I may never eat it again. I'm not sure God could talk me into even letting anyone make it in my kitchen, that's how tired I am of this whole thing. I'm glad we won and now I'm ready to go home, take a long bath, and get the party over with. Next week, I'm more than ready to get my world back into its normal routine."

Alma Grace walked up to them, holding a young police officer's hand. "Mama and Daddy, I want y'all to meet Rick Kelly. Rick, this is my daddy, Jamie Magee, and my mama, Sugar Magee."

Rick kissed Sugar's fingertips and stuck out his hand to Jamie. "Right pleased to meet you both. Alma Grace talks about y'all all the time."

"He's coming to Mother's Day dinner, Mama," Alma Grace said.

"We'll be glad to have you, Rick." Sugar smiled. "Looks like you are about to go on duty."

"Yes, ma'am. I'm going to steal your daughter for a Coke and then I'll be on the night shift. It was right nice meeting y'all."

When they were out of hearing distance, Jamie leaned over and whispered out of the side of his mouth, "Forget normal, darlin'. From the looks on their faces, I'd say we're in for a busy year that could involve wedding cake."

❧

Hank leaned on the fender of his truck and purposely waited on Jack to walk past.

"Hank?" Jack tipped his hat.

"A word, Jack," Hank said.

"Yes, sir?"

"Are you interested in my daughter?" he asked bluntly.

"Yes, sir, I am. I had a crush on her in high school but I wasn't brave enough to ask her out since I'm four years older than her. I've got a little more courage now," Jack said.

"I see. Go slow and be honest. I couldn't stand to see her get another broken heart," Hank said.

"Yes, sir," Jack said.

Carlene slipped up behind Jack. "What are you two talkin' about?"

"I was askin' him to Mother's Day dinner tomorrow. You bring Beulah with you, Jack. Be nice to have her," Hank said smoothly as he got into the truck. "See y'all at the party at Clawdy's. You are coming to it, aren't you, Jack?"

"Wouldn't miss it for the whole world and besides I've got stock to collect on."

∽✦∽

The party was loud and noisy at Clawdy's that night. Jack scanned the room but couldn't find Carlene so he made his way through the crowd. She wasn't in the small dining room off to the side or in the kitchen so he started back through the place and caught a movement in his peripheral vision out the front window.

There she was with her legs drawn up under her on the front porch swing. He slipped out the front door and sat down beside her. "Too much noise?"

"It's been a crazy couple of months," she said. "Hey, did you ever find out who stole all those cookers? They had to have had a list of the teams to even know where to start."

Jack chuckled. "I'd tell you but then…well, you know the rest."

"Hypothetically, then tell me a story."

"Okay." He slipped an arm around her. "But this is hypothetical, remember. About a dozen women came to the police station one night with this idea. I told them that it would never work but they showed me on paper how they'd go about the whole thing. The only place that they actually had to break into was Lenny's. Either they had a key or they knew someone who did for all the rest. They thought it would be a hoot and comeuppance for the way Lenny treated you. You'd be surprised how many friends you have out there who appreciate you for who you are. And I swear the skunk was just an added bonus."

"Wives and ex-wives of the other teams who were sick of hearing about the men's only chili cook-off, hypothetically, of course," she said.

"It could be. But I didn't want your fathers to be blamed so I got Jamie to have a poker party at his house."

"Did they know? I can't see Uncle Jamie agreeing to poker..."

"But I want you to know and remember, Carlene, that among all those people who love you, your daddy is right at the top of the list."

Chapter 21

THE RED-HOT BLOOMERS TEAM picture hung above the credenza that Sunday afternoon. Tansy was bringing the trophy from her house where she said she was working magic and miracles. She finally arrived by way of the back door with her husband right behind her.

Tansy clapped her hands to get everyone's attention. "We're glad that Jack, Yancy, and Rick are here with us today. Now for the big moment we've all been waiting for."

Tansy set the trophy in the middle of the credenza and pulled the white pillowcase away from it.

"It sparkles," Josie said.

The trophy sat in the middle of a footed antique crystal plate that had belonged to Grandma Fannin.

"I remember that plate," Gigi said. "It was the one that set on the credenza in our foyer with one of her candlesticks on either side. Mama kept fruit on the plate or cookies."

"Oatmeal raisin," Jamie said.

Dammit! Now all Carlene could see was those beautiful candlesticks all broken into smithereens.

"Speaking of which, if you will notice the broken bits that are glued to the plate and that surround the trophy," Tansy said.

"I'll be damned," Sugar said.

"Sugar cussed. She did and we all heard it," Gigi said.

"Shhh, no bickering today from any of you," Josie scolded.

"Forgive me, Lord." Sugar looked up at the ceiling. "It's lovely, Tansy. How did you do it?"

"I had it done when the candlesticks came back broken. Took it to a little shop in Dallas and told them what I wanted. If we hadn't won the trophy, we would have put a candle in the middle. They crushed the candlesticks into smaller pieces then coated them with some kind of stuff so the top is smooth and yet we can see the glass sparkling. The trophy fits right well, don't you think?" Tansy beamed.

Gigi wiped at a tear and Hank handed her his handkerchief.

"I love it. This is the best Mother's Day ever. It wasn't just the winning, either. It was all the fun we've had with our girls and together." She sniffed.

Carlene started the applause. "Yes, ma'am. To family and friendships."

When the clapping stopped, Patrice pulled Yancy to the center of the foyer. "I know that thing sparkles like diamonds and speaking of which…" She held out her hand. "Look what I got about thirty minutes ago."

Yancy grinned. "She said yes."

Rick leaned down and whispered in Alma Grace's ear. "We won't steal their thunder but we're next in line, darlin'."

Jack threw an arm around Carlene's shoulders and drew her close to his side. "Family and friends. A wonderful never-ending circle? This feels so right."

Carlene snuggled into his embrace. "Yes, it does. Friends and family—the two best things in the whole world."

THE END

Read on for an excerpt from

The Yellow Rose Barbecue Ball

by Carolyn Brown

Coming April 2015 from Sourcebooks Casablanca

If Nancy Baxter had known what kind of storm she was turning loose, she never would have put Stella's name on the prayer list down at the church in Cadillac, Texas. But she didn't have the benefit of hindsight on that hot southern night and she really did want Stella to get married. So when Heather, the president of the Prayer Angels, asked if anyone wanted to add a name to the list she spoke right up and said, "Pray for my daughter. She needs a husband."

The angels took their spirituality seriously, so the praying began in earnest, and before they were done, God had been petitioned by a dozen women to send a husband to Cadillac and to earmark him special for Stella Baxter. No one dared ask why she needed a husband, but they did have their ideas, which turned into juicy gossip by the next morning.

❧

Stella was humming a song from a Pistol Annie's CD as she opened the door to her beauty shop, the Yellow Rose, that Friday morning. She set the control on the air conditioner back a few notches and swept up a few dead crickets from the waiting area in the front part of the shop.

Blow-dryers heated up the small room, and customers liked

to be cool. If it was this hot the day before the first day of official summer, then by the end of July, it would be even hotter than the famous jalapeño peppers that Cadillac, Texas, was famous for.

The Yellow Rose Beauty Shop had started out fifty years before as a small clothing store, so it had a big display window in the front. It had taken lots of discussion when she, Charlotte, and Piper were designing the shop, but they'd finally decided to carpet the display area with yellow carpet and put a white cast-iron bistro set in it. A galvanized watering can stuffed with a gorgeous arrangement of silk daisies and Queen Anne's lace sat in the middle of the table.

They'd left a wide expanse of floor open between the front door and the three styling stations at the back. Covered in light brown tile that shined like glass, it was easy to clean. On one side was a glass-topped table with four chairs around it, and a soft leather sofa the color of freshly churned butter with a coffee table in front of it occupied the area on the other wall. It was bright and comfortable. Hairstyling magazines were scattered on both tables. Stella stopped long enough to arrange them before she went back to her station.

To the right of the styling stations, three shampoo sinks with chairs had been installed, with a small bookcase separating them from the front area. Above the sinks were posters of their three favorite movies: *Gone with the Wind*, *Steel Magnolias*, and *Something to Talk About*. A swinging door led into a back room that held a weathered wooden table and four mismatched chairs. The table was used for folding towels, doing paperwork, or having lunch. A washer and dryer sat in the corner next to a dorm-sized refrigerator topped with a microwave. And what used to be shoe shelves now held perms, hair dye, shampoo, and racks for towels and capes.

Stella checked her reflection in the mirror while she waited for her first customer of the day. Thank God only her droopy eyes gave away the fact that she'd had a long night of world-class sex in a motel up in Durant, Oklahoma. If someone could look into her face and see both the happiness and the fear, she'd be in big trouble.

If anyone did notice her tired eyes, she'd pass it off as allergies. She would never, ever admit that she'd only slept a few hours between the time she got off work the day before and that morning when the alarm went off. Not even to her two best friends and business partners, Charlotte and Piper. She pulled her naturally curly red hair up into a messy ponytail and tied a bright purple scarf around it, hoping Charlotte and Piper would fuss at her for not fixing her hair and not notice her baggy eyes.

"Hey, are you the only one here?" The bell above the door dinged as Trixie Matthews pushed her way inside. "Ah, cool air. We're in for a scorching-hot summer. I love what y'all did with this old building, Stella. It's light and airy, and I feel like I'm in an uptown salon every time I walk in here. I know I've said it before, but I wish more businesses would refurbish the old part of town."

Stella waved her over to a chair. "Maybe they will. It takes time to rebuild a town when it's got one foot in the grave and the other on a pod of boiled okra. I was just thinking the same thing about this summer. We're due a long, lazy old summer, but it will pass fast, and then it'll be time for the jubilee. Tomorrow is the official first day of the season, and the weatherman says today it's going to reach the three-digit mark for the first time this year. Have a seat, and we'll get you all fixed up. Cut and highlight, right? So what's going on with you and your doctor fellow? Oh, and speaking of the jubilee, how's the jalapeño pepper crop coming along?"

Trixie had to hop to get settled into the chair. She pulled off a baseball cap and set free her light brown hair. She'd always reminded Stella of Ashley Judd in size and looks but maybe with a few more pounds on her curvy body. "We're taking it slow. Besides, I don't have time to plan a wedding, what with all these other ones going on in town. And Cathy keeps those peppers watered every day. I think she might tell them bedtime stories, and that's the secret as to how they get so hot. She might be reading them those erotic romance books she reads all the time. I read one and believe me, if she's reading those to the pepper plants, they'll be plenty hot this year."

Stella whipped a black cape around Trixie's shoulders. "You'll be the prettiest bride Cadillac has ever seen when you do decide to get married again. And I wouldn't doubt anything that Cathy does to make those peppers hot. Daddy says they're the best in the whole world."

"That is so sweet, but, darlin', I had that big wedding thing once. I don't want it again. A trip to the courthouse is more up my alley. I hear that you're on the way to the altar, too. The gossip is hotter than the peppers this morning up at Clawdy's."

Stella's heart stopped, and all the color left her face. The purple scarf didn't even put color into her ashen cheeks.

Trixie reached out from under the cape and touched her arm. "Hey, you look like you've seen a ghost. I was just teasing."

After a couple of good solid thumps, Stella's heart went back to pumping and high color filled her cheeks. She'd been so careful the past six months, mostly because she didn't want to jinx something that was so perfect, and yet so wrong.

"Why would you think such a thing?" Stella whispered.

"It was the gossip from the breakfast crew at Clawdy's this morning. They said that Nancy put you on the prayer list last night."

"I'm not sick, and what does that have to do with marriage!" Stella gasped.

"Maybe you are lovesick," Trixie laughed.

"I can't imagine why she'd do that," Stella said.

"Gossip has it that she just said to pray for you, that you needed a husband, and they prayed. But this morning, everyone is speculating about why you need a husband, and if it's safe to breathe in all these fumes if you are pregnant, and who the father is."

Stella leaned against the counter. "Oh. My. God."

The business. Dammit! The beauty shop would fold. They'd only been open a year. "Everyone in town knows?"

"Probably. Didn't you drive past the church on your way to work this morning?"

Stella shook her head.

Trixie flipped open her phone. "I took a picture."

"Of the church?" Stella asked.

"Of the sign. See."

There it was, right on the big, white wooden sign located at the edge of church lawn in black lettering: PRAY FOR MY DAUGHTER. SHE NEEDS A HUSBAND.

Stella blanched, then blushed.

"It doesn't say whose daughter or why, but someone put it out there for the whole world to see. I bet the church is packed this next Sunday so everyone can see for sure who is at the top of the prayer list. Preacher Jed reads it every Sunday before the sermon, remember?"

Stella tried to speak, but words wouldn't go from brain to mouth. Her face burned. Her hands shook so bad that she laid the scissors down and ran a comb through Stella's hair. No way would she trust her herself to cut hair until she settled down.

"I'd be pissed if I was you," Trixie said.

Piper came through the back door into the shop. "Who's pissed? They can join my club since I'm permanently pissed. Hey, Stella, have you seen the billboard in front of the church? I saw it when I took the boys to day care. Who's got a pregnant daughter in town?"

Instead of a hairdresser, Piper could have been a plus-size model with her height, sexy curves, and big brown eyes. She had a thick mane of gorgeous honey blond hair that fell into soft curls around her face without a bit of styling. She sat down in her swivel chair, threw one long leg decked out in bright yellow leggings over the other, and adjusted the collar of a flowing sleeveless blouse printed with huge sunflowers and green sandals.

Piper looked from Trixie to Stella. "What's going on? I don't think it's ever been this quiet in the shop. Even the crickets are quiet."

"Shhh." Trixie put a finger over her lips. "She's about to explode. I can feel it."

"What happened?" Piper whispered.

Trixie adjusted the cape over her lap. "Nancy put Stella on the prayer list down at the church last night. She's the daughter who needs a husband."

"Holy shit! I told you it was a bad idea to come back here. And what happens when we do? Gene divorces me. Charlotte gets all serious about her knitting again. And now you are pregnant. I bet Nancy is ready to do more than shoot you." Piper finally took a deep breath.

"I am not pregnant!" Stella raised her voice. She gave up on Trixie's hair for the time being and sank into the third swivel chair. This could not have possibly happened at a worse time. What in the hell was her mother thinking?

"Then why would Nancy think you need a husband?" Piper said. "Not that she and I are in agreement on that issue. God only knows if I'd known then what I know now, I damn sure wouldn't have married Gene Stephens when I got pregnant with the twins. Hell, no! I would have just raised them by myself and saved myself the misery. Okay, 'fess up. Why did Nancy do that?"

Trixie answered, "Morning gossip up at Miss Clawdy's Café says that Nancy wants a grandbaby by Mother's Day, which means Stella needs a husband by the first week in August. Evidently she wants a legitimate grandbaby."

"That's right before your birthday, Stella," Piper said.

"Who's getting a grandbaby by Mother's Day?" Charlotte called out from the back door.

"Did you drive past the church this morning?" Piper asked.

Charlotte tucked her purse into the cabinet by Stella's chair and carried her knitting bag to the sofa. She pulled out a set of circular needles and six inches of pale yellow baby blanket. "Yes, I did, and what does that sign mean? Who's pregnant? Who is getting a baby by Mother's Day? Boone and I've decided to wait two years to get pregnant. Mama says that I shouldn't start a family when I'm past thirty, but if we wait two years, I'll still only be twenty-nine when the baby comes."

"Why do women say that?" Trixie asked.

"What?" Piper asked.

"*We* get pregnant? The man in the relationship damn sure doesn't get morning sickness, swollen ankles, and a baby bump. So why does he get to think that he is pregnant?" Trixie asked.

"I don't know, but would somebody please tell me whose daughter needs a husband because she's pregnant?" Charlotte asked.

"Nancy," Piper said.

Charlotte flipped around, wide-eyed, and slapped a hand over her mouth. "You are pregnant? You didn't tell us you were dating. Dear Lord, you are as pale as a sheet. Have you had morning sickness yet?"

Stella stood up and started to pace. "Some friends you are. I'll say it one more time: I'm not pregnant. I can't believe Mama did this. She's lived here her whole life, and she knows how folks talk. This is going to ruin our business. The town is barely big enough for two beauty shops as it is, and we've just now got things built up, and..." Her voice got louder with each word, and the pacing got faster. The lump in her throat was bigger than a grapefruit, and no matter how hard she swallowed, it would not go down.

"Slow down, girl," Trixie said. "It'll all blow over by next week. They'll put something else on the sign and the gossip about you will be old news. You know what they do with yesterday's newspaper, don't you? They wrap raw fish in it or put it on the bottom of bird cages."

"We can always sell out and go back to Dallas," Piper said.

"Or maybe we could go to Walmart in Sherman. I hear they're always looking for good help in the beauty shop up there," Charlotte said.

"I'm not going anywhere," Stella declared. "And I don't need a husband, and I'm pissed, and I could just..." She bolted to the back room, sat down at the old table, and put her head on her arms. She wouldn't cry, not with Trixie there, even if she was a friend. She wouldn't. She refused to let one tear fall. But it did, and then a river washed down her face, taking mascara and blush with it, but none of the pain.

Charlotte and Piper hurried to her side, patting her arm and her knee.

"I've never seen you cry like this," Charlotte said.

"Not since that rotten boy broke up with you our sophomore year," Piper said.

"I'd almost forgotten about that a son of a bitch," Charlotte said.

"You've got every right to be pissed." Trixie followed them back, taking off the cape and laying a hand on Stella's shoulder. "I'll come back later for a cut and highlights. I understand how you feel, but don't worry about the shop. If we've proven anything up at Clawdy's, it's that gossip is damn good for business."

"I'll do your hair, Trixie," Piper said. "I don't have an appointment for another hour, so I can do it with no problem. Just take a seat in my chair, and I'll be right there." Trixie gave Stella an encouraging squeeze and headed into the shop.

"Stella, pull yourself together. This isn't the end of the world," Piper said as she and Charlotte followed Trixie up front.

Charlotte whispered, "What happens if God answers their prayers? We're right in the middle of planning *my* wedding. I don't mean to be selfish, but we've barely gotten started, and those angels are pretty powerful. My aunt is on the team, and she's a true believer."

"She can't get married at all, and neither should any of you," Piper declared as she swung the cape back around Trixie's shoulders.

"It's all real good until about that seventh year, and then he'll decide he wants to be a bachelor again and he's not ready for those two kids you had. No, he doesn't want to share custody. Every other weekend and two weeks in the summer is fine with him because he and the bitch he's sleeping with are too busy to take care of kids any more than that. Then you'll be totally responsible for six-year-old twin boys and all the bills."

Stella heard them talking. She understood that they had her best interests at heart, even if they did disagree. Charlotte wanted her to be as happy as she was with Boone, and Piper wasn't over the pain of a divorce. Stella was happier than she'd ever been in her whole life, but she wasn't ready to tell anyone about her new love...not yet.

Keeping a great big secret from them both was hard enough, but keeping it from her mother had been tougher. Mixed emotions shot through Stella. She was pissed—God Almighty but she was pissed—but a tiny little part of her heart understood that her mama only had her best interests at heart. Too bad that little 10 percent couldn't do anything about the pissed-off 90 percent.

She sat up and said loudly, "I should go down to the church and set that damn sign on fire."

Her forehead made a pop when it hit the table again. When would Jed see that sign, and what would he do? Her gut twisted up tighter than a hangman's noose, and she forgot to inhale until her lungs started to burn.

"The more you stir shit, the worse it smells," Trixie called. "Laugh it off when anyone asks you about it. Tell them you're having triplets and Nancy is going to have to babysit them so you can make a living since you don't have a husband. Spread it around that Nancy will be sorry she ever wanted a grandchild, since they're all going be red-haired demons."

"I'm only twenty-six. I'm not an old maid," Stella said. She emerged from the back room only to slump down on the other end of the sofa from Charlotte, lean her head back, and pinch her nose with two fingers. It didn't erase the headache, but at least she'd stopped seeing red dots in front of her eyes.

"I can't go to church on Sunday with that sign out there, and besides, Jed always reads the prayer list."

"Oh, yes you can, and you will," Trixie said. "If you don't go, the gossip will just get worse. They'll say that you are home with morning sickness. Besides, you'll be at the piano so it's not like anybody will turn around and stare at you when he says your name."

Piper finished the haircut and motioned for Trixie to follow her to the shampoo sink. "I agree with Trixie. Pretend that it's all a big joke. Sit right there on the piano bench and smile. It will take him three minutes to read the whole list and then he'll start preaching. Everyone will forget about it by the time he gets finished."

Trixie nodded. "I think it'll be good for both of our businesses. Folks will flock to the café to gossip, and then they'll come by here to make an appointment and take a look at Stella. The minute they walk out the door, they'll call everyone they know to report that you don't have a baby bump yet. You have just become the brand-new celebrity of Cadillac."

Stella's hand went from the bridge of her nose to her temple. "What if everyone in town starts trying to find a husband for me? Mama has already embarrassed the hell out of me on more than one Sunday, inviting men over to dinner and expecting me to be nice to them. Dear Lord, what has she done?"

Charlotte's needles clicked as she created a lovely cable pattern. "You should have picked one out yourself, then this wouldn't have happened. Now your mama's not the only one looking for a husband for you; the whole town will join in the manhunt. And as far as the preacher reading the list, darlin', I wouldn't care if that man read the dictionary on Sunday morning. I'd drool no matter what he read. He's so sexy, it's a shame he's a preacher."

"The preacher, sexy?" Piper exclaimed.

Charlotte gestured with her knitting. "Yes, ma'am!"

"You are engaged! You shouldn't be looking at other men like that." Stella sat up straight, dry-eyed and unblinking.

"That don't mean I'm dead. I might diet on occasion, but it don't mean I can't look at the ice cream at the grocery store. Mmm, ice cream on the preacher's…"

Stella jumped up, grabbed a bottle of window cleaner, and headed for the shop window. "I've got to do something to keep from taking a sledgehammer to that sign."

Piper hollered across the sound of running water. "I just did those windows yesterday."

"I know you did, but my hands are shaking, and Charlotte talking about the preacher's equipment isn't helping one bit," Stella said.

"I wasn't going to say his equipment," Charlotte giggled. "I was going to say his…Bible. And besides, God is probably too busy scouring the earth for a husband for you to be busy slinging lightning at me, so come on back over here and sit down."

"You're lyin', girlfriend! The look on your face had nothing to do with the Good Book," Piper said.

Stella didn't see anything funny in any of it—not the angels, the sign, or the comments. An ominous black cloud hung above her, and the air was static with electricity. The Yellow Rose might have clean windows and a gorgeous display, but could it withstand all the gossip? Would her clients leave her and go to Ruby's down the street? Worse yet, could her love life withstand the scrutiny? It wouldn't surprise her one bit to be out on the street with nothing but an overdue bank note and a broken heart.

Absolutely nothing could get worse.

And then her mother waved at her from the other side of the window.

About the Author

Carolyn Brown is a *New York Times* and *USA Today* bestselling author with more than sixty books published and credits her eclectic family for her humor and writing ideas. Her books include the cowboy trilogy *Lucky in Love*, *One Lucky Cowboy*, and *Getting Lucky*; the Honky Tonk series, *I Love This Bar*, *Hell, Yeah, Honky Tonk Christmas*, and *My Give a Damn's Busted*; and her bestselling Spikes & Spurs series with *Love Drunk Cowboy*, *Red's Hot Cowboy*, *Darn Good Cowboy Christmas*, *One Hot Cowboy Wedding*, *Mistletoe Cowboy*, *Just a Cowboy and His Baby*, and *Cowboy Seeks Bride*. Carolyn launched into women's fiction with *The Blue-Ribbon Jalapeño Society Jubilee*, first in the Cadillac, Texas, series. She was born in Texas but grew up in southern Oklahoma, where she and her husband, Charles, a retired English teacher, make their home. They have three grown children and enough grandchildren to keep them young.